DOCTOR DOLITTLE

VOL. 1

The COMPLETE COLLECTION

READ ALL OF
DOCTOR DOLITTLE'S ADVENTURES!

DOCTOR DOLITTLE

VOL. 1

The COMPLETE COLLECTION

The Voyages of Doctor Dolittle * *The Story of Doctor Dolittle*
Doctor Dolittle's Post Office

HUGH LOFTING

Aladdin

NEW YORK   LONDON   TORONTO   SYDNEY   NEW DELHI

This book is a work of fiction. Any references to historical events, real people, or real places are used fictitiously. Other names, characters, places, and events are products of the author's imagination, and any resemblance to actual events or places or persons, living or dead, is entirely coincidental.

ALADDIN
An imprint of Simon & Schuster Children's Publishing Division
1230 Avenue of the Americas, New York, New York 10020
First Aladdin edition November 2019
Updated text copyright ©2019 by Christopher Lofting
The Voyages of Doctor Dolittle copyright © 1922 by Hugh Lofting
The Voyages of Doctor Dolittle copyright renewed © 1950 by Josephine Lofting
The Story of Doctor Dolittle copyright © 1920 by Hugh Lofting
The Story of Doctor Dolittle copyright renewed © 1948 by Josephine Lofting
Doctor Dolittle's Post Office copyright © 1923 by Hugh Lofting
Doctor Dolittle's Post Office copyright renewed © 1951 by Josephine Lofting
Cover illustration copyright © 2019 by Anton Petrov

For information about special discounts for bulk purchases, please contact Simon & Schuster
Special Sales at 1-866-506-1949 or business@simonandschuster.com.
The Simon & Schuster Speakers Bureau can bring authors to your live event.
For more information or to book an event contact the Simon & Schuster Speakers
Bureau at 1-866-248-3049 or visit our website at www.simonspeakers.com.
Cover designed by Karin Paprocki
Interior designed by Mike Rosamilia
The text of this book was set in Oneleigh Pro.
Manufactured in the United States of America 0719 FFG
2 4 6 8 10 9 7 5 3 1
Library of Congress Control Number 2018959980
ISBN 978-1-5344-4891-9 (hc)
ISBN 978-1-5344-4890-2 (pbk)
ISBN 978-1-5344-4892-6 (eBook)

These titles were previously published individually with slightly different text and art.

CONTENTS

The VOYAGES of DOCTOR DOLITTLE

ILLUSTRATED BY THE AUTHOR

BY HUGH LOFTING

Contents

PART ONE

PROLOGUE

ALL THAT I HAVE WRITTEN SO FAR ABOUT Doctor Dolittle I heard long after it happened from those who had known him—indeed a great deal of it took place before I was born. But I now come to set down that part of the great man's life that I myself saw and took part in.

Many years ago the Doctor gave me permission to do this. But we were both of us so busy then voyaging around the world, having adventures and filling notebooks full of natural history that I never seemed to get time to sit down and write of our doings.

Now of course, when I am quite an old man, my memory isn't so good anymore. But whenever I am in doubt and have to hesitate and think, I always ask Polynesia, the parrot.

That wonderful bird (she is now nearly two hundred and fifty years old) sits on the top of my desk, usually humming sailor songs to herself, while I write this book. And, as every one who ever met her knows, Polynesia's memory is the most marvelous memory in the world. If there is any happening I am not quite sure of, she is always able to put me right, to tell me exactly how it took place, who was there and everything about it. In fact, sometimes I almost think I ought to say that this book was written by Polynesia instead of me.

Very well then, I will begin. And first of all I must tell you something about myself and how I came to meet the Doctor.

The Cobbler's Son

MY NAME WAS TOMMY STUBBINS, SON OF Jacob Stubbins, the cobbler of Puddleby-on-the-Marsh; and I was nine and a half years old. At that time Puddleby was only quite a small town. A river ran through the middle of it; and over this river there was a very old stone bridge, called Kingsbridge, which led you from the market-place on one side to the churchyard on the other.

Sailing ships came up this river from the sea and anchored near the bridge. I used to go down and watch the sailors unloading the ships upon the river-wall. The sailors sang strange songs as they pulled upon the ropes; and I learned these songs by heart. And I would sit on the river-wall with my feet dangling over the water and sing with the men, pretending to myself that I too was a sailor.

For I longed always to sail away with those brave ships when they turned their backs on Puddleby Church and went creeping down the river again, across the wide, lonely marshes to the sea. I longed to go with them out into the world to seek my fortune

"I would sit on the river-wall with my feet dangling over the water."

in foreign lands—Africa, India, China, and Peru! When they got round the bend in the river and the water was hidden from view, you could still see their huge brown sails towering over the roofs of the town, moving onward slowly—like some gentle giants that walked among the houses without noise. What strange things would they have seen, I wondered, when next they came back to anchor at Kingsbridge! And, dreaming of the lands I had never seen, I'd sit on there, watching till they were out of sight.

Three great friends I had in Puddleby in those days. One was Joe, the mussel man, who lived in a tiny hut by the edge of the water under the bridge. This old man was simply marvelous at making things. I never saw a man so clever with his hands. He used to mend my toy ships for me, which I sailed upon the river; he built windmills out of packing cases and barrel staffs; and he could make the most wonderful kites from old umbrellas.

Joe would sometimes take me in his mussel boat, and when the tide was running out we would paddle down the river as far as the edge of the sea to get mussels and lobsters to sell. And out there on the cold lonely marshes we would see wild geese flying, and curlews and redshanks and many other kinds of seabirds that live among the samfire and the long grass of the great salt fen. And as we crept up the river in the evening, when the tide had turned, we would see the lights on Kingsbridge twinkle in the dusk, reminding us of teatime and warm fires.

Another friend I had was Matthew Mugg, the Cat's-Meat-Man. He was a funny old person with a bad squint. He looked rather awful but he was really quite nice to talk to. He knew everybody in Puddleby; and he knew all the dogs and all the cats. In those times, being a Cat's-Meat-Man was a regular business. And you could see one nearly any day going through the streets with a wooden tray full of pieces of meat stuck on skewers crying, "Meat! M-E-A-T!" People paid him to give this meat to their cats and dogs instead of feeding them dog biscuits or the scraps from the table.

I enjoyed going round with old Matthew and seeing the cats and dogs come running to the garden-gates whenever they heard his call. Sometimes he let me give the meat to the animals myself; and I thought this was great fun. He knew a lot about dogs and he would tell me the names of the different kinds as we went through the town. He had several dogs of his own; one, a whippet, was a very fast runner, and Matthew used to win prizes with her at the Saturday coursing races; another, a terrier, was a fine ratter. The Cat's-Meat-Man used to make a business of rat-catching for the millers and farmers as well as his other trade of selling cat meat.

My third great friend was Luke the Hermit. But of him I will tell you more later on.

I did not go to school, because my father was not rich enough to send me. But I was extremely fond of animals. So I used to spend my time collecting birds' eggs and butterflies, fishing in the river, rambling through the countryside after blackberries and mushrooms and helping the mussel man mend his nets.

Yes, it was a very pleasant life I lived in those days long ago—though of course I did not think so then. I was nine and a half years old; and like all boys, I wanted to grow up—not knowing how well off I was with no cares and nothing to worry me. Always I longed for the time when I should be allowed to leave my father's house, to take passage in one of those brave ships, to sail down the river through the misty marshes to the sea—out into the world to seek my fortune.

I Hear of the Great Naturalist

ONE EARLY MORNING IN THE SPRINGTIME, when I was wandering among the hills at the back of the town, I happened to come upon a hawk with a squirrel in its claws. It was standing on a rock and the squirrel was fighting very hard for its life. The hawk was so frightened when I came upon it suddenly like this, that it dropped the poor creature and flew away. I picked the squirrel up and found that two of its legs were badly hurt. So I carried it in my arms back to the town.

When I came to the bridge I went into the mussel man's hut and asked him if he could do anything for it. Joe put on his spectacles and examined it carefully. Then he shook his head.

"Yon crittur's got a broken leg," he said, "and another badly cut an' all. I can mend you your boats, Tom, but I haven't the tools nor the learning to make a broken squirrel seaworthy. This is a job for a surgeon—and for a right smart one an' all. There be only one man I know who could save yon crittur's life. And that's John Dolittle."

"Who is John Dolittle?" I asked. "Is he a vet?"

"No," said the mussel man. "He's no vet. Doctor Dolittle is a nacheralist."

"What's a nacheralist?"

"A nacheralist," said Joe, putting away his glasses and starting to fill his pipe, "is a man who knows all about animals and butterflies and plants and rocks an' all. John Dolittle is a very great nacheralist. I'm surprised you never heard of him—and you daft over animals. He knows a whole lot about shellfish— that I know from my own knowledge. He's a quiet man and don't talk much; but there's folks who do say he's the greatest nacheralist in the world."

"Where does he live?" I asked.

"Over on the Oxenthorpe Road, t'other side the town. Don't know just which house it is, but 'most anyone 'cross there could tell you, I reckon. Go and see him. He's a great man."

So I thanked the mussel man, took up my squirrel again, and started off toward the Oxenthorpe Road.

The first thing I heard as I came into the marketplace was someone calling "Meat! M-E-A-T!"

"There's Matthew Mugg," I said to myself. "He'll know where this Doctor lives. Matthew knows everyone."

So I hurried across the marketplace and caught him up.

"Matthew," I said, "do you know Doctor Dolittle?"

"Do I know John Dolittle!" said he. "Well, I should think I do! I know him as well as I know my own wife—better, I sometimes think. He's a great man—a very great man."

"Can you show me where he lives?" I asked. "I want to take this squirrel to him. It has a broken leg."

"Certainly," said the Cat's-Meat-Man. "I'll be going right by his house directly. Come along and I'll show you."

So off we went together.

"Oh, I've known John Dolittle for years and years," said Matthew as we made our way out of the marketplace. "But I'm pretty sure he ain't home just now. He's away on a voyage. But he's liable to be back any day. I'll show you his house and then you'll know where to find him."

All the way down the Oxenthorpe Road Matthew hardly stopped talking about his great friend, Doctor John Dolittle—"M. D." He talked so much that he forgot all about calling out "Meat!" until we both suddenly noticed that we had a whole procession of dogs following us patiently.

"Where did the Doctor go to on this voyage?" I asked as Matthew handed round the meat to them.

"I couldn't tell you," he answered. "Nobody never knows where he goes, nor when he's going, nor when he's coming back. He lives all alone except for his pets. He's made some great voyages and some wonderful discoveries. Last time he came back he told me he'd met a native people in the Pacific Ocean—lived on two islands, they did. The husbands lived on one island and the wives lived on the other. Sensible people, them. They only met once a year, when the husbands came over to visit the wives for a great feast—Christmastime, most likely. Yes, he's a wonderful man is the Doctor. And as for animals, well, there ain't no one knows as much about 'em as what he does."

"How did he get to know so much about animals?" I asked.

The Cat's-Meat-Man stopped and leaned down to whisper in my ear.

"He talks their language," he said in a hoarse, mysterious voice.

"The animals' language?" I cried.

"Why certainly," said Matthew. "All animals have some kind of a language. Some sorts talk more than others; some only speak in sign language. But the Doctor, he understands them all—birds as well as animals. We keep it a secret though, him and me, because folks only laugh at you when you speak of it. Why, he can even write animal language. He reads aloud to his pets. He's wrote history books in monkey talk, poetry in canary language, and comic songs for magpies to sing. It's a fact. He's now busy learning the language of the shellfish. But he says it's hard work—and he has caught some terrible colds, holding his head underwater so much. He's a great man."

"He certainly must be," I said. "I do wish he were home so I could meet him."

"Well, there's his house, look," said the Cat's-Meat-Man. "That little one at the bend in the road there—the one high up— like it was sitting on the wall above the street."

We were now beyond the edge of the town. And the house that Matthew pointed out was quite a small one standing by itself. There seemed to be a big garden around it; and this garden was much higher than the road, so you had to go up a flight of steps in the wall before you reached the front gate at the top. I could see that there were many fine fruit trees in the garden, for their branches hung down over the wall in places. But the wall was so high I could not see anything else.

When we reached the house Matthew went up the steps to the front gate and I followed him. I thought he was going to go into the garden; but the gate was locked. A dog came running down from the house; and he took several pieces of meat that the Cat's-Meat-Man pushed through the bars of the gate, and some paper bags full of corn and bran. I noticed that this dog did not stop to eat the meat, as any ordinary dog would have done, but he took all the things back to the house and disappeared. He had a curious, wide collar round his neck, which looked as though it were made of brass or something. Then we left.

"The Doctor isn't back yet," said Matthew, "or the gate wouldn't be locked."

"What were all those things in paper bags you gave the dog?" I asked.

"Oh, those were provisions," said Matthew, "things for the animals to eat. The Doctor's house is simply full of pets. I give the things to the dog, while the Doctor's away, and the dog gives them to the other animals."

"And what was that curious collar he was wearing round his neck?"

"That's a solid-gold dog collar," said Matthew. "It was given to him when he was with the Doctor on one of his voyages long ago. He saved a man's life."

"How long has the Doctor had him?" I asked.

"Oh, a long time. Jip's getting pretty old now. That's why the Doctor doesn't take him on his voyages anymore. He leaves him behind to take care of the house. Every Monday and Thursday I bring the food to the gate here and give it to him through the bars. He never lets anyone come inside the garden while the Doctor's away—not even me, though he knows me well. But you'll always be able to tell if the Doctor's back or not—because if he is, the gate will surely be open."

So I went off home to my father's house and put my squirrel to bed in an old wooden box full of straw. And there I nursed him myself and took care of him as best I could till the time should come when the Doctor would return. And every day I went to the little house with the big garden on the edge of the town and tried the gate to see if it was locked. Sometimes the dog, Jip, would come down to the gate to meet me. But though he always wagged his tail and seemed glad to see me, he never let me come inside the garden.

THE THIRD CHAPTER

The Doctor's Home

ONE MONDAY AFTERNOON TOWARD THE end of April, my father asked me to take some shoes which he had mended to a house on the other side of the town. They were for a Colonel Bellowes, who was very particular.

I found the house and rang the bell at the front door. The Colonel opened it, stuck out a very red face and said, "Go round to the tradesmen's entrance—go to the back door." Then he slammed the door shut.

I felt inclined to throw the shoes into the middle of his flower bed. But I thought my father might be angry, so I didn't. I went round to the back door, and there the colonel's wife met me and took the shoes from me. She looked like a timid little woman and had her hands covered in flour as though she were making bread. She seemed to be terribly afraid of her husband, whom I could still hear stumping round the house somewhere, grunting indignantly because I had come to the front door. Then she asked me in a whisper if I would have a bun and a glass of milk. And I said, "Yes, please."

After I had eaten the bun and milk, I thanked the Colonel's wife and came away. Then I thought that before I went home I would go and see if the Doctor had come back yet. I had been to his house once already that morning. But I thought I'd just like to go and take another look. My squirrel wasn't getting any better and I was beginning to be worried about him.

So I turned into the Oxenthorpe Road and started off toward the Doctor's house. On the way I noticed that the sky was clouding over and that it looked as though it might rain.

I reached the gate and found it still locked. I felt very discouraged. I had been coming here every day for a week now. The dog, Jip, came to the gate and wagged his tail as usual, and then sat down and watched me closely to see that I didn't get in.

I began to fear that my squirrel would die before the Doctor came back. I turned away sadly, went down the steps onto the road, and turned toward home again.

I wondered if it was suppertime yet. Of course I had no watch of my own, but I noticed a gentleman coming toward me down the road; and when he got nearer I saw it was the colonel out for a walk. He was all wrapped up in smart overcoats and mufflers and bright-colored gloves. It was not a very cold day, but he had so many clothes on he looked like a pillow inside a roll of blankets. I asked him if he would please tell me the time.

He stopped, grunted, and glared down at me—his red face growing redder still; and when he spoke it sounded like the cork coming out of a ginger beer bottle.

"Do you imagine for one moment," he spluttered, "that I am going to get myself all unbuttoned just to tell a little boy like you *the time!*" And he went stumping down the street, grunting harder than ever.

I stood still a moment looking after him and wondering how old I would have to be, to have him go to the trouble of getting his watch out. And then, all of a sudden, the rain came down in torrents.

I have never seen it rain so hard. It got dark, almost like night. The wind began to blow; the thunder rolled; the lightning flashed, and in a moment the gutters of the road were flowing like a river. There was no place handy to take shelter, so I put my head down against the driving wind and started to run toward home.

I hadn't gone very far when my head bumped into something soft and I sat down suddenly on the pavement. I looked up to see whom I had run into. And there in front of me, sitting on the wet pavement like myself, was a little round man with a very kind face. He wore a shabby high hat and in his hand he had a small black bag.

"I'm very sorry," I said. "I had my head down and I didn't see you coming."

To my great surprise, instead of getting angry at being knocked down, the little man began to laugh.

"You know this reminds me," he said, "of a time once when I was in India. I ran full tilt into a woman in a thunderstorm. But she was carrying a pitcher of molasses on her head and I had treacle in my hair for weeks afterward—the flies followed me everywhere. I didn't hurt you, did I?"

"No," I said. "I'm all right."

"It was just as much my fault as it was yours, you know," said the little man. "I had my head down too—but look here, we mustn't sit talking like this. You must be soaked. I know I am. How far have you got to go?"

"My home is on the other side of the town," I said, as we picked ourselves up.

"My goodness, but that *was* a wet pavement!" said he. "And I declare it's coming down worse than ever. Come along to my house and get dried. A storm like this can't last."

He took hold of my hand and we started running back down the road together. As we ran I began to wonder who this funny little man could be, and where he lived. I was a perfect stranger to him, and yet he was taking me to his own home to get dried. Such a change, after the old red-faced colonel who had refused even to tell me the time! Presently we stopped.

"Here we are," he said.

I looked up to see where we were and found myself back at the foot of the steps leading to the little house with the big garden! My new friend was already running up the steps and opening the gate with some keys he took from his pocket.

"Surely," I thought, "this cannot be the great Doctor Dolittle himself!"

I suppose after hearing so much about him I had expected someone very tall and strong and marvelous. It was hard to believe that this funny little man with the kind smiling face could really be he. Yet here he was, sure enough, running up the steps and opening the very gate that I had been watching for so many days!

The dog, Jip, came rushing out and started jumping up on him and barking with happiness. The rain was splashing down heavier than ever.

"Are you Doctor Dolittle?" I shouted as we sped up the short garden path to the house.

"Yes, I'm Doctor Dolittle," said he, opening the front door

with the same bunch of keys. "Get in! Don't bother about wiping your feet. Never mind the mud. Take it in with you. Get in out of the rain!"

I popped in, he and Jip following. Then he slammed the door behind us.

The storm had made it dark enough outside; but inside the house, with the door closed, it was as black as night. Then began the most extraordinary noise that I have ever heard. It sounded like all sorts and kinds of animals and birds calling and squeaking and screeching at the same time. I could hear things trundling down the stairs and hurrying along passages. Somewhere in the dark a duck was quacking, a cock was crowing, a dove was cooing, an owl was hooting, a lamb was bleating, and Jip was barking. I felt birds' wings fluttering and fanning near my face. Things kept bumping into my legs and nearly upsetting me. The whole front hall seemed to be filling up with animals. The noise, together with the roaring of the rain, was tremendous; and I was beginning to grow a little bit scared when I felt the Doctor take hold of my arm and shout into my ear.

"Don't be alarmed. Don't be frightened. These are just some of my pets. I've been away three months and they are glad to see me home again. Stand still where you are till I strike a light. My gracious, what a storm! Just listen to that thunder!"

So there I stood in the pitch-black dark, while all kinds of animals that I couldn't see, chattered and jostled around me. It was a curious and a funny feeling. I had often wondered, when I had looked in from the front gate, what Doctor Dolittle would be like and what the funny little house would have inside it. But I never imagined it would be anything like this. Yet somehow, after I had felt the Doctor's hand upon my arm, I was not frightened, only confused.

It all seemed like some strange dream; and I was beginning to wonder if I was really awake, when I heard the Doctor speaking again:

"My blessed matches are all wet. They won't strike. Have you got any?"

"No, I'm afraid I haven't," I called back.

"Never mind," said he. "Perhaps Dab-Dab can raise us a light somewhere."

Then the Doctor made some funny clicking noises with his tongue and I heard someone trundle up the stairs again and start moving about in the rooms above.

Then we waited quite a while without anything happening.

"Will the light be long in coming?" I asked. "Some animal is sitting on my foot and my toes are going to sleep."

"No, only a minute," said the Doctor. "She'll be back in a minute."

And just then I saw the first glimmerings of a light around the landing above. At once all the animals kept quiet.

"I thought you lived alone," I said to the Doctor.

"So I do," said he. "It is Dab-Dab who is bringing the light."

I looked up the stairs, trying to make out who was coming. I could not see around the landing, but I heard the most curious footstep on the upper flight. It sounded like someone hopping down from one step to the other, as though he were using only one leg.

As the light came lower, it grew brighter and began to throw strange, jumping shadows on the walls.

"Ah—at last!" said the Doctor. "Good old Dab-Dab!"

And then I thought I *really* must be dreaming. For there, craning her neck round the bend of the landing, hopping down the stairs on one leg, came a spotless white duck. And in her right foot she carried a lighted candle!

"And in her right foot she carried a lighted candle!"

The Wiff-Waff

WHEN AT LAST I COULD LOOK AROUND me I found that the hall was indeed simply full of animals. It seemed to me that almost every kind of creature from the countryside must be there: a pigeon, a white rat, an owl, a badger, a jackdaw—there was even a small pig, just in from the rainy garden, carefully wiping his feet on the mat while the light from the candle glistened on his wet pink back.

The Doctor took the candlestick from the duck and turned to me.

"Look here," he said. "You must get those wet clothes off—by the way, what is your name?"

"Tommy Stubbins," I said.

"Oh, are you the son of Jacob Stubbins, the shoemaker?"

"Yes," I said.

"Excellent bootmaker, your father," said the Doctor. "You see these?" and he held up his right foot to show me the enormous boots he was wearing. "Your father made me these boots four years ago, and I've been wearing them ever since—perfectly wonderful boots—Well now, look here, Stubbins. You've got to change those wet things—and quick. Wait a moment till I get some more candles lit, and then we'll go upstairs and find some dry clothes. You'll have to wear an old suit of mine till we can get yours dry again by the kitchen fire."

So presently, when more candles had been lit round different parts of the house, we went upstairs; and when we had come into a bedroom, the Doctor opened a big wardrobe and took out two suits of old clothes. These we put on. Then we carried our wet ones down to the kitchen and started a fire in the big chimney. The coat of the Doctor's that I was wearing was so large for me that I kept treading on my own coattails while I was helping to fetch the wood up from the cellar. But very soon we had a huge big fire blazing up the chimney and we hung our wet clothes around on chairs.

"Now let's cook some supper," said the Doctor. "You'll stay and have supper with me, Stubbins, of course?"

Already I was beginning to be very fond of this funny little man who called me "Stubbins," instead of "Tommy" or "little lad" (I did so hate to be called "little lad"!) This man seemed to begin right away treating me as though I were a grown-up friend of his. And when he asked me to stop and have supper with him, I felt terribly proud and happy. But I suddenly remembered that I had not told my mother that I would be out late. So very sadly I answered:

"Thank you very much. I would like to stay, but I am afraid that my mother will begin to worry and wonder where I am if I don't get back."

"Oh, but my dear Stubbins," said the Doctor, throwing another log of wood on the fire, "your clothes aren't dry yet. You'll have to wait for them, won't you? By the time they are ready to put on we will have supper cooked and eaten—Did you see where I put my bag?"

"I think it is still in the hall," I said. "I'll go and see."

I found the bag near the front door. It was made of black leather and looked very, very old. One of its latches was broken and it was tied up round the middle with a piece of string.

"Thank you," said the Doctor when I brought it to him.

"Was that bag all the luggage you had for your voyage?" I asked.

"Yes," said the Doctor, as he undid the piece of string. "I don't believe in a lot of baggage. It's such a nuisance. Life's too short to fuss with it. And it isn't really necessary, you know—Where *did* I put those sausages?"

The Doctor was feeling about inside the bag. First he brought out a loaf of new bread. Next came a glass jar with a curious metal top to it. He held this up to the light very carefully before he set it down upon the table; and I could see that there was some strange little water creature swimming about inside. At last the Doctor brought out a pound of sausages.

"Now," he said, "all we want is a frying pan."

We went into the scullery and there we found some pots and pans hanging against the wall. The Doctor took down the frying pan. It was quite rusty on the inside.

"Dear me, just look at that!" said he. "That's the worst of being away so long. The animals are very good and keep the house wonderfully clean as far as they can. Dab-Dab is a perfect marvel as a housekeeper. But some things of course they can't manage. Never mind, we'll soon clean it up. You'll find some silver-sand down there, under the sink, Stubbins. Just hand it up to me, will you?"

In a few moments we had the pan all shiny and bright, then the sausages were put over the kitchen fire and a beautiful frying smell wafted all through the house.

While the Doctor was busy at the cooking, I went and took another look at the funny little creature swimming about in the glass jar.

"What is this animal?" I asked.

"Oh that," said the Doctor, turning round, "that's a Wiff-Waff. Its full name is *hippocampus pippitopitus*. But the natives just call it a Wiff-Waff—on account of the way it waves its tail, swimming, I imagine. That's what I went on this last voyage for, to get that. You see, I'm very busy just now trying to learn the language of the shell-fish. They *have* languages, of that I feel sure. I can talk a little shark language and porpoise dialect myself. But what I particularly want to learn now is shellfish."

"Why?" I asked.

"Well, you see, some of the shellfish are the oldest kind of animals in the world that we know of. We find their shells in the rocks—turned to stone—thousands of years old. So I feel quite sure that if I could only get to talk their language, I should be able to learn a whole lot about what the world was like ages and ages and ages ago. You see?"

"But couldn't some of the other animals tell you as well?"

"I don't think so," said the Doctor, prodding the sausages with a fork. "To be sure, the monkeys I knew in Africa some time ago were very helpful in telling me about bygone days; but they only went back a thousand years or so. No, I am certain that the oldest history in the world is to be had from the shellfish—and from them only. You see, most of the other animals that were alive in those very ancient times have now become extinct."

"Have you learned any shellfish language yet?" I asked.

"No. I've only just begun. I wanted this particular kind of a pipefish because he is half a shellfish and half an ordinary fish. I went all the way to the eastern Mediterranean after him. But I'm very much afraid he isn't going to be a great deal of help to me. To tell you the truth, I'm rather disappointed in his appearance. He doesn't *look* very intelligent, does he?"

"No, he doesn't," I agreed.

"Ah," said the Doctor. "The sausages are done to a turn. Come along—hold your plate near and let me give you some."

Then we sat down at the kitchen table and started a hearty meal.

It was a wonderful kitchen, that. I had many meals there afterward and I found it a better place to eat in than the grandest dining room in the world. It was so cozy and homelike and warm. It was so handy for the food, too. You took it right off the fire, hot, and put it on the table and ate it. And you could watch your toast toasting at the fender and see it didn't burn while you drank your soup. And if you had forgotten to put the salt on the table, you didn't have to get up and go into another room to fetch it; you just reached round and took the big wooden box off the dresser behind you. Then the fireplace—the biggest fireplace you ever saw—was like a room in itself. You could get right inside it even when the logs were burning and sit on the wide seats on either side and roast chestnuts after the meal was over—or listen to the kettle singing, or tell stories, or look at picture books by the light of the fire. It was a marvelous kitchen. It was like the Doctor—comfortable, sensible, friendly, and solid.

While we were gobbling away, the door suddenly opened and in marched the duck, Dab-Dab, and the dog, Jip, dragging sheets and pillowcases behind them over the clean tiled floor. The Doctor, seeing how surprised I was, explained:

"They're just going to air the bedding for me in front of the fire. Dab-Dab is a perfect treasure of a housekeeper; she never forgets anything. I had a sister once who used to keep house for me (poor, dear Sarah! I wonder how she's getting on—I haven't seen her in many years). But she wasn't nearly as good as Dab-Dab. Have another sausage?"

The Doctor turned and said a few words to the dog and duck in some strange talk and signs. They seemed to understand him perfectly.

"Can you talk in squirrel language?" I asked.

"Oh yes. That's quite an easy language," said the Doctor. "You could learn that yourself without a great deal of trouble. But why do you ask?"

"Because I have a sick squirrel at home," I said. "I took it away from a hawk. But two of its legs are badly hurt and I wanted very much to have you see it, if you would. Shall I bring it tomorrow?"

"Well, if its leg is badly broken I think I had better see it tonight. It may be too late to do much; but I'll come home with you and take a look at it."

So presently we felt the clothes by the fire and mine were found to be quite dry. I took them upstairs to the bedroom and changed, and when I came down the Doctor was already waiting for me with his little black bag full of medicines and bandages.

"Come along," he said. "The rain has stopped now."

Outside it had grown bright again and the evening sky was all red with the setting sun; and thrushes were singing in the garden as we opened the gate to go down onto the road.

Polynesia

I THINK YOUR HOUSE IS THE MOST INTERESTING house I was ever in," I said as we set off in the direction of the town. "May I come and see you again tomorrow?"

"Certainly," said the Doctor. "Come any day you like. Tomorrow I'll show you the garden and my private zoo."

"Oh, have you a zoo?" I asked.

"Yes," said he. "The larger animals are too big for the house, so I keep them in a zoo in the garden. It is not a very big collection, but it is interesting in its way."

"It must be splendid," I said, "to be able to talk all the languages of the different animals. Do you think I could ever learn to do it?"

"Oh surely," said the Doctor, "with practice. You have to be very patient, you know. You really ought to have Polynesia to start you. It was she who gave me my first lessons."

"Who is Polynesia?" I asked.

"Polynesia was a West African parrot I had. She isn't with me anymore now," said the Doctor sadly.

"Why—is she dead?"

"Oh no," said the Doctor. "She is still living, I hope. But when we reached Africa she seemed so glad to get back to her own country. She wept for joy. And when the time came for me to come back here, I had not the heart to take her away from that sunny land—although, it is true, she did offer to come. I left her in Africa—Ah well! I have missed her terribly. She wept again when we left. But I think I did the right thing. She was one of the best friends I ever had. It was she who first gave me the idea of learning the animal languages and becoming an animal doctor. I often wonder if she remained happy in Africa, and whether I shall ever see her funny, old, solemn face again—Good old Polynesia! A most extraordinary bird—Well, well!"

Just at that moment we heard the noise of someone running behind us; and turning round we saw Jip the dog rushing down the road after us, as fast as his legs could bring him. He seemed very excited about something, and as soon as he came up to us, he started barking and whining to the Doctor in a peculiar way. Then the Doctor too seemed to get all worked up and began talking and making odd signs to the dog. At length he turned to me, his face shining with happiness.

"Polynesia has come back!" he cried. "Imagine it. Jip says she has just arrived at the house. My! And it's five years since I saw her. Excuse me a minute."

He turned as if to go back home. But the parrot, Polynesia, was already flying toward us. The Doctor clapped his hands like a child getting a new toy; while the swarm of sparrows in the roadway fluttered, gossiping, up onto the fences, highly scandalized to see a gray-and-scarlet parrot skimming down an English lane.

On she came, straight onto the Doctor's shoulder, where she

immediately began talking a steady stream in a language I could not understand. She seemed to have a terrible lot to say. And very soon the Doctor had forgotten all about me and my squirrel and Jip and everything else; till at length the bird clearly asked him something about me.

"Oh excuse me, Stubbins!" said the Doctor. "I was so interested listening to my old friend here. We must get on and see this squirrel of yours. Polynesia, this is Thomas Stubbins."

The parrot, on the Doctor's shoulder, nodded gravely toward me and then, to my great surprise, said quite plainly in English:

"How do you do? I remember the night you were born. It was a terribly cold winter. You were a very ugly baby."

"Stubbins is anxious to learn animal language," said the Doctor. "I was just telling him about you and the lessons you gave me when Jip ran up and told us you had arrived."

"Well," said the parrot, turning to me, "I may have started the Doctor learning, but I never could have done even that if he hadn't first taught me to understand what *I* was saying when I spoke English. You see, many parrots can talk like a person, but very few of them understand what they are saying. They just say it because— well, because they fancy it is smart or, because they know they will get crackers given them."

By this time we had turned and were going toward my home, with Jip running in front and Polynesia still perched on the Doctor's shoulder. The bird chattered incessantly, mostly about Africa; but now she spoke in English, out of politeness to me.

"How is Prince Bumpo getting on?" asked the Doctor.

"Oh, I'm glad you asked me," said Polynesia. "I almost forgot to tell you. What do you think? *Bumpo is in England!*"

"In England! You don't say!" cried the Doctor. "What on earth is he doing here?"

"His father, the king, sent him here to a place called—er—Bullford, I think it was—to study lessons."

"Bullford! Bullford!" muttered the Doctor. "I never heard of the place—Oh, you mean Oxford."

"Yes, that's the place—Oxford," said Polynesia. "I knew it had cattle in it somewhere. Oxford—that's the place he's gone to."

"Well, well," murmured the Doctor. "Fancy Bumpo studying at Oxford—Well, well!"

"There were great doings in Jolliginki when he left. He was scared to death to come. He was the first man from that country to go abroad. But his father made him come. He said that all the African kings were sending their sons to Oxford now. It was the fashion, and he would have to go. Poor Bumpo went off in tears—and everybody in the palace was crying too. You never heard such a hullabaloo."

"And how is Chee-Chee getting on? Chee-Chee," added the Doctor in explanation to me, "was a pet monkey I had years ago. I left him too in Africa when I came away."

"Well," said Polynesia frowning, "Chee-Chee is not entirely happy. I saw a good deal of him the last few years. He got dreadfully homesick for you and the house and the garden. It's funny, but I was just the same way myself. You remember how crazy I was to get back to the dear old land? And Africa *is* a wonderful country. I thought I was going to have a perfectly grand time. But somehow—I don't know—after a few weeks it seemed to get tiresome. I just couldn't seem to settle down. Well, to make a long story short, one night I made up my mind that I'd come back here and find you. So I hunted up old Chee-Chee and told him about it. He said he didn't blame me a bit—felt exactly the same way himself. Africa was so deadly quiet after the life we had led with you. He missed the stories you used to tell us out of your animal books—and the chats we used to have sitting round the kitchen fire on winter nights. The animals out there were very nice to us and all that. But somehow the dear kind creatures seemed a bit stupid. Chee-Chee said he had noticed it too. But I suppose it wasn't they who had changed; it was we who were different. When I left, poor old Chee-Chee broke down and cried. He said he felt as though his only friend were leaving him— though, as you know, he has simply millions of relatives there. He said it didn't seem fair that I should have wings to fly over here any time I liked, and him with no way to follow me. But mark my words, I wouldn't be a bit surprised if he found a way to come—some day. He's a smart lad, is Chee-Chee."

At this point we arrived at my home. My father's shop was closed and the shutters were up; but my mother was standing at the door, looking down the street.

"Good evening, Mrs. Stubbins," said the Doctor. "It is my fault your son is so late. I made him stay for supper while his clothes were drying. He was soaked to the skin; and so was I. We ran into each other in the storm and I insisted on his coming into my house for shelter."

"I was beginning to get worried about him," said my mother. "I am thankful to you, sir, for looking after him so well and bringing him home."

"Don't mention it—don't mention it," said the Doctor. "We have had a very interesting chat."

"Who might it be that I have the honor of addressing?" asked my mother, staring at the gray parrot perched on the Doctor's shoulder.

"Oh, I'm John Dolittle. I dare say your husband will remember me. He made me some very excellent boots about four years ago. They really are splendid," added the Doctor, gazing down at his feet with great satisfaction.

"The Doctor has come to cure my squirrel, Mother," said I. "He knows all about animals."

"Oh, no," said the Doctor, "not all, Stubbins, not all about them by any means."

"It is very kind of you to come so far to look after his pet," said my mother. "Tom is always bringing home strange creatures from the woods and the fields."

"Is he?" said the Doctor. "Perhaps he will grow up to be a naturalist some day. Who knows?"

"Won't you come in?" asked my mother. "The place is a little untidy because I haven't finished the spring cleaning yet. But there's a nice fire burning in the parlor."

"Thank you!" said the Doctor. "What a charming home you have!"

And after wiping his enormous boots very, very carefully on the mat, the great man passed into the house.

The Wounded Squirrel

INSIDE WE FOUND MY FATHER BUSY PRACTICING on the flute beside the fire. This he always did, every evening, after his work was over.

The Doctor immediately began talking to him about flutes and piccolos and bassoons; and presently my father said:

"Perhaps you perform upon the flute yourself, sir. Won't you play us a tune?"

"Well," said the Doctor, "it is a long time since I touched the instrument. But I would like to try. May I?"

Then the Doctor took the flute from my father and played and played and played. It was wonderful. My mother and father sat as still as statues, staring up at the ceiling as though they were in church; and even I, who didn't bother much about music except on the mouth organ—even I felt all sad and cold and creepy and wished I had been a better boy.

"Oh, I think that was just beautiful!" sighed my mother when at length the Doctor stopped.

"You are a great musician, sir," said my father, "a very great musician. Won't you please play us something else?"

"Why certainly," said the Doctor. "Oh, but look here, I've forgotten all about the squirrel."

"I'll show him to you," I said. "He is upstairs in my room."

So I led the Doctor to my bedroom at the top of the house and showed him the squirrel in the packing case filled with straw.

The animal, who had always seemed very much afraid of me— though I had tried hard to make him feel at home, sat up at once when the Doctor came into the room and started to chatter. The Doctor chattered back in the same way and the squirrel, when he was lifted up to have his leg examined, appeared to be rather pleased than frightened.

I held a candle while the Doctor tied the leg up in what he called "splints," which he made out of matchsticks with his pen-knife.

"I think you will find that his leg will get better now in a very short time," said the Doctor, closing up his bag. "Don't let him run about for at least two weeks yet, but keep him in the open air and cover him up with dry leaves if the nights get cool. He tells me he is rather lonely here, all by himself, and is wondering how his wife and children are getting on. I have assured him you are a man to be trusted; and I will send a squirrel who lives in my garden to find out how his family are and to bring him news of them. He must be kept cheerful at all costs. Squirrels are naturally a very cheerful, active race. It is very hard for them to lie still doing nothing. But you needn't worry about him. He will be all right."

Then we went back again to the parlor and my mother and father kept him playing the flute till after ten o'clock.

Although my parents both liked the Doctor tremendously from the first moment that they saw him, and were very proud to have him come and play to us (for we were really terribly poor), they did not realize then what a truly great man he was one day to become. Of course now, when almost everybody in the whole world has heard about Doctor Dolittle and his books, if you were to go to that little house in Puddleby where my father had his cobbler's shop you would see, set in the wall over the old-fashioned door, a stone with writing on it which says: JOHN DOLITTLE, THE FAMOUS NATURALIST, PLAYED THE FLUTE IN THIS HOUSE IN THE YEAR 1839.

I often look back upon that night long, long ago. And if I close my eyes and think hard, I can see that parlor just as it was then: a funny little man in coattails, with a kind round face, playing away on the flute in front of the fire; my mother on one side of him and my father on the other, holding their breath and listening with their eyes shut; myself, with Jip, squatting on the carpet at his feet, staring into the coals; and Polynesia perched on the mantelpiece beside his shabby high hat, gravely swinging her head from side to side in time to the music. I see it all, just as though it were before me now.

And then I remember how, after we had seen the Doctor out at the front door, we all came back into the parlor and talked about him till it was still later; and even after I did go to bed (I had never stayed up so late in my life before), I dreamed about him and a band of strange, clever animals that played flutes and fiddles and drums the whole night through.

Shellfish Talk

THE NEXT MORNING, ALTHOUGH I HAD GONE to bed so late the night before, I was up frightfully early. The first sparrows were just beginning to chirp sleepily on the slates outside my attic window when I jumped out of bed and scrambled into my clothes.

I could hardly wait to get back to the little house with the big garden—to see the Doctor and his private zoo. For the first time in my life I forgot all about breakfast; and creeping down the stairs on tiptoe, so as not to wake my mother and father, I opened the front door and popped out into the empty, silent street.

When I got to the Doctor's gate I suddenly thought that perhaps it was too early to call on anyone: and I began to wonder if the Doctor would be up yet. I looked into the garden. No one seemed to be about. So I opened the gate quietly and went inside.

As I turned to the left to go down a path between some hedges, I heard a voice quite close to me say:

"Good morning. How early you are!"

I turned around, and there, sitting on the top of a privet hedge, was the gray parrot, Polynesia.

"Good morning," I said. "I suppose I am rather early. Is the Doctor still in bed?"

"Oh no," said Polynesia. "He has been up an hour and a half. You'll find him in the house somewhere. The front door is open. Just push it and go in. He is sure to be in the kitchen cooking breakfast—or working in his study. Walk right in. I am waiting to see the sun rise. But upon my word, I believe it's forgotten to rise. It is an awful climate, this. Now if we were in Africa, the world would be blazing with sunlight at this hour of the morning. Just see that mist rolling over those cabbages. It is enough to give you rheumatism to look at it. Beastly climate—Beastly! Really I don't know why anything but frogs ever stay in England—Well, don't let me keep you. Run along and see the Doctor."

"Thank you," I said. "I'll go and look for him."

When I opened the front door I could smell bacon frying, so I made my way to the kitchen. There I discovered a large kettle boiling away over the fire and some bacon and eggs in a dish upon the hearth. It seemed to me that the bacon was getting all dried up with the heat. So I pulled the dish a little farther away from the fire and went on through the house looking for the Doctor.

I found him at last in the study. I did not know then that it was called the study. It was certainly a very interesting room, with telescopes and microscopes and all sorts of other strange things which I did not understand about but wished I did. Hanging on the walls were pictures of animals and fishes and strange plants and collections of birds' eggs and seashells in glass cases.

The Doctor was standing at the main table in his dressing gown.

At first I thought he was washing his face. He had a square glass box before him full of water. He was holding one ear under the water while he covered the other with his left hand. As I came in he stood up.

"Good morning, Stubbins," said he. "Going to be a nice day, don't you think? I've just been listening to the Wiff-Waff. But he is very disappointing—very."

"Why?" I said. "Didn't you find that he has any language at all?"

"Oh yes," said the Doctor, "he has a language. But it is such a poor language—only a few words, like 'yes' and 'no'—'hot' and 'cold.' That's all he can say. It's very disappointing. You see, he really belongs to two different families of fishes. I thought he was going to be tremendously helpful—Well, well!"

"I suppose," said I, "that means he hasn't very much sense—if his language is only two or three words?"

"Yes, I suppose it does. Possibly it is the kind of life he leads. You see, they are very rare now, these Wiff-Waffs—very rare and very solitary. They swim around in the deepest parts of the ocean entirely by themselves—always alone. So I presume they really don't need to talk much."

"Perhaps some kind of a bigger shellfish would talk more," I said. "After all, he is very small, isn't he?"

"Yes," said the Doctor, "that's true. Oh I have no doubt that there are shellfish who are good talkers—not the least doubt. But the big shellfish—the biggest of them, are so hard to catch. They are only to be found in the deep parts of the sea; and as they don't swim very much, but just crawl along the floor of the ocean most of the time, they are very seldom taken in nets. I do wish I could find some way of going down to the bottom of the sea. I could learn a lot if I could only do that. But we are forgetting all about breakfast— Have you had breakfast yet, Stubbins?"

I told the Doctor that I had forgotten all about it, and he at once led the way into the kitchen.

"Yes," he said, as he poured the hot water from the kettle into the teapot, "if a man could only manage to get right down to the bottom of the sea, and live there a while, he would discover some wonderful things—things that people have never dreamed of."

"But men do go down, don't they?" I asked—"divers and people like that?"

"Oh yes, to be sure," said the Doctor. "Divers go down. I've been down myself in a diving suit, for that matter. But my! They only go where the sea is shallow. Divers can't go down where it is really deep. What I would like to do is to go down to the great depths—where it is miles deep—Well, well, I dare say I shall manage it someday. Let me give you another cup of tea."

Are You a Good Noticer?

JUST AT THAT MOMENT POLYNESIA CAME into the room and said something to the Doctor in bird language. Of course I did not understand what it was. But the Doctor at once put down his knife and fork and left the room.

"You know it is an awful shame," said the parrot as soon as the Doctor had closed the door. "Directly he comes back home, all the animals over the whole countryside get to hear of it, and every sick cat and mangy rabbit for miles around comes to see him and ask his advice. Now there's a big fat hare outside at the back door with a squawking baby. Can she see the Doctor, please! Thinks it's going to have convulsions. Stupid little thing's been eating deadly nightshade again, I suppose. The animals are *so* inconsiderate at times—especially the mothers. They come round and call the Doctor away from his meals and wake him out of his bed at all hours of the night. I don't know how he stands it—really I don't. Why, the poor man never gets any peace at all! I've told him time and again to have special hours for the animals to come. But he is so frightfully kind and considerate. He never refuses to see them if there is anything really wrong with them. He says the urgent cases must be seen at once."

"Why don't some of the animals go and see the other doctors?" I asked.

"Oh, good gracious!" exclaimed the parrot, tossing her head scornfully. "Why, there aren't any other animal doctors—not real doctors. Of course there *are* those vet persons, to be sure. But, bless you, they're no good. You see, they can't understand the animals' language; so how can you expect them to be any use? Imagine yourself, or your father, going to see a doctor who could not understand a word you say—nor even tell you in your own language what you must do to get well! Poof! Those vets! They're that stupid, you've no idea! Put the Doctor's bacon down by the fire, will you?—to keep hot till he comes back."

"Do you think I would ever be able to learn the language of the animals?" I asked, laying the plate upon the hearth.

"Well, it all depends," said Polynesia. "Are you clever at lessons?"

"I don't know," I answered, feeling rather ashamed. "You see, I've never been to school. My father is too poor to send me."

"Well," said the parrot, "I don't suppose you have really missed much—to judge from what *I* have seen of schoolboys. But listen: Are you a good noticer? Do you notice things well? I mean, for instance, supposing you saw two starlings on an apple tree, and you only took one good look at them—would you be able to tell one from the other if you saw them again the next day?"

"I don't know," I said. "I've never tried."

"Well that," said Polynesia, brushing some crumbs off the

corner of the table with her left foot, "that is what you call powers of observation—noticing the small things about birds and animals: the way they walk and move their heads and flip their wings; the way they sniff the air and twitch their whiskers and wiggle their tails. You have to notice all those little things if you want to learn animal language. For you see, lots of the animals hardly talk at all with their tongues; they use their breath or their tails or their feet instead. That is because many of them, in the olden days when lions and tigers were more plentiful, were afraid to make a noise for fear the savage creatures heard them. Birds, of course, didn't care; for they always had wings to fly away with. But that is the first thing to remember: being a good noticer is terribly important in learning animal language."

"It sounds pretty hard," I said.

"You'll have to be very patient," said Polynesia. "It takes a long time to say even a few words properly. But if you come here often, I'll give you a few lessons myself. And once you get started, you'll be surprised how fast you get on. It would indeed be a good thing if you could learn. Because then you could do some of the work for the Doctor—I mean the easier work, like bandaging and giving pills. Yes, yes, that's a good idea of mine. 'Twould be a great thing if the poor man could get some help—and some rest. It is a scandal the way he works. I see no reason why you shouldn't be able to help him a great deal—That is, if you are really interested in animals."

"Oh, I'd love that!" I cried. "Do you think the Doctor would let me?"

"Certainly," said Polynesia, "as soon as you have learned something about doctoring. I'll speak of it to him myself. Sh! I hear him coming. Quick—bring his bacon back to the table."

"Being a good noticer is terribly important."

The Garden
of Dreams

WHEN BREAKFAST WAS OVER THE Doctor took me out to show me the garden. Well, if the house had been interesting, the garden was a hundred times more so. Of all the gardens I have ever seen, his was the most delightful, the most fascinating. At first you did not realize how big it was. You never seemed to come to the end of it. When at last you were quite sure that you had seen it all, you would peer over a hedge, or turn a corner, or look up some steps, and there was a whole new part you never expected to find.

It had everything—everything a garden can have, or ever has had. There were wide, wide lawns with carved stone seats, green with moss. Over the lawns hung weeping willows, and their feathery bough tips brushed the velvet grass when they swung with the wind. The old flagged paths had high, clipped, yew hedges on either side of them, so that they looked like the narrow streets of some old town; and through the hedges, doorways had been made; and over the doorways were shapes like vases and peacocks and half moons all trimmed out of the living trees. There was a lovely marble fishpond with golden carp and blue water lilies and big green frogs. A high brick wall alongside the kitchen garden was all covered with pink and yellow peaches ripening in the sun. There was a wonderful great oak, hollow in the trunk, big enough for four men to hide inside. Many summer houses there were, too—some of wood and some of stone; and one of them was full of books to read. In a corner, among some rocks and ferns, was an outdoor fireplace, where the Doctor used to fry liver and bacon when he had a notion to take his meals in the open air. There was a couch, as well, on which he used to sleep, it seems, on warm summer nights when the nightingales were singing at their best; it had wheels on it so it could be moved about under any tree they sang in. But the thing that fascinated me most of all was a tiny little tree house, high up in the top branches of a great elm, with a long rope ladder leading to it. The Doctor told me he used it for looking at the moon and the stars through a telescope.

It was the kind of a garden where you could wander and explore for days and days—always coming upon something new, always glad to find the old spots over again. That first time that I saw the Doctor's garden I was so charmed by it that I felt I would like to live in it—always and always—and never go outside of it again. For it had everything within its walls to give happiness, to make living pleasant—to keep the heart at peace. It was the Garden of Dreams.

One peculiar thing I noticed immediately when I went into it, and that was what a lot of birds there were about. Every tree seemed to have two or three nests in it. And heaps of other wild creatures appeared to be making themselves at home there, too. Stoats and tortoises and dormice seemed to be quite common, and not in the least shy. Toads of different colors and sizes hopped about the lawn as though it belonged to them. Green lizards (which were very rare in Puddleby) sat up on the stones in the sunlight and blinked at us. Even snakes were to be seen.

"You need not be afraid of them," said the Doctor, noticing that I started somewhat when a large black snake wiggled across the path right in front of us. "These fellows are not poisonous. They do a great deal of good in keeping down many kinds of garden pests. I play the flute to them sometimes in the evening. They love it. Stand right up on their tails and carry on to no end. Funny thing, their taste for music."

"Why do all these animals come and live here?" I asked. "I never saw a garden with so many creatures in it."

"Well, I suppose it's because they get the kind of food they like; and nobody worries or disturbs them. And then, of course, they know me. And if they or their children get sick, I presume they find it handy to be living in a doctor's garden. Look! You see that sparrow on the sundial, swearing at the blackbird down below? Well, he has been coming here every summer for years. He comes from London. The country sparrows round about here are always laughing at him. They say he chirps with such a Cockney accent. He is a most amusing bird—very brave but very cheeky. He loves nothing better than an argument, but he always ends it by getting rude. He is a real city bird. In London he lives around St. Paul's Cathedral. 'Cheapside,' we call him."

"Are all these birds from the country round here?" I asked.

"Most of them," said the Doctor. "But a few rare ones, who ordinarily never come near England at all, visit me every year. For instance, that handsome little fellow hovering over the snapdragon there, he's a ruby-throated hummingbird. Comes from America. Strictly speaking, he has no business in this climate at all. It is too cool. I make him sleep in the kitchen at night. Then every August, about the last week of the month, I have a purple bird-of-paradise come all the way from Brazil to see me. She is a very great swell. Hasn't arrived yet of course. And there are a few others, foreign birds from the tropics mostly, who drop in on me in the course of the summer months. But come, I must show you the zoo."

The Private Zoo

I DID NOT THINK THERE COULD BE ANYTHING left in that garden that we had not seen. But the Doctor took me by the arm and started off down a little narrow path, and after many windings and twistings and turnings we found ourselves before a small door in a high stone wall. The Doctor pushed it open.

Inside was still another garden. I had expected to find cages with animals inside them. But there were none to be seen. Instead there were little stone houses here and there all over the garden; and each house had a window and a door. As we walked in, many of these doors opened and animals came running out to us, evidently expecting food.

"Haven't the doors any locks on them?" I asked the Doctor.

"Oh yes," he said, "every door has a lock. But in my zoo, the doors open from the inside, not from the out. The locks are only there so the animals can go and shut themselves *in* any time they want to get away from the annoyance of other animals or from people who might come here. Every animal in this zoo stays here because he likes it, not because he is forced to."

"They all look very happy and clean," I said. "Would you mind telling me the names of some of them?"

"Certainly. Well now: that funny-looking thing with plates on his back, nosing under the brick over there, is a South American armadillo. The little chap talking to him is a Canadian woodchuck. They both live in those holes you see at the foot of the wall. The two little beasts doing antics in the pond are a pair of Russian minks— and that reminds me: I must go and get them some herring from the town before noon—it is early-closing today. That animal just stepping out of his house is an antelope, one of the smaller South African kinds. Now, let us move to the other side of those bushes there and I will show you some more."

"Are those deer over there?" I asked.

"Deer!" said the Doctor. "Where do you mean?"

"Over there," I said, pointing, "nibbling the grass border of the bed. There are two of them."

"Oh, that," said the Doctor with a smile. "That isn't two animals: that's one animal with two heads—the only two-headed animal in the world. It's called a 'Pushmi-Pullyu.' I brought him from Africa. He's very tame—acts as a kind of night watchman for my zoo. He only sleeps with one head at a time, you see—very handy— the other head stays awake all night."

"Have you any lions or tigers?" I asked as we moved on.

"No," said the Doctor. "It wouldn't be possible to keep them here—and I wouldn't keep them even if I could. If I had my way, Stubbins, there wouldn't be a single lion or tiger in captivity anywhere in the world. They never take to it. They're never happy.

They never settle down. They are always thinking of the big countries they have left behind. You can see it in their eyes, dreaming—
dreaming always of the great open spaces where they were born;
dreaming of the deep, dark jungles where their mothers first taught
them how to scent and track the deer. And what are they given in
exchange for all this?" asked the Doctor, stopping in his walk and
growing all red and angry. "What are they given in exchange for
the glory of an African sunrise, for the twilight breeze whispering
through the palms, for the green shade of the matted, tangled vines,
for the cool, big-starred nights of the desert, for the patter of the
waterfall after a hard day's hunt? What, I ask you, are they given in
exchange for *these*? Why, a bare cage with iron bars; an ugly piece
of dead meat thrust in to their cage once a day; and a crowd of fools
to come and stare at them with open mouths! No, Stubbins. Lions
and tigers, the Big Hunters, should never, never be seen in zoos."

The Doctor seemed to have grown terribly serious—almost
sad. But suddenly his manner changed again and he took me by the
arm with his same old cheerful smile.

"But we haven't seen the butterfly houses yet—nor the aquariums. Come along. I am very proud of my butterfly houses."

Off we went again and came presently into a hedged enclosure.
Here I saw several big huts made of fine wire netting, like cages.
Inside the netting, all sorts of beautiful flowers were growing in the
sun, with butterflies skimming over them. The Doctor pointed to
the end of one of the huts where little boxes with holes in them
stood in a row.

"Those are the hatching boxes," said he. "There I put the different kinds of caterpillars. And as soon as they turn into butterflies
and moths, they come out into these flower gardens to feed."

"Do butterflies have a language?" I asked.

"Oh, I fancy they have," said the Doctor, "and the beetles too. But so far I haven't succeeded in learning much about insect languages. I have been too busy lately trying to master the shellfish talk. I mean to take it up, though."

At that moment Polynesia joined us and said, "Doctor, there are two guinea pigs at the back door. They say they have run away from the boy who kept them because they didn't get the right stuff to eat. They want to know if you will take them in."

"All right," said the Doctor. "Show them the way to the zoo. Give them the house on the left, near the gate—the one the black fox had. Tell them what the rules are and give them a square meal— Now, Stubbins, we will go on to the aquariums. But first of all I must show you my big, glass, seawater tank where I keep the shellfish."

My Schoolmaster, Polynesia

WELL, THERE WERE NOT MANY DAYS after that, you may be sure, when I did not come to see my new friend. Indeed I was at his house practically all day and every day. So much that one evening my mother asked me jokingly why I did not take my bed over there and live at the Doctor's house altogether.

After a while I think I got to be quite useful to the Doctor, feeding his pets for him; helping to make new houses and fences for the zoo; assisting with the sick animals that came; doing all manner of odd jobs about the place. So that although I enjoyed it all very much (it was indeed like living in a new world), I really think the Doctor would have missed me if I had not come so often.

All this time Polynesia came with me wherever I went, teaching me bird language and showing me how to understand the talking signs of the animals. At first I thought I would never be able to learn at all—it seemed so difficult. But the old parrot was wonderfully patient with me—though I could see that occasionally she had hard work to keep her temper.

Soon I began to pick up the strange chatter of the birds and to understand the funny talking antics of the dogs. I used to practice listening to the mice behind the wainscot after I went to bed, and watching the cats on the roofs and pigeons in the market square of Puddleby.

And the days passed very quickly—as they always do when life is pleasant; and the days turned into weeks, and weeks into months; and soon the roses in the Doctor's garden were losing their petals and yellow leaves lay upon the wide green lawn. For the summer was nearly gone.

One day Polynesia and I were talking in the library. This was a fine long room with a grand mantelpiece and the walls were covered from the ceiling to the floor with shelves full of books: books of stories, books on gardening, books about medicine, books of travel; these I loved—and especially the Doctor's great atlas with all its maps of the different countries of the world.

This afternoon Polynesia was showing me the books about animals that John Dolittle had written himself.

"My!" I said. "What a lot of books the Doctor has—all the way around the room! Goodness! I wish I could read! It must be tremendously interesting. Can you read, Polynesia?"

"Only a little," said she. "Be careful how you turn those pages—don't tear them. No, I really don't get time enough for reading—much. That letter there is a *k* and this is a *b*."

"What does this word under the picture mean?" I asked.

"Let me see," she said, and started spelling it out. "B-A-B-O-O-N—that's *monkey*. Reading isn't nearly as hard as it looks, once you know the letters."

"Polynesia," I said, "I want to ask you something very important."

"What is it, my boy?" said she, smoothing down the feathers of her right wing. Polynesia often spoke to me in a very patronizing way. But I did not mind it from her. After all, she was nearly two hundred years old; and I was only ten.

"Listen," I said, "my mother doesn't think it is right that I come here for so many meals. And I was going to ask you: supposing I did a whole lot more work for the Doctor—why couldn't I come and live here altogether? You see, instead of being paid like a regular gardener or workman, I would get my bed and meals in exchange for the work I did. What do you think?"

"You mean you want to be a proper assistant to the Doctor, is that it?"

"Yes. I suppose that's what you call it," I answered. "You know you said yourself that you thought I could be very useful to him."

"Well"—she thought a moment—"I really don't see why not. But is this what you want to be when you grow up, a naturalist?"

"Yes," I said, "I have made up my mind. I would sooner be a naturalist than anything else in the world."

"Humph!—Let's go and speak to the Doctor about it," said Polynesia. "He's in the next room—in the study. Open the door very gently—he may be working and not want to be disturbed."

I opened the door quietly and peeped in. The first thing I saw was an enormous black retriever dog sitting in the middle of the hearth-rug with his ears cocked up, listening to the Doctor who was reading aloud to him from a letter.

"What *is* the Doctor doing?" I asked Polynesia in a whisper.

"Oh, the dog has had a letter from his mistress and he has brought it to the Doctor to read for him. That's all. He belongs to a funny little girl called Minnie Dooley, who lives on the other side of the town. She has pigtails down her back. She and her brother have gone away to the seaside for the summer; and the old retriever is heartbroken while the children are gone. So they write letters to him—in English of course. And as the old dog doesn't understand them, he brings them here, and the Doctor turns them into dog language for him. I think Minnie must have written that she is coming back—to judge from the dog's excitement. Just look at him carrying on!"

Indeed, the retriever seemed to be suddenly overcome with joy. As the Doctor finished the letter, the old dog started barking at the top of his voice, wagging his tail wildly, and jumping about the study. He took the letter in his mouth and ran out of the room snorting hard and mumbling to himself.

"He's going down to meet the coach," whispered Polynesia. "That dog's devotion to those children is more than I can understand. You should see Minnie! She's the most conceited little minx that ever walked. She squints, too."

THE TWELFTH CHAPTER

My Great Idea

P RESENTLY THE DOCTOR LOOKED UP AND saw us at the door.

"Oh—come in, Stubbins," said he, "did you wish to speak to me? Come in and take a chair."

"Doctor," I said, "I want to be a naturalist—like you—when I grow up."

"Oh you do, do you?" murmured the Doctor. "Humph!— Well!—Dear me!—You don't say!—Well, well! Have you, er— have you spoken to your mother and father about it?"

"No, not yet," I said. "I want you to speak to them for me. You would do it better. I want to be your helper—your assistant, if you'll have me. Last night my mother was saying that she didn't consider it right for me to come here so often for meals. And I've been thinking about it a good deal since. Couldn't we make some arrangement—couldn't I work for my meals and sleep here?"

"But my dear Stubbins," said the Doctor, laughing, "you are quite welcome to come here for three meals a day all the year round.

I'm only too glad to have you. Besides, you do do a lot of work, as it is. I've often felt that I ought to pay you for what you do. But what arrangement was it that you thought of?"

"Well, I thought," said I, "that perhaps you would come and see my mother and father and tell them that if they let me live here with you and work hard, that you will teach me to read and write. You see, my mother is awfully anxious to have me learn reading and writing. And besides, I couldn't be a proper naturalist without it, could I?"

"Oh, I don't know so much about that," said the Doctor. "It is nice, I admit, to be able to read and write. But naturalists are not all alike, you know. For example: this young fellow Charles Darwin that people are talking about so much now—he's a Cambridge graduate—reads and writes very well. And then Cuvier—he used to be a tutor. But listen, the greatest naturalist of them all doesn't even know how to write his own name nor to read the ABCs."

"Who is he?" I asked.

"He is a mysterious person," said the Doctor, "a very mysterious person. His name is Long Arrow, the son of Golden Arrow. He is a Native South American."

"Have you ever seen him?" I asked.

"No," said the Doctor, "I've never seen him. I fancy Mr. Darwin doesn't even know that he exists. He lives almost entirely with the animals and with the different native tribes—usually somewhere among the mountains of Peru. Never stays long in one place. Goes from tribe to tribe."

"How do you know so much about him?" I asked, "if you've never even seen him?"

"The purple bird-of-paradise," said the Doctor. "She told

me all about him. She says he is a perfectly marvelous naturalist. I got her to take a message to him for me last time she was here. I am expecting her back any day now. I can hardly wait to see what answer she has brought from him. It is already almost the last week of August. I do hope nothing has happened to her on the way."

"But why do the animals and birds come to you when they are sick?" I said. "Why don't they go to him, if he is so very wonderful?"

"It seems that my methods are more up-to-date," said the Doctor. "But from what the purple bird-of-paradise tells me, Long Arrow's knowledge of natural history must be positively tremendous. His specialty is botany—plants and all that sort of thing. But he knows a lot about birds and animals, too. He's very good on bees and beetles. But now tell me, Stubbins, are you quite sure that you really want to be a naturalist?"

"Yes," said I, "my mind is made up."

"Well you know, it isn't a very good profession for making money. Not at all, it isn't. Most of the good naturalists don't make any money whatsoever. All they do is *spend* money, buying butterfly nets and cases for birds' eggs and things. It is only now, after I have been a naturalist for many years, that I am beginning to make a little money from the books I write."

"I don't care about money," I said. "I want to be a naturalist. Won't you please come and have dinner with my mother and father next Thursday—I told them I was going to ask you—and then you can talk to them about it. You see, there's another thing: if I'm living with you, and sort of belong to your house and business, I shall be able to come with you next time you go on a voyage."

"Oh, I see," said he, smiling. "So you want to come on a voyage with me, do you? Aha!"

"I want to go on all your voyages with you. It would be much easier for you if you had someone to carry the butterfly nets and notebooks. Wouldn't it, now?"

For a long time the Doctor sat thinking, drumming on the desk with his fingers, while I waited, terribly impatiently, to see what he was going to say.

At last he shrugged his shoulders and stood up.

"Well, Stubbins," said he, "I'll come and talk it over with you and your parents next Thursday. And—well, we'll see. We'll see. Give your mother and father my compliments and thank them for their invitation, will you?"

Then I tore home like the wind to tell my mother that the Doctor had promised to come.

A Traveler Arrives

THE NEXT DAY I WAS SITTING ON THE WALL OF the Doctor's garden after tea, talking to Dab-Dab. I had now learned so much from Polynesia that I could talk to most birds and some animals without a great deal of difficulty. I found Dab-Dab a very nice, old, motherly bird—though not nearly so clever and interesting as Polynesia. She had been housekeeper for the Doctor many years now.

Well, as I was saying, the old duck and I were sitting on the flat top of the garden wall that evening, looking down into the Oxenthorpe Road below. We were watching some sheep being driven to market in Puddleby; and Dab-Dab had just been telling me about the Doctor's adventures in Africa. For she had gone on a voyage with him to that country long ago.

Suddenly I heard a curious, distant noise down the road, toward the town. It sounded like a lot of people cheering. I stood up on the wall to see if I could make out what was coming. Presently there appeared round a bend a great crowd of schoolchildren following a very ragged, curious-looking woman.

"What in the world can it be?" cried Dab-Dab.

The children were all laughing and shouting. And certainly the woman they were following was most extraordinary. She had very long arms and the most stooping shoulders I have ever seen. She wore a straw hat on the side of her head with poppies on it; and her skirt was so long for her that it dragged on the ground like a ball gown's train. I could not see anything of her face because of the wide hat pulled over her eyes. But as she got nearer to us and the laughing of the children grew louder, I noticed that her hands were very dark in color, and hairy, like a witch's.

Then all of a sudden Dab-Dab at my side startled me by crying out in a loud voice:

"Why, it's Chee-Chee! Chee-Chee's come back at last! How dare those children tease him! I'll give the little imps something to laugh at!"

And she flew right off the wall down into the road and made straight for the children, squawking away in a most terrifying fashion and pecking at their feet and legs. The children made off down the street back to the town as hard as they could run.

The strange-looking figure in the straw hat stood gazing after them a moment, and then came wearily up to the gate. It didn't bother to undo the latch but just climbed right over the gate as though it were something in the way. And then I noticed that it took hold of the bars with its feet, so that it really had four hands to climb with. But it was only when I at last got a glimpse of the face under the hat that I could be really sure it was a monkey.

Chee-Chee—for it was he—frowned at me suspiciously from

"A traveler arrives."

the top of the gate, as though he thought I was going to laugh at
him like the other boys and girls. Then he dropped into the garden
on the inside and immediately started taking off his clothes. He
tore the straw hat in two and threw it down onto the road. Then he
took off his bodice and skirt, jumped on them savagely, and began
kicking them round the front garden.

Presently I heard a screech from the house, and out flew Polynesia, followed by the Doctor and Jip.

"Chee-Chee! Chee-Chee!" shouted the parrot. "You've come at last! I always told the Doctor you'd find a way. However did you do it?"

They all gathered round him, shaking him by his four hands, laughing and asking him a million questions at once. Then they all started back for the house.

"Run up to my bedroom, Stubbins," said the Doctor, turning to me. "You'll find a bag of peanuts in the small left-hand drawer of the bureau. I have always kept them there in case he might come back unexpectedly someday. And wait a minute—see if Dab-Dab has any bananas in the pantry. Chee-Chee hasn't had a banana, he tells me, in two months."

When I came down again to the kitchen I found everybody listening attentively to the monkey, who was telling the story of his journey from Africa.

Chee-Chee's Voyage

IT SEEMS THAT AFTER POLYNESIA HAD LEFT, Chee-Chee had grown more homesick than ever for the Doctor and the little house in Puddleby. At last he had made up his mind that by hook or crook he would follow her. And one day, going down to the seashore, he saw a lot of people getting onto a ship that was going to England. He tried to get on, too, but they turned him back and drove him away. So he said to himself, "If I could only get some clothes to wear I might easily slip onto the ship among the crowd. Good idea!"

So he went off to a town that was quite close, and hopping in through an open window he found a skirt and bodice lying on a chair. They belonged to a fashionable lady who was taking a bath. Chee-Chee put them on. Next he went back to the seashore, mingled with the crowd there, and at last sneaked safely onto the big ship. Then he thought he had better hide, and he stayed hidden all the time the ship was sailing to England—only coming out at night, when everybody was asleep, to find food.

When he reached England and tried to get off the ship, the sailors saw him; and they wanted to keep him for a pet. But he managed to give them the slip; and once he was onshore, he dived into the crowd and got away. But he was still a long distance from Puddleby and had to come right across the whole breadth of England.

He had a terrible time of it. Whenever he passed through a town, all the children ran after him in a crowd, laughing; and often silly people caught hold of him and tried to stop him, so that he had to run up lampposts and climb up chimney tops to escape from them. At night he used to sleep in ditches or barns or anywhere he could hide; and he lived on the berries he picked from the hedges and the cobnuts that grew in the copses. At length, after many adventures and narrow squeaks, he saw the tower of Puddleby Church and he knew that at last he was near his old home.

When Chee-Chee had finished his story he ate six bananas without stopping and drank a whole bowlful of milk.

"My!" he said. "Why wasn't I born with wings, like Polynesia, so I could fly here? You've no idea how I grew to hate that hat and skirt. I've never been so uncomfortable in my life. All the way from Bristol here, if the wretched hat wasn't falling off my head or catching in the trees, those beastly skirts were tripping me up and getting wound round everything. What on earth do women wear those things for? Goodness, I was glad to see old Puddleby this morning when I climbed over the hill by Bellaby's farm!"

"Your bed on top of the plate rack in the scullery is all ready for you," said the Doctor. "We never had it disturbed, in case you might come back."

"Yes," said Dab-Dab, "and you can have the old smoking jacket of the Doctor's that you used to use as a blanket, in case it is cold in the night."

"Thanks," said Chee-Chee. "It's good to be back in the old house again. Everything's just the same as when I left—except the clean roller towel on the back of the door there—that's new. Well, I think I'll go to bed now. I need sleep."

Then we all went out of the kitchen into the scullery and watched Chee-Chee climb the plate rack like a sailor going up a mast. On the top, he curled himself up, pulled the old smoking jacket over him, and in a minute he was snoring peacefully.

"Good old Chee-Chee!" whispered the Doctor. "I'm glad he's back."

"Yes—good old Chee-Chee!" echoed Dab-Dab and Polynesia.

Then we all tiptoed out of the scullery and closed the door very gently behind us.

THE FIFTEENTH CHAPTER

I Become a Doctor's Assistant

WHEN THURSDAY EVENING CAME THERE was great excitement at our house. My mother had asked me what the Doctor's favorite dishes were, and I had told her: spareribs, sliced beetroot, fried bread, shrimp, and treacle tart. Tonight she had them all on the table waiting for him; and she was now fussing round the house to see if everything was tidy and in readiness for his coming.

At last we heard a knock upon the door, and of course it was I who got there first to let him in.

The Doctor had brought his own flute with him this time. And after supper was over (which he enjoyed very much), the table was cleared away and the washing-up left in the kitchen sink till the next day. Then the Doctor and my father started playing duets.

They got so interested in this that I began to be afraid that they would never come to talking over my business. But at last the Doctor said:

"Your son tells me that he is anxious to become a naturalist."

— 75 —

And then began a long talk that lasted far into the night. At first both my mother and father were rather against the idea—as they had been from the beginning. They said it was only a boyish whim and that I would get tired of it very soon. But after the matter had been talked over from every side, the Doctor turned to my father and said:

"Well now, supposing, Mr. Stubbins, that your son came to me for two years—that is, until he is twelve years old. During those two years he will have time to see if he is going to grow tired of it or not. Also during that time, I will promise to teach him reading and writing and perhaps a little arithmetic as well. What do you say to that?"

"I don't know," said my father, shaking his head. "You are very kind, and it is a handsome offer you make, Doctor. But I feel that Tommy ought to be learning some trade by which he can earn his living later on."

Then my mother spoke up. Although she was nearly in tears at the prospect of my leaving her house while I was still so young, she pointed out to my father that this was a grand chance for me to get learning.

"Now, Jacob," she said, "you know that many lads in the town have been to the grammar school till they were fourteen or fifteen years old. Tommy can easily spare these two years for his education; and if he learns no more than to read and write, the time will not be lost. Though goodness knows," she added, getting out her handkerchief to cry, "the house will seem terribly empty when he's gone."

"I will take care that he comes to see you, Mrs. Stubbins," said the Doctor, "every day, if you like. After all, he will not be very far away."

Well, at length my father gave in; and it was agreed that I was to live with the Doctor and work for him for two years in exchange for learning to read and write and for my board and lodging.

"Of course," added the Doctor, "while I have money I will keep Tommy in clothes as well. But money is a very irregular thing with me; sometimes I have some, and then sometimes I haven't."

"You are very good, Doctor," said my mother, drying her tears. "It seems to me that Tommy is a very fortunate boy."

And then, thoughtless, selfish little imp that I was, I leaned over and whispered in the Doctor's ear:

"Please don't forget to say something about the voyages."

"Oh, by the way," said John Dolittle, "occasionally my work requires me to travel. You will have no objection, I take it, to your son's coming with me?"

My poor mother looked up sharply, more unhappy and anxious than ever at this new turn; while I stood behind the Doctor's chair, my heart thumping with excitement, waiting for my father's answer.

"No," he said slowly after a while. "If we agree to the other arrangement, I don't see that we've the right to make any objection to that."

Well, there surely was never a happier boy in the world than I was at that moment. My head was in the clouds. I trod on air. I could scarcely keep from dancing round the parlor. At last the dream of my life was to come true! At last I was to be given a chance to seek my fortune, to have adventures! For I knew perfectly well that it was now almost time for the Doctor to start upon another voyage. Polynesia had told me that he hardly ever stayed at home for more than six months at a stretch. Therefore he would be surely going again within a fortnight. And I—I, Tommy Stubbins, would go with him! Just to think of it!—to cross the sea, to walk on foreign shores, to roam the world!

PART TWO

The Crew of
The Curlew

FROM THAT TIME ON, OF COURSE, MY POSITION in the town was very different. I was no longer a poor cobbler's son. I carried my nose in the air as I went down the High Street with Jip in his gold collar at my side; and snobbish little boys who had despised me before because I was not rich enough to go to school, now pointed me out to their friends and whispered, "You see him? He's a doctor's assistant—and only ten years old!"

But their eyes would have opened still wider with wonder if they had but known that I and the dog that was with me could talk to one another.

Two days after the Doctor had been to our house to dinner he told me very sadly that he was afraid that he would have to give up trying to learn the language of the shellfish—at all events for the present.

"I'm very discouraged, Stubbins, very. I've tried the mussels and the clams, the oysters and the whelks, cockles and scallops;

seven different kinds of crabs and all the lobster family. I think I'll leave it for the present and go at it again later on."

"What will you turn to now?" I asked.

"Well, I rather thought of going on a voyage, Stubbins. It's quite a time now since I've been away. And there is a great deal of work waiting for me abroad."

"When shall we start?" I asked.

"Well, first I shall have to wait till the purple bird-of-paradise gets here. I must see if she has any message for me from Long Arrow. She's late. She should have been here ten days ago. I hope to goodness she's all right."

"Well, hadn't we better be seeing about getting a boat?" I said. "She is sure to be here in a day or so; and there will be lots of things to do to get ready in the meantime, won't there?"

"Yes, indeed," said the Doctor. "Suppose we go down and see your friend Joe, the mussel man. He will know about boats."

"I'd like to come, too," said Jip.

"All right, come along," said the Doctor, and off we went.

Joe said yes, he had a boat—one he had just bought—but it needed three people to sail her. We told him we would like to see it anyway.

So the mussel man took us off a little way down the river and showed us the neatest, prettiest little vessel that ever was built. She was called the *Curlew*. Joe said he would sell her to us cheap. But the trouble was that the boat needed three people, while we were only two.

"Of course, I shall be taking Chee-Chee," said the Doctor. "But although he is very quick and clever, he is not as strong as a man. We really ought to have another person to sail a boat as big as that."

"I know of a good sailor, Doctor," said Joe, "a first-class seaman who would be glad of the job."

"No thank you, Joe," said Doctor Dolittle. "I don't want any seamen. I couldn't afford to hire them. And then they hamper me so, seamen do, when I'm at sea. They're always wanting to do things the proper way; and I like to do them *my* way. Now, let me see: Who could we take with us?"

"There's Matthew Mugg, the Cat's-Meat-Man," I said.

"No, he wouldn't do. Matthew's a very nice fellow, but he talks too much—mostly about his rheumatism. You have to be frightfully particular whom you take with you on long voyages."

"How about Luke the Hermit?" I asked.

"That's a good idea—splendid—if he'll come. Let's go and ask him right away."

Luke the Hermit

THE HERMIT WAS AN OLD FRIEND OF OURS, AS I have already told you. He was a very peculiar person. Far out on the marshes he lived in a little bit of a shack— all alone except for his brindle bulldog. No one knew where he came from—not even his name. Just "Luke the Hermit" folks called him. He never came into the town; never seemed to want to see or talk to people. His dog, Bob, drove them away if they came near his hut. When you asked anyone in Puddleby who he was or why he lived out in that lonely place by himself, the only answer you got was, "Oh, Luke the Hermit? Well, there's some mystery about him. Nobody knows what it is. But there's a mystery. Don't go near him. He'll set the dog on you."

Nevertheless, there were two people who often went out to that little shack on the fens: the Doctor and myself. And Bob, the bulldog, never barked when he heard us coming. For we liked Luke; and Luke liked us.

This afternoon, crossing the marshes we faced a cold wind blowing from the east. As we approached the hut, Jip put up his ears and said:

"That's funny!"

"What's funny?" asked the Doctor.

"That Bob hasn't come out to meet us. He should have heard us long ago—or smelled us. What's that strange noise?"

"Sounds to me like a gate creaking," said the Doctor. "Maybe it's Luke's door, only we can't see the door from here; it's on the far side of the shack."

"I hope Bob isn't sick," said Jip, and he let out a bark to see if that would call him. But the only answer he got was the wailing of the wind across the wide, salt fen.

We hurried forward, all three of us thinking hard.

When we reached the front of the shack we found the door open, swinging and creaking dismally in the wind. We looked inside. There was no one there.

"Isn't Luke at home, then?" said I. "Perhaps he's out for a walk."

"He is *always* at home," said the Doctor, frowning in a peculiar sort of way. "And even if he were out for a walk, he wouldn't leave his door banging in the wind behind him. There is something odd about this—What are you doing in there, Jip?"

"Nothing much—nothing worth speaking of," said Jip, examining the floor of the hut extremely carefully.

"Come here, Jip," said the Doctor in a stern voice. "You are hiding something from me. You see signs and you know something—or you guess it. What has happened? Tell me. Where is the hermit?"

"I don't know," said Jip, looking very guilty and uncomfortable. "I don't know where he is."

"Well, you know something. I can tell it from the look in your eye. What is it?"

But Jip didn't answer.

For ten minutes the Doctor kept questioning him. But not a word would the dog say.

"Well," said the Doctor at last, "it is no use our standing around here in the cold. The hermit's gone. That's all. We might as well go home to luncheon."

As we buttoned up our coats and started back across the marsh, Jip ran ahead, pretending he was looking for water rats.

"He knows something, all right," whispered the Doctor. "And I think he knows what has happened, too. It's funny, his not wanting to tell me. He has never done that before—not in eleven years. He has always told me everything. Strange—very strange!"

"Do you mean you think he knows all about the hermit, the big mystery about him which folks hint at and all that?"

"I shouldn't wonder if he did," the Doctor answered slowly. "I noticed something in his expression the moment we found that door open and the hut empty. And the way he sniffed the floor, too—it told him something, that floor did. He saw signs we couldn't see. I wonder why he won't tell me. I'll try him again. Here, Jip! Jip! Where is the dog? I thought he went on in front."

"So did I," I said. "He was there a moment ago. I saw him as large as life. Jip—Jip— Jip—JIP!"

But he was gone. We called and called. We even walked back to the hut. But Jip had disappeared.

"Oh well," I said. "Most likely he has just run home ahead of us. He often does that, you know. We'll find him there when we get back to the house."

But the Doctor just closed his coat collar tighter against the wind and strode on, muttering, "Odd—very odd!"

THE THIRD CHAPTER

Jip and the Secret

WHEN WE REACHED THE HOUSE, THE first question the Doctor asked of Dab-Dab in the hall was:

"Is Jip home yet?"

"No," said Dab-Dab, "I haven't seen him."

"Let me know the moment he comes in, will you, please?" said the Doctor, hanging up his hat.

"Certainly I will," said Dab-Dab. "Don't be long over washing your hands; the lunch is on the table."

Just as we were sitting down to luncheon in the kitchen, we heard a great racket at the front door. I ran and opened it. In bounded Jip.

"Doctor!" he cried, "come into the library quick. I've got something to tell you—No, Dab-Dab, the luncheon must wait. Please hurry, Doctor. There's not a moment to be lost. Don't let any of the animals come—just you and Tommy."

"Now," he said, when we were inside the library and the door was closed, "turn the key in the lock and make sure there's no one listening under the windows."

"It's all right," said the Doctor. "Nobody can hear you here. Now, what is it?"

"Well, Doctor," said Jip (he was badly out of breath from running), "I know all about the hermit—I have known for years. But I couldn't tell you."

"Why?" asked the Doctor.

"Because I'd promised not to tell anyone. It was Bob, his dog, that told me. And I swore to him that I would keep the secret."

"Well, and are you going to tell me now?"

"Yes," said Jip, "we've got to save him. I followed Bob's scent just now when I left you out there on the marshes. And I found him. I said to him, 'Is it all right,' I said, 'for me to tell the Doctor now? Maybe he can do something.' And Bob said to me, 'Yes,' said he, 'it's all right because—'"

"Oh, for heaven's sake, go on, go on!" cried the Doctor. "Tell us what the mystery is—not what you said to Bob and what Bob said to you. What has happened? Where *is* the hermit?"

"He's in Puddleby Jail," said Jip. "He's in prison."

"In prison!"

"Yes."

"What for?—What's he done?"

Jip went over to the door and smelled at the bottom of it to see if anyone were listening outside. Then he came back to the Doctor on tiptoe and whispered:

"He killed a man!"

"Lord preserve us!" cried the Doctor, sitting down heavily in a chair and mopping his forehead with a handkerchief. "When did he do it?"

"Fifteen years ago—in a Mexican gold mine. That's why he has been a hermit ever since. He shaved off his beard and kept away from people out there on the marshes so he wouldn't be recognized. But last week, it seems these newfangled policemen came to town, and they heard there was a strange man who kept to himself all alone in a shack on the fen. And they got suspicious. For a long time people had been hunting all over the world for the man that did that killing in the Mexican gold mine fifteen years ago. So these policemen went out to the shack, and they recognized Luke by a mole on his arm. And they took him to prison."

"Well, well!" murmured the Doctor. "Who would have thought it? Luke, the philosopher! Killed a man! I can hardly believe it."

"It's true enough—unfortunately," said Jip. "Luke did it. But it wasn't his fault. Bob says so. And he was there and saw it all. He was scarcely more than a puppy at the time. Bob says Luke couldn't help it. He *had* to do it."

"Where is Bob now?" asked the Doctor.

"Down at the prison. I wanted him to come with me here to see you; but he won't leave the prison while Luke is there. He just sits outside the door of the prison cell and won't move. He doesn't even eat the food they give him. Won't you please come down there, Doctor, and see if there is anything you can do? The trial is to be this afternoon at two o'clock. What time is it now?"

"It's ten minutes past one."

"Bob says he thinks they are going to kill Luke for a punishment if they can prove that he did it—or certainly keep him in prison for the rest of his life. Won't you please come? Perhaps if you spoke to the judge and told him what a good man Luke really is they'd let him off."

"Of course I'll come," said the Doctor, getting up and moving to go. "But I'm very much afraid that I shan't be of any real help." He turned at the door and hesitated thoughtfully.

"And yet—I wonder—"

Then he opened the door and went outside, with Jip and me close at his heels.

THE FOURTH CHAPTER

Bob

DAB-DAB WAS TERRIBLY UPSET WHEN SHE found we were going away again without luncheon; and she made us take some cold pork-pies in our pockets to eat on the way.

When we got to Puddleby Courthouse (it was next door to the prison), we found a great crowd gathered around the building.

This was the week of the assizes—a business which happened every three months, when many pickpockets and other bad characters were tried by a very grand judge who came all the way from London. Anybody in Puddleby who had nothing special to do used to come to the courthouse to hear the trials.

But today it was different. The crowd was not made up of just a few idle people. It was enormous. The news had run through the countryside that Luke the Hermit was to be tried for killing a man, and that the great mystery that had hung over him for so long was to be cleared up at last. The butcher and the baker had closed their shops and taken a holiday. All the farmers from roundabout, and all the townsfolk, were there with their Sunday clothes on, trying to get seats in the courthouse or gossiping outside in low whispers. The High Street was so crowded you could hardly move along it. I had never seen the quiet old town in such a state of excitement before. For Puddleby had not had such an assizes since 1799, when Ferdinand Phipps, the rector's oldest son, had robbed the bank.

If I hadn't had the Doctor with me, I am sure I would never have been able to make my way through the mob packed around the courthouse door. But I just followed behind him, hanging on to his coattails; and at last we got safely into the jail.

"I want to see Luke," said the Doctor to a very grand person in a blue coat with brass buttons standing at the door.

"Ask at the superintendent's office," said the man. "Third door on the left down the corridor."

"Who is that person you spoke to, Doctor?" I asked as we went along the passage.

"He is a policeman."

"And what are policemen?"

"Policemen? They are to keep people in order. They've just been invented—by Sir Robert Peel. That's why they are also called 'peelers' sometimes. It is a wonderful age we live in. They're always thinking of something new. This will be the superintendent's office, I suppose."

From there another policeman was sent with us to show us the way.

Outside the door of Luke's cell we found Bob, the bulldog, who wagged his tail sadly when he saw us. The man who was guiding us took a large bunch of keys from his pocket and opened the door.

I had never been inside a real prison cell before; and I felt quite a thrill when the policeman went out and locked the door after him, leaving us shut in the dimly lighted, little stone room. Before he went, he said that as soon as we had done talking with our friend, we should knock upon the door and he would come and let us out.

At first I could hardly see anything, it was so dim inside. But after a little while I made out a low bed against the wall, under a small barred window. On the bed, staring down at the floor between his feet, sat the hermit, his head resting in his hands.

"Well, Luke," said the Doctor in a kindly voice, "they don't give you much light in here, do they?"

Very slowly the hermit looked up from the floor.

"Hulloa, John Dolittle. What brings you here?"

"I've come to see you. I would have been here sooner, only I didn't hear about all this till a few minutes ago. I went to your hut to ask you if you would join me on a voyage; and when I found it empty, I had no idea where you could be. I am dreadfully sorry to hear about your bad luck. I've come to see if there is anything I can do."

Luke shook his head.

"No, I don't imagine there is anything that can be done. They've caught me at last. That's the end of it, I suppose."

He got up stiffly and started walking up and down the little room.

"In a way I'm glad it's over," said he. "I never got any peace, always thinking they were after me—afraid to speak to anyone. They were bound to get me in the end. Yes, I'm glad it's over."

Then the Doctor talked to Luke for more than half an hour, trying to cheer him up; while I sat around wondering what I ought to say and wishing I could do something.

At last the Doctor said he wanted to see Bob, and we knocked upon the door and were let out by the policeman.

"On the bed sat the hermit."

"Bob," said the Doctor to the big bulldog in the passage, "come out with me into the porch. I want to ask you something."

"How is he, Doctor?" asked Bob as we walked down the corridor into the courthouse porch.

"Oh, Luke's all right. Very miserable, of course, but he's all right. Now tell me, Bob: You saw this business happen, didn't you? You were there when the man was killed, eh?"

"I was, Doctor," said Bob, "and I tell you—"

"All right," the Doctor interrupted, "that's all I want to know for the present. There isn't time to tell me more now. The trial is just going to begin. There are the judge and the lawyers coming up the steps. Now listen, Bob: I want you to stay with me when I go into the courtroom. And whatever I tell you to do, do it. Do you understand? Don't make any scenes. Don't bite anybody, no matter what they may say about Luke. Just behave perfectly quietly and answer any question I may ask you—truthfully. Do you understand?"

"Very well. But do you think you will be able to get him off, Doctor?" asked Bob. "He's a good man, Doctor. He really is. There never was a better."

"We'll see, we'll see, Bob. It's a new thing I'm going to try. I'm not sure the judge will allow it. But—well, we'll see. It's time to go into the courtroom now. Don't forget what I told you. Remember: for heaven's sake, don't start biting anyone or you'll get us all thrown out and spoil everything.

Mendoza

INSIDE THE COURTROOM EVERYTHING WAS very solemn and wonderful. It was a high, big room. Raised above the floor, against the wall was the judge's desk; and here the judge was already sitting—an old, handsome man in a marvelous big wig of gray hair and a gown of black. Below him was another wide, long desk at which lawyers in white wigs sat. The whole thing reminded me of a mixture between a church and a school.

"Those twelve men at the side," whispered the Doctor, "those in pews like a choir, they are what is called the jury. It is they who decide whether Luke is guilty—whether he did it or not."

"And look!" I said. "There's Luke himself in a sort of pulpit thing with policemen each side of him. And there's another pulpit, the same kind, on the other side of the room, see—only that one's empty."

"That one is called the witness-box," said the Doctor. "Now I'm going down to speak to one of those men in white wigs; and I want you to wait here and keep these two seats for us. Bob will stay with you. Keep an eye on him—better hold on to his collar. I shan't be more than a minute or so."

With that the Doctor disappeared into the crowd, which filled the main part of the room.

Then I saw the judge take up a funny little wooden hammer and knock on his desk with it. This, it seemed, was to make people keep quiet, for immediately everyone stopped buzzing and talking and began to listen very respectfully. Then another man in a black gown stood up and began reading from a paper in his hand.

He mumbled away exactly as though he were saying his prayers and didn't want any one to understand what language they were in. But I managed to catch a few words:

"*Biz—biz—biz—biz—biz*—otherwise known as Luke the Hermit, of—*biz—biz—biz—biz*—for killing his partner with—*biz—biz—biz*—otherwise known as Bluebeard Bill on the night of the—*biz—biz—biz*—in the *biz—biz—biz*—of Mexico. Therefore Her Majesty's—*biz—biz—biz*—"

At this moment I felt someone take hold of my arm from the back, and turning round I found the Doctor had returned with one of the men in white wigs.

"Stubbins, this is Mr. Percy Jenkyns," said the Doctor. "He is Luke's lawyer. It is his business to get Luke off—if he can."

Mr. Jenkyns seemed to be an extremely young man with a round, smooth face like a boy. He shook hands with me and then immediately turned and went on talking with the Doctor.

"Oh, I think it is a perfectly precious idea," he was saying. "Of *course* the dog must be admitted as a witness; he was the only one who saw the thing take place. I'm awfully glad you came. I wouldn't have missed this for anything. My hat! Won't it make the old court sit up? They're always frightfully dull, these assizes. But this will stir things. A bulldog witness for the defense! I do hope there are plenty of reporters present—Yes, there's one making a sketch of the prisoner. I shall become known after this—And won't Conkey be pleased? My hat!"

He put his hand over his mouth to smother a laugh and his eyes fairly sparkled with mischief.

"Who is Conkey?" I asked the Doctor.

"Sh! He is speaking of the judge up there, the Honorable Eustace Beauchamp Conckley."

"Now," said Mr. Jenkyns, bringing out a notebook, "tell me a little more about yourself, Doctor. You took your degree as Doctor of Medicine at Durham, I think you said. And the name of your last book was?"

I could not hear any more for they talked in whispers; and I fell to looking round the court again.

Of course I could not understand everything that was going on, though it was all very interesting. People kept getting up in the place the Doctor called the witness-box, and the lawyers at the long table asked them questions about "the night of the twenty-ninth." Then the people would get down again and somebody else would get up and be questioned.

One of the lawyers (who, the Doctor told me afterward, was called the prosecutor) seemed to be doing his best to get the hermit into trouble by asking questions that made it look as though he had always been a very bad man. He was a nasty lawyer, this prosecutor, with a long nose.

Most of the time I could hardly keep my eyes off poor Luke, who sat there between two policemen, staring at the floor as though he weren't interested. The only time I saw him take any notice of at all was when a small dark man with wicked little watery eyes got up into the witness-box. I heard Bob snarl under my chair as this person came into the courtroom, and Luke's eyes just blazed with anger and contempt.

This man said his name was Mendoza, and that he was the one who had guided the Mexican police to the mine after Bluebeard Bill had been killed. And at every word he said I could hear Bob down below me muttering between his teeth:

"It's a lie! It's a lie! I'll chew his face. It's a lie!"

And both the Doctor and I had hard work keeping the dog under the seat.

Then I noticed that our Mr. Jenkyns had disappeared from the Doctor's side. But presently I saw him stand up at the long table to speak to the judge.

"Your Honor," said he, "I wish to introduce a new witness for the defense, Doctor John Dolittle, the naturalist. Will you please step into the witness stand, Doctor?"

There was a buzz of excitement as the Doctor made his way across the crowded room; and I noticed the nasty lawyer with the long nose lean down and whisper something to a friend, smiling in an ugly way that made me want to pinch him.

Then Mr. Jenkyns asked the Doctor a whole lot of questions about himself and made him answer in a loud voice so the whole court could hear. He finished up by saying:

"And you are prepared to swear, Doctor Dolittle, that you understand the language of dogs and can make them understand you. Is that so?"

"Yes," said the Doctor, "that is so."

"And what, might I ask," put in the judge in a very quiet, dignified voice, "has all this to do with the killing of er—er—Bluebeard Bill?"

"This, Your Honor," said Mr. Jenkyns, talking in a very grand manner as though he were on a stage in a theater: "There is in this courtroom at the present moment a bulldog, who is the only living thing that saw the man killed. With the court's permission, I propose to put that dog in the witness stand and have him questioned before you by the eminent scientist, Doctor John Dolittle."

The Judge's Dog

T FIRST THERE WAS A DEAD SILENCE IN THE
court. Then everybody began whispering or giggling
at the same time, till the whole room sounded like
a great hive of bees. Many people seemed to be
shocked; most of them were amused; and a few were angry.

Presently up sprang the nasty lawyer with the long nose.

"I protest, Your Honor," he cried, waving his arms wildly to
the judge. "I object. The dignity of this court is in peril. I protest."

"I am the one to take care of the dignity of this court," said the
judge.

Then Mr. Jenkyns got up again. (If it hadn't been such a serious matter, it was almost like a Punch-and-Judy show: somebody
was always popping down and somebody else popping up).

"If there is any doubt on the score of our being able to do as
we say, Your Honor will have no objection, I trust, to the Doctor's
giving the court a demonstration of his powers—of showing that he
actually can understand the speech of animals?"

I thought I saw a twinkle of amusement come into the old judge's eyes as he sat considering a moment before he answered.

"No," he said at last, "I don't think so." Then he turned to the Doctor.

"Are you quite sure you can do this?" he asked.

"Quite, Your Honor," said the Doctor, "quite sure."

"Very well, then," said the judge. "If you can satisfy us that you really are able to understand canine testimony, the dog shall be admitted as a witness. I do not see, in that case, how I could object to his being heard. But I warn you that if you are trying to make a laughingstock of this court it will go hard with you."

"I protest, I protest!" yelled the long-nosed prosecutor. "This is a scandal, an outrage to the bar!"

"Sit down!" said the judge in a very stern voice.

"What animal does Your Honor wish me to talk with?" asked the Doctor.

"I would like you to talk to my own dog," said the judge. "He is outside in the cloakroom. I will have him brought in; and then we shall see what you can do."

Then someone went out and fetched the judge's dog, a lovely great Russian wolfhound with slender legs and a shaggy coat. He was a proud and beautiful creature.

"Now, Doctor," said the judge, "did you ever see this dog before? Remember you are in the witness stand and under oath."

"No, Your Honor, I never saw him before."

"Very well then, will you please ask him to tell you what I had for supper last night? He was with me and watched me while I ate."

Then the Doctor and the dog started talking to one another in signs and sounds; and they kept at it for quite a long time. And the Doctor began to giggle and get so interested that he seemed to forget all about the court and the judge and everything else.

"What a time he takes!" I heard a woman in front of me whispering. "He's only pretending. Of course he can't do it! Whoever heard of talking to a dog? He must think we're children."

"Haven't you finished yet?" the judge asked the Doctor. "It shouldn't take that long just to ask what I had for supper."

"Oh no, Your Honor," said the Doctor. "The dog told me that long ago. But then he went on to tell me what you did after supper."

"Never mind that," said the judge. "Tell me what answer he gave you to my question."

"He says you had a mutton chop, two baked potatoes, a pickled walnut, and a glass of ale."

The Honorable Eustace Beauchamp Conckley went white to the lips.

"Sounds like witchcraft," he muttered. "I never dreamed—"

"And after your supper," the Doctor went on, "he says you went to see a prizefight and then sat up playing cards for money till twelve o'clock and came home singing, 'We won't get—'"

"That will do," the judge interrupted, "I am satisfied you can do as you say. The prisoner's dog shall be admitted as a witness."

"I protest, I object!" screamed the prosecutor. "Your Honor, this is—"

"Sit down!" roared the judge. "I say the dog shall be heard. That ends the matter. Put the witness in the stand."

And then for the first time in the solemn history of England, a dog was put in the witness stand of Her Majesty's court of assizes. And it was I, Tommy Stubbins (when the Doctor made a sign to me across the room), who proudly led Bob up the aisle, through the astonished crowd, past the frowning, spluttering, long-nosed prosecutor, and made him comfortable on a high chair in the witness-box; from where the old bulldog sat scowling down over the rail upon the amazed and gaping jury.

"Sat scowling down upon the amazed, gaping jury"

The End of the Mystery

THE TRIAL WENT SWIFTLY FORWARD AFTER that. Mr. Jenkyns told the Doctor to ask Bob what he saw on the "night of the twenty-ninth," and when Bob had told all he knew and the Doctor had turned it into English for the judge and the jury, this was what he had to say:

"On the night of the twenty-ninth of November, 1824, I was with my master, Luke Fitzjohn (otherwise known as Luke the Hermit) and his two partners, Manuel Mendoza and William Boggs (otherwise known as Bluebeard Bill) in their gold mine in Mexico. For a long time these three men had been hunting for gold; and they had dug a deep hole in the ground. On the morning of the twenty-ninth, gold was discovered, lots of it, at the bottom of this hole. And all three, my master and his two partners, were very happy about it because now they would be rich. But Manuel Mendoza asked Bluebeard Bill to go for a walk with him. These two men I had always suspected of being bad. So when I noticed that they left my master behind, I followed them secretly to see what they were up to. And in a deep cave in the mountains I heard them arrange together to kill Luke the Hermit so that they should get all the gold and he have none."

At this point the judge asked, "Where is the witness Mendoza? Constable, see that he does not leave the court."

But the wicked little man with the watery eyes had already sneaked out when no one was looking and he was never seen in Puddleby again.

"Then," Bob's statement went on, "I went to my master and tried very hard to make him understand that his partners were dangerous men. But it was no use. He did not understand dog language. So I did the next best thing: I never let him out of my sight, but stayed with him every moment of the day and night.

"Now the hole that they had made was so deep that to get down and up it you had to go in a big bucket tied on the end of a rope; and the three men used to haul one another up and let one another down the mine in this way. That was how the gold was brought up too—in the bucket. Well, about seven o'clock in the evening, my master was standing at the top of the mine, hauling up, Bluebeard Bill who was in the bucket. Just as he had got Bill halfway up, I saw Mendoza come out of the hut where we all lived. Mendoza thought that Bill was away buying groceries. But he wasn't: he was in the bucket. And when Mendoza saw Luke hauling and straining on the rope, he thought he was pulling up a bucketful of gold. So he drew a pistol from his pocket and came sneaking up behind Luke to shoot him.

"I barked and barked to warn my master of the danger he was in; but he was so busy hauling up Bill (who was a heavy man) that he took no notice of me. I saw that if I didn't do something quick, he would surely be shot. So I did a thing I've never done before: suddenly and savagely I bit my master in the leg from behind. Luke was so hurt and startled that he did just what I wanted him to do: he let go the rope with both hands at once and turned round. And then, *Crash!* down went Bill in his bucket to the bottom of the mine and he was killed.

"While my master was busy scolding me, Mendoza put his pistol in his pocket, came up with a smile on his face, and looked down the mine.

"'Why, good gracious!' said he to Luke, 'You've killed Bluebeard Bill. I must go and tell the police'—hoping, you see, to get the whole mine to himself when Luke should be put in prison. Then he jumped on his horse and galloped away.

"And soon my master grew afraid; for he saw that if Mendoza only told enough lies to the police, it *would* look as though he had killed Bill on purpose. So while Mendoza was gone, he and I stole away together secretly and came to England. Here he shaved off his beard and became a hermit. And ever since, for fifteen years, we've remained in hiding. This is all I have to say. And I swear it is the truth, every word."

When the Doctor finished reading Bob's long speech, the excitement among the twelve men of the jury was positively terrific. One, a very old man with white hair, began to weep in a loud voice at the thought of poor Luke hiding on the fen for fifteen years for something he couldn't help. And all the others set to whispering and nodding their heads to one another.

In the middle of all this, up got that horrible prosecutor again, waving his arms more wildly than ever.

"Your Honor," he cried, "I must object to this evidence as

biased. Of course the dog would not tell the truth against his own master. I object. I protest."

"Very well," said the judge, "you are at liberty to cross-examine. It is your duty as prosecutor to prove his evidence untrue. There is the dog: question him, if you do not believe what he says."

I thought the long-nosed lawyer would have a fit. He looked first at the dog, then at the Doctor, then at the judge, then back at the dog scowling from the witness-box. He opened his mouth to say something, but no words came. He waved his arms some more. His face got redder and redder. At last, clutching his forehead, he sank weakly into his seat and had to be helped out of the courtroom by two friends. As he was half carried through the door he was still feebly murmuring, "I protest—I object—I protest!"

The Eighth Chapter

Three Cheers

NEXT THE JUDGE MADE A VERY LONG SPEECH to the jury; and when it was over all the twelve jury-men got up and went out into the next room. And at that point the Doctor came back, leading Bob to the seat beside me.

"What have the jurymen gone out for?" I asked.

"They always do that at the end of a trial—to make up their minds whether the prisoner did it or not."

"Couldn't you and Bob go in with them and help them make up their minds the right way?" I asked.

"No, that's not allowed. They have to talk it over in secret. Sometimes it takes—my gracious, look, they're coming back already! They didn't spend long over it."

Everybody kept quite still while the twelve men came tramping back into their places in the pews. Then one of them, the leader—a little man—stood up and turned to the judge. Everyone was holding his breath, especially the Doctor and myself, to see what he was going to say. You could have heard a pin drop while the whole courtroom, the whole of Puddleby, in fact, waited with craning necks and straining ears to hear the weighty words.

"Your Honor," said the little man, "the jury returns a verdict of *Not Guilty.*"

"What's that mean?" I asked, turning to the Doctor.

But I found Doctor John Dolittle, the famous naturalist, standing on top of a chair, dancing about on one leg like a schoolboy.

"It means he's free!" he cried. "Luke is free!"

"Then he'll be able to come on the voyage with us, won't he?"

But I could not hear his answer; for the whole courtroom seemed to be jumping up on chairs like the Doctor. The crowd had suddenly gone crazy. All the people were laughing and calling and waving to Luke to show him how glad they were that he was free. The noise was deafening.

Then it stopped. All was quiet again; and the people stood up respectfully while the judge left the court. For the trial of Luke the Hermit, that famous trial which to this day they are still talking of in Puddleby, was over.

In the hush while the judge was leaving, a sudden shriek rang out, and there in the doorway stood a woman, her arms outstretched to the hermit.

"Luke!" she cried. "I've found you at last!"

"It's his wife," the woman in front of me whispered. "She ain't seen 'im in fifteen years, poor dear! What a lovely reunion. I'm glad I came. I wouldn't have missed this for anything!"

As soon as the judge had gone the noise broke out again; and now the folks gathered round Luke and his wife and shook them by the hand and congratulated them and laughed over them and cried over them.

"Come along, Stubbins," said the Doctor, taking me by the arm, "let's get out of this while we can."

"But aren't you going to speak to Luke?" I said. "To ask him if he'll come on the voyage?"

"It wouldn't be a bit of use," said the Doctor. "His wife's come for him. No man stands any chance of going on a voyage when his wife hasn't seen him in fifteen years. Come along. Let's get home to tea. We didn't have any lunch, remember. And we've earned something to eat. We'll have one of those mixed meals, lunch and tea combined—with watercress and ham. Nice change. Come along."

Just as we were going to step out a side door, I heard the crowd shouting:

"The Doctor! The Doctor! Where's the Doctor? The hermit would have hanged if it hadn't been for the Doctor. Speech! Speech! The Doctor!"

And a man came running up to us and said:

"The people are calling for you, sir."

"I'm very sorry," said the Doctor, "but I'm in a hurry."

"The crowd won't be denied, sir," said the man. "They want you to make a speech in the marketplace."

"Beg them to excuse me," said the Doctor, "with my compliments. I have an appointment at my house—a very important one that I may not break. Tell Luke to make a speech. Come along, Stubbins, this way."

"Oh, Lord!" he muttered as we got out into the open air and found another crowd waiting for him at the side door. "Let's go up that alleyway—to the left. Quick! Run!"

We took to our heels, darted through a couple of side streets and just managed to get away from the crowd.

It was not till we had reached the Oxenthorpe Road that we dared to slow down to a walk and take our breath. And even when we reached the Doctor's gate and turned to look backward toward the town, the faint murmur of many voices still reached us on the evening wind.

"They're still clamoring for you," I said. "Listen!"

The murmur suddenly swelled into a low distant roar; and although it was a mile and half away, you could distinctly hear the words:

"Three cheers for Luke the Hermit: Hooray! Three cheers for his dog: Hooray! Three cheers for his wife: Hooray! Three cheers for the Doctor: Hooray! Hooray! HOO-R-A-Y!"

The Purple Bird-of-Paradise

P OLYNESIA WAS WAITING FOR US ON THE front porch. She looked full of some important news.

"Doctor," said she, "the purple bird-of-paradise has arrived!"

"At last!" said the Doctor. "I had begun to fear some accident had befallen her. And how is Miranda?"

From the excited way in which the Doctor fumbled his key into the lock, I guessed that we were not going to get our tea right away, even now.

"Oh, she seemed all right when she arrived," said Polynesia, "tired from her long journey, of course, but otherwise all right. But what *do* you think? That mischief-making sparrow, Cheapside, insulted her as soon as she came into the garden. When I arrived on the scene she was in tears and was all for turning round and going straight back to Brazil tonight. I had the hardest work persuading her to wait till you came. She's in the study. I shut Cheapside in one of your bookcases and told him I'd tell you exactly what had happened the moment you got home."

The Doctor frowned, then walked silently and quickly to the study.

Here we found the candles lit; for the daylight was nearly gone. Dab-Dab was standing on the floor mounting guard over one of the glass-fronted bookcases in which Cheapside had been imprisoned. The noisy little sparrow was still fluttering angrily behind the glass when we came in.

In the center of the big table, perched on the inkstand, stood the most beautiful bird I have ever seen. She had a deep violet-colored breast, scarlet wings, and a long, long sweeping tail of gold. She was unimaginably beautiful, but looked dreadfully tired. Already she had her head under her wing; and she swayed gently from side to side on top of the inkstand like a bird that has flown long and far.

"Sh!" said Dab-Dab. "Miranda is asleep. I've got this little imp Cheapside in here. Listen, Doctor: for heaven's sake, send that sparrow away before he does any more mischief. He's nothing but a vulgar little nuisance. We've had a perfectly awful time trying to get Miranda to stay. Shall I serve your tea in here, or will you come into the kitchen when you're ready?"

"We'll come into the kitchen, Dab-Dab," said the Doctor. "Let Cheapside out before you go, please."

Dab-Dab opened the bookcase door and Cheapside strutted out, trying hard not to look guilty.

"Cheapside," said the Doctor sternly, "what did you say to Miranda when she arrived?"

"I didn't say nothing, Doc, straight I didn't. That is, nothing much. I was picking up crumbs off the gravel path when she comes swanking into the garden, turning up her nose in all directions, as though she owned the earth—just because she's got a lot of colored plumage. A London sparrow's as good as her any day. I don't hold by these gawdy bedizened foreigners nohow. Why don't they stay in their own country?"

"But what did you say to her that got her so offended?"

"All I said was, 'You don't belong in an English garden; you ought to be in a milliner's window.' That's all."

"You ought to be ashamed of yourself, Cheapside. Don't you realize that this bird has come thousands of miles to see me, only to be insulted by your impertinent tongue as soon as she reaches my garden? What do you mean by it? If she had gone away again before I got back tonight I would never have forgiven you. Leave the room."

Sheepishly, but still trying to look as though he didn't care, Cheapside hopped out into the passage and Dab-Dab closed the door.

The Doctor went up to the beautiful bird on the inkstand and gently stroked its back. Instantly its head popped out from under its wing.

The Tenth Chapter

Long Arrow, the Son of Golden Arrow

WELL, MIRANDA," SAID THE DOCTOR. "I'm terribly sorry this has happened. But you mustn't mind Cheapside; he doesn't know any better. He's a city bird; and all his life he has had to squabble for a living. You must make allowances. He doesn't know any better."

Miranda stretched her gorgeous wings wearily. Now that I saw her awake and moving, I noticed what a superior, well-bred manner she had. There were tears in her eyes and her beak was trembling.

"I wouldn't have minded so much," she said in a high, silvery voice, "if I hadn't been so dreadfully worn out. That and something else," she added beneath her breath.

"Did you have a hard time getting here?" asked the Doctor.

"The worst passage I ever made," said Miranda. "The weather—Well there. What's the use? I'm here anyway."

"Tell me," said the Doctor, as though he had been impatiently waiting to say something for a long time, "what did Long Arrow say when you gave him my message?"

The purple bird-of-paradise hung her head.

"That's the worst part of it," she said. "I might almost as well have not come at all. I wasn't able to deliver your message. I couldn't find him. *Long Arrow, the son of Golden Arrow, has disappeared!*"

"Disappeared!" cried the Doctor. "Why, what's become of him?"

"Nobody knows," Miranda answered. "He had often disappeared before, as I have told you—so that the tribe didn't know where he was. But it's a mighty hard thing to hide away from the birds. I had always been able to find some owl or martin who could tell me where he was—if I wanted to know. But not this time. That's why I'm nearly a fortnight late in coming to you: I kept hunting and hunting, asking everywhere. I went over the whole length and breadth of South America. But there wasn't a living thing could tell me where he was."

There was a sad silence in the room after she had finished; the Doctor was frowning in a peculiar sort of way, and Polynesia scratched her head.

"Did you ask the black parrots?" asked Polynesia. "They usually know everything."

"Certainly I did," said Miranda. "And I was so upset at not being able to find out anything that I forgot all about observing the weather signs before I started my flight here. I didn't even bother to break my journey at the Azores, but cut right across, making for the Straits of Gibraltar—as though it were June or July. And of course I ran into a perfectly frightful storm in the mid-Atlantic. I really thought I'd never come through it. Luckily I found a piece of a wrecked vessel floating in the sea after the storm had partly died down, and I roosted on it and took some sleep. If I hadn't been able to take that rest I wouldn't be here to tell the tale."

"Poor Miranda! What a time you must have had!" said the Doctor. "But tell me, were you able to find out whereabouts Long Arrow was last seen?"

"Yes. A young albatross told me he had seen him on Spidermonkey Island?"

"Spidermonkey Island? That's somewhere off the coast of Brazil, isn't it?"

"Yes, that's it. Of course I flew there right away and asked every bird on the island—and it is a big island, a hundred miles long. It seems that Long Arrow was visiting some peculiar tribe that lives there, and that when last seen he was going up into the mountains looking for rare medicine plants. I got that from a tame hawk, a pet, which the chief of the tribe keeps for hunting partridges with. I nearly got caught and put in a cage for my pains, too. That's the worst of having beautiful feathers: it's as much as your life is worth to go near most humans. They say, 'Oh how pretty!' and shoot an arrow or a bullet into you. You and Long Arrow were the only two men that I would ever trust myself near—out of all the people in the world."

"But was he never known to have returned from the mountains?"

"No. That was the last that was seen or heard of him. I questioned the seabirds around the shores to find out if he had left the island in a canoe. But they could tell me nothing."

"Do you think that some accident has happened to him?" asked the Doctor in a fearful voice.

"I'm afraid it must have," said Miranda, shaking her head.

"What else can I think?"

"Well," said John Dolittle slowly, "if I could never meet Long Arrow face-to-face it would be the greatest disappointment in my whole life. Not only that, but it would be a great loss to the knowledge of the human race. For, from what you have told me of him, he knew more natural science than all the rest of us put together; and if he has gone without anyone to write it down for him, so the world may be the better for it, it would be a terrible thing. But you don't really think that he is dead, do you?"

"What else can I think?" asked Miranda, bursting into tears, "when for six whole months he has not been seen by flesh, fish, or fowl."

Blind Travel

THIS NEWS ABOUT LONG ARROW MADE US all very sad. And I could see from the silent, dreamy way the Doctor took his tea that he was dreadfully upset. Every once in a while he would stop eating altogether and sit staring at the spots on the kitchen tablecloth as though his thoughts were far away; till Dab-Dab, who was watching to see that he got a good meal, would cough or rattle the pots in the sink.

I did my best to cheer him up by reminding him of all he had done for Luke and his wife that afternoon. And when that didn't seem to work, I went on talking about our preparations for the voyage.

"But you see, Stubbins," said he as we rose from the table and Dab-Dab and Chee-Chee began to clear away the dishes, "I don't know where to go now. I feel sort of lost since Miranda brought me this news. On this voyage I had planned on going to see Long Arrow. I had been looking forward to it for a whole year. I felt he might help me in learning the language of the shellfish—and perhaps in finding some way of getting to the bottom of the sea. But now? He's gone! And all his great knowledge has gone with him."

Then he seemed to fall a-dreaming again.

"Just to think of it!" he murmured. "Long Arrow and I, two students . . . Although I'd never met him, I felt as though I knew him quite well. For, in his way—without any schooling—he has, all his life, been trying to do the very things that I have tried to do in mine. And now he's gone! A whole world lay between us, and only a bird knew us both!"

We went back into the study, where Jip brought the Doctor his slippers and his pipe. And after the pipe was lit and the smoke began to fill the room, the old man seemed to cheer up a little.

"But you will go on some voyage, Doctor, won't you?" I asked. "Even if you can't go to find Long Arrow."

He looked up sharply into my face; and I suppose he saw how anxious I was. Because he suddenly smiled his old, boyish smile and said:

"Yes, Stubbins. Don't worry. We'll go. We mustn't stop working and learning, even if poor Long Arrow has disappeared. But where to go: that's the question. Where shall we go?"

There were so many places that I wanted to go that I couldn't make up my mind right away. And while I was still thinking, the Doctor sat up in his chair and said:

"I'll tell you what we'll do, Stubbins: it's a game I used to play when I was young—before Sarah came to live with me. I used to call it Blind Travel. Whenever I wanted to go on a voyage, and I couldn't make up my mind where to go, I would take the atlas and open it with my eyes shut. Next I'd wave a pencil, still without looking, and stick it down on whatever page had fallen open. Then

I'd open my eyes and look. It's a very exciting game, is Blind Travel. Because you have to swear, before you begin, that you will go to the place the pencil touches, come what may. Shall we play it?"

"Oh, let's!" I almost yelled. "How thrilling! I hope it's China— or Borneo—or Baghdad."

And in a moment I had scrambled up the bookcase, dragged the big atlas from the top shelf, and laid it on the table before the Doctor.

I knew every page in that atlas by heart. How many days and nights I had lingered over its old faded maps, following the blue rivers from the mountains to the sea; wondering what the little towns really looked like, and how wide were the sprawling lakes! I had had a lot of fun with that atlas, traveling, in my mind, all over the world. I can see it now: The first page had no map; it just told you that it was printed in Edinburgh in 1808, and a whole lot more about the book. The next page was the solar system, showing the sun and planets, the stars and the moon. The third page was the chart of the North and South Poles. Then came the hemispheres, the oceans, the continents, and the countries.

As the Doctor began sharpening his pencil, a thought came to me.

"What if the pencil falls upon the North Pole," I asked, "will we have to go there?"

"No. The rules of the game say you don't have to go anyplace you've been to before. You are allowed another try. I've been to the North Pole," he ended quietly, "so we shan't have to go there."

I could hardly speak with astonishment.

"You've been to the North pole!" I managed to gasp out at last. "But I thought it was still undiscovered. The map shows all the

places explorers have reached to, *trying* to get there. Why isn't your name down if you discovered it?"

"I promised to keep it a secret. And you must promise me never to tell anyone. Yes, I discovered the North Pole in April 1809. But shortly after I got there the polar bears came to me in a body and told me there was a great deal of coal there, buried beneath the snow. They knew, they said, that human beings would do anything, and go anywhere, to get coal. So would I please keep it a secret. Because once people began coming up there to start coal mines, their beautiful white country would be spoiled—and there was nowhere else in the world cold enough for polar bears to be comfortable. So of course I had to promise them I would. Ah well, it will be discovered again some day, by somebody else. But I want the polar bears to have their playground to themselves as long as possible. And I daresay it will be a good while yet—for it certainly is a fiendish place to get to. Well now, are we ready? Good! Take the pencil and stand here, close to the table. When the book falls open, wave the pencil round three times and jab it down. Ready? All right. Shut your eyes."

It was a tense and fearful moment—but very thrilling. We both had our eyes shut tight. I heard the atlas fall open with a bang. I wondered what page it was: England or Asia. If it should be the map of Asia, so much would depend on where that pencil would land. I waved three times in a circle. I began to lower my hand. The pencil point touched the page.

"All right," I called out, "it's done."

Destiny and Destination

WE BOTH OPENED OUR EYES; THEN bumped our heads together with a crack in our eagerness to lean over and see where we were to go.

The atlas lay open at a map called *Chart of the South Atlantic Ocean*. My pencil point was resting right in the center of a tiny island. The name of it was printed so small that the Doctor had to get out his strong spectacles to read it. I was trembling with excitement.

"Spidermonkey Island," he read out slowly. Then he whistled softly beneath his breath. "Of all the extraordinary things! You've hit upon the very island where Long Arrow was last seen on earth—I wonder—Well, well! How very singular!"

"We'll go there, Doctor, won't we?" I asked.

"Of course we will. The rules of the game say we've got to."

"I'm so glad it wasn't Oxenthorpe or Bristol," I said. "It'll be a grand voyage, this. Look at all the sea we've got to cross. Will it take us long?"

"Oh no," said the Doctor, "not very. With a good boat and a good wind we should make it easily in four weeks. But isn't it extraordinary? Of all the places in the world, you picked out that one with your eyes shut. Spidermonkey Island after all!—Well, there's one good thing about it: I shall be able to get some Jabizri beetles."

"What are Jabizri beetles?"

"They are a very rare kind of beetle with peculiar habits. I want to study them. There are only three countries in the world where they are to be found. Spidermonkey Island is one of them. But even there they are very scarce."

"What is this little question mark after the name of the island for?" I asked, pointing to the map.

"That means that the island's position in the ocean is not known very exactly—that it is somewhere *about* there. Ships have probably seen it in that neighborhood, that is all, most likely. But I daresay we shall have some difficulty in finding it first."

How like a dream it all sounded! The two of us sitting there at the big study table; the candles lit; the smoke curling toward the dim ceiling from the Doctor's pipe—the two of us sitting there, talking about finding an island in the ocean and being the first Englishmen to land upon it!

"I'll bet it will be a great voyage," I said. "It looks like a lovely island on the map. Will there be people there?"

"Yes. Two tribes of natives live on it, Miranda tells me."

At this point the poor bird-of-paradise stirred and woke up. In our excitement we had forgotten to speak low.

"We are going to Spidermonkey Island, Miranda," said the Doctor. "You know where it is, do you not?"

"I know where it was the last time I saw it," said the bird. "But whether it will be there still, I can't say."

"What do you mean?" asked the Doctor. "It is always in the same place surely?"

"Not by any means," said Miranda. "Why, didn't you know? Spidermonkey Island is a *floating* island. It moves around all over the place—usually somewhere near southern South America. But of course I could surely find it for you if you want to go there."

At this fresh piece of news I could contain myself no longer. I was bursting to tell someone. I ran dancing and singing from the room to find Chee-Chee.

At the door I tripped over Dab-Dab, who was just coming in with her wings full of plates, and fell headlong on my nose.

"Has the boy gone crazy?" cried the duck. "Where do you think you're going, ninny?"

"To Spidermonkey Island!" I shouted, picking myself up and doing cartwheels down the hall. "Spidermonkey Island! Hooray! And it's a *floating* island!"

"You're going to Bedlam, I should say," snorted the housekeeper. "Look what you've done to my best china!"

But I was far too happy to listen to her scolding; and I ran on, singing, into the kitchen to find Chee-Chee.

PART THREE

The Third Man

THAT SAME WEEK WE BEGAN OUR PREPARA-
tions for the voyage.

Joe, the mussel man, had the *Curlew* moved down
the river and tied it up along the river-wall, so it would
be more handy for loading. And for three whole days we carried
provisions down to our beautiful new boat and stowed them away.

I was surprised to find how roomy and big she was inside. There
were three little cabins, a saloon (or dining room), and underneath
all this, a big place called the hold where the food and extra sails and
other things were kept.

I think Joe must have told everybody in the town about our
coming voyage, because there was always a regular crowd watching
us when we brought the things down to put aboard. And of course
sooner or later old Matthew Mugg was bound to turn up.

"My goodness, Tommy," said he, as he watched me carrying
on some sacks of flour, "but that's a pretty boat! Where might the
Doctor be going to this voyage?"

"We're going to Spidermonkey Island," I said proudly.

"And be you the only one the Doctor's taking along?"

"Well, he has spoken of wanting to take another man," I said, "but so far he hasn't made up his mind."

Matthew grunted, then squinted up at the graceful masts of the *Curlew*.

"You know, Tommy," said he, "if it wasn't for my rheumatism, I've half a mind to come with the Doctor myself. There's something about a boat standing ready to sail that always did make me feel venturesome and travelish-like. What's that stuff in the cans you're taking on?"

"This is treacle," I said, "twenty pounds of treacle."

"My Goodness," he sighed, turning away sadly. "That makes me feel more like going with you than ever. But my rheumatism is that bad I can't hardly—"

I didn't hear any more, for Matthew had moved off, still mumbling, into the crowd that stood about the wharf. The clock in Puddleby Church struck noon and I turned back, feeling very busy and important, to the task of loading.

But it wasn't very long before someone else came along and interrupted my work. This was a huge, big, burly man with a red beard and tattoos all over his arms. He wiped his mouth with the back of his hand, spat twice onto the river-wall and said:

"Boy, where's the skipper?"

"The *skipper*!—Who do you mean?" I asked.

"The captain—Where's the captain of this craft?" he said, pointing to the *Curlew*.

"Oh, you mean the Doctor," said I. "Well, he isn't here at present."

At that moment the Doctor arrived with his arms full of note-books and butterfly nets and glass cases and other natural history things. The big man went up to him, respectfully touching his cap.

"Good morning, Captain," said he. "I heard you was in need of hands for a voyage. My name's Ben Butcher, able seaman."

"I am very glad to know you," said the Doctor. "But I'm afraid I shan't be able to take on any more crew."

"Boy, where's the skipper?"

"Why, but Captain," said the able seaman, "you surely ain't going to face deep-sea weather with nothing more than this bit of a lad to help you—and with a cutter that big!"

The Doctor assured him that he was; but the man didn't go away. He hung around and argued. He told us he had known of many ships being sunk through "undermanning." He got out what he called his *stiffikit*—a paper which said what a good sailor he was—and implored us, if we valued our lives, to take him.

But the Doctor was quite firm—polite but determined— and finally the man walked sorrowfully away, telling us he never expected to see us alive again.

Callers of one sort and another kept us quite busy that morning. The Doctor had no sooner gone below to stow away his notebooks than another visitor appeared upon the gangplank. This was a most extraordinary-looking man.

"Pardon me," said he, bowing elegantly, "but is this the ship of the physician Dolittle?"

"Yes," I said, "did you wish to see him?"

"I did—if it will not be inconvenient," he answered.

"Who shall I say it is?"

"I am Bumpo Kahbooboo, Crown Prince of Jolliginki."

I ran downstairs at once and told the Doctor.

"How fortunate!" cried John Dolittle. "My old friend Bumpo! Well, well! He's studying at Oxford, you know. How good of him to come all this way to call on me!" And he tumbled up the ladder to greet his visitor.

Prince Bumpo seemed to be overcome with joy when the Doctor appeared and shook him warmly by the hand.

"News reached me," he said, "that you were about to sail upon a voyage. I hastened to see you before your departure. I am very pleased that I did not miss you."

"You very nearly did miss us," said the Doctor. "As it happened, we were delayed somewhat in getting the necessary number of men to sail our boat. If it hadn't been for that, we would have been gone three days ago."

"How many men does your ship's company yet require?" asked Bumpo.

"Only one," said the Doctor. "But it is so hard to find the right one."

"Methinks I detect something of the finger of Destiny in this," said Bumpo. "How would I do?"

"Splendidly," said the Doctor. "But what about your studies? You can't very well just go off and leave your university career to take care of itself, you know."

"I need a holiday," said Bumpo. "Even had I not gone with you, I intended at the end of this term to take a three-months' leave. But besides, I shall not be neglecting my education if I accompany you. Before I left Jolliginki, my august father, the king, told me to be sure and travel plenty. You are a man of great knowledge. To see the world in your company is an opportunity not to be sneezed upon. No, no, indeed."

"Well," he said slowly, "there is something in what you say, Bumpo, about getting education from the world as well as from the college. And if you are really sure that you want to come, we shall be delighted to have you. Because, to tell you the truth, I think you are exactly the man we need."

Good-Bye!

TWO DAYS AFTER THAT WE HAD ALL IN readiness for our departure.

On this voyage Jip begged so hard to be taken that the Doctor finally gave in and said he could come. Polynesia and Chee-Chee were the only other animals to go with us. Dab-Dab was left in charge of the house and the animal family we were to leave behind.

Of course, as is always the way, at the last moment we kept remembering things we had forgotten; and when we finally closed the house up and went down the steps to the road, we were all burdened with armfuls of odd packages.

Halfway to the river, the Doctor suddenly remembered that he had left the stockpot boiling on the kitchen fire. However, we saw a blackbird flying by who nested in our garden, and the Doctor asked her to go back for us and tell Dab-Dab about it.

Down at the river-wall we found a great crowd waiting to see us off.

Standing right near the gangplank were my mother and father. I hoped that they would not make a scene, or burst into tears or anything like that. But as a matter of fact they behaved quite well—for parents. My mother said something about being sure not to get my feet wet; and my father just smiled a crooked sort of smile, patted me on the back and wished me luck. Good-byes are awfully uncomfortable things, and I was glad when it was over and we boarded the ship.

We were a little surprised not to see Matthew Mugg among the crowd. We had felt sure that he would be there; and the Doctor had intended to give him some extra instructions about the food for the animals we had left at the house.

At last, after much pulling and tugging, we got the anchor up and undid a lot of mooring ropes. Then the *Curlew* began to move gently down the river with the out-running tide, while the people on the wall cheered and waved their handkerchiefs.

We bumped into one or two other boats getting out into the stream; and at one sharp bend in the river we got stuck on a mud-bank for a few minutes. But though the people on the shore seemed to get very excited at these things, the Doctor did not appear to be disturbed by them in the least.

"These little accidents will happen in the most carefully regu-lated voyages," he said as he leaned over the side and fished for his boots, which had gotten stuck in the mud while we were pushing off. "Sailing is much easier when you get out into the open sea. There aren't so many silly things to bump into."

For me indeed it was a great and wonderful feeling, that getting out into the open sea, when at length we passed the little lighthouse at the mouth of the river and found ourselves free of the land. It was all so new and different: just the sky above you and sea below. This ship, which was to be our house and our street, our home and our garden, for so many days to come, seemed so tiny in all this wide water—so tiny and yet so snug, sufficient, safe.

I looked around me and took in a deep breath. The Doctor was at the wheel steering the boat, which was now leaping and plunging gently through the waves. (I had expected to feel seasick at first, but was delighted to find that I didn't.) Bumpo was belowdecks, preparing dinner. Chee-Chee was coiling up ropes in the stern and laying them in neat piles. My work was fastening down the things on the deck so that nothing could roll about if the weather should grow rough when we got farther from the land. Jip was up in the peak of the boat with ears cocked and nose stuck out—like a statue, so still—his keen old eyes keeping a sharp lookout for floating wrecks, sandbars, and other dangers. Each one of us had some special job to do, part of the proper running of a ship. Even old Polynesia was taking the sea's temperature with the Doctor's bath thermometer tied on the end of a string, to make sure there were no icebergs near us. As I listened to her swearing softly to herself because she couldn't read the pesky figures in the fading light, I realized that the voyage had begun in earnest and that very soon it would be night—my first night at sea!

Our Troubles Begin

JUST BEFORE SUPPERTIME BUMPO APPEARED from downstairs and went to the Doctor at the wheel.

"A stowaway in the hold, sir," said he in a very businesslike seafaring voice. "I just discovered him behind the flour bags."

"Dear me!" said the Doctor. "What a nuisance! Stubbins, go down with Bumpo and bring the man up. I can't leave the wheel just now."

So Bumpo and I went down into the hold; and there, behind the flour bags, plastered in flour from head to foot, we found a man. After we had swept most of the flour off him with a broom, we discovered that it was Matthew Mugg. We hauled him upstairs sneezing and took him before the Doctor.

"Why, Matthew!" said John Dolittle. "What on earth are you doing here?"

"The temptation was too much for me, Doctor," said the Cat's-Meat-Man. "You know I've often asked you to take me on voyages with you and you never would. Well, this time, knowing that you needed an extra man, I thought if I stayed hid till the ship was well at sea you would find I came in handylike and keep me. But I had to lie so doubled up, for hours, behind them flour bags, that my rheumatism came on something awful. I just had to change my position; and of course just as I stretched out my legs, along comes this here bloke and sees my feet sticking out. Don't this ship roll something awful! How long has this storm been going on? I reckon this damp sea air wouldn't be very good for my rheumatics."

"No, Matthew, it really isn't. You ought not to have come. You are not in any way suited to this kind of a life. I'm sure you wouldn't enjoy a long voyage a bit. We'll stop in at Penzance and put you ashore. Bumpo, please go downstairs to my bunk: in the pocket of my dressing gown you'll find some maps. Bring me the small one—with blue pencil marks at the top. I know Penzance is over here on our left somewhere. But I must find out what lighthouses there are before I change the ship's course and sail inshore."

"Very good, sir," said Bumpo, turning round smartly and making for the stairway.

"Now, Matthew," said the Doctor, "you can take the coach from Penzance to Bristol. And from there it is not very far to Puddleby, as you know. Don't forget to take the usual provisions to the house every Thursday, and be particularly careful to remember the extra supply of herrings for the baby minks."

While we were waiting for the maps, Chee-Chee and I set about lighting the lamps: a green one on the right side of the ship, a red one on the left, and a white one on the mast.

At last we heard someone trundling on the stairs again and the Doctor said:

"Ah, here's Bumpo with the maps at last!"

But to our great astonishment it was not Bumpo alone that appeared, but *three* people.

"Good Lord deliver us! Who are these?" cried John Dolittle.

"Two more stowaways, sir," said Bumpo stepping forward briskly. "I found them in your cabin hiding under the bunk. One woman and one man, sir. Here are the maps."

"This is too much," said the Doctor feebly. "Who are they? I can't see their faces in this dim light. Strike a match, Bumpo."

You could never guess who it was. It was Luke and his wife. Mrs. Luke appeared to be very miserable and seasick.

They explained to the Doctor that after they had settled down to live together in the little shack out on the fens, so many people came to visit them (having heard about the great trial) that life became impossible; and they had decided to escape from Puddleby in this manner—for they had no money to leave any other way—and try to find some new place to live where they and their story wouldn't be so well known. But as soon as the ship had begun to roll, Mrs. Luke had gotten most dreadfully unwell.

Poor Luke apologized many times for being such a nuisance and said that the whole thing had been his wife's idea.

The Doctor, after he had sent below for his medicine bag and had given Mrs. Luke some *sal volatile* and smelling salts, said he thought the best thing to do would be for him to lend them some money and put them ashore at Penzance with Matthew. He also wrote a letter for Luke to take with him to a friend the Doctor had in the town of Penzance who, it was hoped, would be able to find Luke work to do there.

As the Doctor opened his purse and took out some gold coins,

I heard Polynesia, who was sitting on my shoulder watching the whole affair, mutter beneath her breath:

"There he goes—lending his last blessed penny—three pounds ten—all the money we had for the whole trip! Now we haven't the price of a postage stamp aboard if we should lose an anchor or have to buy a pint of tar. Well, let's pray we don't run out of food. Why doesn't he give them the ship and walk home?"

Presently with the help of the map the course of the boat was changed and, to Mrs. Luke's great relief, we made for Penzance and dry land.

I was tremendously interested to see how a ship could be steered into a port at night with nothing but lighthouses and a compass to guide you. It seemed to me that the Doctor missed all the rocks and sandbars very cleverly.

We got into that funny little Cornish harbor about eleven o'clock that night. The Doctor took his stowaways onshore in our small rowboat, which we kept on the deck of the *Curlew*, and found them rooms at the hotel there. When he got back he told us that Mrs. Luke had gone straight to bed and was feeling much better.

It was now after midnight; so we decided to stay in the harbor and wait till morning before setting out again.

I was glad to get to bed, although I felt that staying up so tremendously late was great fun. As I climbed into the bunk over the Doctor's and pulled the blankets snugly round me, I found I could look out of the porthole at my elbow, and, without raising my head from the pillow, could see the lights of Penzance swinging gently up and down with the motion of the ship at anchor. It was like being rocked to sleep with a little show going on to amuse you. I was just deciding that I liked the life of the sea very much when I fell fast asleep.

THE FOURTH CHAPTER

Our Troubles Continue

HE NEXT MORNING WHEN WE WERE EATING a very excellent breakfast of kidneys and bacon, prepared by Bumpo, the Doctor said to me:

"I was just wondering, Stubbins, whether I should stop at the Capa Blanca Islands or run right across for the coast of Brazil. Miranda said we could expect a spell of excellent weather now—for four and a half weeks at least."

"Well," I said, spooning out the sugar at the bottom of my cocoa cup, "I should think it would be best to make straight across while we are sure of good weather. And besides, the purple bird-of-paradise is going to keep a lookout for us, isn't she? She'll be wondering what's happened to us if we don't get there in about a month."

"True, quite true, Stubbins. On the other hand, the Capa Blancas make a very convenient stopping place on our way across. If we should need supplies or repairs it would be very handy to put in there."

"How long will it take us from here to the Capa Blancas?" I asked.

"About six days," said the Doctor. "Well, we can decide later. For the next two days, at any rate, our direction would be the same practically in either case. If you have finished breakfast let's go and get underway."

Upstairs I found our vessel surrounded by white and gray seagulls who flashed and circled about in the sunny morning air, looking for food scraps thrown out by the ships into the harbor.

By about half past seven we had the anchor up and the sails set to a nice steady breeze; and this time we got out into the open sea without bumping into a single thing. We met the Penzance fishing fleet coming in from the night's fishing, and very trim and neat they looked, in a line like soldiers, with their red-brown sails all leaning over the same way, and the white water dancing before their bows.

For the next three or four days everything went smoothly and nothing unusual happened. During this time we all got settled down into our regular jobs; and in spare moments the Doctor showed each of us how to take our turns at the wheel, the proper manner of keeping a ship on her right course, and what to do if the wind changed suddenly. We divided the twenty-four hours of the day into three spells, and we took it in turns to sleep our eight hours and be awake sixteen. So the ship was well looked after, with two of us always on duty.

Besides that, Polynesia, who was an older sailor than any of us, and really knew a lot about running ships, seemed to be always awake—except when she took her couple of winks in the sun, standing on one leg beside the wheel. You may be sure that no one ever got a chance to stay abed more than his eight hours while Polynesia was around. She used to watch the ship's clock; and if you overslept a half minute, she would come down to the cabin and peck you gently on the nose till you got up.

I very soon grew to be quite fond of our friend Bumpo, with his grand way of speaking and his enormous feet, which someone was always stepping on or falling over. Although he was much older than I was and had been to college, he never tried to lord it over me. He seemed to be forever smiling and kept all of us in good humor. It wasn't long before I began to see the Doctor's good sense in bringing him.

On the morning of the fifth day out, just as I was taking the wheel over from the Doctor, Bumpo appeared and said:

"The salt beef is nearly all gone, sir."

"The salt beef!" cried the Doctor. "Why, we brought a hundred and twenty pounds with us. We couldn't have eaten that in five days. What can have become of it?"

"I don't know, sir, I'm sure. Every time I go down to the stores I find another hunk missing. If it is rats that are eating it, then they are certainly colossal rodents."

Polynesia who was walking up and down a stay rope, taking her morning exercise, put in:

"We must search the hold. If this is allowed to go on, we will all be starving before a week is out. Come downstairs with me, Tommy, and we will look into this matter."

So we went downstairs into the storeroom and Polynesia told us to keep quite still and listen. This we did. And presently we heard from a dark corner of the hold the distinct sound of someone snoring.

"Ah, I thought so," said Polynesia. "It's a man—and a big one. Climb in there, both of you, and haul him out. It sounds as though he were behind that barrel. Gosh! We seem to have brought half of

Puddleby with us. Anyone would think we were a penny ferryboat. Such cheek! Haul him out."

So Bumpo and I lit a lantern and climbed over the stores. And there, behind the barrel, sure enough, we found an enormous bearded man fast asleep with a well-fed look on his face. We woke him up.

"Washamarrer?" he said sleepily.

It was Ben Butcher, the able seaman.

Polynesia spluttered like an angry firecracker.

"This is the last straw," said she. "The one man in the world we least wanted. Shiver my timbers, what cheek!"

"Would it not be, advisable," suggested Bumpo, "while the knave is still sleepy, to strike him on the head with some heavy object and push him through a porthole into the sea?"

"No. We'd get into trouble," said Polynesia. "Besides, there never was a porthole big enough to push that man through. Bring him upstairs to the Doctor."

So we led the man to the wheel, where he respectfully touched his cap to the Doctor.

"Another stowaway, sir," said Bumpo smartly.

I thought the poor Doctor would have a fit.

"Good morning, Captain," said the man. "Ben Butcher, able seaman, at your service. I knew you'd need me, so I took the liberty of stowing away—much against my conscience. But I just couldn't bear to see you poor landsmen set out on this voyage without a single real seaman to help you. You'd never have got home alive if I hadn't come—Why look at your mainsail, sir—all loose at the throat. First gust of wind come along, and away goes your canvas overboard. Well, it's all right now that I'm here. We'll soon get things in shipshape."

"No, it isn't all right," said the Doctor, "it's all wrong. And I'm not at all glad to see you. I told you in Puddleby I didn't want you. You had no right to come."

"But, Captain," said the able seaman, "you can't sail this ship without me. You don't understand navigation. Why, look at the compass now: you've let her swing a point and a half off her course. It's madness for you to try to do this trip alone—if you'll pardon my saying so, sir. Why—why, you'll lose the ship!"

"Look here," said the Doctor, a sudden stern look coming into his eyes, "losing a ship is nothing to me. I've lost ships before and it doesn't bother me in the least. When I set out to go to a place, I get there. Do you understand? I may know nothing whatsoever about sailing and navigation, but I get there just the same. Now you may be the best seaman in the world, but on *this* ship you're just a plain, ordinary nuisance—very plain and very ordinary. And I am now going to call at the nearest port and put you ashore."

"Yes, and think yourself lucky," Polynesia put in, "that you are not locked up for stowing away and eating all our salt beef."

"I don't know what the mischief we're going to do now," I heard her whisper to Bumpo. "We've no money to buy any more; and that salt beef was the most important part of the stores."

"Would it not be good political economy," Bumpo whispered back, "if we salted the able seaman and ate him instead? I should judge that he would weigh more than a hundred and twenty pounds."

"Don't be silly," snapped Polynesia. "Still," she murmured after a moment's thought, "it's an awfully bright idea. I don't suppose anybody saw him come onto the ship—Oh, but heavens! We haven't got enough salt. Besides, he'd be sure to taste of tobacco."

Polynesia Has a Plan

HEN THE DOCTOR TOLD ME TO TAKE THE wheel while he made a little calculation with his map and worked out what new course we should take.

"I shall have to run for the Capa Blancas after all," he told me when the seaman's back was turned. "Dreadful nuisance! But I'd sooner swim back to Puddleby than have to listen to that fellow's talk all the way to Brazil."

Indeed he was a terrible person, this Ben Butcher. You'd think that anyone after being told he wasn't wanted would have had the decency to keep quiet. But not Ben Butcher. He kept going round the deck pointing out all the things we had wrong. According to him, there wasn't a thing right on the whole ship. The anchor was hitched up wrong; the hatches weren't fastened down properly; the sails were put on back to front; all our knots were the wrong kind of knots.

At last the Doctor told him to stop talking and go downstairs. He refused—said he wasn't going to be sunk by landlubbers while he was still able to stay on deck.

This made us feel a little uneasy. He was such an enormous man there was no knowing what he might do if he got really obstreperous.

Bumpo and I were talking about this downstairs in the dining saloon when Polynesia, Jip, and Chee-Chee came and joined us. And, as usual, Polynesia had a plan.

"Listen," she said, "I am certain this Ben Butcher is a smuggler and a bad man. I am a very good judge of seamen, remember, and I don't like the cut of this man's jib. I—"

"Do you really think," I interrupted, "that it *is* safe for the Doctor to cross the Atlantic without any regular seamen on his ship?"

You see, it had upset me quite a good deal to find that all the things we had been doing were wrong; and I was beginning to wonder what might happen if we ran into a storm—particularly as Miranda had only said the weather would be good for a certain time; and we seemed to be having so many delays. But Polynesia merely tossed her head scornfully.

"Oh, bless you, my boy," said she, "you're always safe with John Dolittle. Remember that. Don't take any notice of that stupid old salt. Of course it is perfectly true the Doctor does do everything wrong. But with him it doesn't matter. Mark my words: if you travel with John Dolittle, you always get there, as you heard him say. I've been with him lots of times and I know. Sometimes the ship is upside down when you get there, and sometimes it's right way up. But you get there just the same. And then of course there's another thing about the Doctor," she added thoughtfully, "he always has extraordinary good luck. He may have his troubles, but with him things seem to have a habit of turning out all right in the end. I remember once when we were going through the Straits of Magellan the wind was so strong—"

"But what are we going to do about Ben Butcher?" Jip put in. "You had some plan, Polynesia, hadn't you?"

"Yes. What I'm afraid of is that he may hit the Doctor on the head when he's not looking and make himself captain of the *Curlew*. Bad sailors do that sometimes. Then they run the ship their own way and take it where they want. That's what you call a 'mutiny.'"

"Yes," said Jip, "and we ought to do something pretty quick. We can't reach the Capa Blancas before the day after tomorrow, at best. I don't like to leave the Doctor alone with him for a minute. He smells like a very bad man to me."

"Well, I've got it all worked out," said Polynesia. "Listen: Is there a key in that door?"

We looked outside the dining room and found that there was.

"All right," said Polynesia. "Now Bumpo lays the table for lunch and we all go and hide. Then at twelve o'clock Bumpo rings the dinner bell down here. As soon as Ben hears it he'll come down expecting more salt beef. Bumpo must hide behind the door outside. The moment that Ben is seated at the dining table, Bumpo slams the door and locks it. Then we've got him. See?"

"How ingenious!" Bumpo chuckled. "I'll lay the table at once."

"Yes and take that Worcestershire sauce off the dresser with you when you go out," said Polynesia. "Don't leave any loose eatables around. That fellow has had enough to last any man for three days. Besides, he won't be so inclined to start a fight when we put him ashore at the Capa Blancas if we thin him down a bit before we let him out."

So we all went and hid ourselves in the passage, where we could watch what happened. And presently Bumpo came to the foot of the stairs and rang the dinner bell like mad. Then he hopped behind the dining room door and we all kept still and listened.

Almost immediately, *thump, thump, thump*, down the stairs tramped Ben Butcher, the able seaman. He walked into the dining saloon, sat himself down at the head of the table in the Doctor's place, tucked a napkin under his fat chin and heaved a sigh of expectation.

Then, *bang*! Bumpo slammed the door and locked it.

"That settles *him* for a while," said Polynesia, coming out from her hiding place. "Now let him teach navigation to the sideboard. Gosh, the cheek of the man! I've forgotten more about the sea than that lumbering lout will ever know. Let's go upstairs and tell the Doctor."

And bursting into a rollicking Norwegian sailor song, she climbed up to my shoulder and we went on deck.

The Bed-Maker of Monteverde

W E REMAINED THREE DAYS IN THE Capa Blanca Islands.

There were two reasons why we stayed there so long when we were really in such a hurry to get away. One was the shortage in our provisions caused by the able seaman's enormous appetite. When we came to go over the stores and make a list, we found that he had eaten a whole lot of other things besides the beef. And having no money, we were sorely puzzled how to buy more. The Doctor went through his trunk to see if there was anything he could sell. But the only thing he could find was an old watch with the hands broken and the back dented in; and we decided this would not bring us in enough money to buy much more than a pound of tea.

The other thing that kept us was the bullfight. In these islands, which belonged to Spain, they had bullfights every Sunday. It was on a Friday that we arrived there, and after we had gotten rid of the able seaman we took a walk through the town.

It was a very funny little town, quite different from any that I had ever seen. The streets were all twisty and winding and so narrow that a wagon could only just pass along them. The houses overhung at the top and came so close together that people in the attics could lean out of the windows and shake hands with their neighbors on the opposite side of the street. The Doctor told us the town was very, very old. It was called Monteverde.

As we had no money of course, we did not go to a hotel or anything like that. But on the second evening when we were passing by a bed-maker's shop we noticed several beds, which the man had made, standing on the pavement outside. The Doctor started chatting in Spanish to the bed-maker, who was sitting at his door whistling to a parrot in a cage. The Doctor and the bed-maker got very friendly talking about birds and things. And as it grew near to suppertime, the man asked us to stop and sup with him.

This of course we were very glad to do. And after the meal was over (very nice dishes they were, mostly cooked in olive oil—I particularly liked the fried bananas) we sat outside on the pavement again and went on talking far into the night.

At last when we got up to go back to our ship, this very nice shopkeeper wouldn't hear of our going away on any account. He said the streets down by the harbor were very badly lighted and there was no moon. We would surely get lost. He invited us to spend the night with him and go back to our ship in the morning.

Well, we finally agreed; and as our good friend had no spare bedrooms, the three of us—the Doctor, Bumpo, and I—slept on the beds set out for sale on the pavement before the shop. The night was so hot we needed no coverings. It was great fun to fall asleep out of doors like this, watching the people walking to and fro and the vibrant life of the streets. It seemed to me that Spanish people never went to bed at all. Late as it was, all the little restaurants and cafés around us were wide open, with customers drinking coffee and chatting merrily at the small tables outside. The sound of a guitar strumming softly in the distance mingled with the clatter of china-ware and the babble of voices.

"The Doctor started chatting in Spanish to the bed-maker."

Somehow it made me think of my mother and father far away in Puddleby, with their regular habits, the evening practice on the flute and the rest—doing the same thing every day. I felt sort of sorry for them in a way, because they missed the fun of this traveling life, where we were doing something new all the time—even sleeping differently. But I suppose if they had been invited to go to bed on a pavement in front of a shop, they wouldn't have cared for the idea at all. It is funny how some people are.

The Doctor's Wager

NEXT MORNING WE WERE AWAKENED BY A great racket. There was a procession coming down the street, a number of men in very colorful clothes followed by a large crowd of admiring ladies and cheering children. I asked the Doctor who they were.

"They are the bullfighters," he said. "There is to be a bullfight tomorrow."

"What is a bullfight?" I asked.

To my great surprise the Doctor got red in the face with anger. It reminded me of the time when he had spoken of the lions and tigers in his private zoo.

"A bullfight is a cruel, disgusting business," said he. "These Spanish people are most lovable and hospitable folk. How they can enjoy these wretched bullfights is a thing I will never understand."

Then the Doctor went on to explain to me how a bull was first made very angry by teasing and then allowed to run into a circus where men came out with red cloaks, waved them at him, and ran away. Next the bull was allowed to tire himself out by tossing and killing a lot of poor, old, broken-down horses who couldn't defend themselves. Then, when the bull was thoroughly out of breath and wearied by this, a man came out with a sword and killed the bull.

"Every Sunday," said the Doctor, "in almost every big town in Spain there are six bulls killed like that, and as many horses."

"But aren't the men ever killed by the bull?" I asked.

"Unfortunately, very seldom," said he. "A bull is not nearly as dangerous as he looks, even when he's angry, if you are only quick on your feet and don't lose your head. These bullfighters are very clever and nimble. And the people, especially the Spanish ladies, think no end of them. A famous bullfighter (or matador, as they call them) is a more important man in Spain than a king. Here comes another crowd of them round the corner—look. See the girls throwing kisses to them? Ridiculous business!"

At that moment our friend the bed-maker came out to see the procession go past. And while he was wishing us good morning and inquiring how we had slept, a friend of his walked up and joined us. The bed-maker introduced this friend to us as Don Enrique Cardenas.

Don Enrique, when he heard where we were from, spoke to us in English. He appeared to be a well-educated, gentlemanly sort of person.

"And you go to see the bullfight tomorrow, yes?" he asked the Doctor pleasantly.

"Certainly not," said John Dolittle firmly. "I don't like bullfights—cruel, cowardly shows."

Don Enrique nearly exploded. I never saw a man get so excited. He told the Doctor that he didn't know what he was talking about.

He said bullfighting was a noble sport and that the matadors were the bravest men in the world.

"Oh, rubbish!" said the Doctor. "You never give the poor bull a chance. It is only when he is all tired and dazed that your precious matadors dare to try and kill him."

I thought the Spaniard was going to strike the Doctor he got so angry. While he was still spluttering to find words, the bed-maker came between them and took the Doctor aside. He explained to John Dolittle in a whisper that this Don Enrique Cardenas was a very important person; that he it was who supplied the bulls—a special, strong black kind—from his own farm for all the bullfights in the Capa Blancas. He was a very rich man, the bed-maker said, a most important personage. He mustn't be allowed to take offense on any account.

I watched the Doctor's face as the bed-maker finished, and I saw a flash of boyish mischief come into his eyes as though an idea had struck him. He turned to the angry Spaniard.

"Don Enrique," he said, "you tell me your bullfighters are very brave men and skillful. It seems I have offended you by saying that bullfighting is a poor sport. What is the name of the best matador you have for tomorrow's show?"

"Pepito de Malaga," said Don Enrique, "one of the greatest names, one of the bravest men, in all Spain."

"Very well," said the Doctor, "I have a proposal to make to you. I have never fought a bull in my life. Now supposing I were to go into the ring tomorrow with Pepito de Malaga and any other matadors you choose, and if I can do more tricks with a bull than they can, would you promise to do something for me?"

Don Enrique threw back his head and laughed.

"Man," he said, "you must be mad! You would be killed at once. One has to be trained for years to become a proper bullfighter."

"Supposing I were willing to take the risk of that. You are not afraid, I take it, to accept my offer?"

The Spaniard frowned.

"Afraid!" he cried. "Sir, if you can beat Pepito de Malaga in the bullring I'll promise you anything it is possible for me to grant."

"Very good," said the Doctor. "Now I understand that you are quite a powerful man in these islands. If you wished to stop all bullfighting here after tomorrow, you could do it, couldn't you?"

"Yes," said Don Enrique proudly, "I could."

"Well that is what I ask of you—if I win my wager," said John Dolittle. "If I can do more with angry bulls than can Pepito de Malaga, you are to promise me that there shall never be another bullfight in the Capa Blancas so long as you are alive to stop it. Is it a bargain?"

The Spaniard held out his hand.

"It is a bargain," he said. "I promise. But I must warn you that you are merely throwing your life away, for you will certainly be killed. However, that is no more than you deserve for saying that bullfighting is an unworthy sport. I will meet you here tomorrow morning if you should wish to arrange any particulars. Good day, sir."

As the Spaniard turned and walked into the shop with the bedmaker, Polynesia, who had been listening as usual, flew up onto my shoulder and whispered in my ear:

"I have a plan. Get hold of Bumpo and come someplace where the Doctor can't hear us. I want to talk to you."

I nudged Bumpo's elbow and we crossed the street and pretended to look into a jeweler's window; while the Doctor sat down upon his bed to lace up his boots, the only part of his clothing he had taken off for the night.

"Listen," said Polynesia, "I've been breaking my head trying to think up some way we can get money to buy those stores with; and at last I've got it."

"The money?" said Bumpo.

"No. The idea—to make the money with. Listen: the Doctor is simply bound to win this game tomorrow, sure as you're alive. Now all we have to do is to make a side bet with these Spaniards— they're great on gambling—and the trick's done."

"What's a side bet?" I asked.

"Oh I know what that is," said Bumpo proudly. "We used to have lots of them at Oxford when boat racing was on. I go to Don Enrique and say, 'I bet you a hundred pounds the Doctor wins.' Then if he does win, Don Enrique pays me a hundred pounds; and if he doesn't, I have to pay Don Enrique."

"That's the idea," said Polynesia. "Only don't say a hundred pounds: say two-thousand five-hundred pesetas. Now come and find old Don Ricky-ticky and try to look rich."

So we crossed the street again and slipped into the bed-maker's shop while the Doctor was still busy with his boots.

"Don Enrique," said Bumpo, "allow me to introduce myself. I am the crown prince of Jolliginki. Would you care to have a small bet with me on tomorrow's bullfight?"

Don Enrique bowed.

"Why certainly," he said, "I shall be delighted. But I must warn you that you are bound to lose. How much?"

"Oh, a mere trifle," said Bumpo, "just for the fun of the thing, you know. What do you say to three thousand pesetas?"

"I agree," said the Spaniard, bowing once more. "I will meet you after the bullfight tomorrow."

"So that's all right," said Polynesia as we came out to join the Doctor. "I feel as though quite a load had been taken off my mind."

THE EIGHTH CHAPTER

The Great Bullfight

HE NEXT DAY WAS A GREAT DAY IN Monteverde. All the streets were hung with flags; and everywhere, gaily dressed crowds were to be seen flocking toward the bullring, as the big circus was called where the fights took place.

The news of the Doctor's challenge had gone round the town and, it seemed, had caused much amusement to the islanders. The very idea of a mere foreigner daring to match himself against the great Pepito de Malaga! Serves him right if he got killed!

The Doctor had borrowed a bullfighter's suit from Don Enrique; and very smart and wonderful he looked in it, though Bumpo and I had hard work getting the waistcoat to close in front and even then the buttons kept bursting off it in all directions.

When we set out from the harbor to walk to the bullring, crowds of small boys ran after us making fun of the Doctor's fatness, calling out, *"Juan Hagapoco, el grueso matador!"* which is the Spanish for, "John Dolittle, the fat bullfighter."

As soon as we arrived, the Doctor said he would like to take a look at the bulls before the fight began; and we were at once led to the bull pen where, behind a high railing, six enormous black bulls were tramping around wildly.

In a few hurried words and signs the Doctor told the bulls what he was going to do and gave them careful instructions for their part of the show. The poor creatures were tremendously glad when they heard that there was a chance of bullfighting being stopped; and they promised to do exactly as they were told.

Of course the man who took us in there didn't understand what we were doing. He merely thought the fat Englishman was crazy when he saw the Doctor making signs and talking in ox tongue.

From there the Doctor went to the matadors' dressing rooms while Bumpo and I, with Polynesia, made our way into the bullring and took our seats in the great open-air theater.

It was a very grand sight. Thousands of ladies and gentlemen were there, all dressed in their smartest clothes, and everybody seemed very happy and cheerful.

Right at the beginning Don Enrique got up and explained to the people that the first item on the program was to be a match between the English Doctor and Pepito de Malaga. He told them what he had promised if the Doctor should win. But the people did not seem to think there was much chance of that. A roar of laughter went up at the very mention of such a thing.

When Pepito came into the ring everybody cheered, the ladies blew kisses, and the men clapped and waved their hats.

Presently a large door on the other side of the ring was rolled back and in galloped one of the bulls; then the door was closed again.

At once the matador became very much on the alert. He waved his red cloak and the bull rushed at him. Pepito stepped nimbly aside and the people cheered again.

This game was repeated several times. But I noticed that whenever Pepito got into a tight place and seemed to be in real danger from the bull, an assistant of his, who always hung around somewhere near, drew the bull's attention upon himself by waving another red cloak. Then the bull would chase the assistant and Pepito was left in safety. Most often, as soon as he had drawn the bull off, this assistant ran for the high fence and vaulted out of the ring to save himself. They evidently had it all arranged, these matadors; and it didn't seem to me that they were in any very great danger from the poor clumsy bull so long as they didn't slip and fall.

After about ten minutes of this kind of thing, the small door into the matadors' dressing room opened and the Doctor strolled into the ring. As soon as his fat figure, dressed in sky-blue velvet, appeared, the crowd rocked in their seats with laughter.

Juan Hagapoco, as they had called him, walked out into the center of the ring and bowed ceremoniously to the ladies in the boxes. Then he bowed to the bull. Then he bowed to Pepito. While he was bowing to Pepito's assistant, the bull started to rush at him from behind.

"Look out! Look out! The bull! You will be killed!" yelled the crowd.

But the Doctor calmly finished his bow. Then turning round he folded his arms, fixed the on-rushing bull with his eye, and frowned a terrible frown.

Presently a curious thing happened: the bull's speed got slower and slower. It almost looked as though he were afraid of that frown. Soon he stopped altogether. The Doctor shook his finger at him. He began to tremble. At last, tucking his tail between his legs, the bull turned round and ran away.

The crowd gasped. The Doctor ran after him. Round and round the ring they went, both of them puffing and blowing like grampuses. Excited whispers began to break out among the people. This was something new in bullfighting, to have the bull running away from the man, instead of the man away from the bull. At last in the tenth lap, with a final burst of speed, Juan Hagapoco, the English matador, caught the poor bull by the tail.

Then leading the now-timid creature into the middle of the ring, the Doctor made him do all manner of tricks: standing on the hind legs, standing on the front legs, dancing, hopping, rolling over. He finished up by making the bull kneel down; then he got onto his back and did handsprings and other acrobatics on the beast's horns.

Pepito and his assistant had their noses sadly out of joint. The crowd had forgotten them entirely. They were standing together by the fence not far from where I sat, muttering to one another and slowly growing green with jealousy.

Finally the Doctor turned toward Don Enrique's seat and, bowing, said in a loud voice, "This bull is no good anymore. He's terrified and out of breath. Take him away, please."

"Does the caballero wish for a fresh bull?" asked Don Enrique.

"No," said the Doctor, "I want five fresh bulls. And I would like them all in the ring at once, please."

At this a cry of horror burst from the people. They had been used to seeing matadors escaping from one bull at a time. But *five!*—That must mean certain death.

Pepito sprang forward and called to Don Enrique not to allow it, saying it was against all the rules of bullfighting. ("Ha!" Polynesia chuckled into my ear. "It's like the Doctor's navigation: he breaks all the rules; but he gets there. If they'll only let

"Did acrobatics on the beast's horns"

him, he'll give them the best show for their money they ever saw.") A great argument began. Half the people seemed to be on Pepito's side and half on the Doctor's side. At last the Doctor turned to Pepito and made another very grand bow, which burst the last button off his waistcoat.

"Well, of course if the caballero is afraid—" he began with a bland smile.

"Afraid!" screamed Pepito. "I am afraid of nothing on earth. I am the greatest matador in Spain. With this right hand I have killed nine hundred and fifty-seven bulls."

"All right, then," said the Doctor, "let us see if you can kill five more. Let the bulls in!" he shouted. "Pepito de Malaga is not afraid."

A dreadful silence hung over the great theater as the heavy door into the bull pen was rolled back. Then with a roar the five big bulls bounded into the ring.

"Look fierce," I heard the Doctor call to them in cattle language. "Don't scatter. Keep close. Get ready for a rush. Take Pepito, the one in purple, first. But for heaven's sake don't kill him. Just chase him out of the ring. Now then, all together, go for him!"

The bulls put down their heads and all in line, like a squadron of cavalry, charged across the ring straight for poor Pepito.

For one moment the Spaniard tried his hardest to look brave. But the sight of the five pairs of horns coming at him at full gallop was too much. He turned white to the lips, ran for the fence, vaulted it and disappeared.

"Now the other one," the Doctor hissed. And in two seconds the gallant assistant was nowhere to be seen. Juan Hagapoco, the fat matador, was left alone in the ring with five rampaging bulls.

The rest of the show was really well worth seeing. First, all five bulls went raging round the ring, butting at the fence with their horns, pawing up the sand, hunting for something to kill. Then each one in turn would pretend to catch sight of the Doctor for the first time and giving a bellow of rage, would lower his wicked-looking horns and shoot like an arrow across the ring as though he meant to toss him to the sky.

It was really frightfully exciting. And even I, who knew it was all arranged beforehand, held my breath in terror for the Doctor's life when I saw how near they came to sticking him. But just at the last moment, when the horns' points were two inches from the sky-blue waistcoat, the Doctor would spring nimbly to one side and the great brutes would go thundering harmlessly by, missing him by no more than a hair.

Then all five of them went for him together, completely surrounding him, slashing at him with their horns and bellowing with fury. How he escaped alive I don't know. For several minutes his round figure could hardly be seen at all in that scrimmage of tossing heads, stamping hooves and waving tails. It was, as Polynesia had prophesied, the greatest bullfight ever seen.

One woman in the crowd got quite hysterical and screamed up to Don Enrique:

"Stop the fight! Stop the fight! He is too brave a man to be killed. This is the most wonderful matador in the world. Let him live! Stop the fight!"

But presently the Doctor was seen to break loose from the mob of animals that surrounded him. Then catching each of them by the horns, one after another, he would give their heads a sudden twist and throw them down flat on the sand.

The great fellows acted their parts extremely well. I have never seen trained animals in a circus do better. They lay there panting on the ground where the Doctor threw them as if they were exhausted and completely beaten.

Then with a final bow to the ladies, John Dolittle strolled out of the ring.

The Ninth Chapter

We Depart in a Hurry

S SOON AS THE DOOR CLOSED BEHIND THE Doctor, the most tremendous noise I have ever heard broke loose. Some of the men appeared to be angry (friends of Pepito's, I suppose), but the ladies called and called to have the Doctor come back into the ring.

When at length he did so, the women seemed to go entirely mad over him. They blew kisses to him. They called him a darling. Then they started taking off their flowers, their rings, their necklaces, and their brooches and threw them down at his feet. You never saw anything like it—a perfect shower of jewelry and roses.

But the Doctor just smiled up at them, bowed once more, and backed out.

"Now, Bumpo," said Polynesia, "this is where you go down and gather up all those trinkets and we'll sell 'em. That's what the big matadors do: leave the jewelry on the ground and their assistants collect it for them. We might as well lay in a good supply of money while we've got the chance—you never know when you may need it when you're traveling with the Doctor. Never mind the roses—you can leave them—but don't leave any rings. And when you've finished, go and get your three thousand pesetas out of Don Ricky-ticky. Tommy and I will meet you outside and we'll sell the gewgaws at that pawn shop opposite the bed-maker's. Run along—and not a word to the Doctor, remember."

Outside the bullring we found the crowd still in a great state of excitement. Violent arguments were going on everywhere. Bumpo joined us with his pockets bulging in all directions; and we made our way slowly through the dense crowd to that side of the building where the matadors' dressing room was. The Doctor was waiting at the door for us.

"Good work, Doctor!" said Polynesia, flying onto his shoulder—"Great work!—But listen: I smell danger. *I* think you had better get back to the ship now as quick and as quietly as you can. Put your overcoat on over that giddy suit. I don't like the looks of this crowd. More than half of them are furious because you've won. Don Ricky-ticky must now stop the bullfighting—and you know how they love it. What I'm afraid of is that some of these matadors who are just mad with jealousy may start some dirty work. I think this would be a good time for us to get away."

"I dare say you're right, Polynesia," said the Doctor. "You usually are. The crowd does seem to be a bit restless. I'll slip down to the ship alone—so I shan't be so noticeable—and I'll wait for you there. You come by some different way. But don't be long about it. Hurry!"

As soon as the Doctor had departed, Bumpo sought out Don Enrique and said:

"Honorable sir, you owe me three thousand pesetas."

Without a word, but looking cross-eyed with annoyance, Don Enrique paid his bet.

We next set out to buy the provisions; and on the way we hired a cab and took it along with us.

Not very far away we found a big grocer's shop that seemed to sell everything to eat. We went in and bought up the finest lot of food you ever saw in your life.

As a matter of fact, Polynesia had been right about the danger we were in. The news of our victory must have spread like lightning through the whole town. For as we came out of the shop and loaded the cab up with our stores, we saw various little knots of angry men hunting round the streets, waving sticks and shouting:

"The Englishmen! Where are those accursed Englishmen who stopped the bullfighting? Hang them to a lamppost! Throw them in the sea! The Englishmen! We want the Englishmen!"

After that we didn't waste any time, you may be sure. Bumpo grabbed the Spanish cabdriver and explained to him in signs that if he didn't drive down to the harbor as fast as he knew how and keep his mouth shut the whole way, he would choke the life out of him. Then we jumped into the cab on top of the food, slammed the door, pulled down the blinds, and away we went.

"We won't get a chance to pawn the jewelry now," said Polynesia, as we bumped over the cobbly streets. "But never mind—it may come in handy later on. And anyway, we've got two thousand five hundred pesetas left out of the bet. Don't give the cabby more than two pesetas fifty, Bumpo. That's the right fare, I know."

Well, we reached the harbor all right, and we were mighty glad to find that the Doctor had sent Chee-Chee back with the rowboat to wait for us at the landing-wall.

Unfortunately, while we were in the middle of loading the supplies from the cab onto the boat, the angry mob arrived upon the wharf and made a rush for us. Bumpo snatched up a big beam of wood that lay nearby and swung it round and round his head, letting out dreadful African battle yells all the while. This kept the crowd back while Chee-Chee and I hustled the last of the stores into the boat and clambered in ourselves. Bumpo threw his beam of wood into the thick of the Spaniards and leapt in after us. Then we pushed off and rowed like mad for the *Curlew*.

The mob upon the wall howled with rage, shook their fists and hurled stones and all manner of things after us. Poor old Bumpo got hit on the head with a bottle. But as he had a very strong head it only raised a small bump, while the bottle smashed into a thousand pieces.

When we reached the ship's side, the Doctor had the anchor drawn up and the sails set and everything in readiness to get away. Looking back we saw boats coming out from the harbor-wall after us, filled with angry, shouting men. So we didn't bother to unload our rowboat but just tied it onto the ship's stern with a rope and jumped aboard.

It only took a moment more to swing the *Curlew* round into the wind; and soon we were speeding out of the harbor on our way to Brazil.

"Ha!" sighed Polynesia, as we all flopped down on the deck

to take a rest and get our breath. "That wasn't a bad adventure—quite reminds me of my old seafaring days when I sailed with the smugglers—Golly, that was the life! Never mind your head, Bumpo. It will be all right when the Doctor puts a little arnica on it. Think what we got out of the scrap: a boatload of ship's stores, pockets full of jewelry, and thousands of pesetas. Not bad, you know—not bad."

PART FOUR

THE FIRST CHAPTER

Shellfish Languages Again

IRANDA THE PURPLE BIRD-OF-PARADISE had prophesied rightly when she had foretold a good spell of weather. For three weeks the good ship *Curlew* plowed her way through smiling seas before a steady powerful wind.

I suppose most real sailors would have found this part of the voyage dull. But not I. As we got farther south and farther west, the face of the sea seemed different every day. And all the little things of a voyage that an old hand would have hardly bothered to notice were matters of great interest for my eager eyes.

We did not pass many ships. When we did see one, the Doctor would get out his telescope and we would all take a look at it. Sometimes he would signal to it, asking for news, by hauling up little colored flags upon the mast; and the ship would signal back to us in the same way. The meaning of all the signals was printed in a book that the Doctor kept in the cabin. He told me it was the language of the sea and that all ships could understand it whether they be English, Dutch, or French.

Our greatest happening during those first weeks was passing an iceberg. When the sun shone on it it burst into a hundred colors, sparkling like a jeweled palace in a fairy story. Through the telescope we saw a mother polar bear with a cub sitting on it, watching us. The Doctor recognized her as one of the bears who had spoken to him when he was discovering the North Pole. So he sailed the ship up close and offered to take her and her baby onto the *Curlew* if she wished it. But she only shook her head, thanking him; she said it would be far too hot for the cub on the deck of our ship, with no ice to keep his feet cool. It had been indeed a very hot day; but the nearness of that great mountain of ice made us all turn up our coat collars and shiver with the cold.

During those quiet, peaceful days I improved my reading and writing a great deal with the Doctor's help. I got on so well that he let me keep the ship's log. This is a big book kept on every ship, a kind of diary, in which the number of miles run, the direction of your course, and everything else that happens is written down.

The Doctor, too, in what spare time he had, was nearly always writing—in his notebooks. I used to peep into these sometimes, now that I could read, but I found it hard work to make out the Doctor's handwriting. Many of these notebooks seemed to be about sea things. There were six thick ones filled full with notes and sketches of different seaweeds; and there were others on seabirds; others on sea worms; others on seashells. They were all someday to be rewritten, printed, and bound like regular books.

One afternoon we saw, floating around us, great quantities of stuff that looked like dead grass. The Doctor told me this was gulf weed. A little farther on it became so thick that it covered all the water as far as the eye could reach; it made the *Curlew* look as though she were moving across a meadow instead of sailing the Atlantic.

Crawling about upon this weed, many crabs were to be seen. And the sight of them reminded the Doctor of his dream of learning the language of the shellfish. He fished several of these crabs up with a net and put them in his listening tank to see if he could understand them. Among the crabs he also caught a strange-looking, chubby, little fish which he told me was called a silver fidgit.

After he had listened to the crabs for a while with no success, he put the fidgit into the tank and began to listen to that. I had to leave him at this moment to go and attend to some duties on the deck. But presently I heard him below shouting for me to come down again.

"Stubbins," he cried as soon as he saw me, "a most extraordinary thing—Quite unbelievable—I'm not sure whether I'm dreaming—Can't believe my own senses. I—I—I—"

"Why, Doctor," I said, "what is it? What's the matter?"

"The fidgit," he whispered, pointing with a trembling finger to the listening tank in which the little round fish was still swimming quietly, "he talks English! And—and—*and he whistles tunes*—English tunes!"

"Talks English!" I cried. "Whistles! Why, it's impossible."

"It's a fact," said the Doctor, white in the face with excitement. "It's only a few words, scattered, with no particular sense to them—all mixed up with his own language, which I can't make out yet. But they're English words, unless there's something very wrong with my hearing. And the tune he whistles, it's as plain as anything—always the same tune. Now you listen and tell me what you make of it. Tell me everything you hear. Don't miss a word."

"He talks English!"

I went to the glass tank upon the table while the Doctor grabbed a notebook and a pencil. Undoing my collar, I stood upon the empty packing case he had been using for a stand and put my right ear down under the water.

For some moments I detected nothing at all—except, with my dry ear, the heavy breathing of the Doctor as he waited, all stiff and anxious, for me to say something. At last from within the water, sounding like a child singing miles and miles away, I heard an unbelievably thin, small voice.

"Ah!" I said.

"What is it?" asked the Doctor in a hoarse, trembly whisper. "What does he say?"

"I can't quite make it out," I said. "It's mostly in some strange fish language—Oh, but wait a minute!—Yes, now I get it—'No smoking' . . . 'My, here's a strange one!' 'Popcorn and picture postcards here' . . . 'This way out' . . . 'Don't spit'—What funny things to say, Doctor!—Oh, but wait!—Now he's whistling the tune."

"What tune is it?" gasped the Doctor.

"John Peel."

"Aha," cried the Doctor, "that's what I made it out to be." And he wrote furiously in his notebook.

I went on listening.

"This is most extraordinary," the Doctor kept muttering to himself as his pencil went wiggling over the page. "Most extraordinary—but frightfully thrilling. I wonder where he—"

"Here's some more," I cried, "some more English. . . . *'The big tank needs cleaning'* . . . That's all. Now he's talking fish talk again."

"The big tank!" the Doctor murmured, frowning in a puzzled kind of way. "I wonder where on earth he learned—"

Then he bounded out of his chair.

"I have it!" he yelled. "This fish has escaped from an aquarium. Why, of course! Look at the kind of things he has learned: 'Picture postcards'—they always sell them in aquariums; 'Don't spit'; 'No smoking'; 'This way out'—the things the attendants say.

And then, 'Oh look, here's a strange one!' That's the kind of thing that people exclaim when they look into the tanks. It all fits. There's no doubt about it, Stubbins: we have here a fish who has escaped from captivity. And it's quite possible—not certain, by any means, but quite possible—that I may now, through him, be able to establish communication with the shellfish. This is a great piece of luck."

THE SECOND CHAPTER

The Fidgit's Story

WELL, NOW THAT HE WAS STARTED once more upon his old hobby of the shellfish languages, there was no stopping the Doctor. He worked right through the night.

A little after midnight I fell asleep in a chair; about two in the morning Bumpo fell asleep at the wheel; and for five hours the *Curlew* was allowed to drift where she liked. But still John Dolittle worked on, trying his hardest to understand the fidgit's language, struggling to make the fidgit understand him.

When I woke up it was broad daylight again. The Doctor was still standing at the listening tank, looking as tired as an owl and dreadfully wet. But on his face there was a proud and happy smile.

"Stubbins," he said as soon as he saw me stir, "I've done it. I've got the key to the fidgit's language. It's a frightfully difficult language—quite different from anything I ever heard. The only thing it reminds me of—slightly—is ancient Hebrew. It isn't shellfish; but it's a big step toward it. Now, the next thing, I want you to

take a pencil and a fresh notebook and write down everything I say. The fidgit has promised to tell me the story of his life. I will translate it into English and you put it down in the book. Are you ready?"

Once more the Doctor lowered his ear beneath the level of the water; and as he began to speak, I started to write. And this is the story that the fidgit told us.

THIRTEEN MONTHS IN AN AQUARIUM

"I was born in the Pacific Ocean, close to the coast of Chile. I was one of a family of two-thousand five-hundred and ten. Soon after our mother and father left us, we youngsters got scattered. The family was broken up—by a herd of whales who chased us. I and my sister, Clippa (she was my favorite sister), had a very narrow escape for our lives. As a rule, whales are not very hard to get away from if you are good at dodging—if you've only got a quick swerve. But this one that came after Clippa and myself was a very mean whale. Every time he lost us under a stone or something he'd come back and hunt and hunt till he routed us out into the open again. I never saw such a nasty, persevering brute.

"Well, we shook him at last—though not before he had worried us for hundreds of miles northward, up the west coast of South America. But luck was against us that day. While we were resting and trying to get our breath, another family of fidgits came rushing by, shouting, 'Come on! Swim for your lives! The dogfish are coming!'

"Now dogfish are particularly fond of fidgits. We are, you might say, their favorite food—and for that reason we always keep away from deep, muddy waters. What's more, dogfish are not easy to escape from; they are terribly fast and clever hunters. So up we had to jump and on again.

"After we had gone a few more hundred miles we looked back and saw that the dogfish were gaining on us. So we turned into a harbor. It happened to be one on the West Coast of the United States. Here we guessed, and hoped, the dogfish would not be likely to follow us. As it happened, they didn't even see us turn in, but dashed on northward and we never saw them again. I hope they froze to death in the Arctic Seas.

"But, as I said, luck was against us that day. While I and my sister were cruising gently round the ships anchored in the harbor looking for orange peels, a great delicacy with us—*Swoop! Bang!*—we were caught in a net.

"We struggled for all we were worth; but it was no use. The net was small-meshed and strongly made. Kicking and flipping we were hauled up the side of the ship and dumped down on the deck, high and dry in a blazing noonday sun.

"Here a couple of old men in whiskers and spectacles leaned over us, making strange sounds. Some codling had got caught in the net the same time as we were. These the old men threw back into the sea; but us they seemed to think very precious. They put us carefully into a large jar and after they had taken us onshore they went to a big house and changed us from the jar into glass boxes full of water. This house was on the edge of the harbor; and a small stream of seawater was made to flow through the glass tank so we could breathe properly. Of course we had never lived inside glass walls before; and at first we kept on trying to swim through them and got our noses awfully sore bumping the glass at full speed.

"Then followed weeks and weeks of weary idleness. They treated us well, so far as they knew how. The old fellows in spectacles came and looked at us proudly twice a day and saw that we had the proper food to eat, the right amount of light and that the water was not too hot or too cold. But oh, the dullness of that life! It seemed we were a kind of a show. At a certain hour every morning the big doors of the house were thrown open and everybody in the city who had nothing special to do came in and looked at us. There were other tanks filled with different kinds of fishes all round the walls of the big room. And the crowds would go from tank to tank, looking in at us through the glass—with their mouths open, like half-witted flounders. We got so sick of it that we used to open our mouths back at them; and this they seemed to think highly comical.

"One day my sister said to me, 'Think you, Brother, that these strange creatures who have captured us can talk?'

"'Surely,' said I, 'have you not noticed that some talk with the lips only, some with the whole face, and yet others discourse with the hands? When they come quite close to the glass you can hear them. Listen!'

"At that moment a female, larger than the rest, pressed her nose up against the glass, pointed at me and said to her young behind her, 'Oh look, here's a strange one!'

"And then we noticed that they nearly always said this when they looked in. And for a long time we thought that such was the whole extent of the language, this being a people of but few ideas. To help pass away the weary hours we learned it by heart, 'Oh look, here's a strange one!' But we never got to know what it meant. Other phrases, however, we did get the meaning of; and we even learned to read a little in Man Talk. Many big signs there were, set up upon the walls; and when we saw that the keepers stopped the people from spitting and smoking, pointed to these signs angrily and read them out loud, we knew then that these writings signified, *No Smoking* and *Don't Spit.*

"Then in the evenings, after the crowd had gone, the same-aged male with one leg of wood, swept up the peanut shells with a broom every night. And while he was so doing, he always whistled the same tune to himself. This melody we rather liked; and we learned that, too, by heart—thinking it was part of the language.

"Thus a whole year went by in this dismal place. Some days new fishes were brought in to the other tanks; and other days old fishes were taken out. At first we had hoped we would only be kept here for a while, and that after we had been looked at sufficiently we would be returned to freedom and the sea. But as month after month went by, and we were left undisturbed, our hearts grew heavy within our prison walls of glass and we spoke to one another less and less.

"One day, when the crowd was thickest in the big room, a woman with a red face fainted from the heat. I watched through the glass and saw that the rest of the people got highly excited—though to me it did not seem to be a matter of very great importance. They threw cold water on her and carried her out into the open air.

"This made me think mightily; and presently a great idea burst upon me.

"'Sister,' I said, turning to poor Clippa who was sulking at the bottom of our prison, trying to hide behind a stone from the stupid gaze of the children who thronged about our tank, 'supposing that *we* pretended we were sick: Do you think they would take us also from this stuffy house?'

"'Brother,' said she wearily, 'that they might do. But most likely they would throw us on a rubbish heap, where we would die in the hot sun.'

"'But,' said I, 'why should they go abroad to seek a rubbish heap, when the harbor is so close? While we were being brought here I saw men throwing their rubbish into the water. If they would only throw us also there, we could quickly reach the sea.'

"'The sea!' murmured poor Clippa with a faraway look in her eyes (she had fine eyes, had my sister, Clippa). 'How like a dream it sounds—the sea! Oh, Brother, will we ever swim in it again, think you? Every night as I lie awake on the floor of this evil-smelling dungeon I hear its hearty voice ringing in my ears. How I have longed for it! Just to feel it once again, the nice, big, wholesome homeliness of it all! To jump, just to jump from the crest of an Atlantic wave, laughing in the trade wind's spindrift, down into the blue-green swirling trough! To chase the shrimps on a summer evening, when the sky is red and the light's all pink within the foam! To lie on the top, in the doldrums' noonday calm, and warm your tummy in the tropic sun! To wander hand in hand once more through the giant seaweed forests of the Indian Ocean, seeking the delicious eggs of the pop-pop! To play hide-and-seek among the castles of the coral towns with their pearl and jasper windows spangling the floor of the Spanish Main! To picnic in the anemone-meadows, dim blue and lilac-gray, that lie in the lowlands beyond the South Sea Garden! To throw somersaults on the springy sponge-beds of the Mexican Gulf! To poke about among the dead ships and see what wonders and adventures lie inside! And then, on winter nights when the Northeaster whips the water into froth, to swoop down and down to get away from the cold, down to where the water's warm and dark, down and still down, till we spy the twinkle of the fire eels far below where our friends and cousins sit chatting round the Council Grotto—chatting, Brother, over the news and gossip of *the sea*! . . . Oh—'

"And then she broke down completely, sniffling.

"'Stop it!' I said. 'You make me homesick. Look here: let's pretend we're sick—or better still, let's pretend we're dead; and see what happens. If they throw us on a rubbish heap and we fry in the sun, we'll not be much worse off than we are here in this smelly prison. What do you say? Will you risk it?'

"'I will,' she said, 'and gladly.'

"So next morning two fidgits were found by the keeper floating on the top of the water in their tank, stiff and dead. We gave a mighty good imitation of dead fish—although I say it myself. The keeper ran and got the old gentlemen with spectacles and whiskers. They threw up their hands in horror when they saw us. Lifting us carefully out of the water they laid us on wet cloths. That was the hardest part of all. If you're a fish and get taken out of the water you have to keep opening and shutting your mouth to breathe at all—and even that you can't keep up for long. And all this time we had to stay stiff as sticks and breathe silently through half-closed lips.

"Well, the old fellows poked us and felt us and pinched us till I thought they'd never be done. Then, when their backs were turned a moment, a wretched cat got up on the table and nearly ate us. Luckily the old men turned round in time and shooed her away. You may be sure, though, that we took a couple of good gulps of air while they weren't looking; and that was the only thing that saved us from choking. I wanted to whisper to Clippa to be brave and stick it out. But I couldn't even do that; because, as you know, most kinds of fish talk cannot be heard—not even a shout— unless you're underwater.

"Then, just as we were about to give it up and let on that we were alive, one of the old men shook his head sadly, lifted us up, and carried us out of the building.

"'Now for it!' I thought to myself. 'We'll soon know our fate: liberty or the garbage can.'

"Outside, to our unspeakable horror, he made straight for a large ash-barrel that stood against the wall on the other side of a yard. Most happily for us, however, while he was crossing this yard a very dirty man with a wagon and horses drove up and took the ash-barrel away. I suppose it was his property.

"Then the old man looked around for some other place to throw us. He seemed about to cast us upon the ground. But he evidently thought that this would make the yard untidy and he desisted. The suspense was terrible. He moved outside the yard gate and my heart sank once more as I saw that he now intended to throw us in the gutter of the roadway. But (fortune was indeed with us that day), a large man in blue clothes and silver buttons stopped him in the nick of time. Evidently, from the way the large man lectured and waved a short thick stick, it was against the rules of the town to throw dead fish in the streets.

"At last, to our unutterable joy, the old man turned and moved off with us toward the harbor. He walked so slowly, muttering to himself all the way and watching the man in blue out of the corner of his eye, that I wanted to bite his finger to make him hurry up. Both Clippa and I were actually at our last gasp.

"Finally he reached the seawall and, giving us one last sad look, he dropped us into the waters of the harbor.

"Never had we realized anything like the thrill of that moment, as we felt the salty wetness close over our heads. With one flick of our tails we came to life again. The old man was so surprised that he fell right into the water, almost on top of us. From this he was rescued by a sailor with a boat hook; and the last we saw of him, the man in blue was dragging him away by the coat collar, lecturing him again. Apparently it was also against the rules of the town to throw dead fish into the harbor.

"But we? What time or thought had we for his troubles?

We were free! In lightning leaps, in curving spurts, in crazy zig-zags—whooping, shrieking with delight, we sped for home and the open sea!

"That is all of my story and I will now, as I promised last night, try to answer any questions you may ask about the sea, on condition that I am set at liberty as soon as you have done."

The Doctor: "Is there any part of the sea deeper than that known as the Nero Deep—I mean the one near the Island of Guam?"

The Fidgit: "Why, certainly. There's one much deeper than that, near the mouth of the Amazon River. But it's small and hard to find. We call it 'The Deep Hole.' And there's another in the Antarctic Sea."

The Doctor: "Can you talk any shellfish language yourself?"

The Fidgit: "No, not a word. We regular fishes don't have anything to do with the shellfish. We consider them a low class."

The Doctor: "But when you're near them, can you hear the sound they make talking—I mean without necessarily understanding what they say?"

The Fidgit: "Only with the very largest ones. Shellfish have such weak, small voices it is almost impossible for any but their own kind to hear them. But with the bigger ones it is different. They make a sad, booming noise, rather like an iron pipe being knocked with a stone— only not nearly so loud of course."

The Doctor: "I am most anxious to get down to the bottom

of the sea—to study many things. But we land animals, as you no doubt know, are unable to breathe underwater. Have you any ideas that might help me?"

The Fidgit: "I think that for both your difficulties the best thing for you to do would be to try and get hold of the Great Glass Sea Snail."

The Doctor: "Er—who, or what, is the Great Glass Sea Snail?"

The Fidgit: "He is an enormous saltwater snail, one of the winkle family, but as large as a big house. He talks quite loudly—when he speaks, but this is not often. He can go to any part of the ocean, at all depths, because he doesn't have to be afraid of any creature in the sea. His shell is made of transparent mother-o'-pearl so that you can see through it; but it's thick and strong. When he is out of his shell and he carries it empty on his back, there is room in it for a wagon and a pair of horses. He has been seen carrying his food in it when traveling."

The Doctor: "I feel that that is just the creature I have been looking for. He could take me and my assistant inside his shell and we could explore the deepest depths in safety. Do you think you could get him for me?"

The Fidgit: "Alas, no! I would willingly if I could; but he is hardly ever seen by ordinary fish. He lives at the bottom of the Deep Hole, and seldom comes out. And into the Deep Hole, the lower waters of which are muddy, fishes such as we are afraid to go."

The Doctor: "Dear me! That's a terrible disappointment. Are there many of this kind of snail in the sea?"

The Fidgit: "Oh no. He is the only one in existence, since his second wife died long, long ago. He is the last of the giant shellfish. He belongs to past ages when the whales were land animals and all that. They say he is over seventy thousand years old."

The Doctor: "Good gracious, what wonderful things he could tell me! I do wish I could meet him."

The Fidgit: "Were there any more questions you wished to ask me? This water in your tank is getting quite warm and sickly. I'd like to be put back into the sea as soon as you can spare me."

The Doctor: "Just one more thing: when Christopher Columbus crossed the Atlantic in 1492, he threw overboard two copies of his diary sealed up in barrels. One of them was never found. It must have sunk. I would like to get it for my library. Do you happen to know where it is?"

The Fidgit: "Yes, I do. That, too, is in the Deep Hole. When the barrel sank, the currents drifted it northward down what we call the Orinoco Slope, till it finally disappeared into the Deep Hole. If it was any other part of the sea I'd try and get it for you; but not there."

The Doctor: "Well, that is all, I think. I hate to put you back into the sea, because I know that as soon as I do, I'll think of a hundred other questions I wanted to ask you. But I must keep my promise. Would you care for anything before you go? It seems a cold day—some cracker crumbs or something?"

The Fidgit: "No, I won't stop. All I want just at present is fresh seawater."

The Doctor: "I cannot thank you enough for all the information you have given me. You have been very helpful and patient."

The Fidgit: "Pray, do not mention it. It has been a real pleasure to be of assistance to the great John Dolittle. You are, as of course you know, already quite famous among the better class of fishes. Good-bye!—and good luck to you, to your ship, and to all your plans!"

The Doctor carried the listening tank to a porthole, opened it, and emptied the tank into the sea.

"Good-bye!" he murmured as a faint splash reached us from without.

I dropped my pencil on the table and leaned back with a sigh. My fingers were so stiff with writer's cramp that I felt as though I should never be able to open my hand again. But I, at least, had had a night's sleep. As for the poor Doctor, he was so weary that he had hardly put the tank back upon the table and dropped into a chair, when his eyes closed and he began to snore.

In the passage outside, Polynesia scratched angrily at the door. I rose and let her in.

"A nice state of affairs!" she stormed. "What sort of a ship is this? There's Bumpo upstairs asleep under the wheel; the Doctor asleep down here; and you making pothooks in a copybook with a pencil! Expect the ship to steer herself to Brazil? We're just drifting around the sea like an empty bottle—and a week behind time as it is. What's happened to you all?"

She was so angry that her voice rose to a scream. But it would have taken more than that to wake the Doctor.

I put the notebook carefully in a drawer and went on deck to take the wheel.

Bad Weather

AS SOON AS I HAD THE *CURLEW* SWUNG round upon her course again I noticed something peculiar: we were not going as fast as we had been. Our favorable wind had almost entirely disappeared.

This, at first, we did not worry about, thinking that at any moment it might spring up again. But the whole day went by; then two days; then a week—ten days, and the wind grew no stronger. The *Curlew* just dawdled along at the speed of a toddling babe.

I now saw that the Doctor was becoming uneasy. He kept getting out his sextant (an instrument that tells you what part of the ocean you are in) and making calculations. He was forever looking at his maps and measuring distances on them. The far edge of the sea, all around us, he examined with his telescope a hundred times a day.

"But, Doctor," I said when I found him one afternoon mumbling to himself about the misty appearance of the sky, "it wouldn't matter so much, would it, if we did take a little longer over the trip?

We've got plenty to eat on board now; and the purple bird-of-paradise will know that we have been delayed by something that we couldn't help."

"Yes, I suppose so," he said thoughtfully. "But I hate to keep her waiting. At this season of the year she generally goes to the Peruvian Mountains—for her health. And besides, the good weather she prophesied is likely to end any day now and delay us still further. If we could only keep moving at even a fair speed, I wouldn't mind. It's this hanging around, almost dead still, that gets me restless—Ah, here comes a wind—Not very strong—but maybe it'll grow."

A gentle breeze from the northeast came singing through the ropes; and we smiled up hopefully at the *Curlew*'s leaning masts.

"We've only got another hundred and fifty miles to make, to sight the coast of Brazil," said the Doctor. "If that wind would just stay with us, steady for a full day, we'd see land."

But suddenly the wind changed, swung to the east, then back to the northeast—then to the north. It came in fitful gusts, as though it hadn't made up its mind which way to blow; and I was kept busy at the wheel, swinging the *Curlew* this way and that to keep the right side of it.

Presently we heard Polynesia, who was in the rigging keeping a lookout for land or passing ships, screech down to us:

"Bad weather coming. That jumpy wind is an ugly sign. And look! Over there in the east—see that black line, low down? If that isn't a storm I'm a landlubber. The gales round here are fierce, when they do blow—tear your canvas out like paper. You take the wheel, Doctor: it'll need a strong arm if it's a real storm. I'll go wake Bumpo and Chee-Chee. This looks bad to me. We'd best get all the sails down right away, till we see how strong she's going to blow."

Indeed the whole sky was now beginning to take on a very threatening look. The black line to the eastward grew blacker as it came nearer and nearer. A low, rumbly, whispering noise went moaning over the sea. The water that had been so blue and smiling turned to a ruffled ugly gray. And across the darkening sky, shreds of cloud swept like tattered witches flying from the storm.

I must confess I was frightened. You see, I had only so far seen the sea in friendly moods: sometimes quiet and lazy; sometimes laughing, venturesome and reckless; sometimes brooding and poetic, when moonbeams turned her ripples into silver threads and dreaming, snowy night clouds piled up fairy castles in the sky. But as yet I had not known, or even guessed at, the terrible strength of the sea's wild anger.

When that storm finally struck us we leaned right over flatly on our side, as though some invisible giant had slapped the poor *Curlew* on the cheek.

After that, things happened so thick and so fast that what with the wind that stopped your breath, the driving, blinding water, the deafening noise and the rest, I haven't a very clear idea of how our shipwreck came about.

I remember seeing the sails, which we were now trying to roll up upon the deck, torn out of our hands by the wind and go overboard like a penny balloon—very nearly carrying Chee-Chee with them. And I have a dim recollection of Polynesia screeching somewhere for one of us to go downstairs and close the portholes.

In spite of our masts being bare of sail, we were now scudding along to the southward at a great pace. But every once in a while huge gray-black waves would arise from under the ship's side like nightmare monsters, swell and climb, then crash down upon us, pressing us into the sea; and the poor *Curlew* would come to a standstill, half under water, like a gasping, drowning pig.

While I was clambering along toward the wheel to see the Doctor, clinging like a leech with hands and legs to the rails lest I be blown overboard, one of these tremendous seas tore loose my hold, filled my throat with water, and swept me like a cork the full length of the deck. My head struck a door with an awful bang. And then I fainted.

Wrecked!

WHEN I AWOKE I WAS VERY HAZY IN MY head. The sky was blue and the sea was calm. At first I thought that I must have fallen asleep in the sun on the deck of the *Curlew*. And thinking that I would be late for my turn at the wheel, I tried to rise to my feet. I found I couldn't; my arms were tied to something behind me with a piece of rope. By twisting my neck around I found this to be a mast, broken off short. Then I realized that I wasn't sitting on a ship at all; I was only sitting on a piece of one. I began to feel uncomfortably scared. Screwing up my eyes, I searched the rim of the sea north, east, south, and west: no land; no ships; nothing was in sight. I was alone in the ocean!

At last, little by little, my bruised head began to remember what had happened: first, the coming of the storm; the sails going overboard; then the big wave which had banged me against the door. But what had become of the Doctor and the others? What day was this, tomorrow or the day after? And why was I sitting on only part of a ship?

"I was alone in the ocean!"

Working my hand into my pocket, I found my penknife and cut the rope that tied me. This reminded me of a shipwreck story which Joe had once told me, of a captain who had tied his son to a mast in order that he shouldn't be washed overboard by the gale. So of course it must have been the Doctor who had done the same to me.

But where was he?

The awful thought came to me that the Doctor and the rest

of them must be drowned, since there was no other wreckage to be seen upon the waters. I got to my feet and stared around the sea again—Nothing—nothing but water and sky!

A long way off I saw the small dark shape of a bird skimming low down over the swell. When it came quite close I saw it was a stormy petrel. I tried to talk to it, to see if it could give me news. But unluckily I hadn't learned much seabird language and I couldn't even attract its attention, much less make it understand what I wanted.

Twice it circled round my raft, lazily, with hardly a flip of the wing. And I could not help wondering, in spite of the distress I was in, where it had spent last night—how it, or any other living thing, had weathered such a smashing storm. It made me realize the great big difference between different creatures; and that size and strength are not everything. To this petrel, a frail little thing of feathers, much smaller and weaker than I, the sea could do anything she liked, it seemed; and his only answer was a lazy, saucy flip of the wing! *He* was the one who should be called the *able* seaman. For, come raging gale, come sunlit calm, this wilderness of water was his home.

After swooping over the sea around me (just looking for food, I supposed) he went off in the direction from which he had come. And I was alone once more.

I found I was somewhat hungry—and a little thirsty, too. I began to think all sorts of miserable thoughts, the way one does when he is lonesome and has missed breakfast. What was going to become of me now, if the Doctor and the rest were drowned? I would starve to death or die of thirst. Then the sun went behind some clouds and I felt cold. How many hundreds or thousands of miles was I from any land? What if another storm should come and smash up even this poor raft on which I stood?

I went on like this for a while, growing gloomier and gloomier, when suddenly I thought of Polynesia. "You're always safe with the Doctor," she had said. "He gets there. Remember that."

I'm sure I wouldn't have minded so much if he had been here with me. It was this being all alone that made me want to weep. And yet the petrel was alone! What a baby I was, I told myself, to be scared to the verge of tears just by loneliness! I was quite safe where I was—for the present anyhow. John Dolittle wouldn't get scared by a little thing like this. He only got excited when he made a discovery, found a new bug or something. And if what Polynesia had said was true, he couldn't be drowned and things would come out all right in the end somehow.

I threw out my chest, buttoned up my collar, and began walking up and down the short raft to keep warm. I would be like John Dolittle. I wouldn't cry—And I wouldn't get excited.

How long I paced back and forth I don't know. But it was a long time—for I had nothing else to do.

At last I got tired and lay down to rest. And in spite of all my troubles, I soon fell fast asleep.

This time when I woke up, stars were staring down at me out of a cloudless sky. The sea was still calm; and my strange craft was rocking gently under me on an easy swell. All my fine courage left me as I gazed up into the big silent night and felt the pains of hunger and thirst set to work in my stomach harder than ever.

"Are you awake?" said a high silvery voice at my elbow.

I sprang up as though someone had stuck a pin in me. And

there, perched at the very end of my raft, her beautiful golden tail glowing dimly in the starlight, sat Miranda, the purple bird-of-paradise!

Never have I been so glad to see anyone in my life. I almost fell into the water as I leapt to hug her.

"I didn't want to wake you," said she. "I guessed you must be tired after all you've been through—Don't squash the life out of me, boy: I'm not a stuffed duck, you know."

"Oh, Miranda, you dear old thing," said I, "I'm so glad to see you. Tell me, where is the Doctor? Is he alive?"

"Of course he's alive—and it's my firm belief he always will be. He's over there, about forty miles to the west."

"What's he doing there?"

"He's sitting on the other half of the *Curlew,* shaving himself—or he was when I left him."

"Well, thank heaven he's alive!" said I. "Bumpo—and the animals, are they all right?"

"Yes, they're with him. Your ship broke in half in the storm. The Doctor had tied you down when he found you stunned. And the part you were on got separated and floated away. Golly, it *was* a storm! One has to be a gull or an albatross to stand that sort of weather. I had been watching for the Doctor for three weeks from a clifftop; but last night I had to take refuge in a cave to keep my tail feathers from blowing out. As soon as I found the Doctor, he sent me off with some porpoises to help us in our search. There had been quite a gathering of seabirds waiting to greet the Doctor; but the rough weather sort of broke up the arrangements that had been made to welcome him properly. It was the petrel that first gave us the tip where you were."

"Well, but how can I get to the Doctor, Miranda? I haven't any oars."

"Get to him! Why, you're going to him now. Look behind you."

I turned around. The moon was just rising on the sea's edge. And I now saw that my raft was moving through the water, but so gently that I had not noticed it before.

"What's moving us?" I asked.

"The porpoises," said Miranda.

I went to the back of the raft and looked down into the water. And just below the surface I could see the dim forms of four big porpoises, their sleek skins glinting in the moonlight, pushing at the raft with their noses.

"They're old friends of the Doctor's," said Miranda. "They'd do anything for John Dolittle. We should see his party soon now. We're pretty near the place I left them—Yes, there they are! See that dark shape? No, more to the right of where you're looking. Can't you make out the figure of the man standing against the sky? Now Chee-Chee spies us—he's waving. Don't you see them?"

I didn't—for my eyes were not as sharp as Miranda's. But presently from somewhere in the murky dusk I heard Bumpo singing his African songs with the full force of his enormous voice. And in a little, by peering and peering in the direction of the sound, I at last made out a dim mass of tattered, splintered wreckage—all that remained of the poor *Curlew* —floating low down upon the water.

A hulloa came through the night. And I answered it. We kept it up, calling to one another back and forth across the calm night sea. And a few minutes later the two halves of our brave little ruined ship bumped gently together again.

Now that I was nearer and the moon was higher I could see more plainly. Their half of the ship was much bigger than mine.

It lay partly upon its side; and most of them were perched upon the top, munching ship's biscuit.

But close down to the edge of the water, using the sea's calm surface for a mirror and a piece of broken bottle for a razor, John Dolittle was shaving his face by the light of the moon.

THE FIFTH CHAPTER

Land!

THEY ALL GAVE ME A GREAT GREETING AS I clambered off my half of the ship onto theirs. Bumpo brought me a wonderful drink of fresh water that he drew from a barrel; and Chee-Chee and Polynesia stood around me feeding me ship's biscuit.

But it was the sight of the Doctor's smiling face—just knowing that I was with him once again—that cheered me more than anything else. As I watched him carefully wipe his glass razor and put it away for future use, I could not help comparing him in my mind with the stormy petrel. Indeed, the vast strange knowledge which he had gained from his speech and friendship with animals had brought him the power to do things that no other human being would dare to try. Like the petrel, he could apparently play with the sea in all her moods. And ridiculous though it was, I could quite understand what Miranda meant when she said she firmly believed that he could never die. Just to be with him gave you a wonderful feeling of comfort and safety.

Except for his appearance (his clothes were crumpled and damp and his battered high hat was stained with saltwater), that storm which had so terrified me had disturbed him no more than getting stuck on the mudbank in Puddleby River.

Politely thanking Miranda for getting me so quickly, he asked her if she would now go ahead of us and show us the way to Spidermonkey Island. Next, he gave orders to the porpoises to leave my old piece of the ship and push the bigger half wherever the bird-of-paradise should lead us.

How much he had lost in the wreck besides his razor I did not know—everything, most likely, together with all the money he had saved up to buy the ship with. And still he was smiling as though he wanted for nothing in the world. The only things he had saved, as far as I could see—beyond the barrel of water and bag of biscuit— were his precious notebooks. These, I saw when he stood up, he had strapped around his waist with yards and yards of twine. He was, as old Matthew Mugg used to say, a great man. He was unbelievable.

And now for three days we continued our journey slowly but steadily—southward.

The only inconvenience we suffered from was the cold. This seemed to increase as we went forward. The Doctor said that the island, disturbed from its usual paths by the great gale, had evidently drifted farther south than it had ever been before.

On the third night poor Miranda came back to us nearly frozen. She told the Doctor that in the morning we would find the island quite close to us, though we couldn't see it now as it was a misty, dark night. She said that she must hurry back at once to a warmer climate; and that she would visit the Doctor in Puddleby next August as usual.

"Don't forget, Miranda," said John Dolittle, "if you should hear anything of what happened to Long Arrow, to get word to me."

The bird-of-paradise assured him she would. And after the Doctor had thanked her again and again for all that she had done for us, she wished us good luck and disappeared into the night.

We were all awake early in the morning, long before it was light, waiting for our first glimpse of the country we had come so far to see. And as the rising sun turned the eastern sky to gray, of course it was old Polynesia who first shouted that she could see palm trees and mountaintops.

With the growing light it became plain to all of us: a long island with high rocky mountains in the middle—and so near to us that you could almost throw your hat upon the shore.

The porpoises gave us one last push and our strange-looking craft bumped gently on a low beach. Then, thanking our lucky stars for a chance to stretch our cramped legs, we all bundled off onto the land—the first land, even though it was floating land, that we had trodden for six weeks. What a thrill I felt as I realized that Spidermonkey Island, the little spot in the atlas that my pencil had touched, lay at last beneath my feet!

When the light increased still further, we noticed that the palms and grasses of the island seemed withered and almost dead. The Doctor said that it must be on account of the cold that the island was now suffering from in its new climate. These trees and grasses, he told us, were the kind that belonged to warm, tropical weather.

The porpoises asked if we wanted them any further. And the Doctor said that he didn't think so, not for the present—nor the raft either, he added; for it was already beginning to fall to pieces and could not float much longer.

As we were preparing to go inland and explore the island, we suddenly noticed a whole band of natives watching us with great curiosity from among the trees. The Doctor went forward to talk to them. But he could not make them understand. He tried by signs to show them that he had come on a friendly visit. The natives didn't seem to like us, however. They had bows and arrows and long hunting spears, with stone points, in their hands; and they made signs back to the Doctor to tell him that if he came a step nearer they would kill us all. They evidently wanted us to leave the island at once. It was a very uncomfortable situation.

At last the Doctor made them understand that he only wanted to see the island all over and that then he would go away—though how he meant to do it, with no boat to sail in, was more than I could imagine.

While they were talking among themselves another man arrived—apparently with a message that they were wanted in some other part of the island. Because presently, shaking their spears threateningly at us, they went off with the newcomer.

"What discourteous chaps!" said Bumpo. "Did you ever see such inhospitability? Never even asked us if we'd had breakfast, the benighted bounders!"

"Sh! They're going off to their village," said Polynesia. "I'll bet there's a village on the other side of those mountains. If you take my advice, Doctor, you'll get away from this beach while their backs are turned. Let us go up into the higher land for the present—someplace where they won't know where we are. They may grow friendlier when they see we mean no harm. They have honest, open faces and look like a decent crowd to me."

So, feeling a little bit discouraged by our first reception, we moved off toward the mountains in the center of the island.

The Jabizri

WE FOUND THE WOODS AT THE FEET OF the hills thick and tangly and somewhat hard to get through. On Polynesia's advice, we kept away from all paths and trails, feeling it best to avoid meeting any natives for the present.

But she and Chee-Chee were good guides and splendid jungle hunters; and the two of them set to work at once looking for food for us. In a very short space of time they had found quite a number of different fruits and nuts that made for excellent eating, though none of us knew the names of any of them. We discovered a nice clean stream of good water that came down from the mountains; so we were supplied with something to drink, as well.

We followed the stream up toward the heights. And presently we came to parts where the woods were thinner and the ground rocky and steep. Here we could get glimpses of wonderful views all over the island, with the blue sea beyond.

While we were admiring one of these the Doctor suddenly said, "Sh! A Jabizri! Don't you hear it?"

We listened and heard, somewhere in the air about us, an extraordinarily musical hum—like a bee, but not just one note. This hum rose and fell, up and down—almost like someone singing.

"No other insect but the Jabizri beetle hums like that," said the Doctor. "I wonder where he is—quite near, by the sound—flying among the trees probably. Oh, if I only had my butterfly net! Why didn't I think to strap that around my waist too. Confound the storm: I may miss the chance of a lifetime now of getting the rarest beetle in the world. Oh look! There he goes!"

A huge beetle, easily three inches long I should say, suddenly flew by our noses. The Doctor got frightfully excited. He took off his hat to use as a net, swooped at the beetle and caught it. He nearly fell down a precipice onto the rocks below in his wild hurry, but that didn't bother him in the least. He knelt down, chortling, upon the ground with the Jabizri safe under his hat. From his pocket he brought out a glass-topped box, and into this he very skilfully made the beetle walk from under the rim of the hat. Then he rose up, happy as a child, to examine his new treasure through the glass lid.

It certainly was a most beautiful insect. It was pale blue underneath, but its back was glossy black with huge red spots on it.

"There isn't an entymologist in the whole world who wouldn't give all he has to be in my shoes today," said the Doctor. "Hulloa! This Jabizri's got something on his leg—Doesn't look like mud. I wonder what it is."

He took the beetle carefully out of the box and held it by its back in his fingers, where it waved its six legs slowly in the air. We all crowded about him, peering at it. Rolled around the middle section of its right foreleg was something that looked like a thin dried leaf. It was bound on very neatly with strong spiderwebbing.

It was marvelous to see how John Dolittle with his fat heavy fingers undid that cobweb cord and unrolled the leaf, whole, without tearing it or hurting the precious beetle. The Jabizri he put back into the box. Then he spread the leaf out flat and examined it.

You can imagine our surprise when we found that the inside of the leaf was covered with signs and pictures, drawn so tiny that you almost needed a magnifying glass to tell what they were. Some of the signs we couldn't make out at all; but nearly all the pictures were quite plain, figures of men and mountains mostly. The whole was done in a curious sort of brown ink.

For several moments there was a dead silence while we all stared at the leaf, fascinated and mystified.

"I think this is written in blood," said the Doctor at last. "It turns that color when it's dry. Somebody pricked his finger to make these pictures. It's an old dodge when you're short of ink—but highly unsanitary. What an extraordinary thing to find tied to a beetle's leg! I wish I could talk beetle language and find out where the Jabizri got it from."

"But what is it?" I asked. "Rows of little pictures and signs. What do you make of it, Doctor?"

"It's a letter," he said, "a picture letter. All these little things put together mean a message. But why give a message to a beetle to carry—and to a Jabizri, the rarest beetle in the world?—What an extraordinary thing!"

Then he fell to muttering over the pictures.

"I wonder what it means: men walking up a mountain; men walking into a hole in a mountain; a mountain falling down—it's a good drawing, that; men pointing to their open mouths; bars—prison bars, perhaps; men praying; men lying down—they look as though they might be sick; and last of all, just a mountain—a peculiar-shaped mountain."

All of a sudden the Doctor looked up sharply at me, a wonderful smile of delighted understanding spreading over his face.

"*Long Arrow!*" he cried. "Don't you see, Stubbins? Why, of course! Only a naturalist would think of doing a thing like this: giving his letter to a beetle—not to a common beetle, but to the rarest of all, one that other naturalists would try to catch—Well, well! Long Arrow! A picture letter from Long Arrow. For pictures are the only writing that he knows."

"Yes, but who is the letter to?" I asked.

"It's to me very likely. Miranda had told him, I know, years ago, that someday I meant to come here. But if not for me, then it's for anyone who caught the beetle and read it. It's a letter to the world."

"Well, but what does it say? It doesn't seem to me that it's much good to you now that you've got it."

"Yes, it is," he said, "because, look, I can read it now. First picture: men walking up a mountain—that's Long Arrow and his party; men going into a hole in a mountain—they enter a cave looking for medicine plants or mosses; a mountain falling down—some hanging rocks must have slipped and trapped them, imprisoned them in the cave. And this was the only living creature that could carry a message for them to the outside world—a beetle, who could *burrow* his way into the open air. Of course it was only a slim chance that the beetle would ever be caught and the letter read. But it *was* a chance; and when men are in great danger, they grab at any straw of hope. . . . All right. Now look at the next picture: men pointing to their open mouths—they are hungry; men praying—begging anyone who finds this letter to come to their assistance; men lying down—they are sick, or starving. This letter, Stubbins, is their last cry for help."

He sprang to his feet as he finished, snatched out a notebook, and put the letter between the leaves. His hands were trembling with haste and agitation.

"Come on," he cried, "up the mountain—all of you! There's not a moment to lose. Bumpo, bring the water and nuts with you. heaven only knows how long they've been pining underground. Let's hope and pray we're not too late!"

"But where are you going to look?" I asked. "Miranda said the island was a hundred miles long and the mountains seem to run all the way down the center of it."

"Didn't you see the last picture?" he said, grabbing up his hat from the ground and cramming it on his head. "It was an oddly shaped mountain—looked like a hawk's head. Well, there's where he is—if he's still alive. First thing for us to do is to get up on a high peak and look around the island for a mountain shaped like a hawk's head. Just think of it! There's a chance of my meeting Long Arrow, the son of Golden Arrow, after all! Come on! Hurry! To delay may mean death to the greatest naturalist ever born!"

Hawk's-Head Mountain

WE ALL AGREED AFTERWARD THAT none of us had ever worked so hard in our lives before as we did that day. For my part, I know I was often on the point of dropping exhausted with fatigue; but I just kept on going—like a machine—determined that, whatever happened, *I* would not be the first to give up.

When we had scrambled to the top of a high peak, almost instantly we saw the strange mountain pictured in the letter. In shape it was the perfect image of a hawk's head, and was, as far as we could see, the second highest summit in the island.

Although we were all out of breath from our climb, the Doctor didn't let us rest a second as soon as he had sighted it. With one look at the sun for direction, down he dashed again, breaking through thickets, splashing over brooks, taking all the shortcuts. For a fat man, he was certainly the swiftest cross-country runner I ever saw.

We floundered after him as fast as we could. When I say *we*,

I mean Bumpo and myself; for the animals—Jip, Chee-Chee, and Polynesia—were a long way ahead—even beyond the Doctor— enjoying the hunt like a paper chase.

At length we arrived at the foot of the mountain we were making for; and we found its sides very steep. Said the Doctor:

"Now we will separate and search for caves. This spot where we now are, will be our meeting place. If anyone finds anything like a cave or a hole where the earth and rocks have fallen in, he must shout and hulloa to the rest of us. If we find nothing we will all gather here in about an hour's time. Everybody understand?"

Then we all went off our different ways.

Each of us, you may be sure, was anxious to be the one to make a discovery. And never was a mountain searched so thoroughly. But alas, nothing could we find that looked in the least like a fallen-in cave. There were plenty of places where rocks had tumbled down to the foot of the slopes; but none of these appeared as though caves or passages could possibly lie behind them.

One by one, tired and disappointed, we straggled back to the meeting place. The Doctor seemed gloomy and impatient but by no means inclined to give up.

"Jip," he said, "couldn't you *smell* anything like a person anywhere?"

"No," said Jip. "I sniffed at every crack on the mountainside. But I am afraid my nose will be of no use to you here, Doctor. The trouble is, the whole air is so saturated with the smell of spider monkeys that it drowns every other scent—And besides, it's too cold and dry for good smelling."

"It is certainly that," said the Doctor, "and getting colder all the time. I'm afraid the island is still drifting to the south. Let's hope it stops before long or we won't be able to get even nuts and fruit to eat—everything in the island will perish—Chee-Chee, what luck did you have?"

"None, Doctor. I climbed to every peak and pinnacle I could see. I searched every hollow and cleft. But not one place could I find where men might be hidden."

"And Polynesia," asked the Doctor, "did you see nothing that might put us on the right track?"

"Not a thing, Doctor, but I have a plan."

"Oh good!" cried John Dolittle, full of hope renewed. "What is it? Let's hear it."

"You still have that beetle with you," she asked, "the Biz-biz, or whatever it is you call the wretched insect?"

"Yes," said the Doctor, producing the glass-topped box from his pocket, "here it is."

"All right. Now listen," said she. "If what you have supposed is true—that is, that Long Arrow had been trapped inside the mountain by falling rock, he probably found that beetle inside the cave—perhaps many other different beetles too, eh? He wouldn't have been likely to take the Biz-biz in with him, would he? He was hunting plants, you say, not beetles. Isn't that right?"

"Yes," said the Doctor, "that's probably so."

"Very well. It is fair to suppose then that the beetle's home, or his hole, is in that place—the part of the mountain where Long Arrow and his party are imprisoned, isn't it?"

"Quite, quite."

"All right. Then the thing to do is to let the beetle go—and watch him; and sooner or later he'll return to his home in Long Arrow's cave. And there we will follow him, or at all events," she added, smoothing down her wing feathers with a very superior air, "we will follow him till the miserable bug starts nosing under the earth. But at least he will show us what part of the mountain Long Arrow is hidden in."

"But he may fly, if I let him out," said the Doctor. "Then we shall just lose him and be no better off than we were before."

"*Let* him fly," snorted Polynesia scornfully. "A parrot can wing it as fast as a Biz-biz, I fancy. If he takes to the air, I'll guarantee not to let the little devil out of my sight. And if he just crawls along the ground you can follow him yourself."

"Splendid!" cried the Doctor. "Polynesia, you have a great brain. I'll set him to work at once and see what happens."

Again we all clustered round the Doctor as he carefully lifted off the glass lid and let the big beetle climb out upon his finger.

"Ladybug, Ladybug, fly away home!" crooned Bumpo. "Your house is on fire and your chil—"

"Oh, be quiet!" snapped Polynesia crossly. "Stop insulting him! Don't you suppose he has wits enough to go home without your telling him?"

"I thought perchance he might be of a philandering disposition," said Bumpo humbly. "It could be that he is tired of his home and needs to be encouraged. Shall I sing him 'Home Sweet Home,' think you?"

"No. Then he'd never go back. Your voice needs a rest. Don't sing to him: just watch him—Oh, and Doctor, why not tie another message to the creature's leg, telling Long Arrow that we're doing our best to reach him and that he mustn't give up hope?"

"I will," said the Doctor. And in a minute he had pulled a dry leaf from a bush nearby and was covering it with little pictures in pencil.

At last, neatly fixed up with his new mailbag, Mr. Jabizri crawled off the Doctor's finger to the ground and looked about him. He stretched his legs, polished his nose with his front feet, and then moved off leisurely to the west.

We had expected him to walk *up* the mountain; instead, he walked *around* it. Do you know how long it takes a beetle to walk round a mountain? Well, I assure you it takes an unbelievably long time. As the hours dragged by, we hoped and hoped that he would get up and fly the rest, and let Polynesia carry on the work of following him. But he never opened his wings once. I had not realized before how hard it is for a human being to walk slowly enough to keep up with a beetle. It was the most tedious thing I have ever gone through. And as we dawdled along behind, watching him like hawks lest we lose him under a leaf or something, we all got so cross and ill-tempered we were ready to bite one another's heads off. And when he stopped to look at the scenery or polish his nose some more, I could hear Polynesia behind me letting out the most dreadful seafaring swear words you ever heard.

After he had led us the whole way round the mountain, he brought us to the exact spot where we started from, and there he came to a dead stop.

"Well," said Bumpo to Polynesia, "what do you think of the beetle's sense now? You see, he *doesn't* know enough to go home."

"Oh, be still!" snapped Polynesia. "Wouldn't *you* want to stretch your legs for exercise if you'd been shut up in a box all day. Probably his home is near here, and that's why he's come back."

"But why," I asked, "did he go the whole way round the mountain first?"

Then the three of us got into a violent argument. But in the middle of it all the Doctor suddenly called out:

"Look, look!"

We turned and found that he was pointing to the Jabizri, who was now walking *up* the mountain at a much faster and more businesslike gait.

"Well," said Bumpo, sitting down wearily, "if he is going to walk *over* the mountain and back, for more exercise, I'll wait for him here. Chee-Chee and Polynesia can follow him."

Indeed it would have taken a monkey or a bird to climb the place which the beetle was now walking up. It was a smooth, flat part of the mountain's side, steep as a wall.

But presently, when the Jabizri was no more than ten feet above our heads, we all cried out together. For, even while we watched him, he had disappeared into the face of the rock like a raindrop soaking into sand.

"He's gone," cried Polynesia. "There must be a hole up there." And in a twinkling she had fluttered up the rock and was clinging to the face of it with her claws.

"Yes," she shouted down, "we've run him to earth at last. His hole is right here, behind a patch of lichen—big enough to get two fingers in."

"Ah," cried the Doctor, "this great slab of rock must have slid down from the summit and shut off the mouth of the cave like a door. Poor fellows! What a dreadful time they must have spent in there! Oh, if we only had some picks and shovels now!"

"Picks and shovels wouldn't do much good," said Polynesia. "Look at the size of the slab: a hundred feet high and as many broad. You would need an army for a week to make any impression on it."

"I wonder how thick it is," said the Doctor; and he picked up a big stone and banged it with all his might against the face of the rock. It made a hollow booming sound, like a giant drum. We all stood still listening while the echo of it died slowly away.

And then a cold shiver ran down my spine. For, from within the mountain, back came three answering knocks: *Boom!* . . . *Boom!* . . . *Boom!*

Wide-eyed, we looked at one another as though the earth itself had spoken. And the solemn little silence that followed was broken by the Doctor.

"Thank heaven," he said in a hushed, reverent voice, "some of them at least are alive!"

PART FIVE

A Great Moment

THE NEXT PART OF OUR PROBLEM WAS THE hardest of all: how to roll aside, pull down, or break open that gigantic slab. As we gazed up at it towering above our heads, it looked indeed a hopeless task for our tiny strength.

But the sounds of life from inside the mountain had put new heart in us. And in a moment we were all scrambling around trying to find any opening or crevice that would give us something to work on. Chee-Chee scaled up the sheer wall of the slab and examined the top of it where it leaned against the mountain's side; I uprooted bushes and stripped off hanging creepers that might conceal a weak place; the Doctor got more leaves and composed new picture letters for the Jabizri to take in if he should turn up again; while Polynesia carried up a handful of nuts and pushed them into the beetle's hole, one by one, for the prisoners inside to eat.

"Nuts are so nourishing," she said.

But Jip it was who, scratching at the foot of the slab like a good ratter, made the discovery which led to our final success.

"Doctor," he cried, running up to John Dolittle with his nose all covered with black mud, "this slab is resting on nothing but a bed of soft earth. You never saw such easy digging. I guess the cave behind must be just too high up for the men inside to reach the earth with their hands, or they could have scraped a way out long ago. If we can only scratch the earthbed away from under, the slab might drop a little. Then maybe they can climb out over the top."

The Doctor hurried to examine the place where Jip had dug.

"Why, yes," he said, "if we can get the earth away from under this front edge, the slab is standing up so straight, we might even make it fall right down in this direction. It's well worth trying. Let's get at it, quick."

We had no tools but the sticks and slivers of stone that we could find around. A strange sight we must have looked, the whole crew of us squatting down on our heels, scratching and burrowing at the foot of the mountain, like six badgers in a row.

After about an hour, during which in spite of the cold the sweat fell from our foreheads in all directions, the Doctor said:

"Be ready to jump from under, clear out of the way, if she shows signs of moving. If this slab falls on anybody, it will squash him flatter than a pancake."

Presently there was a grating, grinding sound.

"Look out!" yelled John Dolittle. "Here she comes! Scatter!"

We ran for our lives, outward, toward the sides. The big rock slid gently down, about a foot, into the trough that we had made beneath it. For a moment I was disappointed, for like that, it was as hopeless as before—no signs of a cave mouth showing above it. But as I looked upward, I saw the top coming very slowly away from the mountainside. We had unbalanced it below. As it moved apart from the face of the mountain, sounds of human voices, crying gladly in a strange tongue, issued from behind. Faster and faster the top swung forward, downward. Then, with a roaring crash that shook the whole mountain range beneath our feet, it struck the earth and cracked in halves.

How can I describe to anyone that first meeting between the two greatest naturalists the world ever knew: Long Arrow, the son of Golden Arrow, and John Dolittle, M. D., of Puddleby-on-the-Marsh? The scene rises before me now, plain and clear in every detail, though it took place so many, many years ago. But when I come to write of it, words seem such poor things with which to tell you of that great occasion.

I know that the Doctor, whose life was surely full enough of big happenings, always counted the setting free of the scientist as the greatest thing he ever did. For my part, knowing how much this meeting must mean to him, I was on pins and needles of expectation and curiosity as the great stone finally thundered down at our feet and we gazed across it to see what lay behind.

The gloomy black mouth of a tunnel, full twenty feet high, was revealed. In the center of this opening stood an enormous man, seven feet tall, handsome, muscular, slim and naked—but for a beaded cloth about his middle and an eagle's feather in his hair. He held one hand across his face to shield his eyes from the blinding sun, which he had not seen in many days.

"It is he!" I heard the Doctor whisper at my elbow. "I know him by his great height and the scar upon his chin."

And he stepped forward slowly across the fallen stone with his hand outstretched to him.

"It was a great moment."

Presently the man uncovered his eyes. And I saw that they had a curious piercing gleam in them—like the eyes of an eagle, but kinder and more gentle. He slowly raised his right arm, the rest of him still and motionless like a statue, and took the Doctor's hand in his. It was a great moment. Polynesia nodded to me in a knowing, satisfied kind of way. And I heard old Bumpo sniffle sentimentally.

Then the Doctor tried to speak to Long Arrow. But he knew no English, of course, and the Doctor knew none of his tongue. Presently, to my surprise, I heard the Doctor trying him in different animal languages.

"How do you do?" he said in dog talk; "I am glad to see you," in horse signs; "How long have you been buried?" in deer language. Still the man made no move, but stood there, straight and stiff, understanding not a word.

The Doctor tried again, in several other animal dialects. But with no result.

Till at last he came to the language of eagles.

"Great Long Arrow," he said in the fierce screams and short grunts that the big birds use, "never have I been so glad in all my life as I am today to find you still alive."

In a flash Long Arrow's stony face lit up with a smile of understanding; and back came the answer in eagle tongue:

"Mighty Friend, I owe my life to you. For the remainder of my days I am in your debt."

Afterward Long Arrow told us that this was the only bird or animal language that he had ever been able to learn. But that he had not spoken it in a long time, for no eagles ever came to this island.

Then the Doctor signaled to Bumpo, who came forward with the nuts and water. But Long Arrow neither ate nor drank. Taking the supplies with a nod of thanks, he turned and carried them into the inner dimness of the cave. We followed him.

Inside we found nine other men, women, and boys, lying on the rock floor in a dreadful state of thinness and exhaustion.

Some had their eyes closed, as if dead. Quickly the Doctor went round them all and listened to their hearts. They were all alive; but one woman was too weak even to stand upon her feet.

At a word from the Doctor, Chee-Chee and Polynesia sped off into the jungles after more fruit and water.

While Long Arrow was handing round what food we had to his starving friends, we suddenly heard a sound outside the cave. Turning about we saw, clustered at the entrance, the band of people who had met us so inhospitably at the beach.

They peered into the dark cave cautiously at first. But as soon as they saw Long Arrow and the others with us, they came rushing in, laughing, clapping their hands with joy and talking at a tremendous rate.

Long Arrow explained to the Doctor that the nine people we had found in the cave with him were two families who had accompanied him into the mountains to help him gather medicine plants. And while they had been searching for a kind of moss—good for indigestion—which grows only inside of damp caves, the great rock slab had slid down and shut them in. Then for two weeks they had lived on the medicine moss and such fresh water as could be found dripping from the damp walls of the cave. The natives on the island had given them up for lost and mourned them as dead; and they were now very surprised and happy to find their relatives alive.

When Long Arrow turned to the newcomers and told them in their own language that it was the Doctor who had found and freed their relatives, they gathered round John Dolittle, all talking at once.

Long Arrow said they were apologizing and trying to tell the

Doctor how sorry they were that they had seemed unfriendly to him at the beach.

Then they went outside and looked at the great stone we had thrown down, big as a meadow; and they walked round and round it, pointing to the break running through the middle and wondering how the trick of felling it was done.

Travelers who have since visited Spidermonkey Island tell me that that huge stone slab is now one of the regular sights of the island. And that the native guides, when showing it to visitors, always tell *their* story of how it came there. They say that when the Doctor found that the rocks had entrapped his friend, Long Arrow, he was so angry that he ripped the mountain in half with his bare hands and let him out.

THE SECOND CHAPTER

"The People of the Moving Land"

FROM THAT TIME ON, THE ISLANDERS' TREAT-
ment of us was very different. We were invited to their
village for a feast to celebrate the recovery of the lost
families. And after we had made a litter from saplings
to carry the sick woman in, we all started off down the mountain.

On the way, the natives told Long Arrow something that
appeared to be sad news, for on hearing it, his face grew very grave.
The Doctor asked him what was wrong. And Long Arrow said he
had just been informed that the chief of the tribe, an old man of
eighty, had died early that morning.

"That," Polynesia whispered in my ear, "must have been what
they went back to the village for, when the messenger fetched them
from the beach. Remember?"

"What did he die of?" asked the Doctor.

"He died of cold," said Long Arrow.

Indeed, now that the sun was setting, we were all shivering.

"This is a serious thing," said the Doctor to me. "The island is still in the grip of that wretched current flowing southward. We will have to look into this tomorrow. If nothing can be done about it, the natives had better take to canoes and leave the island. The chance of being wrecked will be better than getting frozen to death in the ice floes of the Antarctic."

Presently we came over a saddle in the hills, and looking downward on the far side of the island, we saw the village—a large cluster of grass huts and brightly colored totem poles close by the edge of the sea.

"How artistic!" said the Doctor. "Delightfully situated. What is the name of the village?"

"Popsipetel," said Long Arrow. "That is the name also of the tribe. The word signifies in their tongue, *The People of The Moving Land*. There are two tribes on the island: the Popsipetels at this end and the Bag-jagderags at the other."

"Which is the larger of the two peoples?"

"The Bag-jagderags, by far. Their city covers two square leagues. But," added Long Arrow, a slight frown darkening his handsome face, "for me, I would rather have one Popsipetel than a hundred Bag-jagderags."

The news of the rescue we had made had evidently gone ahead of us. For as we drew nearer to the village we saw crowds streaming out to greet the friends and relatives whom they had never thought to see again.

These good people, when they, too, were told how the rescue had been the work of the strange visitor to their shores, all gathered round the Doctor, shook him by the hands, patted him and hugged him. Then they lifted him up upon their strong shoulders and carried him down the hill into the village.

There the welcome we received was even more wonderful. In spite of the cold air of the coming night, the villagers, who had all been shivering within their houses, threw open their doors and came out in hundreds. I had no idea that the little village could hold so many. They thronged about us, smiling and nodding and waving their hands; and as the details of what we had done were recited by Long Arrow, they kept shouting strange singing noises, which we supposed were words of gratitude or praise.

We were next escorted to a brand-new grass house, clean and sweet-smelling within, and informed that it was ours. Six boys offered to assist us.

On our way through the village we noticed a house, larger than the rest, standing at the end of the main street. Long Arrow pointed to it and told us it was the chief's house, but that it was now empty—no new chief having yet been elected to take the place of the old one who had died.

THE THIRD CHAPTER

What Makes an Island Float

VERY EARLY IN OUR EXPERIENCE OF POPSIPETEL kindness we saw that if we were to get anything done at all, we would almost always have to do it secretly. The Doctor was so popular and loved by all that as soon as he showed his face at his door in the morning, crowds of admirers, waiting patiently outside, flocked about him and followed him wherever he went.

It was only with great difficulty that we escaped from the crowd the first morning and set out with Long Arrow to explore the island at our leisure.

In the interior we found that not only the plants and trees were suffering from the cold: the animal life was in even worse straits. Shivering birds were to be seen everywhere, their feathers all fluffed out, gathering together for flight to summer lands. And many lay dead upon the ground. Going down to the shore, we watched land crabs in large numbers taking to the sea to find some better home. While away to the southeast we could see many icebergs floating—a sign that we were now not far from the terrible region of the Antarctic.

As we were looking out to sea, we noticed our friends the porpoises jumping through the waves. The Doctor hailed them and they came ashore.

He asked them how far we were from the South Polar Continent.

About a hundred miles, they told him. And then they asked why he wanted to know.

"Because this floating island we are on," said he, "is drifting southward all the time in a current. It's an island that ordinarily belongs somewhere in the tropic zone—real sultry weather, sunstrokes and all that. If it doesn't stop going southward pretty soon, everything on it is going to perish."

"Well," said the porpoises, "then the thing to do is to get it back into a warmer climate, isn't it?"

"Yes, but how?" said the Doctor. "We can't *row* it back."

"No," said they, "but whales could push it—if you only got enough of them."

"What a splendid idea! Whales, the very thing!" said the Doctor. "Do you think you could get me some?"

"Why, certainly," said the porpoises, "we passed one herd of them out there, sporting about among the icebergs. We'll ask them to come over. And if they aren't enough, we'll try and hunt up some more. Better have plenty."

"Thank you," said the Doctor. "You are very kind. By the way, do you happen to know how this island came to be a floating island? At least half of it, I notice, is made of stone. It is very odd that it floats at all, isn't it?"

"It is unusual," they said. "But the explanation is quite simple. It used to be a mountainous part of South America—an overhanging part—sort of an awkward corner, you might say. Way back in the glacial days, thousands of years ago, it broke off from the mainland; and by some curious accident the inside of it, which is hollow, got filled with air as it fell into the ocean. You can only see less than half of the island: the bigger half is underwater. And in the middle of it, underneath, is a huge rock air chamber, running right up inside the mountains. And that's what keeps it floating."

"What a peculiar phenomenon!" said Bumpo.

"It is indeed," said the Doctor. "I must make a note of that." And out came the everlasting notebook.

The porpoises went bounding off toward the icebergs. And not long after, we saw the sea heaving and frothing as a big herd of whales came toward us at full speed.

They certainly were enormous creatures; and there must have been a good two hundred of them.

"Here they are," said the porpoises, poking their heads out of the water.

"Good!" said the Doctor. "Now just explain to them, will you please? that this is a very serious matter for all the living creatures in this land. And ask them if they will be so good as to go down to the far end of the island, put their noses against it, and push it back near the coast of Southern Brazil."

The porpoises evidently succeeded in persuading the whales to do as the Doctor asked; for presently we saw them thrashing through the seas, going off toward the south end of the island.

Then we lay down upon the beach and waited.

After about an hour the Doctor got up and threw a stick into the water. For a while this floated motionless. But soon we saw it begin to move gently down the coast.

"Ah!" said the Doctor. "See that? The island is going north at last. Thank goodness!"

Faster and faster we left the stick behind; and smaller and dimmer grew the icebergs on the skyline.

The Doctor took out his watch, threw more sticks into the water, and made a rapid calculation.

"Humph! Fourteen and a half knots an hour," he murmured. "A very nice speed. It should take us about five days to get back near Brazil. Well, that's that—Quite a load off my mind. I declare I feel warmer already. Let's go and get something to eat."

THE FOURTH CHAPTER

War!

O N OUR WAY BACK TO THE VILLAGE THE
Doctor began discussing natural history with Long
Arrow. But their most interesting talk, mainly about
plants, had hardly begun when a runner came dashing
up to us with a message.

Long Arrow listened gravely to the breathless, babbled words,
then turned to the Doctor and said in eagle tongue:

"Great Friend, an evil thing has befallen the Popsipetels. Our
neighbors to the south, the thievish Bag-jagderags, who for so long
have cast envious eyes on our stores of ripe corn, have gone upon
the warpath; and even now are advancing to attack us."

"Evil news indeed," said the Doctor. "Yet let us not judge
harshly. Perhaps it is that they are desperate for food, having their
own crops frost-killed before harvest. For are they not even nearer
the cold south than you?"

"Make no excuses for any man of the tribe of the
Bag-jagderags," said Long Arrow, shaking his head. "They are an

idle, shiftless race. They do but see a chance to get corn without the labor of husbandry. If it were not that they are a much bigger tribe and hope to defeat their neighbor by sheer force of numbers, they would not have dared to make open war upon the brave Popsipetels."

When we reached the village we found it in a great state of excitement. Everywhere men were seen putting their bows in order, sharpening spears, grinding battle-axes and making arrows by the hundred. Women were raising a high fence of bamboo poles all round the village. Scouts and messengers kept coming and going, bringing news of the movements of the enemy. While high up in the trees and hills about the village we could see lookouts watching the mountains to the south.

Long Arrow brought another man, short but enormously broad, and introduced him to the Doctor as Big Teeth, the chief warrior of the Popsipetels.

The Doctor volunteered to go and see the enemy and try to argue the matter out peacefully with them instead of fighting; for war, he said, was at best a stupid wasteful business. But the two shook their heads. Such a plan was hopeless, they said. The last time they had sent a messenger to do peaceful arguing, the enemy had merely hit him with an ax.

While the Doctor was asking Big Teeth how he meant to defend the village against attack, a cry of alarm was raised by the lookouts.

"They're coming! The Bag-jagderags—swarming down the mountains in thousands!"

"Well," said the Doctor, "it's all in the day's work, I suppose. I don't believe in war; but if the village is attacked, we must help defend it."

And he picked up a club from the ground and tried the heft of it against a stone.

"This," he said, "seems like a pretty good tool to me." And he walked to the bamboo fence and took his place among the other waiting fighters.

Then we all got hold of some kind of weapon with which to help our friends, the gallant Popsipetels: I borrowed a bow and a quiver full of arrows; Jip was content to rely upon his old, but still strong teeth; Chee-Chee took a bag of rocks and climbed a palm where he could throw them down upon the enemies' heads; and Bumpo marched after the Doctor to the fence, armed with a young tree in one hand and a doorpost in the other.

When the enemy drew near enough to be seen from where we stood, we all gasped with astonishment. The hillsides were actually covered with them—thousands upon thousands. They made our small army within the village look like a mere handful.

"Saints alive!" muttered Polynesia. "Our little lot will stand no chance against that swarm. This will never do. I'm going off to get some help."

Where she was going and what kind of help she meant to get, I had no idea. She just disappeared from my side. But Jip, who had heard her, poked his nose between the bamboo bars of the fence to get a better view of the enemy and said:

"Likely enough she's gone after the black parrots. Let's hope she finds them in time. Just look at those ugly ruffians climbing down the rocks—millions of 'em! This fight's going to keep us all hopping."

And Jip was right. Before a quarter of an hour had gone by,

our village was completely surrounded by one huge mob of yelling, raging Bag-jagderags.

I now come again to a part in the story of our voyages where things happened so quickly, one upon the other, that looking backward I see the picture only in a confused kind of way. I know that if it had not been for the Terrible Three—as they came afterward to be fondly called in Popsipetel history—Long Arrow, Bumpo, and the Doctor, the war would have been soon over and the whole island would have belonged to the worthless Bag-jagderags. But the Englishman, the African, and the South American were a regiment unto themselves; and between them they made that village a dangerous place for any man to try to enter.

The bamboo fencing that had been hastily set up around the town was not a very strong affair; and right from the start it gave way in one place after another as the enemy thronged and crowded against it. Then the Doctor, Long Arrow, and Bumpo would hurry to the weak spot, a terrific hand-to-hand fight would take place, and the enemy would be thrown out. But almost instantly a cry of alarm would come from some other part of the village wall; and the three would have to rush off and do the same thing all over again.

The Popsipetels were themselves no mean fighters; but the strength and weight of those three men of different lands, standing close together, swinging their enormous war clubs, was really a sight for the wonder and admiration of anyone.

Many weeks later when I was passing a campfire at night, I heard this song being sung. It has since become one of the traditional folksongs of the Popsipetels.

THE SONG OF THE TERRIBLE THREE

Oh hear ye the Song of the Terrible Three
And the fight that they fought by the edge of the sea.
Down from the mountains, the rocks and the crags,
Swarming like wasps, came the Bag-jagderags.
Surrounding our village, our walls they broke down.
Oh, sad was the plight of our men and our town!
But heaven determined our land to set free
And sent us the help of the Terrible Three.
Shoulder to shoulder, they hammered and hit.
Like demons of fury they kicked and they bit.
Like a wall of destruction they stood in a row,
Flattening enemies, six at a blow.
And long shall we sing of the Terrible Three
And the fight that they fought by the edge of the sea.

General Polynesia

BUT ALAS! EVEN THE THREE, MIGHTY THOUGH they were, could not last forever against an army that seemed to have no end. In one of the hottest scrimmages, when the enemy had broken a particularly wide hole through the fence, I saw Long Arrow's great figure topple and come down with a spear sticking in his broad chest.

For another half hour Bumpo and the Doctor fought on side by side. How their strength held out so long I cannot tell, for never a second were they given to get their breath or rest their arms.

The Doctor—the quiet, kindly, peaceable, little Doctor!— well, you wouldn't have known him if you had seen him that day, dealing out whacks you could hear a mile off, walloping and swatting in all directions.

As for Bumpo, with staring eyeballs and grim set teeth, he was a veritable demon. None dared come within yards of that wicked, wide-circling doorpost. But a stone, skilfully thrown, struck him at last in the center of the forehead. And down went the second of the Three. John Dolittle, the last of the Terribles, was left fighting alone.

Jip and I rushed to his side and tried to take the places of the fallen ones. But, far too light and too small, we made but a poor exchange. Another length of the fence crashed down, and through the widened gap the Bag-jagderags poured in on us like a flood.

"To the canoes! To the sea!" shouted the Popsipetels. "Fly for your lives! All is over! The war is lost!"

But the Doctor and I never got a chance to fly for our lives. We were swept off our feet and knocked down flat by the sheer weight of the mob. And once down, we were unable to get up again. I thought we would surely be trampled to death.

But at that moment, above the din and racket of the battle, we heard the most terrifying noise that ever assaulted human ears: the sound of millions and millions of parrots all screeching with fury together.

The army, which in the nick of time Polynesia had brought to our rescue, darkened the whole sky to the west. I asked her afterward, how many birds there were; she said she didn't know exactly, but that they certainly numbered somewhere between sixty and seventy millions. In that extraordinarily short space of time she had brought them from the mainland of South America.

If you have ever heard a parrot screech with anger you will know that it makes a truly frightful sound; and if you have ever been bitten by one, you will know that its bite can be a nasty and a painful thing.

The black parrots (coal black all over, they were—except for a scarlet beak and a streak of red in wing and tail) on the word of

command from Polynesia set to work upon the Bag-jagderags who
were now pouring through the village looking for plunder.

And the black parrots' method of fighting was peculiar. This
is what they did: on the head of each Bag-jagderag, three or four
parrots settled and took a good foothold in his hair with their claws;
then they leaned down over the sides of his head and began clipping
snips out of his ears, for all the world as though they were punching tickets. That is all they did. They never bit them anywhere else
except the ears. But it won the war for us.

With howls pitiful to hear, the Bag-jagderags fell over one
another in their haste to get out of that accursed village. It was no
use their trying to pull the parrots off their heads; because for each
head there were always four more parrots waiting impatiently to
get on.

Some of the enemy were lucky; with only a snip or two they
managed to get outside the fence—where the parrots immediately
left them alone. But with most, before the black birds had done with
them, the ears presented a very singular appearance—like the edge
of a postage-stamp. This treatment, very painful at the time, did
not, however, do them any permanent harm beyond the change in
looks. And it later got to be the tribal mark of the Bag-jagderags.
No really smart young lady of this tribe would be seen walking with
a man who did not have scalloped ears—for such was a proof that
he had been in the Great War. And that (though it is not generally
known to scientists) is how this people came to be called by the
other nations, the *Ragged-Eared Bag-jagderags* .

As soon as the village was cleared of the enemy, the Doctor
turned his attention to the wounded.

In spite of the length and fierceness of the struggle, there were surprisingly few serious injuries. Poor Long Arrow was the worst off. However, after the Doctor had washed his wound and got him to bed, he opened his eyes and said he already felt better. Bumpo was only badly stunned.

With this part of the business over, the Doctor called to Polynesia to have the black parrots drive the enemy right back into their own country and to wait there, guarding them all night.

Polynesia gave the short word of command; and like one bird, those millions of parrots opened their red beaks and let out once more their terrifying battle scream.

The Bag-jagderags didn't wait to be bitten a second time, but fled helter-skelter over the mountains from which they had come; while Polynesia and her victorious army followed watchfully behind like a great, threatening, black cloud.

The Doctor picked up his high hat, which had been knocked off in the fight, dusted it carefully, and put it on.

"Tomorrow," he said, shaking his fist toward the hills, "we will arrange the terms of peace—and we will arrange them—in the City of Bag-jagderag!"

His words were greeted with cheers of triumph from the admiring Popsipetels. The war was over.

The Peace of
the Parrots

HE NEXT DAY WE SET OUT FOR THE FAR END of the island, and reaching it in canoes (for we went by sea) after a journey of twenty-five hours, we remained no longer than was necessary in the city of Bag-jagderag.

When he threw himself into that fight at Popsipetel, I saw the Doctor really angry for the first time in my life. But his anger, once aroused, was slow to die. All the way down the coast of the island he never ceased to rail against this cowardly people who had attacked his friends, the Popsipetels, for no other reason but to rob them of their corn, because they were too idle to till the land themselves. And he was still angry when he reached the city of Bag-jagderag.

Long Arrow had not come with us, for he was as yet too weak from his wound. But the Doctor—always clever at languages—was already getting familiar with the native tongue. Besides, among the half-dozen Popsipetels who accompanied us to paddle the canoes, was one boy to whom we had taught a little English. He and the Doctor between them managed to make themselves understood to the Bag-jagderags. This people, with the terrible parrots still blackening the hills about their stone town, waiting for the word to descend and attack, were, we found, in a very humble mood.

Leaving our canoes we passed up the main street to the palace of the chief. Bumpo and I couldn't help smiling with satisfaction as we saw how the waiting crowds that lined the roadway bowed their heads to the ground, as the little, round, angry figure of the Doctor strutted ahead of us with his chin in the air.

At the foot of the palace steps the chief and all the more important personages of the tribe were waiting to meet him, smiling humbly and holding out their hands in friendliness. The Doctor took not the slightest notice. He marched right by them, up the steps to the door of the palace. There he turned around and at once began to address the people in a firm voice.

I never heard such a speech in my life—and I am quite sure that they never did either. First he called them a long string of names: cowards, loafers, thieves, vagabonds, good-for-nothings, bullies, and whatnot. Then he said he was still seriously thinking of allowing the parrots to drive them on into the sea, in order that this pleasant land might be rid, once for all, of their worthless carcases.

At this a great cry for mercy went up, and the chief and all of them fell on their knees, calling out that they would submit to any conditions of peace he wished.

Then the Doctor called for one of their scribes—that is, a man who did picture writing. And on the stone walls of the palace of Bag-jagderag he bade him write down the terms of the peace as he dictated it. This peace is known as *The Peace of the Parrots*, and—unlike most peaces—was, and is, strictly kept—even to this day.

It was quite long in words. The half of the palace front was covered with picture writing, and fifty pots of paint were used, before the weary scribe had done. But the main part of it all was that there should be no more fighting; and that the two tribes should give solemn promise to help one another whenever there was corn famine or other distress in the lands belonging to either.

This greatly surprised the Bag-jagderags. They had expected from the Doctor's angry face that he would at least chop a couple of hundred heads off—and probably make the rest of them slaves for life.

But when they saw that he only meant kindly by them, their great fear of him changed to a tremendous admiration. And as he ended his long speech and walked briskly down the steps again on his way back to the canoes, the group of chieftains threw themselves at his feet and cried:

"Do but stay with us, Great Lord, and all the riches of Bag-jagderag shall be poured into your lap. Gold mines we know of in the mountains and pearl beds beneath the sea. Only stay with us, that your all-powerful wisdom may lead our council and our people in prosperity and peace."

The Doctor held up his hand for silence.

"No man," said he, "would wish to be the guest of the Bag-jagderags till they had proved by their deeds that they are an honest people. Be true to the terms of the peace and from yourselves shall come good government and prosperity—Farewell!"

Then he turned and, followed by Bumpo, the Popsipetels and myself, walked rapidly down to the canoes.

The Hanging Stone

BUT THE CHANGE OF HEART IN THE BAG-jagderags was really sincere. The Doctor had made a great impression on them—a deeper one than even he himself realized at the time. In fact, I sometimes think that that speech of his from the palace steps had more effect upon the peoples of Spidermonkey Island than had any of his great deeds which, great though they were, were always magnified and exaggerated when the news of them was passed from mouth to mouth.

A sick girl was brought to him as he reached the place where the boats lay. She turned out to have some quite simple ailment which he quickly gave the remedy for. But this increased his popularity still more. And when he stepped into his canoe, the people all around us actually burst into tears. It seems (I learned this afterward) that they thought he was going away across the sea, for good, to the mysterious foreign lands from which he had come.

Some of the chieftains spoke to the Popsipetels as we pushed off. What they said I did not understand; but we noticed that several canoes filled with Bag-jagderags followed us at a respectful distance all the way back to Popsipetel.

The Doctor had determined to return by the other shore, so that we should be thus able to make a complete trip round the island's shores.

Shortly after we started, while still off the lower end of the island, we sighted a steep point on the coast where the sea was in a great state of turmoil, white with soapy froth. On going nearer, we found

"Working away with their noses against the end of the island"

that this was caused by our friendly whales who were still faithfully working away with their noses against the end of the island, driving us northward. We had been kept so busy with the war that we had forgotten all about them. But as we paused and watched their mighty tails lashing and churning the sea, we suddenly realized that we had not felt cold in quite a long while. Speeding up our boat lest the island be carried away from us altogether, we passed on up the coast; and here and there we noticed that the trees on the shore already looked greener and more healthy. Spidermonkey Island was getting back into her home climates.

About halfway to Popsipetel we went ashore and spent two or three days exploring the central part of the island. Our paddlers took us up into the mountains, very steep and high in this region, overhanging the sea. And they showed us what they called the Whispering Rocks.

This was a very peculiar and striking piece of scenery. It was like a great vast basin, or circus, in the mountains, and out of the center of it there rose a table of rock with an ivory chair upon it. All around this the mountains went up like stairs, or theater seats, to a great height—except at one narrow end that was open to a view of the sea. You could imagine it a council meeting place or concert hall for giants, and the rock table in the center the stage for performers or the stand for the speaker.

We asked our guides why it was called the Whispering Rocks, and they said, "Go down into it and we will show you."

The great bowl was miles deep and miles wide. We scrambled down the rocks and they showed us how, even when you stood far, far apart from one another, you merely had to whisper in that great place and everyone in the theater could hear you. This was, the

"The Whispering Rocks"

Doctor said, on account of the echoes that played backward and forward between the high walls of rock.

Our guides told us that it was here, in days long gone by, when the Popsipetels owned the whole of Spidermonkey Island, that the kings were crowned. The ivory chair upon the table was the throne in which they sat. And so great was the big theater that all the people in the island were able to get seats in it to see the ceremony.

They showed us also an enormous hanging stone perched on the edge of a volcano's crater—the highest summit in the whole island.

Although it was very far below us, we could see it quite plainly; and it looked wobbly enough to be pushed off its perch with the hand. There was a legend among the people, they said, that when the greatest of all Popsipetel kings should be crowned in the ivory chair, this hanging stone would tumble into the volcano's mouth and go straight down to the center of the earth.

The Doctor said he would like to go and examine it closer.

And when we were standing at the lip of the volcano (it took us half a day to get up to it), we found the stone was unbelievably large—big as a cathedral. Underneath it we could look right down into a black hole that seemed to have no bottom. The Doctor explained to us that volcanoes sometimes spurted up fire from these holes in their tops; but that those on floating islands were always cold and dead.

"Stubbins," he said, looking up at the great stone towering above us, "do you know what would most likely happen if that boulder should fall in?"

"No," said I, "what?"

"You remember the air chamber that the porpoises told us lies under the center of the island?"

"Yes."

"Well, this stone is heavy enough, if it fell into the volcano, to break through into that air chamber from above. And once it did, the air would escape and the floating island would float no more. It would sink."

"But then everybody on it would be drowned, wouldn't they?" said Bumpo.

"Oh no, not necessarily. That would depend on the depth of the sea where the sinking took place. The island might touch bottom when it had only gone down, say, a hundred feet. But there would be lots of it still sticking up above the water then, wouldn't there?"

"Yes," said Bumpo, "I suppose there would. Well, let us hope that the ponderous fragment does *not* lose its equilibrium, for I don't believe it would stop at the center of the earth—more likely it would fall right through the world and come out the other side."

Many other wonders there were which these men showed us in the central regions of their island. But I have not time or space to tell you of them now.

Descending toward the shore again, we noticed that we were still being watched, even here among the highlands, by the Bagjagderags who had followed us. And when we put to sea once more, a boatload of them proceeded to go ahead of us in the direction of Popsipetel. Having lighter canoes, they traveled faster than our party; and we judged that they should reach the village—if that was where they were going—many hours before we could.

The Doctor was now becoming anxious to see how Long Arrow was getting on, so we all took turns at the paddles and went on traveling by moonlight through the whole night.

We reached Popsipetel just as the dawn was breaking.

To our great surprise we found that not only we, but the whole village also, had been up all night. A great crowd was gathered about the dead chief's house. And as we landed our canoes upon the beach we saw a large number of old men, the seniors of the tribe, coming out at the main door.

We inquired what was the meaning of all this; and were told that the election of a new chief had been going on all through the whole night. Bumpo asked the name of the new chief; but this, it seemed, had not yet been given out. It would be announced at midday.

As soon as the Doctor had paid a visit to Long Arrow and seen that he was doing nicely, we proceeded to our own house at the far end of the village. Here we ate some breakfast and then lay down to take a good rest.

Rest, indeed, we needed; for life had been strenuous and busy for us ever since we had landed on the island. And it wasn't many minutes after our weary heads struck the pillows that the whole crew of us were sound asleep.

The Election

W E WERE AWAKENED BY MUSIC. THE glaring noonday sunlight was streaming in at our door, outside of which some kind of a band appeared to be playing. We got up and looked out. Our house was surrounded by the whole population of Popsipetel. We were used to having quite a number of curious and admiring locals waiting at our door at all hours, but this was quite different. The vast crowd was dressed in its best clothes. Bright beads, gawdy feathers, and festive blankets gave cheerful color to the scene. Everyone seemed in very good humor, singing or playing on musical instruments—mostly painted wooden whistles or drums made from skins.

We found Polynesia—who had arrived back from Bag-jagderag while we slept—sitting on our doorpost watching the show. We asked her what all the holiday-making was about.

"The result of the election has just been announced," said she. "The name of the new chief was given out at noon."

"And who is the new chief?" asked the Doctor.

"You are," said Polynesia quietly.

"*I!*" gasped the Doctor. "Well, of all things!"

"Yes," said she. "You're the one. And what's more, they've changed your surname for you. They didn't think that Dolittle was a proper or respectful name for a man who had done so much. So you are now to be known as Jong Thinkalot. How do you like it?"

"But I don't *want* to be a chief," said the Doctor in an irritable voice.

"I'm afraid you'll have hard work to get out of it now," said she, "unless you're willing to put to sea again in one of their rickety canoes. You see, you've been elected not merely the chief of the Popsipetels; you're to be a king—the king of the whole of Spidermonkey Island. The Bag-jagderags, who were so anxious to have you govern them, sent spies and messengers ahead of you; and when they found that you had been elected chief of the Popsipetels overnight, they were bitterly disappointed. However, rather than lose you altogether, the Bag-jagderags were willing to give up their independence, and insisted that they and their lands be united to the Popsipetels in order that you could be made king of both. So now you're in for it."

"Oh, Lord!" groaned the Doctor, "I do wish they wouldn't be so enthusiastic! Bother it, I don't *want* to be a king!"

"I should think, Doctor," said I, "you'd feel rather proud and glad. I wish *I* had a chance to be a king."

"Oh I know it sounds grand," said he, pulling on his boots miserably. "But the trouble is, you can't take up responsibilities and then just drop them again when you feel like it. I have my own work to do. Scarcely one moment have I had to give to natural history since I landed on this island. I've been doing someone else's business all the time. And now they want me to go on doing it! Why, once I'm made king of the Popsipetels, that's the end of me as a useful naturalist. I'd be too busy for anything. All I'd be then is just a er—er—just a king."

"Well, that's something!" said Bumpo. "My father is a king and has a hundred and twenty wives."

"That would make it worse," said the Doctor—"a hundred and twenty times worse. I have my work to do. I don't want to be a king."

"Look," said Polynesia, "here come the head men to announce your election. Hurry up and get your boots laced."

The throng before our door had suddenly parted asunder, making a long lane; and down this we now saw a group of personages coming toward us. The man in front, a handsome old fellow with a wrinkled face, carried in his hands a wooden crown—a truly beautiful and gorgeous crown, even though of wood. Wonderfully carved and painted, it had two lovely blue feathers springing from the front of it. Behind the old man came eight strong men bearing a litter, a sort of chair with long handles underneath to carry it by.

Kneeling down on one knee, bending his head almost to the ground, the old man addressed the Doctor, who now stood in the doorway putting on his collar and tie.

"Oh, Mighty One," said he, "we bring you word from the Popsipetel people. Great are your deeds beyond belief, kind is your heart and your wisdom, deeper than the sea. Our chief is dead. The people clamor for a worthy leader. Our old enemies, the Bagjagderags are become, through you, our brothers and good friends. They too desire to bask beneath the sunshine of your smile. Behold then, I bring to you the Sacred Crown of Popsipetel which, since ancient days when this island and its peoples were one, beneath one monarch, has rested on no kingly brow. Oh Kindly One, we are bidden by the united voices of the peoples of this land to carry you to the Whispering Rocks, that there, with all respect and majesty, you may be crowned our king—King of all the Moving Land."

The good people did not seem to have even considered the possibility of John Dolittle's refusing. As for the poor Doctor, I never saw him so upset by anything. It was, in fact, the only time I have known him to get thoroughly fussed.

"Oh dear!" I heard him murmur, looking around wildly for some escape. "What *shall* I do?—Did any of you see where I laid that stud of mine?—How on earth can I get this collar on without a stud? What a day this is, to be sure!—Maybe it rolled under the bed, Bumpo—I do think they might have given me a day or so to think it over in. Whoever heard of waking a man right out of his sleep and telling him he's got to be a king, before he has even washed his face? Can't any of you find it? Maybe you're standing on it, Bumpo. Move your feet."

"Oh don't bother about your stud," said Polynesia. "You will have to be crowned without a collar. They won't know the difference."

"I tell you I'm not going to be crowned," cried the Doctor, "not if I can help it. I'll make them a speech. Perhaps that will satisfy them."

He turned back to the men at the door.

"My friends," he said, "I am not worthy of this great honor you would do me. Little or no skill have I in the arts of kingcraft. Assuredly among your own brave men you will find many better fitted to lead you. For this compliment, this confidence and trust, I thank you. But, I pray you, do not think of me for such high duties which I could not possibly fulfill."

The old man repeated his words to the people behind him in a louder voice. Stolidly they shook their heads, moving not an inch. The old man turned back to the Doctor.

"You are the chosen one," said he. "They will have none but you."

Into the Doctor's perplexed face suddenly there came a flash of hope.

"I'll go and see Long Arrow," he whispered to me. "Perhaps he will know of some way to get me out of this."

And asking the personages to excuse him a moment, he left them there, standing at his door, and hurried off in the direction of Long Arrow's house. I followed him.

We found our big friend lying on a grass bed outside his home, where he had been moved so he might witness the holiday-making.

"Long Arrow," said the Doctor speaking, quickly in eagle tongue so that the bystanders should not overhear, "in dire peril I come to you for help. These men would make me their king. If such a thing befalls me, all the great work I hoped to do must go undone, for who is there unfreer than a king? I pray you speak with them and persuade their kind, well-meaning hearts that what they plan to do would be unwise."

Long Arrow raised himself upon his elbow.

"Oh Kindly One," said he (this seemed now to have become the usual manner of address when speaking to the Doctor), "sorely it grieves me that the first wish you ask of me I should be unable to grant. Alas! I can do nothing. These people have so set their hearts on keeping you for king that if I tried to interfere they would drive me from their land and likely crown you in the end in any case. A king you must be, if only for a while. We must so arrange the business of governing that you may have time to give to nature's secrets. Later we may be able to hit upon some plan to relieve you of the burden of the crown. But for now you must be king. These people are a headstrong tribe and they will have their way. There is no other course."

Sadly the Doctor turned away from the bed and faced about. And there behind him stood the old man again, the crown still held in his wrinkled hands and the royal litter waiting at his elbow. With a deep reverence the bearers motioned toward the seat of the chair, inviting him to get in.

Once more the poor Doctor looked wildly, hopelessly about him for some means of escape. For a moment I thought he was going to take to his heels and run for it. But the crowd around us was far too thick and densely packed for anyone to break through it. A band of whistles and drums nearby suddenly started the music of a solemn processional march. He turned back pleadingly again to Long Arrow in a last appeal for help. But the big man merely shook his head and pointed, like the bearers, to the waiting chair.

At last, almost in tears, John Dolittle stepped slowly into the litter and sat down. As he was hoisted onto the broad shoulders of the bearers, I heard him still feebly muttering beneath his breath:

"Botheration take it! I don't *want* to be a king!"

"Farewell!" called Long Arrow from his bed. "And may good fortune ever stand within the shadow of your throne!"

"He comes!—He comes!" murmured the crowd. "Away! Away!—To the Whispering Rocks!"

And as the procession formed up to leave the village, the crowd about us began hurrying off in the direction of the mountains to make sure of good seats in the giant theater where the crowning ceremony would take place.

THE NINTH CHAPTER

The Coronation of King Jong

I N MY LONG LIFETIME I HAVE SEEN MANY GRAND and inspiring things, but never anything that impressed me half as much as the sight of the Whispering Rocks as they looked on the day King Jong was crowned. As Bumpo, Chee-Chee, Polynesia, Jip, and I finally reached the dizzying edge of the great bowl and looked down inside it, it was like gazing over a never-ending ocean of copper-colored faces; for every seat in the theater was filled, every man, woman, and child in the island—including Long Arrow, who had been carried up on his sick bed—was there to see the show.

Yet not a sound, not a pin drop, disturbed the solemn silence of the Whispering Rocks. It was quite creepy and sent chills running up and down your spine. Bumpo told me afterward that it took his breath away too much for him to speak, but that he hadn't known before that there were that many people in the world.

Away down by the Table of the Throne stood a brand-new, brightly colored totem pole. All the families had totem poles and kept them set up before the doors of their houses. The idea of a totem pole is something like a doorplate or a visiting card. It represents in its carvings the deeds and qualities of the family to which it belongs. This one, beautifully decorated and much higher than any other, was the Dolittle or, as it was to be henceforth called, the Royal Thinkalot totem. It had nothing but animals on it, to signify the Doctor's great knowledge of creatures. And the animals chosen to be shown were those which to the Islanders were supposed to represent good qualities of character, such as, the deer for speed; the ox for perseverance; the fish for discretion, and so on. But at the top of the totem is always placed the sign or animal by which the family is most proud to be known. This, on the Thinkalot pole, was an enormous parrot, in memory of the famous Peace of the Parrots.

The ivory throne had been all polished with scented oil and it glistened white in the strong sunlight. At the foot of it there had been strewn great quantities of branches of flowering trees, which with the new warmth of milder climates were now blossoming in the valleys of the island.

Soon we saw the royal litter, with the Doctor seated in it, slowly ascending the winding steps to the table. Reaching the flat top at last, it halted and the Doctor stepped out upon the flowery carpet. So still and perfect was the silence that even at that distance above I distinctly heard a twig snap beneath his tread.

Walking to the throne accompanied by the old man, the Doctor got up upon the stand and sat down. How tiny his little round figure looked when seen from that tremendous height! The throne had been made for longer-legged kings; and when he was seated, his feet did not reach the ground, but dangled six inches from the top step.

Then the old man turned round and, looking up at the people, began to speak in a quiet even voice; but every word he said was easily heard in the farthest corner of the Whispering Rocks.

First he recited the names of all the great Popsipetel kings who in days long ago had been crowned in this ivory chair. He spoke of the greatness of the Popsipetel people, of their triumphs, of their hardships. Then waving his hand toward the Doctor he began recounting the things that this king-to-be had done. And I am bound to say that they easily outmatched the deeds of those who had gone before him.

As soon as he started to speak of what the Doctor had achieved for the tribe, the people, still strictly silent, all began waving their right hands toward the throne. This gave to the vast theater a very singular appearance: acres and acres of something moving—with never a sound.

At last the old man finished his speech and, stepping up to the chair, very respectfully removed the Doctor's battered high hat. He was about to put it upon the ground, but the Doctor took it from him hastily and kept it on his lap. Then taking up the Sacred Crown he placed it upon John Dolittle's head. It did not fit very well (for it had been made for smaller-headed kings), and when the wind blew in freshly from the sunlit sea the Doctor had some difficulty in keeping it on. But it looked very splendid.

Turning once more to the people, the old man said:

"People of Popsipetel, behold your elected king!—Are you content?"

And then at last the voice of the people broke loose.

"JONG! JONG!" they shouted. "LONG LIVE KING JONG!"

The sound burst upon the solemn silence with the crash of a hundred cannon. There, where even a whisper carried miles, the shock of it was like a blow in the face. Back and forth the mountains threw it to one another. I thought the echoes of it would never die away as it passed rumbling through the whole island, jangling among the lower valleys, booming in the distant sea caves.

Suddenly I saw the old man point upward, to the highest mountain in the island; and looking over my shoulder, I was just in time to see the Hanging Stone topple slowly out of sight—down into the heart of the volcano.

"See ye, Men of the Moving Land!" the old man cried. "The stone has fallen and our legend has come true: the King of Kings is crowned this day!"

The Doctor, too, had seen the stone fall and he was now standing up looking at the sea expectantly.

"He's thinking of the air chamber," said Bumpo in my ear. "Let us hope that the sea isn't very deep in these parts."

After a full minute (so long did it take the stone to fall that depth) we heard a muffled, distant, crunching thud—and then immediately after, a great hissing of escaping air. The Doctor, his face tense with anxiety, sat down in the throne again, still watching the blue water of the ocean with staring eyes.

Soon we felt the island slowly sinking beneath us. We saw the sea creep inland over the beaches as the shores went down— one foot, three feet, ten feet, twenty, fifty, a hundred. And then, thank goodness, gently as a butterfly alighting on a rose, it stopped! Spidermonkey Island had come to rest on the sandy bottom of the Atlantic, and earth was joined to earth once more.

Of course, many of the houses near the shores were now

underwater. Popsipetel Village itself had entirely disappeared. But it didn't matter. No one was drowned; for every soul in the island was high up in the hills, watching the coronation of King Jong.

The natives themselves did not realize at the time what was taking place, though of course they had felt the land sinking beneath them. The Doctor told us afterward that it must have been the shock of that tremendous shout, coming from a million throats at once, which had toppled the Hanging Stone off its perch. But in Popsipetel history the story was handed down (and it is firmly believed to this day) that when King Jong sat upon the throne, so great was his mighty weight, that the very island itself sank down to do him honor and never moved again.

PART SIX

New Popsipetel

JONG THINKALOT HAD NOT BEEN IN HIS NEW position for more than a couple of days before my notions about kings and the kind of lives they led changed very considerably. I had thought that all that kings had to do was to sit on a throne and have people bow down before them several times a day. I now saw that a king can be the hardest-working man in the world—if he attends properly to his business.

From the moment that he got up, early in the morning, till the time he went to bed, late at night—seven days in the week—John Dolittle was busy, busy, busy. First of all there was the new town to be built. The village of Popsipetel had disappeared: the city of New Popsipetel must be made. With great care a place was chosen for it—and a very beautiful position it was, at the mouth of a large river. The shores of the island at this point formed a lovely wide bay where canoes—and ships, too, if they should ever come—could lie peacefully at anchor without danger from storms.

The Doctor tried his hardest to do away with most of the

old-fashioned pomp and grandeur of a royal court. As he said to Bumpo and me, if he must be a king, he meant to be a thoroughly democratic one, that is a king who is chummy and friendly with his subjects and doesn't put on airs. And when he drew up the plans for the city of New Popsipetel he had no palace shown of any kind. A little cottage in a back street was all that he had provided for himself.

But this the natives would not permit on any account. They had been used to having their kings rule in a truly grand and kingly manner; and they insisted that he have built for himself the most magnificent palace ever seen. In all else they let him have his own way absolutely; but they wouldn't allow him to wriggle out of any of the ceremony or show that goes with being a king. A thousand servants he had to keep in his palace, night and day, to wait on him. The Royal Canoe had to be kept up—a gorgeous, polished mahogany boat, seventy feet long, inlaid with mother-of-pearl and paddled by the hundred strongest men in the island. The palace gardens covered a square mile and employed a hundred and sixty gardeners.

Even in his dress the poor man was compelled always to be grand and elegant and uncomfortable. The beloved and battered high hat was put away in a closet and only looked at secretly. State robes had to be worn on all occasions. And when the Doctor did once in a while manage to sneak off for a short, natural-history expedition he never dared to wear his old clothes, but had to chase his butterflies with a crown upon his head and a scarlet cloak flying behind him in the wind.

There was no end to the kinds of duties the Doctor had to perform and the questions he had to decide upon—everything, from settling disputes about lands and boundaries, to making peace

"Had to chase his butterflies with a crown upon his head"

between a husband and wife who had been throwing shoes at one another. In the east wing of the royal palace was the Hall of Justice. And here King Jong sat every morning from nine to eleven passing judgment on all cases that were brought before him.

Then in the afternoon he taught school. The sort of things he taught were not always those you find in ordinary schools.

Bumpo and I helped with the teaching as far as we could— simple arithmetic, and easy things like that. But the classes in astronomy, farming science, and a host of other subjects, the Doctor had to teach himself. The people were tremendously keen about the schooling and they came in droves and crowds; so that even with the open-air classes (a schoolhouse was impossible of course), the Doctor had to take them in relays and batches of five or six thousand at a time and used a big megaphone or trumpet to make himself heard.

The rest of his day was more than filled with road-making, building watermills, attending the sick, and a million other things.

In spite of his being so unwilling to become a king, John Dolittle made a very good one—once he got started. He may not have been as dignified as many kings in history who were always running off to war and getting themselves into romantic situations; but since I have grown up and seen something of foreign lands and governments, I have often thought that Popsipetel under the reign of Jong Thinkalot was perhaps the best ruled state in the history of the world.

The Doctor's birthday came round after we had been on the island six months and a half. The people made a great public holiday of it and there was much feasting, dancing, fireworks, speech-making, and jollification.

Toward the close of the day the chief men of the two tribes formed a procession and passed through the streets of the town, carrying a very gorgeously painted tablet of ebony wood, ten feet high. This was a picture history, such as they preserved for each of the ancient kings of Popsipetel to record their deeds.

With great and solemn ceremony it was set up over the door of the new palace: and everybody then clustered round to look at it. It had six pictures on it commemorating the six great events in the life of King Jong, and beneath were written the verses that explained them. They were composed by the court poet; and this is a translation:

I

(His Landing on the Island)

Heaven-sent,
In his dolphin-drawn canoe
From worlds unknown
He landed on our shores.
The very palms
Bowed down their heads
In welcome to the coming King.

II

(His Meeting with the Beetle)

By moonlight in the mountains
He communed with beasts.
The shy Jabizri brings him picture words
Of great distress.

III

(He Liberates the Lost Families)

Big was his heart with pity;
Big were his hands with strength.
See how he tears the mountain like a yam!

See how the lost ones
Dance forth to greet the day!

IV
(He Brings Warmth)
Our land was cold and dying.
He waved his hand and lo!
The sun leaned down;
Then while we crowded round
The grateful glow, pushed he
Our wayward, floating land
Back to peaceful anchorage
In sunny seas.

V

(He Leads the People to Victory in War)
Once only
Was his kindly countenance
Darkened by a deadly frown.
Woe to the wicked enemy
That dares attack
The tribe with Thinkalot for Chief!

VI
(He Is Crowned King)
The birds of the air rejoiced;
The sea laughed and gamboled with her shores;
All people wept for joy
The day we crowned him King.

He is the Builder, the Healer, the Teacher and the Prince;
He is the greatest of them all.
May he live a thousand thousand years,
Happy in his heart,
To bless our land with Peace.

The Second Chapter

Thoughts of Home

IN THE ROYAL PALACE BUMPO AND I HAD A BEAU-tiful suite of rooms of our very own—which Polynesia, Jip, and Chee-Chee shared with us. Officially Bumpo was minister of the interior; while I was First Lord of the Treasury. Long Arrow also had quarters there; but at present he was absent, traveling abroad.

One night after supper, when the Doctor was away in the town somewhere visiting a newborn baby, we were all sitting round the big table in Bumpo's reception room. This we did every evening, to talk over the plans for the following day and various affairs of state. It was a kind of cabinet meeting.

Tonight, however, we were talking about England—and also about things to eat. We had gotten a little tired of the local food. Often we got so hungry for something different that the Doctor would sneak downstairs with us into the palace basement, after all the cooks were safe in bed, and fry pancakes secretly over the dying embers of the fire. The Doctor himself was the finest cook that ever lived. But he used to make a terrible mess of the kitchen; and of course we had to be awfully careful that we didn't get caught.

Well, as I was saying, tonight food was the subject of discussion at the cabinet meeting; and I had just been reminding Bumpo of the nice dishes we had had at the bed-maker's house in Monteverde.

"I tell you what I would like now," said Bumpo. "A large cup of cocoa with whipped cream on the top of it. In Oxford we used to be able to get the most wonderful cocoa. It is really too bad they haven't any cocoa trees in this island, or cows to give cream."

"When do you suppose," asked Jip, "the Doctor intends to move on from here?"

"I was talking to him about that only yesterday," said Polynesia. "But I couldn't get any satisfactory answer out of him. He didn't seem to want to speak about it."

There was a pause in the conversation.

"Do you know what I believe?" she added presently. "I believe the Doctor has given up even thinking of going home."

"Good Lord!" cried Bumpo. "You don't say!"

"Sh!" said Polynesia. "What's that noise?"

We listened; and away off in the distant corridors of the palace we heard the sentries crying,

"The King! Make way! The King!"

"It's he—at last," whispered Polynesia, "late, as usual. Poor man, how he does work! Chee-Chee, get the pipe and tobacco out of the cupboard and lay the dressing gown ready on his chair."

When the Doctor came into the room he looked serious and thoughtful. Wearily he took off his crown and hung it on a peg behind the door. Then he exchanged the royal cloak for the dressing gown, and dropped into his chair at the head of the table with a deep sigh and started to fill his pipe.

"Well," asked Polynesia quietly, "how did you find the baby?"

"The baby?" he murmured—his thoughts still seemed to be very far away. "Ah yes. The baby was much better, thank you. It has cut its second tooth."

Then he was silent again, staring dreamily at the ceiling through a cloud of tobacco smoke, while we all sat round quite still, waiting.

"We were wondering, Doctor," said I at last, "just before you came in—when you would be returning home again. We will have been on this island seven months tomorrow."

The Doctor sat forward in his chair looking rather uncomfortable.

"Well, as a matter of fact," said he after a moment, "I meant to speak to you myself this evening on that very subject. But it's—er—a little hard to make anyone exactly understand the situation. I am afraid that it would be impossible for me to leave the work I am now engaged on. . . . You remember, when they first insisted on making me king, I told you it was not easy to shake off responsibilities, once you had taken them up.

"I would like to continue my voyages and my natural history work; and I would like to go back to Puddleby—as much as any of you. This is March, and the crocuses will be showing in the lawn. . . . But that which I feared has come true: I cannot close my eyes to what might happen if I should leave these people and run away. They like me; they trust me. And no man wants to be unfair to those who trust him. . . . And then again, I like *them*. Don't you see what I mean? How can I possibly run away and leave them in the lurch? . . . No. I have thought it over a good deal and tried to decide what was best. And I am afraid that the work I took up when I assumed the crown I must stick to. I'm afraid—I've got to stay."

"For good—for your whole life?" asked Bumpo in a low voice.

For some moments the Doctor, frowning, made no answer.

"I don't know," he said at last. "Anyhow, for the present there is certainly no hope of my leaving. It wouldn't be right."

The sad silence that followed was broken finally by a knock upon the door.

With a patient sigh the Doctor got up and put on his crown and cloak again.

"Come in," he called, sitting down in his chair once more.

The door opened and a footman—one of the hundred and forty-three who were always on night duty—stood bowing in the entrance.

"Oh, Kindly One," said he, "there is a traveler at the palace gate who would have speech with Your Majesty."

"Another baby's been born, I'll bet a shilling," muttered Polynesia.

"Did you ask the traveler's name?" inquired the Doctor.

"Yes, Your Majesty," said the footman. "It is Long Arrow, the son of Golden Arrow."

Long Arrow's Science

L ONG ARROW!" CRIED THE DOCTOR. "HOW splendid! Show him in—show him in at once."

"I'm so glad," he continued, turning to us as soon as the footman had gone. "I've missed Long Arrow terribly. He's an awfully good man to have around—even if he doesn't talk much. Let me see: it's five months now since he went off to Brazil. I'm so glad he's back safe. He does take such tremendous chances with that canoe of his—clever as he is. It's no joke, crossing a hundred miles of open sea in a twelve-foot canoe. I wouldn't care to try it."

Another knock; and when the door swung open in answer to the Doctor's call, there stood our big friend on the threshold, a smile upon his strong, bronzed face. Behind him appeared two porters carrying loads done up in palm matting. These, when the first salutations were over, Long Arrow ordered to lay their burdens down.

"Behold, oh Kindly One," said he, "I bring you, as I promised, my collection of plants that I had hidden in a cave in the Andes. These treasures represent the labors of my life."

The packages were opened; and inside were many smaller packages and bundles. Carefully they were laid out in rows upon the table.

It appeared at first a large but disappointing display. There were plants, flowers, fruits, leaves, roots, nuts, beans, honeys, gums, bark, seeds, bees, and a few kinds of insects.

The study of plants—or botany, as it is called—was a kind of natural history that had never interested me very much. I had considered it, compared with the study of animals, a dull science. But as Long Arrow began taking up the various things in his collection and explaining their qualities to us, I became more and more fascinated. And before he had done I was completely absorbed by the wonders of the Vegetable Kingdom that he had brought so far.

"These," said he, taking up a little packet of big seeds, "are what I have called laughing beans.'"

"What are they for?" asked Bumpo.

"To cause mirth," said Long Arrow.

Bumpo, while the other man's back was turned, took three of the beans and swallowed them.

"Alas!" said the botanist when he discovered what Bumpo had done. "If he wished to try the powers of these seeds he should have eaten no more than a quarter of one. Let us hope that he does not die of laughter."

The beans' effect upon Bumpo was most extraordinary. First he broke into a broad smile; then he began to giggle; finally he burst into such prolonged roars of hearty laughter that we had to carry him into the next room and put him to bed. The Doctor said afterward that he probably would have died laughing if he had not had such a strong constitution. All through the night he gurgled happily in his sleep. And even when we woke him up the next morning, he rolled out of bed still chuckling.

Returning to the Reception Room, we were shown some red roots which Long Arrow told us had the property, when made into a soup with sugar and salt, of causing people to dance with extraordinary speed and endurance. He asked us to try them; but we refused, thanking him. After Bumpo's exhibition, we were a little afraid of any more experiments for the present.

There was no end to the curious and useful things that Long Arrow had collected: an oil from a vine that would make hair grow in one night; an orange as big as a pumpkin, which he had raised in his own mountain garden in Peru; a black honey (he had brought the bees that made it, too, and the seeds of the flowers they fed on) that would put you to sleep, just with a teaspoonful, and make you wake up fresh in the morning; a nut that made the voice beautiful for singing; a water weed that stopped cuts from bleeding; a moss that cured snakebite; a lichen that prevented seasickness.

The Doctor of course was tremendously interested. Well into the early hours of the morning he was busy going over the articles on the table one by one, listing their names and writing their properties and descriptions into a notebook as Long Arrow dictated.

"There are things here, Stubbins," he said as he ended, "which in the hands of skilled druggists will make a vast difference to the medicine and chemistry of the world. I suspect that this sleeping-honey by itself will take the place of half the bad drugs we have had to use so far. Long Arrow has discovered a pharmacopoeia of his own. Miranda was right: he is a great naturalist. His name deserves to be placed beside Linnaeus. Someday I must get all these things to England. But when?" he added sadly. "Yes, that's the problem: When?"

The Sea-Serpent

F OR A LONG TIME AFTER THAT CABINET MEET-
ing of which I have just told you we did not ask the Doctor
anything further about going home. Life in Spidermonkey
Island went forward, month in month out, busily and pleasantly. The winter, with Christmas celebrations, came and went, and
summer was with us once again before we knew it.

As time passed, the Doctor became more and more taken up
with the care of his big family; and the hours he could spare for his
natural history work grew fewer and fewer. I knew that he often still
thought of his house and garden in Puddleby and of his old plans and
ambitions; because once in a while we would notice his face grow
thoughtful and a little sad when something reminded him of England
or his old life. But he never spoke of these things. And I truly believe
he would have spent the remainder of his days on Spidermonkey
Island if it hadn't been for an accident—and for Polynesia.

The old parrot had grown very tired of the place and she made
no secret of it.

"The very idea," she said to me one day as we were walking on the seashore, "the idea of the famous John Dolittle wasting his valuable life here! Why, it's preposterous!"

All that morning we had been watching the Doctor supervise the building of the new theater in Popsipetel—there was already an opera house and a concert hall; and finally she had got so grouchy and annoyed at the sight that I had suggested her taking a walk with me.

"Do you really think," I asked as we sat down on the sands, "that he will never go back to Puddleby again?"

"I don't know," said she. "At one time I felt sure that the thought of the pets he had left behind at the house would take him home soon. But since Miranda brought him word last August that everything was all right there, that hope's gone. For months and months I've been racking my brains to think up a plan. If we could only hit upon something that would turn his thoughts back to natural history again—I mean something big enough to get him really excited—we might manage it. But how?"—she shrugged her shoulders in disgust—"How?—when all he thinks of now is paving streets and teaching babies that twice one are two!"

It was a perfect Popsipetel day, bright and hot, blue and yellow. Drowsily I looked out to sea thinking of my mother and father. I wondered if they were getting anxious over my long absence. Beside me, old Polynesia went on grumbling away in low, steady tones; and her words began to mingle and mix with the gentle lapping of the waves upon the shore. It may have been the even murmur of her voice, helped by the soft and balmy air, that lulled me to sleep. I don't know. Anyhow, I presently dreamed that the island had moved again—not floating as before, but suddenly, jerkily, as though something enormously powerful had heaved it up from its bed just once and let it down.

How long I slept after that I have no idea. I was awakened by a gentle pecking on the nose.

"Tommy! Tommy!" (it was Polynesia's voice) "Wake up! Gosh, what a boy, to sleep through an earthquake and never notice it! Tommy, listen: here's our chance now. Wake *up*, for goodness' sake!"

"What's the matter?" I asked, sitting up with a yawn.

"Sh! Look!" whispered Polynesia, pointing out to sea.

Still only half awake, I stared before me with bleary, sleep-laden eyes. And in the shallow water, not more than thirty yards from shore, I saw an enormous pale pink shell. Dome-shaped, it towered up in a graceful rainbow curve to a tremendous height; and round its base the surf broke gently in little waves of white. It could have belonged to the wildest dream.

"What in the world is it?" I asked.

"That," whispered Polynesia, "is what sailors for hundreds of years have called the *Sea-serpent*. I've seen it myself more than once from the decks of ships, at long range, curving in and out of the water. But now that I see it close and still, I very strongly suspect that the Sea-serpent of history is none other than the Great Glass Sea Snail that the fidgit told us of. If that isn't the only fish of its kind in the seven seas, call me a carrion crow— Tommy, we're in luck. Our job is to get the Doctor down here to look at that prize specimen before it moves off to the Deep Hole. If we can, then trust me, we may leave this blessed island yet. You stay here and keep an eye on it while I go after the Doctor. Don't move or speak—don't even breathe heavy: he might get scared—awful timid things, snails. Just watch him; and I'll be back in two shakes."

Stealthily creeping up the sands till she could get behind the cover of some bushes before she took to her wings, Polynesia went off in the direction of the town; while I remained alone upon the shore, fascinatedly watching this unbelievable monster wallowing in the shallow sea.

It moved very little. From time to time it lifted its head out of the water, showing its enormously long neck and horns. Occasionally it would try and draw itself up, the way a snail does when he goes to move, but almost at once it would sink down again as if exhausted. It seemed to me to act as though it were hurt underneath; but the lower part of it, which was below the level of the water, I could not see.

I was still absorbed in watching the great beast when Polynesia returned with the Doctor. They approached so silently and so cautiously that I neither saw nor heard them coming till I found them crouching beside me on the sand.

One sight of the snail changed the Doctor completely. His eyes just sparkled with delight. I had not seen him so thrilled and happy since the time we caught the Jabizri beetle when we first landed on the island.

"It is he!" the Doctor whispered. "The Great Glass Sea Snail himself—not a doubt of it. Polynesia, go down the shore a way and see if you can find any of the porpoises for me. Perhaps they can tell us what the snail is doing here. It's very unusual for him to be in shallow water like this. And Stubbins, you go over to the harbor and bring me a small canoe. But be most careful how you paddle it round into this bay. If the snail should take fright and go out into the deeper water, we may never get a chance to see him again."

"And don't tell any of the locals," Polynesia added in a whisper as I moved to go. "We must keep this a secret or we'll have a crowd of sightseers round here in five minutes. It's mighty lucky we found the snail in a quiet bay."

Reaching the harbor, I picked out a small light canoe from among the number that were lying there and, without telling anyone what I wanted it for, got in and started off to paddle it down the shore.

I was mortally afraid that the snail might have left before I got back. And you can imagine how delighted I was when I rounded a rocky cape and came in sight of the bay, to find he was still there.

Polynesia, I saw, had gotten her errand done and returned ahead of me, bringing with her a pair of porpoises. These were already conversing in low tones with John Dolittle. I beached the canoe and went up to listen.

"What I want to know," the Doctor was saying, "is how the snail comes to be here. I was given to understand that he usually stayed in the Deep Hole; and that when he did come to the surface, it was always in mid-ocean."

"Oh, didn't you know? Haven't you heard?" the porpoises replied. "You covered up the Deep Hole when you sank the island. Why yes: you let it down right on top of the mouth of the hole— sort of put the lid on, as it were. The fishes that were in it at the time have been trying to get out ever since. The Great Snail had the worst luck of all: the island nipped him by the tail just as he was leaving the hole for a quiet evening stroll. And he was held there for six months trying to wriggle himself free. Finally he had to heave the whole island up at one end to get his tail loose. Didn't you feel a sort of an earthquake shock about an hour ago?"

"Yes I did," said the Doctor, "it shook down part of the theater I was building."

"Well, that was the snail heaving up the island to get out of the hole," they said. "All the other fishes saw their chance and escaped when he raised the lid. It was lucky for them he's so big and strong. But the strain of that terrific heave took its toll on him: he sprained a muscle in his tail and it started swelling rather badly. He wanted some quiet place to rest up; and seeing this soft beach handy he crawled in here."

"Dear me!" said the Doctor. "I'm terribly sorry. I suppose I should have given some sort of notice that the island was going to be let down. But to tell the truth, we didn't know it ourselves; it happened by a kind of an accident. Do you imagine the poor fellow is hurt very badly?"

"We're not sure," said the porpoises, "because none of us can speak his language. But we swam right around him on our way in here, and he did not seem to be really seriously injured."

"Can't any of your people speak shellfish?" the Doctor asked.

"Not a word," said they. "It's a most frightfully difficult language."

"Do you think that you might be able to find me some kind of a fish that could?"

"We don't know," said the porpoises. "We might try."

"I should be extremely grateful to you if you would," said the Doctor. "There are many important questions I want to ask this snail. And besides, I would like to do my best to cure his tail for him. It's the least I can do. After all, it was my fault, indirectly, that he got hurt."

"Well, if you wait here," said the porpoises, "we'll see what can be done."

The Shellfish Riddle Solved at Last

S O DOCTOR DOLITTLE, WITH A CROWN ON HIS head, sat down upon the shore like King Knut, and waited. And for a whole hour the porpoises kept going and coming, bringing up different kinds of sea beasts from the deep to see if they could help him.

Many and curious were the creatures they produced. It would seem however that there were very few things that spoke shellfish except the shellfish themselves. Still, the porpoises grew a little more hopeful when they discovered a very old sea urchin (a funny, ball-like, little fellow with long whiskers all over him) who said he could not speak pure shellfish, but he used to understand starfish— enough to get along—when he was young. This was coming nearer, even if it wasn't anything to go crazy about. Leaving the urchin with us, the porpoises went off once more to hunt up a starfish.

They were not long getting one, for they were quite common in those parts. Then, using the sea urchin as an interpreter, they questioned the starfish. He was a rather stupid sort of creature; but he tried his best to be helpful. And after a little patient examination we found to our delight that he could speak shellfish moderately well.

Feeling quite encouraged, the Doctor and I now got into the canoe; and, with the porpoises, the urchin, and the starfish swimming alongside, we paddled very gently out till we were close under the towering shell of the Great Snail.

And then began the most curious conversation I have ever witnessed. First the starfish would ask the snail something; and whatever answer the snail gave, the starfish would tell it to the sea urchin, the urchin would tell it to the porpoises, and the porpoises would tell it to the Doctor.

In this way we obtained considerable information, mostly about the very ancient history of the animal kingdom; but we missed a good many of the finer points in the snail's longer speeches on account of the stupidity of the starfish and all this translating from one language to another.

While the snail was speaking, the Doctor and I put our ears against the wall of his shell and found that we could in this way hear the sound of his voice quite plainly. It was, as the fidgit had described, deep and bell-like. But of course we could not understand a single word he said. However the Doctor was by this time terrifically excited about getting near to learning the language he had sought so long. And presently, by making the other fishes repeat over and over again short phrases which the snail used, he began to put words together for himself. You see, he was already familiar with one or two fish languages; and that helped him quite a little. After he had practiced for a while like this, he leaned over the side of the canoe and, putting his face below the water, tried speaking to the snail directly.

It was hard and difficult work; and hours went by before he got any results. But presently I could tell by the happy look on his face that little by little he was succeeding.

The sun was low in the west and the cool evening breeze was beginning to rustle softly through the bamboo groves when the Doctor finally turned from his work and said to me:

"Stubbins, I have persuaded the snail to come in onto the dry part of the beach and let me examine his tail. Will you please go back to the town and tell the workmen to stop working on the theater for today? Then go on to the palace and get my medicine bag. I think I left it under the throne in the Audience Chamber."

"And remember," Polynesia whispered as I turned away, "not a word to a soul. If you get asked questions, keep your mouth shut. Pretend you have a toothache or something."

This time when I got back to the shore—with the medicine bag—I found the snail high and dry on the beach. Seeing him in his full length like this, it was easy to understand how old-time, superstitious sailors had called him the Sea-serpent. He certainly was gigantic, and in his own way, a graceful, beautiful creature. John Dolittle was examining a swelling on his tail.

From the bag which I had brought, the Doctor took a large bottle of liniment and began rubbing the sprain. Next he took all the bandages he had in the bag and fastened them end to end. But even like that they were not long enough to go more than halfway round the enormous tail. The Doctor insisted that he must get the swelling strapped tight somehow. So he sent me off to the palace once more to get all the sheets from the royal linen closet. These Polynesia and I tore into bandages for him. And at last, after terrific exertions, we got the sprain strapped to his satisfaction.

The snail really seemed to be quite pleased with the attention he had received; and he stretched himself in lazy comfort when the Doctor was done. In this position, when the shell on his back was empty, you could look right through it to the palm trees on the other side.

"I think one of us had better sit up with him all night," said the Doctor. "We might put Bumpo on that duty; he's been napping all day, I know—in the summer house. It's a pretty bad sprain, that; and if the snail shouldn't be able to sleep, he'll be happier with someone with him for company. He'll get all right though—in a few days, I should judge. If I wasn't so confoundedly busy I'd sit up with him myself. I wish I could, because I still have a lot of things to talk over with him."

"But, Doctor," said Polynesia as we prepared to go back to the town, "you ought to take a holiday. All kings take holidays once in the while—every one of them. King Charles, for instance—of course, Charles was before your time—but he!—why, he was *always* holiday-making. Not that he was ever what you would call a model king. But just the same, he was frightfully popular. Everybody liked him—even the golden carp in the fishpond at Hampton Court. As a king, the only thing I had against him was his inventing those stupid little snappy dogs they call King Charles Spaniels. There are lots of stories told about poor Charles; but that, in my opinion, is the worst thing he did. However, all this is beside the point. As I was saying, kings have to take holidays the same as anybody else. And you haven't taken one since you were crowned, have you now?"

"No," said the Doctor, "I suppose that's true."

"Well now I'll tell you what you do," said she. "As soon as you get back to the palace, you publish a royal proclamation that you are going away for a week into the country for your health. And you're going *without any servants*, you understand—just like a plain person. It's called traveling incognito, when kings go off like that. They all do it—It's the only way they can ever have a good time. Then the week you're away you can spend lolling on the beach back there with the snail. How's that?"

"I'd like to," said the Doctor. "It sounds most attractive. But there's that new theater to be built; none of our carpenters would know how to get those rafters on without me to show them. And then there are the babies—"

"Oh bother the theater—and the babies, too," snapped Polynesia. "The theater can wait a week. And as for babies, they never have anything more than colic. How do you suppose babies got along before you came here, for heaven's sake? Take a holiday. . . . You need it."

The Last Cabinet Meeting

F ROM THE WAY POLYNESIA TALKED, I GUESSED that this idea of a holiday was part of her plan.

The Doctor made no reply; and we walked on silently toward the town. I could see, nevertheless, that her words had made an impression on him.

After supper he disappeared from the palace without saying where he was going—a thing he had never done before. Of course we all knew where he had gone: back to the beach to sit up with the snail. We were sure of it, because he had said nothing to Bumpo about attending to the matter.

As soon as the doors were closed upon the cabinet meeting that night, Polynesia addressed the ministry:

"Look here, you fellows," said she, "we've simply got to get the Doctor to take this holiday somehow—unless we're willing to stay in this blessed island for the rest of our lives."

"But what difference," Bumpo asked, "is his taking a holiday going to make?"

Impatiently Polynesia turned upon the minister of the interior.

"Don't you see? If he has a clear week to get thoroughly inter-ested in his natural history again—marine stuff, his dream of seeing the floor of the ocean and all that—there may be some chance of his consenting to leave this pesky place. But while he is here on duty as king, he never gets a moment to think of anything outside of the business of government."

"Yes, that's true. He's far too conscientious," Bumpo agreed.

"And besides," Polynesia went on, "his only hope of ever get-ting away from here would be to escape secretly. He's got to leave while he is holiday-making incognito—when no one knows where he is or what he's doing, but us. If he built a ship big enough to cross the sea in, all the locals would see it and hear it, being built; and they'd ask what it was for. They would interfere. They'd sooner have anything happen than lose the Doctor. Why, I believe if they thought he had any idea of escaping they would put chains on him."

"Yes, I really think they would," I agreed. "Yet without a ship of some kind I don't see how the Doctor is going to get away, even secretly."

"Well, I'll tell you," said Polynesia. "If we do succeed in mak-ing him take this holiday, our next step will be to get the sea snail to promise to take us all in his shell and carry us to the mouth of Puddleby River. If we can get the snail willing, the temptation will be too much for John Dolittle and he'll come, I know— especially as he'll be able to take those new plants and drugs of Long Arrow's to the English doctors, as well as see the floor of the ocean on the way."

"How thrilling!" I cried. "Do you mean the snail could take us under the sea all the way back to Puddleby?"

"Certainly," said Polynesia. "A little trip like that is nothing to him. He would crawl along the floor of the ocean and the Doctor could see all the sights. Perfectly simple. Oh, John Dolittle will come, all right, if we can only get him to take that holiday—*and* if the snail will consent to give us the ride."

"Golly, I hope he does!" sighed Jip. "I'm sick of these beastly tropics—they make you feel so lazy and good-for-nothing. And there are no rats or anything here—not that a fellow would have the energy to chase 'em even if there were. My, wouldn't I be glad to see old Puddleby and the garden again! And won't Dab-Dab be glad to have us back!"

"By the end of next month," said I, "it will be two whole years since we left England—since we pulled up the anchor at Kingsbridge and bumped our way out into the river."

"And got stuck on the mudbank," added Chee-Chee in a dreamy, faraway voice.

"Do you remember how all the people waved to us from the river-wall?" I asked.

"Yes. And I suppose they've often talked about us in the town since," said Jip, "wondering whether we're dead or alive."

"Stop," said Bumpo, "I feel I am about to weep."

The Doctor's Decision

ELL, YOU CAN GUESS HOW GLAD WE were when the next morning the Doctor, after his all-night conversation with the snail, told us that he had made up his mind to take the holiday. A proclamation was published right away by the town crier that His Majesty was going into the country for a seven-day rest, but that during his absence the palace and the government offices would be kept open as usual.

Polynesia was immensely pleased. She at once set quietly to work making arrangements for our departure—taking good care all the while that no one should get an inkling of where we were going, what we were taking with us, the hour of our leaving, or which of the palace gates we would go out by.

Cunning old schemer that she was, she forgot nothing. And not even we, who were of the Doctor's party, could imagine what reasons she had for some of her preparations. She took me inside and told me that the one thing I must remember to bring with me was *all* of the Doctor's notebooks. Long Arrow, who was let into the secret of our destination, said he would like to come with us as far as the beach to see the Great Snail; and Polynesia told him to be sure and bring his collection of plants. Bumpo she ordered to carry the Doctor's high hat—carefully hidden under his coat. She sent off nearly all the footmen who were on night duty to do errands in the town, so that there should be as few servants as possible to see us leave. And midnight, the hour when most of the townspeople would be asleep, she finally chose for our departure.

We had to take a week's food supply with us for the royal holiday. So, with our other packages, we were heavily laden when on the stroke of twelve we opened the west door of the palace and stepped cautiously and quietly into the moonlit garden.

"Tiptoe incognito," whispered Bumpo as we gently closed the heavy doors behind us.

No one had seen us leave.

At the foot of the stone steps leading from the Peacock Terrace to the Sunken Rosary, something made me pause and look back at the magnificent palace that we had built in this strange, far-off land. Somehow I felt it in my bones that we were leaving it tonight, never to return again. And I wondered what other kings and ministers would dwell in its splendid halls when we were gone. The air was hot; and everything was deadly still but for the gentle splashing of the tame flamingoes paddling in the lily pond. Suddenly the twinkling lantern of a night watchman appeared round the corner of a cypress hedge. Polynesia plucked at my stocking and, in an impatient whisper, bade me hurry before our flight be discovered.

On our arrival at the beach we found the snail already feeling much better and now able to move his tail without pain.

The porpoises (who are by nature inquisitive creatures) were still hanging about in the offing to see if anything of interest was going to happen. Polynesia, the plotter, while the Doctor was occupied with his new patient, signaled to them and drew them aside for a little private chat.

"Now see here, my friends," she said, speaking low, "you know how much John Dolittle has done for the animals—given his whole life up to them, one might say. Well, here is your chance to do something for him. Listen: he got made king of this island against his will, see? And now that he has taken the job on, he feels that he can't leave it—thinks the people won't be able to get along without him and all that—which is nonsense, as you and I very well know. All right. Then here's the point: if this snail were only willing to take him and us—and a little baggage—not very much, thirty or forty pieces, say—inside his shell and carry us to England, we feel sure that the Doctor would go; because he's just crazy to mess about on the floor of the ocean. What's more, this would be his one and only chance of escape from the island. Now, it is highly important that the Doctor return to his own country to carry on his proper work, which means such a lot to the animals of the world. So what we want you to do is to tell the sea urchin to tell the starfish to tell the snail to take us in his shell and carry us to Puddleby River. Is that plain?"

"Quite, quite," said the porpoises. "And we will willingly do our very best to persuade him—for it is, as you say, a perfect shame for the great man to be stuck here when he is so much needed by the animals."

"And don't let the Doctor know what you're about," said Polynesia as they started to move off. "He might balk if he thought we had any hand in it. Get the snail to offer on his own account to take us. See?"

John Dolittle, unaware of anything save the work he was engaged on, was standing knee-deep in the shallow water, helping the snail try out his mended tail to see if it were well enough to travel on. Bumpo and Long Arrow, with Chee-Chee and Jip, were lolling at the foot of a palm a little way up the beach. Polynesia and I now went and joined them.

Half an hour passed.

What success the porpoises had met with, we did not know, till suddenly the Doctor left the snail's side and came splashing out to us, quite breathless.

"What *do* you think?" he cried. "While I was talking to the snail just now he offered, of his own accord, to take us all back to England inside his shell. He says he has got to go on a voyage of discovery anyway, to hunt up a new home, now that the Deep Hole is closed. Said it wouldn't be much out of his way to drop us at Puddleby River, if we cared to come along. Goodness, what a chance! I'd love to go. To examine the floor of the ocean all the way from Brazil to Europe! No man ever did it before. What a glorious trip! Oh, that I had never allowed myself to be made king! Now I must see the chance of a lifetime slip by."

He turned from us and moved down the sands again to the middle beach, gazing wistfully, longingly out at the snail. There was something peculiarly sad and forlorn about him as he stood there on the lonely, moonlit shore, the crown upon his head, his figure showing sharply black against the glittering sea behind.

Out of the darkness at my elbow Polynesia rose and quietly moved down to his side.

"Now, Doctor," said she in a soft persuasive voice as though she were talking to a wayward child, "you know this king business is not your real work in life. These natives will be able to get along without you—not so well as they do with you of course—but they'll manage—the same as they did before you came. Nobody can say you haven't done your duty by them. It was their fault: they made you king. Why not accept the snail's offer and just drop everything now and go? The work you'll do, the information you'll carry home, will be of far more value than what you're doing here."

"Good friend," said the Doctor, turning to her sadly, "I cannot. I began life as a people's doctor: I seem to have come back to it in the end. I cannot desert them. Later, perhaps something will turn up. But I cannot leave them now."

"That's where you're wrong, Doctor," said she. "Now is when you should go. Nothing will 'turn up.' The longer you stay, the harder it will be to leave—Go now. Go tonight."

"What, steal away without even saying good-bye to them! Why, Polynesia, what a thing to suggest!"

"A fat chance they would give you to say good-bye!" snorted Polynesia, growing impatient at last. "I tell you, Doctor, if you go back to that palace tonight, for goodbys or anything else, you will stay there. Now—this moment—is the time for you to go."

The truth of the old parrot's words seemed to be striking home, for the Doctor stood silent a minute, thinking.

"But there are the notebooks," he said presently. "I would have to go back to fetch them."

"I have them here, Doctor," said I, speaking up, "all of them."

Again he pondered.

"And Long Arrow's collection," he said. "I would have to take that also with me."

"It is here, Oh Kindly One," came the botanist's deep voice from the shadow beneath the palm.

"But what about provisions," asked the Doctor, "food for the journey?"

"We have a week's supply with us, for our holiday," said Polynesia. "That's more than we will need."

For a third time the Doctor was silent and thoughtful.

"And then there's my hat," he said fretfully at last. "That settles it: I'll *have* to go back to the palace. I can't leave without my hat. How could I appear in Puddleby with this crown on my head?"

"Here it is, Doctor," said Bumpo, producing the hat, old, battered, and beloved, from under his coat.

Polynesia had indeed thought of everything.

Yet even now we could see the Doctor was still trying to think up further excuses.

"Oh Kindly One," said Long Arrow, "why tempt ill fortune? Your way is clear. Your future and your work beckon you back to your foreign home beyond the sea. With you will go also what lore I too have gathered for mankind—to lands where it will be of wider use than it can ever be here. I see the glimmerings of dawn in the eastern heaven. Day is at hand. Go before your subjects are abroad. Go before your project is discovered. For truly I believe that if you go not now, you will linger the remainder of your days a captive king in Popsipetel."

Great decisions often take no more than a moment in the making. Against the now paling sky I saw the Doctor's figure suddenly stiffen. Slowly he lifted the Sacred Crown from off his head and laid it on the sands.

And when he spoke his voice was choked with tears.

"They will find it here," he murmured, "when they come to search for me. And they will know that I have gone. . . . I wonder if they will ever understand—and forgive."

He took his old hat from Bumpo; then facing Long Arrow, gripped his outstretched hand in silence.

"You decide aright, oh Kindly One," said the naturalist, "though none will miss and mourn you more than Long Arrow, the son of Golden Arrow. Farewell, and may good fortune ever lead you by the hand!"

It was the first and only time I ever saw the Doctor weep. Without a word to any of us, he turned and moved down the beach into the shallow water of the sea.

The snail humped up its back and made an opening between its shoulders and the edge of its shell. The Doctor clambered up and passed within. We followed him, after handing up the baggage. The opening shut tight with a whistling suction noise.

Then, turning in the direction of the east, the great creature began moving smoothly forward, down the slope into the deeper waters.

Just as the swirling dark green surf was closing in above our heads, the big morning sun popped his rim up over the edge of the ocean. And through our transparent walls of pearl we saw the watery world about us suddenly light up with that most wondrously colorful of visions, a daybreak beneath the sea.

* * *

The rest of the story of our homeward voyage is soon told.

Our new quarters we found very satisfactory. Inside the spacious shell, the snail's wide back was extremely comfortable to sit and lounge on—better than a sofa, when you once got accustomed to the damp and clammy feeling of it. He asked us, shortly after we started, if we wouldn't mind taking off our boots, as the hobnails in them hurt his back as we ran excitedly from one side to another to see the different sights.

The motion was not unpleasant, very smooth and even; in fact, but for the landscape passing outside, you would not know, on the level going, that you were moving at all.

I had always thought for some reason or other that the bottom of the sea was flat. I found that it was just as irregular and changeful as the surface of the dry land. We climbed over great mountain ranges, with peaks towering above peaks. We threaded our way through dense forests of tall sea plants. We crossed wide, empty stretches of sandy mud, like deserts—so vast that you went on for a whole day with nothing ahead of you but a dim horizon. Sometimes the scene was moss-covered, rolling country, green and restful to the eye like rich pastures; so that you almost looked to see sheep cropping on these underwater downs. And sometimes the snail would roll us forward inside him like peas, when he suddenly dipped downward to descend into some deep secluded valley with steeply sloping sides.

In these lower levels we often came upon the shadowy shapes of dead ships, wrecked and sunk heaven only knows how many years ago; and passing them we would speak in hushed whispers like children seeing monuments in churches.

Here, too, in the deeper, darker waters, monstrous fishes, feeding quietly in caves and hollows would suddenly spring up, alarmed at our approach, and flash away into the gloom with the speed of an arrow. While other bolder ones, all sorts of unearthly shapes and colors, would come right up and peer in at us through the shell.

"I suppose they think we are a sort of aquarium," said Bumpo. "I'd hate to be a fish."

It was a thrilling and ever-changing show. The Doctor wrote or sketched incessantly. Before long we had filled all the blank note-books we had left. Then we searched our pockets for any odd scraps of paper on which to jot down still more observations. We even went through the used books a second time, writing in between the lines, scribbling all over the covers, back and front.

Our greatest difficulty was getting enough light to see by. In the lower waters it was very dim. On the third day we passed a band of fire eels, a sort of large, marine glowworm; and the Doctor asked the snail to get them to come with us for a way. This they did, swimming alongside, and their light was very helpful, though not brilliant.

How our giant shellfish found his way across that vast and gloomy world was a great puzzle to us. John Dolittle asked him by what means he navigated—how he knew he was on the right road to Puddleby River. And what the snail said in reply got the Doctor so excited, that having no paper left, he tore out the lining of his precious hat and covered it with notes.

By night of course it was impossible to see anything; and during the hours of darkness the snail used to swim instead of crawl. When he did so he could travel at a terrific speed, just by waggling that long tail of his. This was the reason why we completed the trip in so short a time—five and a half days.

The air of our chamber, not having a change in the whole voyage, got very close and stuffy; and for the first two days we all had headaches. But after that we got used to it and didn't mind it in the least.

Early in the afternoon of the sixth day, we noticed we were climbing a long gentle slope. As we went upward it grew lighter. Finally we saw that the snail had crawled right out of the water altogether and had now come to a dead stop on a long strip of gray sand.

Behind us we saw the surface of the sea rippled by the wind. On our left was the mouth of a river with the tide running out. While in front, the low, flat land stretched away into the mist—which prevented one from seeing very far in any direction. A pair of wild ducks with craning necks and whirring wings passed over us and disappeared like shadows, seaward.

As a landscape, it was a great change from the hot, brilliant sunshine of Popsipetel.

With the same whistling suction sound, the snail made the opening for us to crawl out by. As we stepped down upon the marshy land we noticed that a fine, drizzling autumn rain was falling.

"Can this be Merrie England?" asked Bumpo, peering into the fog. "Doesn't look like any place in particular. Maybe the snail hasn't brought us right after all."

"Yes," sighed Polynesia, shaking the rain off her feathers, "this is England all right. You can tell it by the beastly climate."

"Oh, but fellows," cried Jip, as he sniffed up the air in great gulps, "it has a *smell*—a good and glorious smell! Excuse me a minute: I see a water rat."

"Sh! Listen!" said Chee-Chee through teeth that chattered with the cold. "There's Puddleby Church's clock striking four.

Why don't we divide up the baggage and get moving. We've got a long way to foot it home across the marshes."

"Let's hope," I put in, "that Dab-Dab has a nice fire burning in the kitchen."

"I'm sure she will," said the Doctor as he picked out his old medicine bag from among the bundles. "With this wind from the east, she'll need it to keep the animals in the house warm. Come on. Let's hug the riverbank so we don't miss our way in the fog. You know, there's something rather attractive in the bad weather of England—when you've got a kitchen fire to look forward to. . . . Four o'clock! Come along—we'll just be in nice time for tea."

The End

THE
Story of
DOCTOR DOLITTLE

BEING THE
HISTORY OF HIS PECULIAR LIFE
AT HOME AND ASTONISHING ADVENTURES
IN FOREIGN PARTS.   NEVER BEFORE PRINTED.

TOLD BY HUGH LOFTING   ILLUSTRATED BY THE AUTHOR

Contents

Puddleby

ONCE UPON A TIME, MANY YEARS AGO—WHEN our grandfathers were little children—there was a doctor; and his name was Dolittle—John Dolittle, M. D. "M. D." means that he was a proper doctor and knew a whole lot.

He lived in a little town called, Puddleby-on-the-Marsh. All the folks, young and old, knew him well by sight. And whenever he walked down the street in his high hat everyone would say, "There goes the Doctor! He's a clever man." And the dogs and the children would all run up and follow behind him; and even the crows that lived in the church tower would caw and nod their heads.

The house he lived in, on the edge of the town, was quite small; but his garden was very large and had a wide lawn and stone seats and weeping willows hanging over. His sister, Sarah Dolittle, was housekeeper for him; but the Doctor looked after the garden himself.

He was very fond of animals and kept many kinds of pets. Besides the goldfish in the pond at the bottom of his garden, he had rabbits in the pantry, white mice in his piano, a squirrel in the linen closet, and a hedgehog in the cellar. He had a cow with a calf, too, and an old lame horse—twenty-five years of age—and chickens, and pigeons, and two lambs, and many other animals. But his favorite pets were Dab-Dab the duck, Jip the dog, Gub-Gub the baby pig, Polynesia the parrot, and the owl Too-Too.

His sister used to grumble about all these animals and said they made the house untidy. And one day when an old lady with rheumatism came to see the Doctor, she sat on the hedgehog who was sleeping on the sofa, and never came to see him anymore but drove every Saturday all the way to Oxenthorpe, another town ten miles off, to see a different doctor.

Then his sister, Sarah Dolittle, came to him and said, "John, how can you expect sick people to come and see you when you keep all these animals in the house? It's a fine doctor would have his parlor full of hedgehogs and mice! That's the fourth personage these animals have driven away. Squire Jenkins and the parson say they wouldn't come near your house again—no matter how sick they are. We are getting poorer every day. If you go on like this, none of the best people will have you for a doctor."

"But I like the animals better than the 'best people,'" said the Doctor.

"You are ridiculous," said his sister, and walked out of the room.

So as time went on, the Doctor got more and more animals; and the people who came to see him got less and less. Till at last he had no one left—except the Cat's-Meat-Man, who didn't mind any kind of animal. But the Cat's-Meat-Man wasn't very rich and he only got sick once a year—at Christmastime, when he used to give the Doctor sixpence for a bottle of medicine.

"And she never came to see him anymore."

Sixpence a year wasn't enough to live on—even in those days, long ago; and if the Doctor hadn't had some money saved up in his money box, no one knows what would have happened.

And he kept on getting still more pets; and of course it cost a lot to feed them. And the money he had saved up grew littler and littler.

Then he sold his piano, and let the mice live in a bureau drawer. But the money he got for that too began to go, so he sold the brown suit he wore on Sundays and went on becoming poorer and poorer.

And now, when he walked down the street in his high hat, people would say to one another, "There goes John Dolittle, M. D.! There was a time when he was the best known doctor in the West Country—Look at him now—He hasn't any money and his stockings are full of holes!"

But the dogs and the cats and the children still ran up and followed him through the town—the same as they had done when he was rich.

Animal Language

I T HAPPENED ONE DAY THAT THE DOCTOR WAS sitting in his kitchen talking with the Cat's-Meat-Man who had come to see him with a stomachache.

"Why don't you give up being a people's doctor and be an animal doctor?" asked the Cat's-Meat-Man.

The parrot, Polynesia, was sitting in the window looking out at the rain and singing a sailor song to herself. She stopped singing and started to listen.

"You see, Doctor," the Cat's-Meat-Man went on, "you know all about animals—much more than what these here vets do. That book you wrote—about cats, why, it's wonderful! I can't read or write myself—or maybe I'd write some books. But my wife, Theodosia, she's a scholar, she is. And she read your book to me. Well, it's wonderful—that's all I can say—wonderful. You might have been a cat yourself. You know the way they think. And listen: you can make a lot of money doctoring animals. Do you know that? You see, I'd send all the old women who had sick cats or dogs to you. And if they didn't get sick fast enough, I could put something in the meat I sell 'em to make 'em sick, see?"

"Oh no," said the Doctor quickly. "You mustn't do that. That wouldn't be right."

"Oh, I didn't mean real sick," answered the Cat's-Meat-Man. "Just a little something to make them droopylike was what I had reference to. But as you say, maybe it ain't quite fair on the animals. But they'll get sick anyway, because the old women always give 'em too much to eat. And look, all the farmers round about who had lame horses and weak lambs—they'd come. Be an animal doctor."

When the Cat's-Meat-Man had gone, the parrot flew off the window onto the Doctor's table and said:

"That man's got sense. That's what you ought to do. Be an animal doctor. Give the silly people up if they haven't brains enough to see you're the best doctor in the world. Take care of animals instead—*they'll* soon find it out. Be an animal doctor."

"Oh, there are plenty of animal doctors," said John Dolittle, putting the flowerpots outside on the windowsill to get the rain.

"Yes, there *are* plenty," said Polynesia. "But none of them are any good at all. Now listen, Doctor, and I'll tell you something. Did you know that animals can talk?"

"I knew that parrots can talk," said the Doctor.

"Oh, we parrots can talk in two languages—people's language and bird language," said Polynesia proudly. "If I say, 'Polly wants a cracker,' you understand me. But hear this: *Ka-ka oi-ee, fee-fee?*"

"Good gracious!" cried the Doctor. "What does that mean?"

"That means, 'Is the porridge hot yet?'—in bird language."

"My! You don't say so!" said the Doctor. "You never talked that way to me before."

"What would have been the good?" said Polynesia, dusting some cracker crumbs off her left wing. "You wouldn't have understood me if I had."

"Tell me some more," said the Doctor, all excited; and he rushed over to the dresser drawer and came back with the butcher's book and a pencil. "Now don't go too fast—and I'll write it down. This is interesting—very interesting—something quite new. Give me the birds' ABCs first—slowly now."

So that was the way the Doctor came to know that animals had a language of their own and could talk to one another. And all that afternoon, while it was raining, Polynesia sat on the kitchen table giving him bird words to put down in the book.

At teatime, when the dog, Jip, came in, the parrot said to the Doctor, "See, *he's* talking to you."

"Looks to me as though he were scratching his ear," said the Doctor.

"But animals don't always speak with their mouths," said the parrot in a high voice, raising her eyebrows. "They talk with their ears, with their feet, with their tails—with everything. Sometimes they don't *want* to make a noise. Do you see now the way he's twitching up one side of his nose?"

"What's that mean?" asked the Doctor.

"That means, 'Can't you see that it has stopped raining?'" Polynesia answered. "He is asking you a question. Dogs nearly always use their noses for asking questions."

After a while, with the parrot's help, the Doctor got to learn the language of the animals so well that he could talk to them himself and understand everything they said. Then he gave up being a people's doctor altogether.

As soon as the Cat's-Meat-Man had told everyone that John Dolittle was going to become an animal doctor, old ladies began to bring him their pet pugs and poodles who had eaten too much cake; and farmers came many miles to show him sick cows and sheep.

One day a plow horse was brought to him; and the poor thing was terribly glad to find a man who could talk in horse language.

"You know, Doctor," said the horse, "that vet over the hill knows nothing at all. He has been treating me six weeks now— for spavins. What I need is *spectacles*. I am going blind in one eye. There's no reason why horses shouldn't wear glasses, the same as people. But that stupid man over the hill never even looked at my eyes. He kept on giving me big pills. I tried to tell him; but he couldn't understand a word of horse language. What I need is spectacles."

"Of course—of course," said the Doctor. "I'll get you some at once."

"I would like a pair like yours," said the horse, "only green. They'll keep the sun out of my eyes while I'm plowing the fifty-acre field."

"Certainly," said the Doctor. "Green ones you shall have."

"You know, the trouble is, sir," said the plow horse as the Doctor opened the front door to let him out, "the trouble is that *anybody* thinks he can doctor animals—just because the animals don't complain. As a matter of fact, it takes a much cleverer man to be a really good animal doctor than it does to be a good people's doctor. My farmer's boy thinks he knows all about horses. I wish you could see him—his face is so fat he looks as though he had no eyes—and he has got as much brain as a potato bug. He tried to put a mustard-plaster on me last week."

"Where did he put it?" asked the Doctor.

"Oh, he didn't put it anywhere—on me," said the horse. "He only tried to. I kicked him into the duck pond."

"Well, well!" said the Doctor.

"I'm a pretty quiet creature as a rule," said the horse. "Very patient with people—don't make much fuss. But it was bad enough to have that vet giving me the wrong medicine. And when that red-faced clown started to monkey with me, I just couldn't bear it anymore."

"Did you hurt the boy much?" asked the Doctor.

"Oh no," said the horse. "I kicked him in the right place. The vet's looking after him now. When will my glasses be ready?"

"I'll have them for you next week," said the Doctor. "Come in again Tuesday—good morning!"

Then John Dolittle got a fine, big pair of green spectacles; and the plow horse stopped going blind in one eye and could see as well as ever.

"He could see as well as ever."

And soon it became a common sight to see farm animals wearing glasses in the country round Puddleby; and a blind horse was a thing unknown.

And so it was with all the other animals that were brought to him. As soon as they found that he could talk their language, they told him where the pain was and how they felt, and of course it was easy for him to cure them.

Now all these animals went back and told their brothers and friends that there was a doctor in the little house with the big garden who really *was* a doctor. And whenever any creatures got sick—not only horses and cows and dogs—but all the little things of the fields, like harvest mice and water voles, badgers and bats, they came at once to his house on the edge of the town, so that his big garden was nearly always crowded with animals trying to get in to see him.

There were so many that came that he had to have special doors made for the different kinds. He wrote "HORSES" over the front door, "COWS" over the side door, and "SHEEP" on the kitchen door. Each kind of animal had a separate door—even the mice had a tiny tunnel made for them into the cellar, where they waited patiently in rows for the Doctor to come round to them.

And so, in a few years' time, every living thing for miles and miles got to know about John Dolittle, M. D. And the birds who flew to other countries in the winter told the animals in foreign lands of the wonderful doctor of Puddleby-on-the-Marsh, who could understand their talk and help them in their troubles. In this way he became famous among the animals—all over the world— better known even than he had been among the folks of the West Country. And he was happy and liked his life very much.

"They came at once to his house on the edge of the town."

One afternoon when the Doctor was busy writing in a book, Polynesia sat in the window—as she nearly always did—looking out at the leaves blowing about in the garden. Presently she laughed aloud.

"What is it, Polynesia?" asked the Doctor, looking up from his book.

"I was just thinking," said the parrot; and she went on looking at the leaves.

"What were you thinking?"

"I was thinking about people," said Polynesia. "People make me sick. They think they're so wonderful. The world has been going on now for thousands of years, hasn't it? And the only thing in animal language that *people* have learned to understand is that when a dog wags his tail he means 'I'm glad!' It's funny, isn't it?

You are the very first man to talk like us. Oh, sometimes people annoy me dreadfully—such airs they put on—talking about 'the dumb animals.' *Dumb*, huh? Why, I knew a macaw once who could say 'Good morning!' in seven different ways without once opening his mouth. He could talk every language—and Greek. An old professor with a gray beard bought him. But he didn't stay. He said the old man didn't talk Greek right, and he couldn't stand listening to him teach the language wrong. I often wonder what's become of him. That bird knew more geography than people will ever know. *People!* Golly, I suppose if people ever learn to fly—like any common hedge sparrow—we shall never hear the end of it!"

"You're a wise old bird," said the Doctor. "How old are you really? I know that parrots and elephants sometimes live to be very, very old."

"I can never be quite sure of my age," said Polynesia. "It's either a hundred and eighty-three or a hundred and eighty-two. But I know that when I first came here from Africa, King Charles was still hiding in the oak tree—because I saw him. He looked scared to death."

THE THIRD CHAPTER

More Money Troubles

AND SOON THE DOCTOR BEGAN TO MAKE money again; and his sister, Sarah, bought a new dress and was happy.

Some of the animals who came to see him were so sick that they had to stay at the Doctor's house for a week. And when they were getting better they used to sit in chairs on the lawn.

And often, even after they got well, they did not want to go away—they liked the Doctor and his house so much. And he never had the heart to refuse them when they asked if they could stay with him. So in this way he went on getting more and more pets.

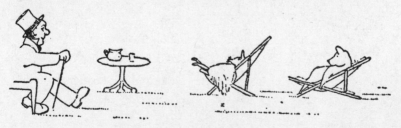

"They used to sit in chairs on the lawn."

Once when he was sitting on his garden wall smoking a pipe in the evening, an Italian organ-grinder came round with a monkey on a string. The Doctor saw at once that the monkey's collar was too tight and that he was dirty and unhappy. So he took the monkey away from the Italian, gave the man a shilling and told him to go. The organ-grinder got awfully angry and said that he wanted to keep the monkey. But the Doctor told him that if he didn't go away, he would punch him on the nose. John Dolittle was a strong man, though he wasn't very tall. So the Italian went away saying rude things and the monkey stayed with Doctor Dolittle and had a good home. The other animals in the house called him "Chee-Chee"—which is a common word in monkey language, meaning "ginger."

And another time, when the circus came to Puddleby, the crocodile who had a bad toothache escaped at night and came into the Doctor's garden. The Doctor talked to him in crocodile language and took him into the house and made his tooth better. But when the crocodile saw what a nice house it was—with all the different places for the different kinds of animals—he too wanted to live with the Doctor. He asked if he could sleep in the fishpond at the bottom of the garden, if he promised not to eat the fish. When the circus men came to take him back, he got so wild and savage that he frightened them away. But to everyone in the house he was always as gentle as a kitten.

But now the old ladies grew afraid to send their lapdogs to Doctor Dolittle because of the crocodile; and the farmers wouldn't believe that he would not eat the lambs and sick calves they brought to be cured. So the Doctor went to the crocodile and told him he must go back to his circus. But he wept such big tears, and begged so hard to be allowed to stay, that the Doctor hadn't the heart to turn him out.

So then the Doctor's sister came to him and said:

"John, you must send that creature away. Now the farmers and the old ladies are afraid to send their animals to you—just as we were beginning to be well off again. Now we shall be ruined entirely. This is the last straw. I will no longer be housekeeper for you if you don't send away that alligator."

"It isn't an alligator," said the Doctor, "it's a crocodile."

"I don't care what you call it," said his sister. "It's a nasty thing to find under the bed. I won't have it in the house."

"But he has promised me," the Doctor answered, "that he will not bite anyone. He doesn't like the circus; and I haven't the money to send him back to Africa where he comes from. He minds his own business and on the whole is very well behaved. Don't be so fussy."

"I tell you I *will not* have him around," said Sarah. "He eats the linoleum. If you don't send him away this minute I'll—I'll go and get married!"

"All right," said the Doctor, "go and get married. It can't be helped." And he took down his hat and went out into the garden.

So Sarah Dolittle packed up her things and went off; and the Doctor was left all alone with his animal family.

And very soon he was poorer than he had ever been before. With all these mouths to fill, and the house to look after, and no one to do the mending, and no money coming in to pay the butcher's bill, things began to look very difficult. But the Doctor didn't worry at all.

"Money is a nuisance," he used to say. "We'd all be much better off if it had never been invented. What does money matter, so long as we are happy?"

But soon the animals themselves began to get worried. And one evening when the Doctor was asleep in his chair before the kitchen fire they began talking it over among themselves in whispers. And the owl, Too-Too, who was good at arithmetic, figured it out that there was only money enough left to last another week—if they each had one meal a day and no more.

Then the parrot said, "I think we all ought to do the housework ourselves. At least we can do that much. After all, it is for our sakes that the old man finds himself so lonely and so poor."

So it was agreed that the monkey, Chee-Chee, was to do the cooking and mending; the dog was to sweep the floors; the duck was to dust and make the beds; the owl, Too-Too, was to keep the

"One evening when the Doctor was asleep in his chair"

accounts, and the pig was to do the gardening. They made Polynesia, the parrot, housekeeper and laundress, because she was the oldest.

Of course at first they all found their new jobs very hard to do—all except Chee-Chee, who had hands, and could do things like a man. But they soon got used to it; and they used to think it great fun to watch Jip, the dog, sweeping his tail over the floor with a rag tied onto it for a broom. After a little while they got to do the work so well that the Doctor said that he had never had his house kept so tidy or so clean before.

In this way things went along all right for a while; but without money they found it very hard.

Then the animals made a vegetable and flower stall outside the garden gate and sold radishes and roses to the people that passed by along the road.

But still they didn't seem to make enough money to pay all the bills—and still the Doctor wouldn't worry. When the parrot came to him and told him that the fishmonger wouldn't give them any more fish, he said:

"Never mind. So long as the hens lay eggs and the cow gives milk we can have omelettes and junket. And there are plenty of vegetables left in the garden. The winter is still a long way off. Don't fuss. That was the trouble with Sarah—she would fuss. I wonder how Sarah's getting on—an excellent woman—in some ways—Well, well!"

But the snow came earlier than usual that year; and although the old lame horse hauled in plenty of wood from the forest outside the town so they could have a big fire in the kitchen, most of the vegetables in the garden were gone, and the rest were covered with snow; and many of the animals were really hungry.

THE FOURTH CHAPTER

A Message
From Africa

THAT WINTER WAS A VERY COLD ONE. AND one night in December, when they were all sitting round the warm fire in the kitchen and the Doctor was reading aloud to them out of books he had written himself in animal language, Too-Too the owl suddenly said:

"Sh! What's that noise outside?"

They all listened; and presently they heard the sound of someone running. Then the door flew open and the monkey, Chee-Chee, ran in, badly out of breath.

"Doctor!" he cried. "I've just had a message from a cousin of mine in Africa. There is a terrible sickness among the monkeys out there. They are all catching it—and they are dying in hundreds. They have heard of you, and beg you to come to Africa to stop the sickness."

"Who brought the message?" asked the Doctor, taking off his spectacles and laying down his book.

"A swallow," said Chee-Chee. "She is outside on the rain-butt."

"Bring her in by the fire," said the Doctor. "She must be perished with the cold. The swallows flew south six weeks ago!"

So the swallow was brought in, all huddled and shivering; and although she was a little afraid at first, she soon got warmed up and sat on the edge of the mantelpiece and began to talk.

When she had finished, the Doctor said:

"I would gladly go to Africa—especially in this bitter weather. But I'm afraid we haven't money enough to buy the tickets. Get me the money box, Chee-Chee."

So the monkey climbed up and got it off the top shelf of the dresser.

There was nothing in it—not one single penny!

"I felt sure there was twopence left," said the Doctor.

"There *was*," said the owl. "But you spent it on a rattle for that badger's baby when he was teething."

"Did I?" said the Doctor. "Dear me, dear me! What a nuisance money is, to be sure! Well, never mind. Perhaps if I go down to the seaside I shall be able to borrow a boat that will take us to Africa. I knew a seaman once who brought his baby to me with measles. Maybe he'll lend us his boat—the baby got well."

So early the next morning the Doctor went down to the seashore. And when he came back he told the animals it was all right—the sailor was going to lend them the boat.

Then the crocodile and the monkey and the parrot were very glad and began to sing, because they were going back to Africa, their real home. And the Doctor said:

"I shall only be able to take you three—with Jip the dog, Dab-Dab the duck, Gub-Gub the pig, and Too-Too the owl. The rest of the animals, like the dormice and the water voles and the bats, they

"I felt sure there was twopence left."

will have to go back and live in the fields where they were born till
we come home again. But as most of them sleep through the winter,
they won't mind that—and besides, it wouldn't be good for them to
go to Africa."

So then the parrot, who had been on long sea voyages before,
began telling the Doctor all the things he would have to take with
him on the ship.

"You must have plenty of pilot-bread," she said, "'hardtack'
they call it. And you must have beef in cans—and an anchor."

"I expect the ship will have its own anchor," said the Doctor.

"Well, make sure," said Polynesia. "Because it's very important.
You can't stop if you haven't got an anchor. And you'll need a bell."

"What's that for?" asked the Doctor.

"To tell the time by," said the parrot. "You go and ring it every
half hour and then you know what time it is. And bring a whole lot
of rope—it always comes in handy on voyages."

Then they began to wonder where they were going to get the money from to buy all the things they needed.

"Oh, bother it! Money again," cried the Doctor. "Goodness! I shall be glad to get to Africa where we don't have to have any! I'll go and ask the grocer if he will wait for his money till I get back—No, I'll send the sailor to ask him."

So the sailor went to see the grocer. And presently he came back with all the things they wanted.

Then the animals packed up; and after they had turned off the water so the pipes wouldn't freeze, and put up the shutters, they closed the house and gave the key to the old horse who lived in the stable. And when they had seen that there was plenty of hay in the loft to last the horse through the winter, they carried all their luggage down to the seashore and got onto the boat.

The Cat's-Meat-Man was there to see them off; and he brought a large suet pudding as a present for the Doctor because, he said he had been told, you couldn't get suet pudding in foreign parts.

As soon as they were on the ship, Gub-Gub the pig asked where the beds were, for it was four o'clock in the afternoon and he wanted his nap. So Polynesia took him downstairs into the inside of the ship and showed him the beds, set all on top of one another like bookshelves against a wall.

"Why, that isn't a bed!" cried Gub-Gub. "That's a shelf!"

"Beds are always like that on ships," said the parrot. "It isn't a shelf. Climb up into it and go to sleep. That's what you call 'a bunk.'"

"I don't think I'll go to bed yet," said Gub-Gub. "I'm too excited. I want to go upstairs again and see them start."

"Well, this is your first trip," said Polynesia. "You will get used

"And the voyage began."

to the life after a while." And she went back up the stairs of the ship, humming this song to herself:

> I've seen the Black Sea and the Red Sea;
>   I rounded the Isle of Wight;
> I discovered the Yellow River,
>   And the Orange too—by night.
> Now Greenland drops behind again,
>   And I sail the ocean Blue.
> I'm tired of all these colors, Jane,
>   So I'm coming back to you.

They were just going to start on their journey, when the Doctor said he would have to go back and ask the sailor the way to Africa.

But the swallow said she had been to that country many times and would show them how to get there.

So the Doctor told Chee-Chee to pull up the anchor, and the voyage began.

The Great Journey

NOW FOR SIX WHOLE WEEKS THEY WENT sailing on and on, over the rolling sea, following the swallow who flew before the ship to show them the way. At night she carried a tiny lantern, so they should not miss her in the dark; and the people on the other ships that passed said that the light must be a shooting star.

As they sailed farther and farther into the south, it got warmer and warmer. Polynesia, Chee-Chee, and the crocodile enjoyed the hot sun to no end. They ran about laughing and looking over the side of the ship to see if they could see Africa yet.

The pig and the dog and the owl, Too-Too, could do nothing in such weather, but sat at the end of the ship in the shade of a big barrel, with their tongues hanging out, drinking lemonade.

Dab-Dab the duck used to keep herself cool by jumping into the sea and swimming behind the ship. And every once in a while, when the top of her head got too hot, she would dive under the ship and come up on the other side. In this way, too, she used to catch herrings on Tuesdays and Fridays—when everybody on the boat ate fish to make the beef last longer.

When they got near to the equator they saw some flying fishes coming toward them. And the fishes asked the parrot if this was Doctor Dolittle's ship. When she told them it was, they said they were glad, because the monkeys in Africa were getting worried that he would never come. Polynesia asked them how many miles they had yet to go; and the flying fishes said it was only fifty-five miles now to the coast of Africa.

And another time a whole school of porpoises came dancing through the waves; and they too asked Polynesia if this was the ship of the famous doctor. And when they heard that it was, they asked the parrot if the Doctor wanted anything for his journey.

And Polynesia said, "Yes. We have run short of onions."

"There is an island not far from here," said the porpoises, "where the wild onions grow tall and strong. Keep straight on—we will get some and catch up to you."

So the porpoises dashed away through the sea. And very soon the parrot saw them again, coming up behind, dragging the onions through the waves in big nets made of seaweed.

The next evening, as the sun was going down, the Doctor said:

"Get me the telescope, Chee-Chee. Our journey is nearly ended. Very soon we should be able to see the shores of Africa."

And about half an hour later, sure enough, they thought they could see something in front that might be land. But it began to get darker and darker and they couldn't be sure.

Then a great storm came up, with thunder and lightning. The wind howled; the rain came down in torrents; and the waves got so high they splashed right over the boat.

Presently there was a big BANG! The ship stopped and rolled over on its side.

"What's happened?" asked the Doctor, coming up from downstairs.

"I'm not sure," said the parrot; "but I think we're shipwrecked. Tell the duck to get out and see."

So Dab-Dab dived right down under the waves. And when she came up she said they had struck a rock; there was a big hole in the bottom of the ship; the water was coming in; and they were sinking fast.

"We must have run into Africa," said the Doctor. "Dear me, dear me! Well—we must all swim to land."

But Chee-Chee and Gub-Gub did not know how to swim.

"We must have run into Africa."

"Get the rope!" said Polynesia. "I told you it would come in handy. Where's that duck? Come here, Dab-Dab. Take this end of the rope, fly to the shore, and tie it onto a palm tree, and we'll hold the other end on the ship here. Then those that can't swim must climb along the rope till they reach the land. That's what you call a 'lifeline.'"

So they all got safely to the shore—some swimming, some flying; and those that climbed along the rope brought the Doctor's trunk and medicine bag with them.

But the ship was no good anymore—with the big hole in the bottom; and presently the rough sea beat it to pieces on the rocks and the timbers floated away.

Then they all took shelter in a nice dry cave they found, high up in the cliffs, till the storm was over.

When the sun came out the next morning, they went down to the sandy beach to dry themselves.

"Dear old Africa!" sighed Polynesia. "It's good to get back. Just think—it'll be a hundred and sixty-nine years tomorrow since I was here! And it hasn't changed a bit! Same old palm trees; same old red earth; same old black ants! There's no place like home!"

And the others noticed she had tears in her eyes—she was so pleased to see her country once again.

Then the Doctor missed his high hat; for it had been blown into the sea during the storm. So Dab-Dab went out to look for it. And presently she saw it, a long way off, floating on the water like a toy boat.

When she flew down to get it, she found one of the white mice, very frightened, sitting inside it.

"What are you doing here?" asked the duck. "You were told to stay behind in Puddleby."

"I didn't want to be left behind," said the mouse. "I wanted to see what Africa was like—I have relatives there. So I hid in the baggage and was brought onto the ship with the hardtack. When the ship sank I was terribly frightened—because I cannot swim far. I swam as long as I could, but I soon got all exhausted and thought I was going to sink. And then, just at that moment, the old man's hat came floating by; and I got into it because I did not want to be drowned."

So the duck took up the hat with the mouse in it and brought it to the Doctor on the shore. And they all gathered round to have a look.

"I got into it because I did not want to be drowned."

"That's what you call a 'stowaway,'" said the parrot.

Presently, when they were looking for a place in the trunk where the white mouse could travel comfortably, the monkey, Chee-Chee, suddenly said:

"Sh! I hear footsteps in the jungle!"

They all stopped talking and listened. And soon a man came down out of the woods and asked them what they were doing there.

"My name is John Dolittle—M. D.," said the Doctor. "I have been asked to come to Africa to cure the monkeys who are sick."

"You must all come before the king," said the man.

"What king?" asked the Doctor, who didn't want to waste any time.

"The king of the Jolliginki," the man answered. "All these lands belong to him; and all strangers must be brought before him. Follow me."

So they gathered up their baggage and went off, following the man through the jungle.

Polynesia and the King

WHEN THEY HAD GONE A LITTLE WAY through the thick forest, they came to a wide, clear space; and they saw the king's palace.

This was where the king lived with his queen, Ermintrude, and their son, Prince Bumpo. The prince was away fishing for salmon in the river. But the king and queen were sitting under an umbrella before the palace door. And Queen Ermintrude was asleep.

When the Doctor had come up to the palace the king asked him his business; and the Doctor told him why he had come to Africa.

"You may not travel through my lands," said the king. "Many years ago a visitor came to these shores and I was very kind to him. But after he had dug holes in the ground to get the gold, and killed all the elephants to get their ivory tusks, he went away secretly in his ship—without so much as saying 'Thank you.' Never again shall a stranger travel through the lands of Jolliginki."

Then the king turned to some of the men who were standing near and said, "Take away this medicine man—with all his animals, and lock them up in my strongest prison."

So six of the men led the Doctor and all his pets away and shut them up in a stone dungeon. The dungeon had only one little window, high up in the wall, with bars in it; and the door was strong and thick.

Then they all grew very sad; and Gub-Gub the pig began to cry. But Chee-Chee said he would spank him if he didn't stop that horrible noise; and he kept quiet.

"Are we all here?" asked the Doctor, after he had gotten used to the dim light.

"Yes, I think so," said the duck, who started to count them.

"Where's Polynesia?" asked the crocodile. "She isn't here."

"Are you sure?" said the Doctor. "Look again. Polynesia! Polynesia! Where are you?"

"I suppose she escaped," grumbled the crocodile. "Well, that's just like her! Sneaked off into the jungle as soon as her friends got into trouble."

"I'm not that kind of a bird," said the parrot, climbing out of the pocket in the tail of the Doctor's coat. "You see, I'm small enough to get through the bars of that window; and I was afraid they would put me in a cage instead. So while the king was busy talking, I hid in the Doctor's pocket—and here I am! That's what you call a 'ruse,'" she said, smoothing down her feathers with her beak.

"Good Gracious!" cried the Doctor. "You're lucky I didn't sit on you."

"Now listen," said Polynesia, "tonight, as soon as it gets dark, I am going to creep through the bars of that window and fly over to the palace. And then—you'll see—I'll soon find a way to make the king let us all out of prison."

"Oh, what can *you* do?" said Gub-Gub, turning up his nose and beginning to cry again. "You're only a bird!"

"Quite true," said the parrot. "But do not forget that although I am only a bird, *I can talk like a man*—and I know these people."

So that night, when the moon was shining through the palm trees and all the king's men were asleep, the parrot slipped out through the bars of the prison and flew across to the palace. The pantry window had been broken by a tennis ball the week before; and Polynesia popped in through the hole in the glass.

She heard Prince Bumpo snoring in his bedroom at the back of the palace. Then she tiptoed up the stairs till she came to the king's bedroom. She opened the door gently and peeped in.

The queen was away at a dance that night at her cousin's; but the king was in bed fast asleep.

Polynesia crept in, very softly, and got under the bed.

Then she coughed—just the way Doctor Dolittle used to cough. Polynesia could mimic anyone.

The king opened his eyes and said sleepily: "Is that you, Ermintrude?" (He thought it was the queen come back from the dance.)

Then the parrot coughed again—loud, like a man. And the king sat up, wide awake, and said, "Who's that?"

"I am Doctor Dolittle," said the parrot—just the way the Doctor would have said it.

"What are you doing in my bedroom?" cried the king. "How dare you get out of prison! Where are you?—I don't see you."

But the parrot just laughed—a long, deep, jolly laugh, like the Doctor's.

"Stop laughing and come here at once, so I can see you," said the king.

"Foolish king!" answered Polynesia. "Have you forgotten that you are talking to John Dolittle, M. D.—the most wonderful man on earth? Of course you cannot see me. I have made myself invisible. There is nothing I cannot do. Now listen: I have come here tonight to warn you. If you don't let me and my animals travel through your kingdom, I will make you and all your people sick like the monkeys. For I can make people well: and I can make people ill—just by raising my little finger. Send your soldiers at once to open the dungeon door, or you shall have mumps before the morning sun has risen on the hills of Jolliginki."

Then the king began to tremble and was very much afraid.

"Doctor," he cried, "it shall be as you say. Do not raise your little finger, please!" And he jumped out of bed and ran to tell the soldiers to open the prison door.

As soon as he was gone, Polynesia crept downstairs and left the palace by the pantry window.

But the queen, who was just letting herself in at the back door with a latchkey, saw the parrot getting out through the broken glass. And when the king came back to bed she told him what she had seen.

Then the king understood that he had been tricked, and he was dreadfully angry. He hurried back to the prison at once.

But he was too late. The door stood open. The dungeon was empty. The Doctor and all his animals were gone.

The Bridge of Apes

Q UEEN ERMINTRUDE HAD NEVER IN HER LIFE seen her husband so terrible as he got that night. He gnashed his teeth with rage. He called everybody a fool. He threw his toothbrush at the palace cat. He rushed round in his nightshirt and woke up all his army and sent them into the jungle to catch the Doctor. Then he made all his servants go too—his cooks and his gardeners and his barber and Prince Bumpo's tutor—even the queen, who was tired from dancing in a pair of tight shoes, was packed off to help the soldiers in their search.

All this time the Doctor and his animals were running through the forest toward the land of the monkeys as fast as they could go.

Gub-Gub, with his short legs, soon got tired; and the Doctor had to carry him—which made it pretty hard when they had the trunk and the medicine bag with them as well.

The king of the Jolliginki thought it would be easy for his army to find them, because the Doctor was in a strange land and would not know his way. But he was wrong; because the monkey,

Chee-Chee, knew all the paths through the jungle—better even than the king's men did. And he led the Doctor and his pets to the very thickest part of the forest—a place where no man had ever been before—and hid them all in a big hollow tree between high rocks.

"We had better wait here," said Chee-Chee, "till the soldiers have gone back to bed. Then we can go on into the land of the monkeys."

So there they stayed the whole night through.

They often heard the king's men searching and talking in the jungle round about. But they were quite safe, for no one knew of that hiding place but Chee-Chee—not even the other monkeys.

At last, when daylight began to come through the thick leaves overhead, they heard Queen Ermintrude saying in a very tired voice that it was no use looking anymore—that they might as well go back and get some sleep.

As soon as the soldiers had all gone home, Chee-Chee brought the Doctor and his animals out of the hiding place and they set off for the land of the monkeys.

It was a long, long way, and they often got very tired—especially Gub-Gub. But when he cried they gave him milk out of the coconuts, which he was very fond of.

They always had plenty to eat and drink; because Chee-Chee and Polynesia knew all the different kinds of fruits and vegetables that grow in the jungle, and where to find them—like dates and figs and groundnuts and ginger and yams. They used to make their lemonade out of the juice of wild oranges, sweetened with honey that they got from the bees' nests in hollow trees. No matter what it was they asked for, Chee-Chee and

Polynesia always seemed to be able to get it for them—or something like it.

At night they slept in tents made of palm leaves, on thick, soft beds of dried grass. And after a while they got used to walking such a lot and did not get so tired and enjoyed the life of travel very much.

But they were always glad when the night came and they stopped for their resting. Then the Doctor used to make a little fire of sticks; and after they had had their supper, they would sit round it in a ring, listening to Polynesia singing songs about the sea, or to Chee-Chee telling stories of the jungle.

And many of the tales that Chee-Chee told were very interesting. Because although the monkeys had no history books of their own before Doctor Dolittle came to write them for them, they remember everything that happens by telling stories to their children. And Chee-Chee spoke of many things his grandmother had told him—tales of long, long, long ago, before Noah and the Flood—of the days when men dressed in bearskins and lived in holes in the rock and ate their mutton raw, because they did not know what cooking was—having never seen a fire. And he told them of the great mammoths and lizards, as long as a train, that wandered over the mountains in those times, nibbling from the tree-tops. And often they got so interested listening, that when he had finished they found their fire had gone right out, and they had to scurry round to get more sticks and build a new one.

Now when the king's army had gone back and told the king that they couldn't find the Doctor, the king sent them out again and told them they must stay in the jungle till they caught him. So all this time, while the Doctor and his animals were going along toward the land of the monkeys, thinking themselves quite safe, they were still being followed by the king's men. If Chee-Chee had known this, he would most likely have hidden them again. But he didn't know it.

One day Chee-Chee climbed up a high rock and looked out over the treetops. And when he came down he said they were now quite close to the land of the monkeys and would soon be there.

And that same evening, sure enough, they saw Chee-Chee's cousin and a lot of other monkeys, who had not yet got sick, sitting in the trees by the edge of a swamp, looking and waiting for them. And when they saw the famous doctor really come, these monkeys made a tremendous noise, cheering and waving leaves and swinging out of the branches to greet him.

They wanted to carry his bag and his trunk and everything he had—and one of the bigger ones even carried Gub-Gub, who had gotten tired again. Then two of them rushed on in front to tell the sick monkeys that the great doctor had come at last.

But the king's men, who were still following, had heard the noise of the monkeys cheering; and they at last knew where the Doctor was, and hastened on to catch him.

The big monkey carrying Gub-Gub was coming along behind slowly, and he saw the captain of the army sneaking through the trees. So he hurried after the Doctor and told him to run.

Then they all ran harder than they had ever run in their lives; and the king's men, coming after them, began to run, too; and the captain ran hardest of all.

Then the Doctor tripped over his medicine bag and fell down

in the mud, and the captain thought he would surely catch him this time.

But the captain had very long ears—though his hair was very short. And as he sprang forward to take hold of the Doctor, one of his ears caught fast in a tree; and the rest of the army had to stop and help him.

By this time the Doctor had picked himself up, and on they went again, running and running. And Chee-Chee shouted:

"It's all right! We haven't far to go now!"

But before they could get into the land of the monkeys, they came to a steep cliff with a river flowing below. This was the end of the Kingdom of Jolliginki; and the land of the monkeys was on the other side—across the river.

And Jip the dog looked down over the edge of the steep, steep cliff and said:

"Golly! How are we ever going to get across?"

"Oh, dear!" said Gub-Gub. "The king's men are quite close now—Look at them! I am afraid we are going to be taken back to prison again." And he began to weep.

But the big monkey who was carrying the pig dropped him on the ground and cried out to the other monkeys:

"Boys—a bridge! Quick!—Make a bridge! We've only a minute to do it. They've got the captain loose, and he's coming on like a deer. Get lively! A bridge! A bridge!"

The Doctor began to wonder what they were going to make a bridge out of, and he gazed around to see if they had any boards hidden anyplace.

But when he looked back at the cliff, there, hanging across the river, was a bridge all ready for him—made of living monkeys! For while his back was turned, the monkeys—quick as a flash—had made themselves into a bridge, just by holding hands and feet.

And the big one shouted to the Doctor, "Walk over! Walk over—all of you—hurry!"

Gub-Gub was a bit scared, walking on such a narrow bridge at that dizzy height above the river. But he got over all right; and so did all of them.

John Dolittle was the last to cross. And just as he was getting to the other side, the king's men came rushing up to the edge of the cliff.

Then they shook their fists and yelled with rage. For they saw they were too late. The Doctor and all his animals were safe in the land of the monkeys and the bridge was pulled across to the other side.

Then Chee-Chee turned to the Doctor and said:

"John Dolittle was the last to cross."

"Many great explorers and gray-bearded naturalists have lain long weeks hidden in the jungle waiting to see the monkeys do that trick. But we never let a foreigner get a glimpse of it before. You are the first to see the famous 'Bridge of Apes.'"

And the Doctor felt very pleased.

The Leader of the Lions

J OHN DOLITTLE NOW BECAME DREADFULLY, awfully busy. He found hundreds and thousands of monkeys sick—gorillas, orangutans, chimpanzees, dog-faced baboons, marmosettes, gray monkeys, red ones—all kinds. And many had died.

The first thing he did was to separate the sick ones from the well ones. Then he got Chee-Chee and his cousin to build him a little house of grass. The next thing: he made all the monkeys who were still well come and be vaccinated.

And for three days and three nights the monkeys kept coming from the jungles and the valleys and the hills to the little house of grass, where the Doctor sat all day and all night, vaccinating and vaccinating.

Then he had another house made—a big one, with a lot of beds in it; and he put all the sick ones in this house.

But so many were sick, there were not enough well ones to do the nursing. So he sent messages to the other animals, like the lions and the leopards and the antelopes, to come and help with the nursing.

"He made all the monkeys who were still well come and be vaccinated."

But the leader of the lions was a very proud creature. And when he came to the Doctor's big house full of beds he seemed angry and scornful.

"Do you dare to ask me, sir?" he said, glaring at the Doctor. "Do you dare to ask me—*ME, the king of beasts*, to wait on a lot of dirty monkeys? Why, I wouldn't even eat them between meals!"

Although the lion looked very terrible, the Doctor tried hard not to seem afraid of him.

"I didn't ask you to eat them," he said quietly. "And besides, they're not dirty. They've all had a bath this morning. *Your* coat looks as though it needed brushing—badly. Now listen, and I'll tell you something: the day may come when the lions get sick. And if you don't help the other animals now, the lions may find themselves left all alone when *they* are in trouble. That often happens to proud people."

"The lions are never *in* trouble—they only *make* trouble," said the leader, turning up his nose. And he stalked away into the jungle, feeling he had been rather smart and clever.

"ME, the king of beasts, to wait on a lot of dirty monkeys?"

Then the leopards got proud too and said they wouldn't help. And then of course the antelopes—although they were too shy and timid to be rude to the Doctor like the lion—*they* pawed the ground and smiled foolishly, and said they had never been nurses before.

And now the poor Doctor was worried frantic, wondering where he could get help enough to take care of all these thousands of monkeys in bed.

But the leader of the lions, when he got back to his den, saw his wife, the queen lioness, come running out to meet him with her hair untidy.

"One of the cubs won't eat," she said. "I don't know *what* to do with him. He hasn't taken a thing since last usness—for she was

And she began to cry and shake with

a good mother, even though she was at his children—two

So the leader went into his den. And one of them seen

very cunning little cubs, lying on

quite poorly.

Then the lion told his wife, quite proudly, just what he had said to the Doctor. And she got so angry she nearly drove him out of the den.

"You never *did* have a grain of sense!" she screamed. "All the animals from here to the Indian Ocean are talking about this wonderful man, and how he can cure any kind of sickness, and how kind he is—the only man in the whole world who can talk the language of the animals! And now, *now*—when we have a sick baby on our hands, you must go and offend him! You great idiot! Nobody but a fool is ever rude to a *good* doctor. You—" and she started pulling her husband's hair.

"Go back to that man at once," she yelled, "and tell him you're sorry. And take all the other empty-headed lions with you—and those stupid leopards and antelopes. Then do everything the Doctor tells you. Work hard! And perhaps he will be kind enough to come and see the cub later. Now be off! *Hurry*, I tell you! You're not fit to be a father!"

And she went into the den next door, where another mother lion lived, and told her all about it.

So the leader of the lions went back to the Doctor and said, "I happened to be passing this way and thought I'd look in. Got any help yet?"

"No," said the Doctor. "I haven't. And I'm dreadfully worried."

"Help's hard to get these days," said the lion. "Animals don't seem to want to work anymore. You can't blame them—in a way. Well, seeing you're in difficulties, I don't mind doing what I can—just to oblige you—so long as I don't have to wash the creatures. And I have told all the other hunting animals to come and do their share. The leopards should be here any minute now. . . . Oh, and by the way, we've got a sick cub at home. I don't think there's much the matter with him myself. But the wife is anxious. If you are around that way this evening, you might take a look at him, will you?"

Then the Doctor was very happy; for all the lions and the leopards and the antelopes and the giraffes and the zebras—all the animals of the forests and the mountains and the plains—came to help him in his work. There were so many of them that he had to send some away, and only kept the cleverest.

And now very soon the monkeys began to get better. At the end of a week the big house full of beds were half-empty. And at the end of the second week, the last monkey had gotten well.

Then the Doctor's work was done; and he was so tired he went to bed and slept for three days without even turning over.

THE NINTH CHAPTER

The Monkeys' Council

CHEE-CHEE STOOD OUTSIDE THE DOCTOR'S door, keeping everybody away till he woke up. Then John Dolittle told the monkeys that he must now go back to Puddleby.

They were very surprised at this; for they had thought that he was going to stay with them forever. And that night all the monkeys got together in the jungle to talk it over.

And the Chief Chimpanzee rose up and said:

"Why is it the good man is going away? Is he not happy here with us?"

But none of them could answer him.

Then the Grand Gorilla got up and said, "I think we all should go to him and ask him to stay. Perhaps if we make him a new house and a bigger bed, and promise him plenty of monkey servants to work for him and to make life pleasant for him—perhaps then he will not wish to go."

Then Chee-Chee got up; and all the others whispered, "Sh! Look! Chee-Chee, the great traveler, is about to speak!"

And Chee-Chee said to the other monkeys:

"My friends, I am afraid it is useless to ask the Doctor to stay.

"*Then the Grand Gorilla got up.*"

He owes money in Puddleby; and he says he must go back and pay it."

And the monkeys asked him, "What is *money?*"

Then Chee-Chee told them that in the Doctor's land you could get nothing without money; you could *do* nothing without money—that it was almost impossible to *live* without money.

And some of them asked, "But can you not even eat and drink without paying?"

But Chee-Chee shook his head. And then he told them that even he, when he was with the organ-grinder, had been made to ask the children for money.

And the chief chimpanzee turned to the oldest orangutan and said, "Cousin, surely these men be strange creatures! Who would wish to live in such a land? My gracious, how paltry!"

Then Chee-Chee said, "When we were coming to you we

had no boat to cross the sea in and no money to buy food to eat on our journey. So a man lent us some biscuits; and we said we would pay him when we came back. And we borrowed a boat from a sailor, but it was broken on the rocks when we reached the shores of Africa. Now the Doctor says he must go back and get the sailor another boat—because the man was poor and his ship was all he had."

And the monkeys were all silent for a while, sitting quite still upon the ground and thinking hard.

At last the biggest baboon got up and said:

"I do not think we ought to let this good man leave our land till we have given him a fine present to take with him, so that he may know we are grateful for all that he has done for us."

And a little, tiny red monkey who was sitting up in a tree shouted down:

"I think that too!"

And then they all cried out, making a great noise, "Yes, yes. Let us give him the finest present a man ever had!"

Now they began to wonder and ask one another what would be the best thing to give him. And one said, "Fifty bags of coconuts!" And another—"A hundred bunches of bananas!—At least he shall not have to buy his fruit in the Land Where You Pay to Eat!"

But Chee-Chee told them that all these things would be too heavy to carry so far and would go bad before half was eaten.

"If you want to please him," he said, "give him an animal. You may be sure he will be kind to it. Give him some rare animal they have not got in the menageries."

And the monkeys asked him, "What are *menageries*?"

Then Chee-Chee explained to them that menageries were places in the Doctor's land where animals were put in cages for people to come and look at. And the monkeys were very shocked and said to one another:

"These men are like thoughtless young ones—stupid and easily amused. Sh! It is a prison he means."

So then they asked Chee-Chee what rare animal it could be that they should give the Doctor—one he had not seen before. And the major of the marmosettes asked, "Have they an iguana over there?"

But Chee-Chee said, "Yes, there is one in the London Zoo."

And another asked, "Have they an okapi?"

But Chee-Chee said, "Yes. In Belgium, where my organ-grinder took me five years ago, they had an okapi in a big city they call Antwerp."

And another asked, "Have they a Pushmi-Pullyu?"

Then Chee-Chee said, "No. No foreigner has ever seen a Pushmi-Pullyu. Let us give him that."

The Rarest Animal of All

PUSHMI-PULLYUS ARE NOW EXTINCT. THAT means there aren't any more. But long ago, when Doctor Dolittle was alive, there were some of them still left in the deepest jungles of Africa; and even then they were very, very scarce. They had no tail, but a head at each end, and sharp horns on each head. They were very shy and terribly hard to catch. The Africans get most of their animals by sneaking up behind them while they are not looking. But you could not do this with the Pushmi-Pullyu—because, no matter which way you came toward him, he was always facing you. And besides, only one half of him slept at a time. The other head was always awake—and watching. This was why they were never caught and never seen in zoos. Though many of the greatest huntsmen and the cleverest menagerie-keepers spent years of their lives searching through the jungles in all weathers for Pushmi-Pullyus, not a single one had ever been caught. Even then, years ago, he was the only animal in the world with two heads.

Well, the monkeys set out hunting for this animal through the forest. And after they had gone a good many miles, one of them found peculiar footprints near the edge of a river; and they knew that a Pushmi-Pullyu must be very near that spot.

Then they went along the bank of the river a little way and they saw a place where the grass was high and thick; and they guessed that he was in there.

So they all joined hands and made a great circle round the high grass. The Pushmi-Pullyu heard them coming; and he tried hard to break through the ring of monkeys. But he couldn't do it. When he saw that it was no use trying to escape, he sat down and waited to see what they wanted.

They asked him if he would go with Doctor Dolittle and be put on show in his homeland.

But he shook both his heads hard and said, "Certainly not!"

They explained to him that he would not be shut up in a menagerie but would just be looked at. They told him that the Doctor was a very kind man but hadn't any money, and people would pay to see a two-headed animal and the Doctor would get rich and could pay for the boat he had borrowed to come to Africa in.

But he answered, "No. You know how shy I am—I hate being stared at." And he almost began to cry.

Then for three days they tried to persuade him.

And at the end of the third day he said he would come with them and see what kind of a man the Doctor was, first.

So the monkeys traveled back with the Pushmi-Pullyu. And when they came to where the Doctor's little house of grass was, they knocked on the door.

The duck, who was packing the trunk, said, "Come in!"

And Chee-Chee very proudly took the animal inside and showed him to the Doctor.

"What in the world is it?" asked John Dolittle, gazing at the strange creature.

"Lord save us!" cried the duck. "How does it make up its mind?"

"It doesn't look to me as though it had any," said Jip the dog.

"This, Doctor," said Chee-Chee, "is the Pushmi-Pullyu—the rarest animal of the African jungles, the only two-headed beast in the world! Take him home with you and your fortune's made. People will pay any money to see him."

"But I don't want any money," said the Doctor.

"Yes you do," said Dab-Dab the duck. "Don't you remember how we had to pinch and scrape to pay the butcher's bill in Puddleby? And how are you going to get the sailor the new boat you spoke of—unless we have the money to buy it?"

"I was going to make him one," said the Doctor.

"How does it make up its mind?"

"Oh, do be sensible!" cried Dab-Dab. "Where would you get all the wood and the nails to make one with? And besides, what are we going to live on? We shall be poorer than ever when we get back. Chee-Chee's perfectly right: take the funny-looking thing along, do!"

"Well, perhaps there is something in what you say," murmured the Doctor. "It certainly would make a nice new kind of pet. But does the, er—what-do-you-call-it really want to go abroad?"

"Yes, I'll go," said the Pushmi-Pullyu who saw at once, from the Doctor's face, that he was a man to be trusted. "You have been so kind to the animals here—and the monkeys tell me that I am the only one who will do. But you must promise me that if I do not like it in your land you will send me back."

"Why, certainly—of course, of course," said the Doctor. "Excuse me, surely you are related to the deer family, are you not?"

"Yes," said the Pushmi-Pullyu—"to the Abyssinian gazelles and the Asiatic chamois—on my mother's side. My father's great-grandfather was the last of the unicorns."

"Most interesting!" murmured the Doctor; and he took a book out of the trunk, which Dab-Dab was packing, and began turning the pages. "Let us see if Buffon says anything—"

"I notice," said the duck, "that you only talk with one of your mouths. Can't the other head talk as well?"

"Oh yes," said the Pushmi-Pullyu. "But I keep the other mouth for eating—mostly. In that way I can talk while I am eating without being rude. Our people have always been very polite."

When the packing was finished and everything was ready to start, the monkeys gave a grand party for the Doctor, and all the animals of the jungle came. And they had pineapples and mangoes and honey and all sorts of good things to eat and drink.

After they had all finished eating, the Doctor got up and said:

"My friends: I am not clever at speaking long words after dinner, like some men; and I have just eaten many fruits and much honey. But I wish to tell you that I am very sad at leaving your beautiful country. Because I have things to do at home, I must go. After I have gone, remember never to let the flies settle on your food before you eat it; and do not sleep on the ground when the rains are coming. I—er—er—I hope you will all live happily ever after."

When the Doctor stopped speaking and sat down, all the monkeys clapped their hands a long time and said to one another, "Let it be remembered always among our people that he sat and ate with us, here, under the trees. For surely he is the greatest of men!"

And the Grand Gorilla, who had the strength of seven horses in his hairy arms, rolled a great rock up to the head of the table and said:

"This stone for all time shall mark the spot."

And even to this day, in the heart of the jungle, that stone is still there. And monkey mothers, passing through the forest with their families, still point down at it from the branches and whisper to their children, "Sh! There it is—look—where the good man sat and ate food with us in the Year of the Great Sickness!"

Then, when the party was over, the Doctor and his pets started out to go back to the seashore. And all the monkeys went with him as far as the edge of their country, carrying his trunk and bags, to see him off.

THE ELEVENTH CHAPTER

The Prince

BY THE EDGE OF THE RIVER THEY STOPPED and said farewell.

This took a long time, because all those thousands of monkeys wanted to shake John Dolittle by the hand.

Afterward, when the Doctor and his pets were going on alone, Polynesia said:

"We must tread softly and talk low as we go through the land of the Jolliginki. If the king should hear us, he will send his soldiers to catch us again; for I am sure he is still very angry over the trick I played on him."

"What I am wondering," said the Doctor, "is where we are going to get another boat to go home in. . . . Oh well, perhaps we'll find one lying about on the beach that nobody is using. 'Never lift your foot till you come to the stile.'"

One day, while they were passing through a very thick part of the forest, Chee-Chee went ahead of them to look for coconuts. And while he was away, the Doctor and the rest of the animals, who did not know the jungle paths so well, got lost in the deep woods. They wandered around and around but could not find their way down to the seashore.

Chee-Chee, when he could not see them anywhere, was terribly upset. He climbed high trees and looked out from the top branches to try and see the Doctor's high hat; he waved and shouted; he called to all the animals by name. But it was no use. They seemed to have disappeared altogether.

Indeed, they had lost their way very badly. They had strayed a long way off the path, and the jungle was so thick with bushes and creepers and vines that sometimes they could hardly move at all, and the Doctor had to take out his pocketknife and cut his way along. They stumbled into wet, boggy places; they got all tangled up in thick convolvulus runners; they scratched themselves on thorns, and twice they nearly lost the medicine bag in the underbrush. There seemed no end to their troubles; and nowhere could they come upon a path.

At last, after blundering about like this for many days, getting their clothes torn and their faces covered with mud, they walked right into the king's backyard garden by mistake. The king's men came running up at once and caught them.

But Polynesia flew into a tree in the garden, without anybody seeing her, and hid herself. The Doctor and the rest were taken before the king.

"Ha, ha!" cried the king. "So you are caught again! This time you shall not escape. Take them all back to prison and put double locks on the door. This prisoner shall scrub my kitchen floor for the rest of his life!"

So the Doctor and his pets were led back to prison and locked up. And the Doctor was told that in the morning he must begin scrubbing the kitchen floor.

They were all very unhappy.

"This is a great nuisance," said the Doctor. "I really must get back to Puddleby. That poor sailor will think I've stolen his ship if I don't get home soon. . . . I wonder if those hinges are loose."

But the door was very strong and firmly locked. There seemed no chance of getting out. Then Gub-Gub began to cry again.

All this time Polynesia was still sitting in the tree in the palace garden. She was saying nothing and blinking her eyes.

This was always a very bad sign with Polynesia. Whenever she said nothing and blinked her eyes, it meant that somebody had been making trouble, and she was thinking out some way to put things right. People who made trouble for Polynesia or her friends were nearly always sorry for it afterward.

Presently she spied Chee-Chee swinging through the trees, still looking for the Doctor. When Chee-Chee saw her, he came into her tree and asked her what had become of him.

"The Doctor and all the animals have been caught by the king's men and locked up again," whispered Polynesia. "We lost our way in the jungle and blundered into the palace garden by mistake."

"But couldn't you guide them?" asked Chee-Chee; and he began to scold the parrot for letting them get lost while he was away looking for the coconuts.

"It was all that stupid pig's fault," said Polynesia. "He would keep running off the path, hunting for gingerroots. And I was kept so busy catching him and bringing him back, that I turned to the left, instead of the right, when we reached the swamp. Sh! Look!

There's Prince Bumpo coming into the garden! He must not see us. Don't move, whatever you do!"

And there, sure enough, was Prince Bumpo, the king's son, opening the garden gate. He carried a book of fairy tales under his arm. He came strolling down the gravel walk, humming a sad song, till he reached a stone seat right under the tree where the parrot and the monkey were hiding. Then he lay down on the seat and began reading the fairy stories to himself.

Chee-Chee and Polynesia watched him, keeping very quiet and still.

"Chee-Chee!" Polynesia whispered. "I have an idea. Maybe I can hypnotize him!"

"What good will that do?" Chee-Chee whispered back.

"When you've been hypnotized, you sort of go to sleep and you'll do whatever you've been told to do, even after you wake up. If I can put the prince in a trance, I'll tell him to unlock the prison and let the Doctor out!"

"Well, it's worth a try," Chee-Chee said. "How will you do it?"

"Just watch me and don't move," Polynesia whispered, and she slid very quietly down the branch on which she was perched until she was closer to the prince. Clutching a smaller twig, she slowly began waving it in front of him and making a low humming sound in her throat.

Prince Bumpo saw the twig swinging to and fro, and soon his eyes started to close. After a moment, Polynesia spoke in a quiet, soothing voice: "Bumpo, Prince Bumpo, there is something you must do."

Prince Bumpo smiled gently in his sleep.

"In thy father's prison," said the parrot, "there lies a famous man, John Dolittle by name. Many things he knows about medicine, and mighty deeds has he performed. Yet thy kingly father leaves him languishing long and lingering hours. Go to him, brave Bumpo, secretly, when the sun has set. But first, prepare him a ship in which he may sail away, far from these shores. Then go and unlock the prison doors. Let the great man and his animals go free!"

Again, the sleeping prince smiled.

The Escape

VERY, VERY QUIETLY, MAKING SURE THAT no one should see her, Polynesia then slipped out of the garden and flew across to the prison.

She found Gub-Gub poking his nose through the bars of the window, trying to sniff the cooking smells that came from the palace kitchen. She told the pig to bring the Doctor to the window because she wanted to speak to him. So Gub-Gub went and woke the Doctor, who was taking a nap.

"Listen," whispered the parrot, when John Dolittle's face appeared: "Prince Bumpo is going to find a ship for you, and then he will come here tonight to unlock the prison doors. Have everyone ready to leave."

"How on earth—" the Doctor started to ask, but Polynesia quickly hissed, "Quiet! The guards are coming!" and she flew off.

The prince was as good as his (or Polynesia's) word, and late that night he came to the prison.

"Oh, great Doctor," he said, "I have come to set you free and have made ready a ship for you."

Then the prince, taking a bunch of copper keys from his pocket, undid the great double locks. And the Doctor, with all his animals, ran as fast as they could down to the seashore; while Bumpo leaned against the wall of the empty dungeon, smiling after them happily.

When they came to the beach they saw Polynesia and Chee-Chee waiting for them on the rocks near the ship. Then the Pushmi-Pullyu, the white mouse, Gub-Gub, Dab-Dab, Jip, and Too-Too went onto the ship with the Doctor. But Chee-Chee, Polynesia, and the crocodile stayed behind, because Africa was their proper home, the land where they were born.

And when the Doctor stood upon the boat, he looked over the side across the water. And then he remembered that they had no one with them to guide them back to Puddleby.

The wide, wide sea looked terribly big and lonesome in the moonlight; and he began to wonder if they would lose their way when they passed out of sight of land.

But even while he was wondering, they heard a strange whispering noise, high in the air, coming through the night. And the animals all stopped saying good-bye and listened.

The noise grew louder and bigger. It seemed to be coming nearer to them—a sound like the autumn wind blowing through the leaves of a poplar tree, or a great, great rain beating down upon a roof.

And Jip, with his nose pointing and his tail quite straight, said: "Birds!—millions of them—flying fast—that's it!"

And then they all looked up. And there, streaming across the face of the moon, like a huge swarm of tiny ants, they could see thousands and thousands of little birds. Soon the whole sky seemed full of them, and still more kept coming—more and more. There were so many that for a little they covered the whole moon so it could not shine, and the sea grew dark and black—like when a storm cloud passes over the sun.

And presently all these birds came down close, skimming over the water and the land; and the night sky was left clear above, and the moon shone as before. Still never a call nor a cry nor a song they made—no sound but this great rustling of feathers that grew greater now than ever. When they began to settle on the sands, along the ropes of the ship—anywhere and everywhere except the trees—the Doctor could see that they had blue wings and white breasts and very short, feathered legs. As soon as they had all found a place to sit, suddenly there was no noise left anywhere—all was quiet; all was still.

"Crying bitterly and waving till the ship was out of sight"

And in the silent moonlight John Dolittle spoke:

"I had no idea that we had been in Africa so long. It will be nearly summer when we get home. For these are the swallows going back. Swallows, I thank you for waiting for us. It is very thoughtful of you. Now we need not be afraid that we will lose our way upon the sea. . . . Pull up the anchor and set the sail!"

When the ship moved out upon the water, those who stayed behind—Chee-Chee, Polynesia, and the crocodile—grew terribly sad. For never in their lives had they known anyone they liked so well as Doctor John Dolittle of Puddleby-on-the-Marsh.

And after they had called good-bye to him again and again and again, they still stood there upon the rocks, crying bitterly and waving till the ship was out of sight.

Red Sails and
Blue Wings

SAILING HOMEWARD, THE DOCTOR'S SHIP HAD
to pass the coast of Barbary. This coast is the seashore of
the Great Desert. It is a wild, lonely place—all sand and
stones. And it was here that the Barbary pirates lived.

These pirates, a bad lot of men, used to wait for sailors to
be shipwrecked on their shores. And often, if they saw a boat
passing, they would come out in their fast-sailing ships and chase
it. When they caught a boat like this at sea, they would steal
everything on it; and after they had taken the people off, they
would sink the ship and sail back to Barbary singing songs and
feeling proud of the mischief they had done. Then they used to
make the people they had caught write home to their friends for
money. And if the friends sent no money, the pirates often threw
the people into the sea.

Now one sunshiny day the Doctor and Dab-Dab were walking
up and down on the ship for exercise; a nice fresh wind was blowing
the boat along, and everybody was happy. Presently Dab-Dab saw

the sail of another ship a long way behind them on the edge of the sea. It was a red sail.

"I don't like the look of that sail," said Dab-Dab. "I have a feeling it isn't a friendly ship. I am afraid there is more trouble coming to us."

Jip, who was lying nearby taking a nap in the sun, began to growl and talk in his sleep.

"I smell roast beef cooking," he mumbled, "underdone roast beef—with brown gravy over it."

"Good gracious!" cried the Doctor. "What's the matter with the dog? Is he *smelling* in his sleep—as well as talking?"

"I suppose he is," said Dab-Dab. "All dogs can smell in their sleep."

"But what is he smelling?" asked the Doctor. "There is no roast beef cooking on our ship."

"No," said Dab-Dab. "The roast beef must be on that other ship over there."

"But that's ten miles away," said the Doctor. "He couldn't smell that far surely!"

"Oh, yes, he could," said Dab-Dab. "You ask him."

Then Jip, still fast asleep, began to growl again, and his lip curled up angrily, showing his clean, white teeth.

"I smell bad men," he growled. "The worst men I ever smelled. I smell trouble. I smell a fight—six bad scoundrels fighting against one brave man. I want to help him. Woof—oo—WOOF!" Then he barked, loud, and woke himself up with a surprised look on his face.

"See!" cried Dab-Dab. "That boat is nearer now. You can count its three big sails—all red. Whoever it is, they are coming after us. . . . I wonder who they are."

"They are surely the pirates of Barbary."

"They are bad sailors," said Jip, "and their ship is very swift. They are surely the pirates of Barbary."

"Well, we must put up more sails on our boat," said the Doctor, "so we can go faster and get away from them. Run downstairs, Jip, and fetch me all the sails you see."

The dog hurried downstairs and dragged up every sail he could find.

But even when all these were put up on the masts to catch the wind, the boat did not go nearly as fast as the pirates'—which kept coming on behind, closer and closer.

"This is a poor ship the prince gave us," said Gub-Gub the pig. "The slowest he could find, I should think. Might as well try to win a race in a soup tureen as hope to get away from them in this old barge. Look how near they are now! You can see the mustaches on the faces of the men—six of them. What are we going to do?"

Then the Doctor asked Dab-Dab to fly up and tell the swallows that pirates were coming after them in a swift ship, and what should he do about it.

When the swallows heard this, they all came down onto the Doctor's ship; and they told him to unravel some pieces of long rope and make them into a lot of thin strings as quickly as he could. Then the ends of these strings were tied onto the front of the ship; and the swallows took hold of the strings with their feet and flew off, pulling the boat along.

And although swallows are not very strong when only one or two are by themselves, it is different when there are a great lot of them together. And there, tied to the Doctor's ship, were a thousand strings; and two thousand swallows were pulling on each string—all terribly swift fliers.

And in a moment the Doctor found himself traveling so fast he had to hold his hat on with both hands; for he felt as though the ship itself were flying through waves that frothed and boiled with speed.

And all the animals on the ship began to laugh and dance about in the rushing air, for when they looked back at the pirates' ship, they could see that it was growing smaller now, instead of bigger. The red sails were being left far, far behind.

The Rats' Warning

RAGGING A SHIP THROUGH THE SEA IS HARD work. And after two or three hours, the swallows began to get tired in the wings and short of breath. Then they sent a message down to the Doctor to say that they would have to take a rest soon; and that they would pull the boat over to an island not far off and hide it in a deep bay till they had breath enough to go on.

And presently the Doctor saw the island they had spoken of. It had a very beautiful, high green mountain in the middle of it.

When the ship had sailed safely into the bay where it could not be seen from the open sea, the Doctor said he would get off onto the island to look for water—because there was none left to drink on his ship. And he told all the animals to get out too and romp on the grass to stretch their legs.

Now as they were getting off, the Doctor noticed that a whole lot of rats were coming up from downstairs and leaving the ship as well. Jip started to run after them, because chasing rats had always been his favorite game. But the Doctor told him to stop.

And one big black rat, who seemed to want to say something to the Doctor, now crept forward timidly along the rail, watching the dog out of the corner of his eye. And after he had coughed nervously two or three times, and cleaned his whiskers and wiped his mouth, he said:

"Ahem—er—you know of course that all ships have rats in them, Doctor, do you not?"

And the Doctor said, "Yes."

"And you have heard that rats always leave a sinking ship?"

"Yes," said the Doctor, "so I've been told."

"People," said the rat, "always speak of it with a sneer—as though it were something disgraceful. But you can't blame us, can you? After

"And have you heard that rats always leave a sinking ship?"

all, who would stay on a sinking ship if he could get off it?"

"It's very natural," said the Doctor, "very natural. I quite understand. . . . Was there—Was there anything else you wished to say?"

"Yes," said the rat. "I've come to tell you that we are leaving this one. But we wanted to warn you before we go. This is a bad ship you have here. It isn't safe. The sides aren't strong enough. Its boards are rotten. Before tomorrow night, it will sink to the bottom of the sea."

"But how do you know?" asked the Doctor.

"We always know," answered the rat. "The tips of our tails get that tingly feeling—like when your foot's asleep. This morning, at six o'clock, while I was getting breakfast, my tail suddenly began to tingle. At first I thought it was my rheumatism coming back. So I went and asked my aunt how she felt—you remember her?—the long, piebald rat, rather skinny, who came to see you in Puddleby last spring with jaundice? Well, she said her tail was tingling like everything! Then we knew, for sure, that this boat was going to sink in less than two days; and we all made up our minds to leave it as soon as we got near enough to any land. It's a bad ship, Doctor. Don't sail in it anymore or you'll be surely drowned. . . . Good-bye! We are now going to look for a good place to live on this island."

"Good-by!" said the Doctor. "And thank you very much for coming to tell me. Very considerate of you—very! Give my regards to your aunt. I remember her perfectly. . . . Leave that rat alone, Jip! Come here! Lie down!"

So then the Doctor and all his animals went off, carrying pails and saucepans, to look for water on the island, while the swallows took their rest.

"I wonder what is the name of this island," said the Doctor, as he was climbing up the mountainside. "It seems a pleasant place. What a lot of birds there are!"

"Why, these are the Canary Islands," said Dab-Dab. "Don't you hear the canaries singing?"

The Doctor stopped and listened.

"Why, to be sure—of course!" he said. "How stupid of me! I wonder if they can tell us where to find water."

And presently the canaries, who had heard all about Doctor Dolittle from birds of passage, came and led him to a beautiful spring of cool, clear water where the canaries used to take their bath; and they showed him lovely meadows where the birdseed grew and all the other sights of their island.

And the Pushmi-Pullyu was glad they had come; because he liked the green grass so much better than the dried apples he had been eating on the ship. And Gub-Gub squeaked for joy when he found a whole valley full of wild sugarcane.

A little later, when they had all had plenty to eat and drink, and were lying on their backs while the canaries sang for them, two of the swallows came hurrying up, very flustered and excited.

"Doctor!" they cried, "the pirates have come into the bay; and they've all got onto your ship. They are downstairs looking for things to steal. They have left their own ship with nobody on it. If you hurry and come down to the shore, you can get onto their ship—which is very fast—and escape. But you'll have to hurry."

"That's a good idea," said the Doctor. "Splendid!"

And he called his animals together at once, said good-bye to the canaries and ran down to the beach.

When they reached the shore they saw the pirate ship, with the three red sails, standing in the water; and—just as the swallows had said—there was nobody on it; all the pirates were downstairs in the Doctor's ship, looking for things to steal.

So John Dolittle told his animals to walk very softly, and they all crept onto the pirate ship.

The Barbary Dragon

E VERYTHING WOULD HAVE GONE ALL RIGHT if the pig had not caught a cold in his head while eating the damp sugarcane on the island. This is what happened:

After they had pulled up the anchor without a sound, and were moving the ship very, very carefully out of the bay, Gub-Gub suddenly sneezed so loud that the pirates on the other ship came rushing upstairs to see what the noise was.

As soon as they saw that the Doctor was escaping, they sailed the other boat right across the entrance to the bay so that the Doctor could not get out into the open sea.

Then the leader of these bad men (who called himself "Ben Ali, the Dragon") shook his fist at the Doctor and shouted across the water:

"Ha! Ha! You are caught, my fine friend! You were going to run off in my ship, eh? But you are not a good enough sailor to beat Ben Ali, the Barbary Dragon. I want that duck you've got—and the pig, too. We'll have pork chops and roast duck for supper tonight. And before I let you go home, you must make your friends send me a trunk-full of gold."

Poor Gub-Gub began to weep; and Dab-Dab made ready to fly to save her life. But the owl, Too-Too, whispered to the Doctor:

"Keep him talking, Doctor. Be pleasant to him. Our old ship is bound to sink soon—the rats said it would be at the bottom of the sea before tomorrow night—and the rats are never wrong. Be pleasant, till the ship sinks under him. Keep him talking."

"What, until tomorrow night!" said the Doctor. "Well, I'll do my best. . . . Let me see—What shall I talk about?"

"Oh, let them come on," said Jip. "We can fight the dirty rascals. There are only six of them. Let them come on. I'd love to tell that collie next door, when we get home, that I had bitten a real pirate. Let 'em come. We can fight them."

"But they have pistols and swords," said the Doctor. "No, that would never do. I must talk to him. . . . Look here, Ben Ali—"

But before the Doctor could say any more, the pirates began to sail the ship nearer, laughing with glee, and saying one to another, "Who shall be the first to catch the pig?"

Poor Gub-Gub was dreadfully frightened; and the Pushmi-Pullyu began to sharpen his horns for a fight by rubbing them on the mast of the ship; while Jip kept springing into the air and barking and calling Ben Ali bad names in dog language.

But presently something seemed to go wrong with the pirates; they stopped laughing and cracking jokes; they looked puzzled; something was making them uneasy.

Then Ben Ali, staring down at his feet, suddenly bellowed out: "Thunder and Lightning! Men, *the boat's leaking!*"

And then the other pirates peered over the side and they saw

"Look here, Ben Ali—"

that the boat was indeed getting lower and lower in the water. And one of them said to Ben Ali:

"But surely if this old boat were sinking, we should see the rats leaving it."

And Jip shouted across from the other ship:

"You great duffers, there are no rats there to leave! They left two hours ago! 'Ha! Ha!' to you, 'my fine friends!'"

But of course the men did not understand him.

Soon the front end of the ship began to go down and down, faster and faster—till the boat looked almost as though it were standing on its head; and the pirates had to cling to the rails and the masts and the ropes and anything to keep from sliding off. Then the sea rushed roaring in through all the windows and the doors. And at last the ship plunged right down to the bottom of the sea, making a dreadful gurgling sound; and the six bad men were left bobbing about in the deep water of the bay.

Some of them started to swim for the shores of the island; while others came and tried to get onto the boat where the Doctor was. But Jip kept snapping at their noses, so they were afraid to climb up the side of the ship.

Then suddenly they all cried out in great fear:

"*The sharks!* The sharks are coming! Let us get onto the ship before they eat us! Help, help! The sharks! The sharks!"

And now the Doctor could see, all over the bay, the backs of big fishes swimming swiftly through the water.

And one great shark came near to the ship, and poking his nose out of the water he said to the Doctor:

"Are you John Dolittle, the famous animal doctor?"

"Yes," said Doctor Dolittle. "That is my name."

"Well," said the shark, "we know these pirates to be a bad lot—especially Ben Ali. If they are annoying you, we will gladly eat them up for you—and then you won't be troubled anymore."

"Thank you," said the Doctor. "This is really most attentive. But I don't think it will be necessary to eat them. Don't let any of them reach the shore until I tell you—just keep them swimming about, will you? And please make Ben Ali swim over here that I may talk to him."

So the shark went off and chased Ben Ali over to the Doctor.

"Listen, Ben Ali," said John Dolittle, leaning over the side. "You have been a very bad man; and I understand that you have killed many people. These good sharks here have just offered to eat you up for me—and 'twould indeed be a good thing if the seas were rid of you. But if you will promise to do as I tell you, I will let you go in safety."

"What must I do?" asked the pirate, looking down sideways at the big shark who was smelling his leg under the water.

"You must kill no more people," said the Doctor. "You must stop stealing; you must never sink another ship; you must give up being a pirate altogether."

"But what shall I do then?" asked Ben Ali. "How shall I live?"

"You and all your men must go onto this island and be birdseed farmers," the Doctor answered. "You must grow birdseed for the canaries."

The Barbary Dragon turned pale with anger. *"Grow birdseed!"* he groaned in disgust. "Can't I be a sailor?"

"No," said the Doctor, "you cannot. You have been a sailor long enough—and sent many stout ships and good men to the bottom of the sea. For the rest of your life you must be a peaceful farmer. The shark is waiting. Do not waste any more of his time. Make up your mind."

"Thunder and Lightning!" Ben Ali muttered. *"Birdseed!"* Then he looked down into the water again and saw the great fish smelling his other leg.

"Very well," he said sadly. "We'll be farmers."

"And remember," said the Doctor, "that if you do not keep your promise—if you start killing and stealing again, I shall hear of it, because the canaries will come and tell me. And be very sure that I will find a way to punish you. For though I may not be able to sail a ship as well as you, so long as the birds and the beasts and the fishes are my friends, I do not have to be afraid of a pirate chief—even though he calls himself 'the Dragon of Barbary.' Now go and be a good farmer and live in peace."

Then the Doctor turned to the big shark, and waving his hand he said:

"All right. Let them swim safely to the land."

THE SIXTEENTH CHAPTER

Too-Too, the Listener

HAVING THANKED THE SHARKS AGAIN FOR their kindness, the Doctor and his pets set off once more on their journey home in the swift ship with the three red sails.

As they moved out into the open sea, the animals all went downstairs to see what their new boat was like inside; while the Doctor leaned on the rail at the back of the ship with a pipe in his mouth, watching the Canary Islands fade away in the blue dusk of the evening.

While he was standing there, wondering how the monkeys were getting on—and what his garden would look like when he got back to Puddleby, Dab-Dab came tumbling up the stairs, all smiles and full of news.

"Doctor!" she cried. "This ship of the pirates is simply beautiful—absolutely. The beds downstairs are made of primrose silk—with hundreds of big pillows and cushions; there are thick, soft carpets on the floors; the dishes are made of silver; and there are all sorts of good things to eat and drink—special things; the larder—well, it's just like a shop, that's all. You never saw anything like it in your life. Just think—they kept five different kinds of sardines, those men! Come and look. . . . Oh, and we found a little room down there with the door locked; and we are all crazy to get in and see what's inside. Jip says it must be where the pirates kept their treasure. But we can't open the door. Come down and see if you can let us in."

So the Doctor went downstairs and he saw that it was indeed a beautiful ship. He found the animals gathered round a little door, all talking at once, trying to guess what was inside. The Doctor turned the handle but it wouldn't open. Then they all started to hunt for the key. They looked under the mat; they looked under all the carpets; they looked in all the cupboards and drawers and lockers—in the big chests in the ship's dining room; they looked everywhere.

While they were doing this they discovered a lot of new and wonderful things that the pirates must have stolen from other ships: Kashmir shawls as thin as a cobweb, embroidered with flowers of gold; carved ivory boxes full of Russian tea; an old violin with a string broken and a picture on the back; a set of big chessmen, carved out of coral and amber; a walking stick which had a sword inside it when you pulled the handle; six wineglasses with tourquoise and silver round the rims; and a lovely great sugar bowl, made of mother-of-pearl. But nowhere in the whole boat could they find a key to fit that lock.

So they all came back to the door, and Jip peered through the keyhole. But something had been set against the wall on the inside, and he could see nothing.

"Sh! Listen! I do believe there's someone in there!"

While they were standing around, wondering what they should do, the owl, Too-Too, suddenly said, "Sh! Listen! I do believe there's someone in there!"

They all kept still a moment. Then the Doctor said, "You must be mistaken, Too-Too. I don't hear anything."

"I'm sure of it," said the owl. "Sh! There it is again. Don't you hear that?"

"No, I do not," said the Doctor. "What kind of a sound is it?"

"I hear the noise of someone putting his hand in his pocket," said the owl.

"But that makes hardly any sound at all," said the Doctor. "You couldn't hear that out here."

"Pardon me, but I can," said Too-Too. "I tell you there is someone on the other side of that door putting his hand in his pocket. Almost everything makes *some* noise—if your ears are only sharp enough to catch it. Bats can hear a mole walking in his tunnel under the earth—and they think they're good hearers. But we owls can tell you, using only one ear, the color of a kitten from the way it winks in the dark."

"Well, well!" said the Doctor. "You surprise me. That's very interesting. . . . Listen again and tell me what he's doing now."

"I'm not sure yet," said Too-Too, "if it's a man at all. Maybe it's a woman. Lift me up and let me listen at the keyhole and I'll soon tell you."

So the Doctor lifted the owl up and held him close to the lock of the door.

After a moment Too-Too said:

"Now he's rubbing his face with his left hand. It is a small hand and a small face. It *might* be a woman—no. Now he pushes his hair back off his forehead. It's a man, all right."

"Women sometimes do that," said the Doctor.

"True," said the owl. "But when they do, their long hair makes quite a different sound. . . . Sh! Make that fidgety pig keep still. Now all hold your breath a moment so I can listen well. This is very difficult, what I'm doing now—and the pesky door is so thick! Sh! Everybody quite still—shut your eyes and don't breathe."

Too-Too leaned down and listened again very hard and long.

At last he looked up into the Doctor's face and said:

"The man in there is unhappy. He weeps. He has taken care not to blubber or sniffle, lest we should find out that he is crying. But I heard—quite distinctly—the sound of a tear falling on his sleeve."

"How do you know it wasn't a drop of water falling off the ceiling on him?" asked Gub-Gub.

"Pshaw! Such ignorance!" sniffed Too-Too. "A drop of water falling off the ceiling would have made ten times as much noise!"

"Well," said the Doctor, "if the poor fellow's unhappy, we've got to get in and see what's the matter with him. Find me an ax, and I'll chop the door down."

The Seventeenth Chapter

The Ocean Gossips

RIGHT AWAY AN AX WAS FOUND. AND THE Doctor soon chopped a hole in the door big enough to clamber through.

At first he could see nothing at all, it was so dark inside. So he struck a match.

The room was quite small; no window; the ceiling, low. For furniture there was only one little stool. All round the room big barrels stood against the walls, fastened at the bottom so they wouldn't tumble with the rolling of the ship; and above the barrels, pewter jugs of all sizes hung from wooden pegs. There was a strong, winey smell. And in the middle of the floor sat a little boy, about eight years old, crying bitterly.

"I declare, it is the pirates' rum room!" said Jip in a whisper.

"Yes. Very rum!" said Gub-Gub. "The smell makes me giddy."

The little boy seemed rather frightened to find a man standing there before him, and of all those animals staring in through the hole in the broken door. But as soon as he saw John Dolittle's face by the light of the match, he stopped crying and got up.

"You aren't one of the pirates, are you?" he asked.

And when the Doctor threw back his head and laughed long and loud, the little boy smiled too and came and took his hand.

"You laugh like a friend," he said, "not like a pirate. Could you tell me where my uncle is?"

"I am afraid I can't," said the Doctor. "When did you see him last?"

"It was the day before yesterday," said the boy. "I and my uncle were out fishing in our little boat when the pirates came and caught us. They sunk our fishing boat and brought us both onto this ship. They told my uncle that they wanted him to be a pirate like them—for he was clever at sailing a ship in all weathers. But he said he didn't want to be a pirate, because killing people and stealing was no work for a good fisherman to do. Then the leader, Ben Ali, got very angry and gnashed his teeth, and said they would throw my uncle into the sea if he didn't do as they said. They sent me downstairs; and I heard the noise of a fight going on above. And when they let me come up again next day, my uncle was nowhere to be seen. I asked the pirates where he was, but they wouldn't tell me. I am very much afraid they threw him into the sea and drowned him."

And the little boy began to cry again.

"Well now—wait a minute," said the Doctor. "Don't cry. Let's go and have tea in the dining room, and we'll talk it over. Maybe your uncle is quite safe all the time. You don't *know* that he was drowned, do you? And that's something. Perhaps we can find him for you. First we'll go and have tea—with strawberry jam; and then we will see what can be done."

All the animals had been standing around listening with great curiosity. And when they had gone into the ship's dining room and were having tea, Dab-Dab came up behind the Doctor's chair and whispered:

"Ask the porpoises if the boy's uncle was drowned—they'll know."

"All right," said the Doctor, taking a second piece of bread-and-jam.

"What are those funny, clicking noises you are making with your tongue?" asked the boy.

"Oh, I just said a couple of words in duck language," the Doctor answered. "This is Dab-Dab, one of my pets."

"I didn't even know that ducks had a language," said the boy. "Are all these other animals your pets, too? What is that strange-looking thing with two heads?"

"Sh!" the Doctor whispered. "That is the Pushmi-Pullyu. Don't let him see we're talking about him—he gets so dreadfully embarrassed. . . . Tell me, how did you come to be locked up in that little room?"

"The pirates shut me in there when they were going off to steal things from another ship. When I heard someone chopping on the door, I didn't know who it could be. I was very glad to find it was you. Do you think you will be able to find my uncle for me?"

"Well, we are going to try very hard," said the Doctor. "Now what was your uncle like to look at?"

"He had red hair," the boy answered, "very red hair, and the picture of an anchor tattooed on his arm. He was a strong man, a kind uncle and the best sailor in the South Atlantic. His fishing boat was called *The Saucy Sally*—a cutter-rigged sloop."

"What's 'cutterigsloop'?" whispered Gub-Gub, turning to Jip.

"Sh! That's the kind of a ship the man had," said Jip. "Keep still, can't you?"

"Oh," said the pig, "is that all? I thought it was something to drink."

So the Doctor left the boy to play with the animals in the dining room, and went upstairs to look for passing porpoises.

And soon a whole school came dancing and jumping through the water, on their way to Brazil.

When they saw the Doctor leaning on the rail of his ship, they came over to see how he was getting on.

And the Doctor asked them if they had seen anything of a man with red hair and an anchor tattooed on his arm.

"Do you mean the master of *The Saucy Sally*?" asked the porpoises.

"Yes," said the Doctor. "That's the man. Has he been drowned?"

"His fishing sloop was sunk," said the porpoises, "for we saw it lying on the bottom of the sea. But there was nobody inside it, because we went and looked."

"His little nephew is on the ship with me here," said the Doctor. "And he is terribly afraid that the pirates threw his uncle into the sea. Would you be so good as to find out for me, for sure, whether he has been drowned or not?"

"Oh, he isn't drowned," said the porpoises. "If he were, we would be sure to have heard of it from the deep-sea decapods. We hear all the saltwater news. The shellfish call us 'The Ocean Gossips.' No—tell the little boy we are sorry we do not know where his uncle is; but we are quite certain he hasn't been drowned in the sea."

So the Doctor ran downstairs with the news and told the nephew, who clapped his hands with happiness. And the Pushmi-Pullyu took the little boy on his back and gave him a ride round the dining room table; while all the other animals followed behind, beating the dish covers with spoons, pretending it was a parade.

Smells

"YOUR UNCLE MUST NOW BE *FOUND*," SAID THE Doctor. "That is the next thing—now that we know he wasn't thrown into the sea."

Then Dab-Dab came up to him again and whispered: "Ask the eagles to look for the man. No living creature can see better than an eagle. When they are miles high in the air they can count the ants crawling on the ground. Ask the eagles."

So the Doctor sent one of the swallows off to get some eagles.

And in about an hour the little bird came back with six different kinds of eagles: a black eagle, a bald eagle, a fish eagle, a golden eagle, an eagle-vulture, and a white-tailed sea eagle. Twice as high as the boy they were, each one of them. And they stood on the rail of the ship, like round-shouldered soldiers all in a row, stern and still and stiff; while their great, gleaming, black eyes shot darting glances here and there and everywhere.

Gub-Gub was scared of them and got behind a barrel. He said

he felt as though those terrible eyes were looking right inside him to see what he had stolen for lunch.

And the Doctor said to the eagles:

"A man has been lost—a fisherman with red hair and an anchor marked on his arm. Would you be so kind as to see if you can find him for us? This boy is the man's nephew."

Eagles do not talk very much. And all they answered in their husky voices was:

"You may be sure that we will do our best—for John Dolittle."

Then they flew off—and Gub-Gub came out from behind his barrel to see them go. Up and up and up they went—higher and higher and higher still. Then, when the Doctor could only just see them, they parted company and started going off all different ways—north, east, south, and west, looking like tiny grains of black sand creeping across the wide, blue sky.

"My gracious!" said Gub-Gub in a hushed voice. "What a height! I wonder they don't scorch their feathers—so near the sun!"

They were gone a long time. And when they came back it was almost night.

And the eagles said to the Doctor:

"We have searched all the seas and all the countries and all the islands and all the cities and all the villages in this half of the world. But we have failed. In the main street of Gibraltar we saw three red hairs lying on a wheelbarrow before a baker's door. But they were not the hairs of a man—they were the hairs out of a fur coat. Nowhere, on land or water, could we see any sign of this boy's uncle. And if *we* could not see him, then he is not to be seen. . . . For John Dolittle—we have done our best."

Then the six great birds flapped their big wings and flew back to their homes in the mountains and the rocks.

"Well," said Dab-Dab, after they had gone, "what are we going to do now? The boy's uncle *must* be found—there's no two ways about that. The lad isn't old enough to be knocking around the world by himself. Boys aren't like ducklings—they have to be taken care of till they're quite old. . . . I wish Chee-Chee were here. He would soon find the man. Good old Chee-Chee! I wonder how he's getting on!"

"If we only had Polynesia with us," said the white mouse. "*She* would soon think of some way. Do you remember how she got us all out of prison—the second time? My, but she was a clever one!"

"I don't think so much of those eagle fellows," said Jip. "They're just conceited. They may have very good eyesight and all that; but when you ask them to find a man for you, they can't do it—and they have the cheek to come back and say that nobody else could do it. They're just conceited—like that collie in Puddleby. And I don't think a whole lot of those gossipy old porpoises, either. All they could tell us was that the man isn't in the sea. We don't want to know where he *isn't*—we want to know where he is."

"Oh, don't talk so much," said Gub-Gub. "It's easy to talk; but it isn't so easy to find a man when you have got the whole world to hunt him in. Maybe the fisherman's hair has turned white, worrying about the boy; and that was why the eagles didn't find him. You don't know everything. You're just talking. You are not doing anything to help. You couldn't find the boy's uncle any more than the eagles could—you couldn't do as well."

"You stupid piece of warm bacon!"

"Couldn't I?" said the dog. "That's all you know, you stupid piece of warm bacon! I haven't begun to try yet, have I? You wait and see!"

Then Jip went to the Doctor and said:

"Ask the boy if he has anything in his pockets that belonged to his uncle, will you, please?"

So the Doctor asked him. And the boy showed them a gold ring which he wore on a piece of string around his neck because it was too big for his finger. He said his uncle gave it to him when they saw the pirates coming.

Jip smelled the ring and said:

"That's no good. Ask him if he has anything else that belonged to his uncle."

Then the boy took from his pocket a great big red handkerchief and said, "This was my uncle's too."

As soon as the boy pulled it out, Jip shouted:

"*Snuff*, by Jingo! Black Rappee snuff. Don't you smell it? His uncle took snuff. Ask him, Doctor."

The Doctor questioned the boy again; and he said, "Yes. My uncle took a lot of snuff."

"Fine!" said Jip. "The man's as good as found. 'Twill be as easy as stealing milk from a kitten. Tell the boy I'll find his uncle for him in less than a week. Let us go upstairs and see which way the wind is blowing."

"But it is dark now," said the Doctor. "You can't find him in the dark!"

"I don't need any light to look for a man who smells of Black Rappee snuff," said Jip as he climbed the stairs. "If the man had a hard smell, like string, now—or hot water, it would be different. But *snuff*! Tut, tut!"

"Does hot water have a smell?" asked the Doctor.

"Certainly it has," said Jip. "Hot water smells quite different from cold water. It is warm water—or ice—that has the really difficult smell. Why, I once followed a man for ten miles on a dark night by the smell of the hot water he had used to shave with—for the poor fellow had no soap. . . . Now then, let us see which way the wind is blowing. Wind is very important in long-distant smelling. It mustn't be too fierce a wind—and of course it must blow the right way. A nice, steady, damp breeze is the best of all. . . . Ha! This wind is from the North."

Then Jip went up to the front of the ship and smelled the wind, and he started muttering to himself:

"Tar; Spanish onions; kerosene oil; wet raincoats; crushed laurel leaves; rubber burning; lace curtains being washed—No, my mistake, lace curtains hanging out to dry; and foxes—hundreds of 'em—cubs; and—"

"Can you really smell all those different things in this one wind?" asked the Doctor.

"Why, of course!" said Jip. "And those are only a few of the easy smells—the strong ones. Any mongrel could smell those with a cold in the head. Wait now, and I'll tell you some of the harder scents that are coming on this wind—a few of the dainty ones."

Then the dog shut his eyes tight, poked his nose straight up in the air, and sniffed hard with his mouth half-open.

For a long time he said nothing. He kept as still as a stone. He hardly seemed to be breathing at all. When at last he began to speak, it sounded almost as though he were singing, sadly, in a dream.

"Bricks," he whispered, very low, "old yellow bricks, crumbling with age in a garden wall; the sweet breath of young cows standing in a mountain stream; the lead roof of a dovecote—or perhaps a granary—with the midday sun on it; black kid gloves lying in a bureau drawer of walnut wood; a dusty road with a horses' drinking trough beneath the sycamores; little mushrooms bursting through the rotting leaves; and—and—and—"

"Any parsnips?" asked Gub-Gub.

"No," said Jip. "You always think of things to eat. No parsnips whatsoever. And no snuff—plenty of pipes and cigarettes, and a few cigars. But no snuff. We must wait till the wind changes to the south."

"Yes, it's a poor wind, that," said Gub-Gub. "I think you're a fake, Jip. Whoever heard of finding a man in the middle of the ocean just by smell! I told you you couldn't do it."

"Look here," said Jip, getting really angry. "You're going to get a bite on the nose in a minute! You needn't think that just because the Doctor won't let us give you what you deserve, that you can be as cheeky as you like!"

"Stop quarreling!" said the Doctor. "Stop it! Life's too short. Tell me, Jip, where do you think those smells are coming from?"

"From Devon and Wales—most of them," said Jip. "The wind is coming that way."

"Well, well!" said the Doctor. "You know that's really quite remarkable—quite. I must make a note of that for my new book. I wonder if you could train me to smell as well as that. . . . But no—perhaps I'm better off the way I am. 'Enough is as good as a feast,' they say. Let's go down to supper. I'm quite hungry."

"So am I," said Gub-Gub.

The Rock

U P THEY GOT, EARLY NEXT MORNING, OUT OF the silken beds; and they saw that the sun was shining brightly and that the wind was blowing from the south.

Jip smelled the south wind for half an hour. Then he came to the Doctor, shaking his head.

"I smell no snuff as yet," he said. "We must wait till the wind changes to the east."

But even when the east wind came, at three o'clock that afternoon, the dog could not catch the smell of snuff.

The little boy was terribly disappointed and began to cry again, saying that no one seemed to be able to find his uncle for him. But all Jip said to the Doctor was:

"Tell him that when the wind changes to the west, I'll find his uncle even if he is in China—so long as he is still taking Black Rappee snuff."

Three days they had to wait before the west wind came. This was on a Friday morning, early—just as it was getting light. A fine, rainy mist lay on the sea like a thin fog. And the wind was soft and warm and wet.

As soon as Jip awoke he ran upstairs and poked his nose in the air. Then he got most frightfully excited and rushed down again to wake the Doctor up.

"Doctor!" he cried. "I've got it! Doctor! Doctor! Wake up! Listen! I've got it! The wind's from the west and it smells of nothing but snuff. Come upstairs and start the ship—quick!"

So the Doctor tumbled out of bed and went to the rudder to steer the ship.

"Now I'll go up to the front," said Jip, "and you watch my nose—whichever way I point it, you turn the ship the same way. The man cannot be far off—with the smell as strong as this. And the wind's all lovely and wet. Now watch me!"

So all that morning Jip stood in the front part of: the ship, sniffing the wind and pointing the way for the Doctor to steer, while all

"'Doctor!' he cried. 'I've got it!'"

the animals and the little boy stood round with their eyes wide open, watching the dog in wonder.

About lunchtime Jip asked Dab-Dab to tell the Doctor that he was getting worried and wanted to speak to him. So Dab-Dab went and fetched the Doctor from the other end of the ship and Jip said to him:

"The boy's uncle is starving. We must make the ship go as fast as we can."

"How do you know he is starving?" asked the Doctor.

"Because there is no other smell in the west wind but snuff," said Jip. "If the man were cooking or eating food of any kind, I would be bound to smell it, too. But he hasn't even fresh water to drink. All he is taking is snuff—in large pinches. We are getting nearer to him all the time, because the smell grows stronger every minute. But make the ship go as fast as you can, for I am certain that the man is starving."

"All right," said the Doctor, and he sent Dab-Dab to ask the swallows to pull the ship, the same as they had done when the pirates were chasing them.

So the stout little birds came down and once more harnessed themselves to the ship.

And now the boat went bounding through the waves at a terrible speed. It went so fast that the fishes in the sea had to jump for their lives to get out of the way and not be run over.

And all the animals got tremendously excited; and they gave up looking at Jip and turned to watch the sea in front, to spy out any land or islands where the starving man might be.

But hour after hour went by and still the ship went rushing on, over the same flat, flat sea; and no land anywhere came into sight.

And now the animals gave up chattering and sat around silent, anxious, and miserable. The little boy again grew sad. And on Jip's face there was a worried look.

At last, late in the afternoon, just as the sun was going down, the owl, Too-Too, who was perched on the tip of the mast, suddenly startled them all by crying out at the top of his voice:

"Jip! Jip! I see a great, great rock in front of us—look—way out there where the sky and the water meet. See the sun shine on it—like gold! Is the smell coming from there?"

And Jip called back:

"Yes. That's it. That is where the man is. At last, at last!"

And when they got nearer they could see that the rock was very large—as large as a big field. No trees grew on it, no grass—nothing. The great rock was as smooth and as bare as the back of a tortoise.

Then the Doctor sailed the ship right round the rock. But nowhere on it could a man be seen. All the animals screwed up their eyes and looked as hard as they could; and John Dolittle got a telescope from downstairs.

But not one living thing could they spy—not even a gull, nor a starfish, nor a shred of seaweed.

They all stood still and listened, straining their ears for any sound. But the only noise they heard was the gentle lapping of the little waves against the sides of their ship.

Then they all started calling, "Hulloa, there! HULLOA!" till their voices were hoarse. But only the echo came back from the rock.

And the little boy burst into tears and said:

"I am afraid I shall never see my uncle anymore! What shall I tell them when I get home!"

But Jip called to the Doctor:

"He must be there—he must—*he must*! The smell goes on no farther. He must be there, I tell you! Sail the ship close to the rock and let me jump out onto it."

So the Doctor brought the ship as close as he could and let down the anchor. Then he and Jip got out of the ship, onto the rock.

Jip at once put his nose down close to the ground and began to run all over the place. Up and down he went, back and forth—zigzagging, twisting, doubling, and turning. And everywhere he went, the Doctor ran behind him, close at his heels—till he was terribly out of breath.

At last Jip let out a great bark and sat down. And when the Doctor came running up to him, he found the dog staring into a big, deep hole in the middle of the rock.

"The boy's uncle is down there," said Jip quietly. "No wonder those silly eagles couldn't see him! It takes a dog to find a man."

So the Doctor got down into the hole, which seemed to be a kind of cave, or tunnel, running a long way under the ground. Then he struck a match and started to make his way along the dark passage, with Jip following behind.

The Doctor's match soon went out; and he had to strike another and another and another.

At last the passage came to an end; and the Doctor found himself in a kind of tiny room with walls of rock.

And there, in the middle of the room, his head resting on his arms, lay a man with very red hair—fast asleep!

Jip went up and sniffed at something lying on the ground beside him. The Doctor stooped and picked it up. It was an enormous snuffbox. And it was full of Black Rappee!

The Twentieth Chapter

The Fisherman's Town

GENTLY THEN—VERY GENTLY, THE DOCTOR woke the man up.

But just at that moment the match went out again. And the man thought it was Ben Ali coming back, and he began to punch the Doctor in the dark.

But when John Dolittle told him who it was, and that he had his little nephew safe on his ship, the man was tremendously glad and said he was sorry he had fought the Doctor. He had not hurt him much, though—because it was too dark to punch properly. Then he gave the Doctor a pinch of snuff.

And the man told how the Barbary Dragon had put him on to this rock and left him there, when he wouldn't promise to become a pirate; and how he used to sleep down in this hole because there was no house on the rock to keep him warm.

And then he said:

"For four days I have had nothing to eat or drink. I have lived on snuff."

"There you are!" said Jip. "What did I tell you?"

So they struck some more matches and made their way out through the passage into the daylight; and the Doctor hurried the man down to the boat to get some soup.

When the animals and the little boy saw the Doctor and Jip coming back to the ship with a redheaded man, they began to cheer and yell and dance about the boat. And the swallows up above started whistling at the top of their voices—thousands and millions of them—to show that they too were glad that the boy's brave uncle had been found. The noise they made was so great that sailors far out at sea thought that a terrible storm was coming. "Hark to that gale howling in the east!" they said.

And Jip was awfully proud of himself—though he tried hard not to look conceited. When Dab-Dab came to him and said, "Jip, I had no idea you were so clever!" he just tossed his head and answered:

"Oh, that's nothing special. But it takes a dog to find a man, you know. Birds are no good for a game like that."

Then the Doctor asked the red-haired fisherman where his home was. And when he had told him, the Doctor asked the swallows to guide the ship there first.

And when they had come to the land that the man had spoken of, they saw a little fishing town at the foot of a rocky mountain; and the man pointed out the house where he lived.

And while they were letting down the anchor, the little boy's mother (who was also the man's sister) came running down to the shore to meet them, laughing and crying at the same time. She had been sitting on a hill for twenty days, watching the sea and waiting for them to return.

And she kissed the Doctor many times, so that he giggled and blushed like a schoolgirl. And she tried to kiss Jip, too, but he ran away and hid inside the ship.

"It's a silly business, this kissing," he said. "I don't hold by it. Let her go and kiss Gub-Gub—if she *must* kiss something."

The fisherman and his sister didn't want the Doctor to go away again in a hurry. They begged him to spend a few days with them. So John Dolittle and his animals had to stay at their house a whole Saturday and Sunday and half of Monday.

And all the little boys of the fishing village went down to the beach and pointed at the great ship anchored there, and said to one another in whispers:

"Look! That was a pirate ship—Ben Ali's—the most terrible pirate that ever sailed the Seven Seas! That old gentleman with the high hat, who's staying up at Mrs. Trevelyan's, *he* took the ship away from the Barbary Dragon—and made him into a farmer. Who'd have thought it of him—him so gentle-like and all! . . . Look at the

"And she kissed the Doctor many times."

great red sails! Ain't she a wicked-looking ship—and fast? My!"

All those two days and a half that the Doctor stayed at the little fishing town, the people kept asking him out to teas and luncheons and dinners and parties; all the ladies sent him boxes of flowers and candies; and the village band played tunes under his window every night.

At last the Doctor said:

"Good people, I must go home now. You have really been most kind. I shall always remember it. But I must go home—for I have things to do."

Then, just as the Doctor was about to leave, the mayor of the town came down the street and a lot of other people in grand clothes with him. And the mayor stopped before the house where the Doctor was living; everybody in the village gathered round to see what was going to happen.

After six page boys had blown on shining trumpets to make the people stop talking, the Doctor came out onto the steps and the mayor spoke.

"Doctor John Dolittle," said he. "It is a great pleasure for me to present to the man who rid the seas of the Dragon of Barbary this little token from the grateful people of our worthy town."

And the mayor took from his pocket a little tissue-paper packet, and opening it, he handed to the Doctor a perfectly beautiful watch with real diamonds in the back.

Then the mayor pulled out of his pocket a still larger parcel and said:

"Where is the dog?"

Then everybody started to hunt for Jip. And at last Dab-Dab found him on the other side of the village in a stable yard, where all the dogs of the countryside were standing round him speechless with admiration and respect.

When Jip was brought to the Doctor's side, the mayor opened the larger parcel; and inside was a dog collar made of solid gold! And a great murmur of wonder went up from the village folk as the mayor bent down and fastened it round the dog's neck with his own hands.

For written on the collar in big letters were these words: JIP— THE CLEVEREST DOG IN THE WORLD.

Then the whole crowd moved down to the beach to see them off. And after the red-haired fisherman and his sister and the little boy had thanked the Doctor and his dog over and over and over again, the great, swift ship with the red sails was turned once more toward Puddleby and they sailed out to sea, while the village band played music on the shore.

Home Again

MARCH WINDS HAD COME AND GONE; April's showers were over; May's buds had opened into flower; and the June sun was shining on the pleasant fields, when John Dolittle at last got back to his own country.

But he did not yet go home to Puddleby. First he went traveling through the land with the Pushmi-Pullyu in a caravan, stopping at all the country fairs. And there, with the acrobats on one side of them and the Punch-and-Judy show on the other, they would hang out a big sign that read, COME AND SEE THE MARVELOUS TWO-HEADED ANIMAL FROM THE JUNGLES OF AFRICA. ADMISSION SIXPENCE.

And the Pushmi-Pullyu would stay inside the wagon, while the other animals would lie about underneath. The Doctor sat in a chair in front taking the sixpences and smiling on the people as they went in; and Dab-Dab was kept busy all the time scolding him because he would let the children in for nothing when she wasn't looking.

And menagerie-keepers and circus men came and asked the Doctor to sell them the strange creature, saying they would pay a tremendous lot of money for him. But the Doctor always shook his head and said:

"No. The Pushmi-Pullyu shall never be shut up in a cage. He shall be free always to come and go, like you and me."

Many curious sights and happenings they saw in this wandering

"The Doctor sat in a chair in front."

life; but they all seemed quite ordinary after the great things they had seen and done in foreign lands. It was very interesting at first, being sort of part of a circus; but after a few weeks they all got dreadfully tired of it and the Doctor and all of them were longing to go home.

But so many people came flocking to the little wagon and paid the sixpence to go inside and see the Pushmi-Pullyu that very soon the Doctor was able to give up being a showman.

And one fine day, when the hollyhocks were in full bloom, he came back to Puddleby a rich man, to live in the little house with the big garden.

And the old lame horse in the stable was glad to see him; and so were the swallows who had already built their nests under the eaves of his roof and had young ones. And Dab-Dab was glad, too, to get back to the house she knew so well—although there was a terrible lot of dusting to be done, with cobwebs everywhere.

And after Jip had gone and shown his golden collar to the conceited collie next door, he came back and began running round the garden like a crazy thing, looking for the bones he had buried long ago, and chasing the rats out of the toolshed; while Gub-Gub dug up the horseradishes, which had grown three feet high in the corner by the garden wall.

The Doctor went and saw the sailor who had lent him the boat, and he bought two new ships for him and a rubber doll for his baby; and he paid the grocer for the food he had lent him for the journey to Africa. Then he bought another piano and put the white mice back in it—because they said the bureau drawer was drafty.

"He began running around the garden like a crazy thing."

Even when the Doctor had filled the old money box on the dresser shelf, he still had a lot of money left; and he had to get three more money boxes, just as big, to put the rest in.

"Money," he said, "is a terrible nuisance. But it's nice not to have to worry."

"Yes," said Dab-Dab, who was toasting muffins for his tea, "it is indeed!"

And when the winter came again and the snow flew against the kitchen window, the Doctor and his animals would sit round the big, warm fire after supper, and he would read aloud to them out of his books.

But far away in Africa, where the monkeys chattered in the palm trees before they went to bed under the big yellow moon, they would say to one another:

"I wonder what the Good Man's doing now—over there, in England! Do you think he ever will come back?"

And Polynesia would squeak out from the vines:

"I think he will—I guess he will—I hope he will!"

And then the crocodile would grunt up at them from the black mud of the river:

"I'm SURE he will. Go to sleep!"

The End

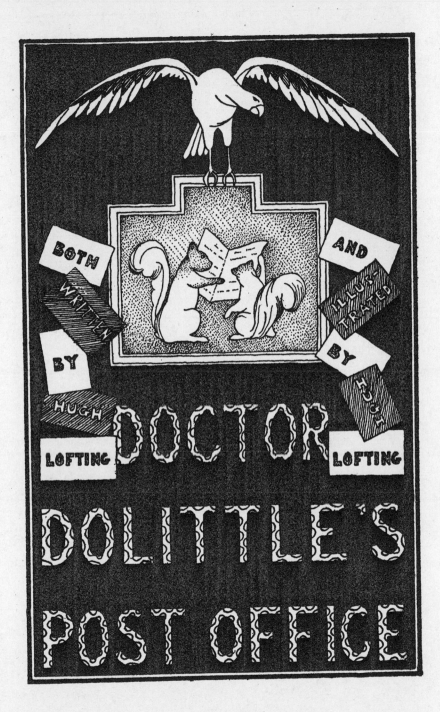

BOTH WRITTEN BY HUGH LOFTING

AND ILLUSTRATED BY HUGH LOFTING

DOCTOR DOLITTLE'S POST OFFICE

Contents

PROLOGUE

NEARLY ALL OF THE HISTORY OF DOCTOR Dolittle's Post Office took place when he was returning from a voyage to West Africa. Therefore I will begin (as soon as I have told you a little about how he came to take the journey) from where he turned his ship toward home again and set sail for Puddleby-on-the-Marsh.

Sometime before this the Pushmi-Pullyu, after a long stay in England, had grown a little homesick for Africa. And although he was tremendously fond of the Doctor and never wanted to leave him altogether, he asked him one winter day when the weather was particularly cold and disagreeable if he would mind running down to Africa for a holiday—just for a week or two.

The Doctor readily agreed because he hadn't been on a voyage in a long while and he felt he too needed a change from the chilly December days of England.

So he started off. Besides the Pushmi-Pullyu, he took Dab-Dab the duck, Jip the dog, Gub-Gub the pig, Too-Too the owl, and the white mouse—the same good company he had had with him on his adventurous return from the land of the monkeys. For this trip the Doctor bought a little sailing boat—very old and battered and worn, but a good sound craft for bad weather.

They sailed away down to the south coast of the Bight of Benin. There they visited many African kingdoms. And while they were ashore, the Pushmi-Pullyu had a chance to wander freely through his old grazing grounds. And he enjoyed his holiday thoroughly.

One morning the Doctor was delighted to see his old friends the swallows gathering once more about his ship at anchor for their yearly flight to England. They asked him whether he too was returning; because if so, they said, they would accompany him, the same as they had done when he was escaping from the kingdom of Jolliginki.

As the Pushmi-Pullyu was now quite ready to leave, the Doctor thanked the swallows and told them he would be delighted to have their company. Then for the remainder of that day all was hustle and hurry and bustle, getting the ship provisioned and making preparations for the long trip back to England.

By the following morning everything was in readiness to put to sea. The anchor was drawn up and with all sail set, the Doctor's ship moved northward before a favorable wind. And it is from this point that my story begins.

PART ONE

THE FIRST CHAPTER

Zuzana

ONE MORNING IN THE FIRST WEEK OF THE return voyage, when John Dolittle and his animals were all sitting at breakfast round the big table in the cabin, one of the swallows came down and said that he wanted to speak to the Doctor.

John Dolittle at once left the table and went out into the passage where he found the swallow leader himself, a very neat, trim little bird with long, long wings and sharp, snappy, black eyes. Speedy-the-Skimmer he was called—a name truly famous throughout the whole of the feathered world. He was the champion flycatcher and aerial acrobat of Europe, Africa, Asia, and America. For years every summer he had won all the flying races, having broken his own record only last year by crossing the Atlantic in eleven and a half hours—at a speed of over two hundred miles an hour.

"Well, Speedy," said John Dolittle. "What is it?"

"Doctor," said the little bird in a mysterious whisper, "we

have sighted a canoe about a mile ahead of the ship and a little to the east, with only a woman in it. She is weeping bitterly and isn't paddling the canoe at all. She is several miles from land—ten, at least, I should say—because at the moment we are crossing the Bay of Fantippo and can only just see the shore of Africa. She is really in dangerous straits, with such a little bit of a boat that far out at sea. But she doesn't seem to care. She's just sitting in the bottom of the canoe, crying as if she doesn't mind what happens to her. I wish you would come and speak to her, for we fear she is in great trouble."

"All right," said the Doctor. "Fly slowly on to where the canoe is and I will steer the ship to follow you."

So John Dolittle went up on deck and by steering the boat after the guiding swallows, he presently saw a small, dark canoe rising and falling on the waves. It looked so tiny on the wide face of the waters that it could be taken for a log or a stick—or, indeed, missed altogether, unless you were close enough to see it. In the canoe sat a woman with her head bowed down upon her knees.

"What's the matter?" shouted the Doctor, as soon as he was near enough to make the woman hear. "Why have you come so far from the land? Don't you know that you are in great danger if a storm should come up?"

Slowly the woman raised her head.

"Go away," said she, "and leave me to my sorrow. Haven't I suffered enough harm?"

John Dolittle steered the boat up closer still and continued to talk to the woman in a kindly way. But she seemed for a long time to mistrust him. Little by little, however, the Doctor won her confidence, and at last, still weeping bitterly, she told him her story.

Her name was Zuzana, and she belonged to a tribe that had been at war. In this war, her husband had been captured and then sold into slavery.

Zuzana described to the Doctor how she had followed the slave ship a long way out in a canoe, imploring them to give her back her husband. But they had only laughed at her and gone on their way. And their ship had soon passed out of sight.

The Doctor was dreadfully angry when he heard the story. And he asked Zuzana how long ago it was that the slaver's ship bearing her husband had left.

She told him it was half an hour ago. Without her husband, she said, life meant nothing to her, and when the ship had passed from view, going northward along the coast, she had burst into tears and just let the canoe drift, not even having the heart to paddle back to land.

The Doctor told the woman that no matter what it cost, he was going to help her. And he was all for speeding up his ship and going in chase of the slave boat right away. But Dab-Dab the duck warned him that his boat was very slow and that its sails could be easily seen by the slavers, who would never allow it to come near them.

So the Doctor put down his anchor and, leaving the ship where it was, got into the woman's canoe. Then, calling to the swallows to help him as guides, he set off northward along the coast, looking into all the bays and behind all the islands for the slave ship that had taken Zuzana's husband.

But after many hours of fruitless search, night began to come on and the swallows who were acting as guides could no longer see big distances, for there was no moon.

Poor Zuzana began weeping some more when the Doctor said he would have to give up for the night.

"By morning," said she, "the ship of the wicked slave dealers will be many miles away and I shall never get my husband back. Alas! Alas!"

Some of the swallows were still with the Doctor, sitting on the edge of the canoe. And the famous Skimmer, the leader, was also there. They and the Doctor were talking over what they could do, when suddenly the Skimmer said, "Sh! Look!" and pointed out to the west over the dark, heaving sea.

Even Zuzana stopped her wailing and turned to look. And there, way out on the dim, black edge of the ocean, they could see a tiny light.

"A ship!" cried the Doctor.

"Yes," said Speedy, "that's a ship, sure enough. I wonder if it's another slave ship."

"Well, if it's a slave ship, it's not the one we're looking for," said the Doctor, "because it's in the wrong direction. The one we're after went north."

"Listen, Doctor," said Speedy-the-Skimmer, "suppose I fly over to it and see what kind of a ship it is and come back and tell you. Who knows? It might be able to help us."

"All right, Speedy. Thank you," said the Doctor.

So the Skimmer sped off into the darkness toward the tiny light far out to sea, while the Doctor fell to wondering how his own ship was getting on, which he had left at anchor some miles down the coast to the south.

After twenty minutes had gone by, John Dolittle began to get worried, because the Skimmer, with his tremendous speed, should have had time to get there and back long ago.

But soon with a flirt of the wings the famous leader made a neat circle in the darkness overhead and dropped, light as a feather, onto the Doctor's knee.

"Well," said John Dolittle, "what kind of a ship was it?"

"It's a big ship," panted the Skimmer, "with tall, high masts and, I should judge, a fast one. But it is coming this way and it is sailing with great care, afraid, I imagine, of shallows and sandbars. It is a very neat ship, smart and new-looking all over. And there are great big guns—cannons—looking out of little doors in her sides. The men on her are all well dressed in smart blue clothes—not like ordinary seamen at all. And on the ship's hull was painted some lettering—her name, I suppose. Of course, I couldn't read it. But I remember what it looked like. Give me your hand and I'll show you."

Then the Skimmer, with one of his claws, began tracing out some letters on the Doctor's palm. Before he had gotten very far, John Dolittle sprang up, nearly overturning the canoe.

"H.M.S.!" he cried. "That means Her Majesty's Ship. It's a man-o'-war—a navy vessel. The very thing we want to deal with slave traders!"

The Doctor's Reception
on the Warship

THEN THE DOCTOR AND ZUZANA STARTED TO
paddle their canoe for all they were worth in the direction of the light. The night was calm, but the long swell
of the ocean swung the little canoe up and down like a
seesaw, and it took all Zuzana's skill to keep it in a straight line.

After about an hour had gone by, the Doctor noticed that the
ship they were trying to reach was no longer coming toward them,
but seemed to have stopped. And when he finally came up beneath
its towering shape in the darkness, he saw the reason why—the man-
o'-war had run into his own ship, which he had left at anchor with no
lights. However, the navy vessel had fortunately been going so carefully that no serious damage, it seemed, had been done to either ship.

Finding a rope ladder hanging on the side of the man-o'-war,
John Dolittle climbed up it, with Zuzana, and went aboard to see
the captain.

He found the captain strutting the quarterdeck, mumbling to
himself.

"Good evening," said the Doctor politely. "Nice weather we're having."

The Captain came up to him and shook his fist in his face.

"Are you the owner of that Noah's ark down there?" he stormed, pointing to the other ship alongside.

"Er—yes—temporarily," said the Doctor. "Why?"

"Well, will you be so good," snarled the captain, his face all out of shape with rage, "as to tell me what in thunder you mean by leaving your old junk at anchor on a dark night without any lights? What kind of a sailor are you? Here I bring Her Majesty's latest cruiser after Jimmie Bones, the slave trader—been hunting him for weeks, I have—and, as though the beastly coast wasn't difficult enough as it is, I bump into a craft riding at anchor with no lights. Luckily, I was going slow, taking soundings, or we might have gone down with all hands. I hallooed to your ship and got no answer. So I go aboard her, with pistols ready, thinking maybe she's a slaver, trying to play tricks on me. I creep all over the ship, but not a soul do I meet. At last in the cabin I find a pig—*asleep in an armchair!* Do you usually leave your craft in the charge of a pig, with orders to go to sleep? If you own the ship, why aren't you on her? Where have you been?"

"I was out canoeing with a lady," said the Doctor, and he smiled comfortingly at Zuzana, who was beginning to weep again.

"*Canoeing with a lady!*" spluttered the captain. "Well, I'll be—"

"Yes," said the Doctor. "Let me introduce you. This is Zuzana, Captain—er—"

But the captain interrupted him by calling for a sailor, who stood near.

"I'll teach you to leave Noah's ark at anchor on the high seas

"Where have you been?"

for the navy to bump into, my fine deep-sea philanderer! Think the shipping laws are made for a joke? Here," he turned to the sailor, who had come in answer to his call, "Master-at-Arms, put this man under arrest."

"Aye-aye, sir," said the master-at-arms. And before the Doctor knew it, he had handcuffs fastened firmly on his wrists.

"But this lady was in distress," said the Doctor. "I was in such a hurry I forgot all about lighting the ship. In fact, it wasn't dark yet when I left."

"Take him below!" roared the captain. "Take him below before I kill him."

And the poor Doctor was dragged away by the master-at-arms toward a stair leading to the lower decks. But at the head of the stairs he caught hold of the handrail and hung on long enough to shout back to the captain:

"I could tell you where Jimmie Bones is, if I wanted to."

"What's that?" snorted the captain. "Here, bring him back! What was that you said?"

"I said," murmured the Doctor, getting his handkerchief out and blowing his nose with his handcuffed hands, "that I could tell you where Jimmie Bones is—if I wanted to."

"Where is he?" cried the captain.

"My memory doesn't work very well while my hands are tied," said the Doctor quietly, nodding toward the handcuffs. "Possibly if you took these things off I might remember."

"Oh, excuse me," said the captain, his manner changing at once. "Master-at-Arms, release the prisoner."

"Aye-aye, sir," said the sailor, removing the handcuffs from the Doctor's wrists and turning to go.

"Oh, and by the way," the captain called after him, "bring a chair up on deck. Perhaps our visitor is tired."

Then John Dolittle told the captain the whole story of Zuzana and her troubles. And all the other officers on the ship gathered around to listen.

"And I have no doubt," the Doctor ended, "that this slaver who took away the woman's husband was no other than Jimmie Bones, the man you are after."

"Quite so," said the captain. "I know he is somewhere around the coast. But where is he now? He's a difficult fish to catch."

"He has gone northward," said the Doctor. "But your ship is

fast and should be able to overtake him. If he hides in some of these bays and creeks, I have several birds here with me who can, as soon as it is light, seek him out for us and tell us where he is."

The Captain looked with astonishment into the faces of his listening officers, who all smiled unbelievingly.

"What do you mean—birds?" the captain asked. "Pigeons—trained canaries, or something?"

"No," said the Doctor, "I mean the swallows who are going back to England for the summer. They very kindly offered to guide my ship home. They're friends of mine, you see."

This time the officers all burst out laughing and tapped their foreheads knowingly, to show they thought the Doctor was crazy. And the captain, thinking he was being made a fool of, flew into a rage once more and was all for having the Doctor arrested again.

But the officer who was second in command whispered in the captain's ear:

"Why not take the old fellow along and let him try, sir? Our course was northward, anyway. I seem to remember hearing something, when I was attached to the Home Fleet, about an old chap in the west counties who had some strange powers with beasts and birds. I have no doubt this is he. Dolittle, he was called. He seems harmless enough. There's just a chance he may be of some assistance to us. The natives evidently trust him or the woman wouldn't have come with him."

After a moment's thought the captain turned to the Doctor again.

"You sound clean crazy to me, my good man. But if you can put me in the way of capturing Jimmie Bones the slaver, I don't care what means you use to do it. As soon as the day breaks we will get underway. But if you are just amusing yourself at the expense of Her Majesty's Navy I warn you it will be the worst day's work for yourself you ever did. Now go and put riding lights on that ark of yours and tell the pig that if he lets them go out he shall be made into rashers of bacon for the officers' mess."

There was much laughter and joking as the Doctor climbed over the side and went back to his own ship to get his lights lit. But the next morning when he came back to the man-o'-war—and about a thousand swallows came with him—the officers of Her Majesty's Navy were not nearly so inclined to make fun of him.

The sun was just rising over the distant coast of Africa and it was as beautiful a morning as you could wish to see.

Speedy-the-Skimmer had arranged plans with the Doctor overnight. And long before the great warship pulled up her anchor and swung around upon her course, the famous swallow leader was miles ahead, with a band of picked hunters, exploring up creeks and examining all the hollows of the coast where the slave trader might be hiding.

Speedy had agreed with the Doctor upon a sort of overhead telegraph system to be carried on by the swallows. And as soon as the millions of little birds had spread themselves out in a line along the coast, so that the sky was speckled with them as far as the eye could reach, they began passing messages, by whistling to one another, all the way from the scouts in front back to the Doctor on the warship, to give news of how the hunt was progressing.

And somewhere about noon word came through that Bones's slave ship had been sighted behind a long, high cape. Great care must be taken, the message said, because the slave ship was in all

"The birds spread themselves out along the coast"

readiness to sail at a moment's notice. The slavers had only stopped to get water and lookouts were posted to warn them to return at once, if necessary.

When the Doctor told this to the captain, the man-o'-war changed her course still closer inshore, to keep behind the cover of the long cape. All the sailors were warned to keep very quiet, so the navy ship could sneak up on the slaver unawares.

Now the captain, expecting the slavers to put up a fight, also gave orders to get the guns ready. And just as they were about to round the long cape, one of the silly gunners let a gun off by accident.

"*Boom!*" . . . The shot went rolling and echoing over the silent sea like angry thunder.

Instantly word came back over the swallows' telegraph line that the slavers were warned and were escaping. And, sure enough, when the warship rounded the cape at last, there was the slave ship putting out to sea, with all sail set and a good ten-mile start on the man-o'-war.

A Great Gunner

AND THEN BEGAN A MOST EXCITING SEA race. It was now two o'clock in the afternoon and there were not many hours of daylight left.

The Captain (after he had done swearing at the stupid gunner who had let off the gun by accident) realized that if he did not catch up to the slaver before dark came on, he would probably lose him altogether. For this Jim Bones was a very sly and clever rascal and he knew the West Coast of Africa (it is sometimes called to this day *The Slave Coast*) very well. After dark, by running without lights, he would easily find some nook or corner to hide in—or double back on his course and be miles away before morning came.

So the captain gave orders that all possible speed was to be made. These were the days when steam was first used on ships. But at the beginning it was only used together with the sails, to help the power of the wind. Of this vessel, HMS *Violet*, the captain was very proud. And he was most anxious that the *Violet* should have the honor of catching Bones the slaver, who for so long had been defying the navy by carrying on slave trade after it had been forbidden. So the *Violet's* steam engines were put to work their hardest. And thick, black smoke rolled out of her funnels and darkened the blue sea and smudged up her lovely white sails humming tight in the breeze.

Then the engine boy, also anxious that his ship should have the honor of capturing Bones, tied down the safety valve on the steam engine to make her go faster, and then went up on deck to see the show. And soon, of course, one of the *Violet's* brand-new boilers burst with a terrific bang and made an awful mess of the engine room.

But, being a full-rigged man-o'-war, the *Violet* was still a pretty speedy sailor. And on she went, furiously plowing the waves and slowly gaining on the slave ship.

However, the crafty Bones, with so big a start, was not easy to overtake. And soon the sun began to set and the captain frowned and stamped his feet. For with darkness he knew his enemy would be safe.

Down below among the crew, the man who had fired the gun by accident was having a terrible time. All his companions were setting on him and mobbing him for being such a duffer as to warn Bones—who would now almost certainly escape. The distance from the slaver was still too great to use the kind of guns they had in those days. But when the captain saw darkness creeping over the sea and his enemy escaping, he gave orders to man the guns anyway— although he hadn't the least hope that his shots would hit the slaver at that distance.

Now, Speedy-the-Skimmer, as soon as the race had begun, had come on to the warship to take a rest. And he happened to be talking to the Doctor when the order to man the guns came down from the captain. So the Doctor and Speedy went below to watch the guns being fired.

They found an air of quiet but great excitement there. Each gunner was leaning on his gun, aiming it, watching the enemy's ship in the distance, and waiting for the order to fire. The poor man who had been mobbed by his fellows was still almost in tears at his own stupid mistake.

Suddenly an officer shouted, *"Fire!"* And with a crash that shook the ship from stem to stern, eight big cannon balls went whistling out across the water.

But not one hit the slave ship. *Splash! Splash! Splash!* They fell harmlessly into the water.

"The light's too bad," grumbled the gunners. "Who could hit anything two miles away in this rotten light?"

Then Speedy whispered in the Doctor's ear, "Ask them to let me fire a gun. My sight is better than theirs for bad light."

But just at that moment the order came from the captain, *"Cease firing!"* And the men left their places.

As soon as their backs were turned, Speedy jumped on top of one of the guns and, straddling his short, white legs apart, he cast his beady little black eyes along the aiming sights. Then with his wings he signaled to the Doctor behind him to swing the gun this way and that, so as to aim it the way he wanted.

"Fire!" said Speedy. And the Doctor fired.

"What in thunder's this?" roared the captain from the quarterdeck as the shot rang out. "Didn't I give the order to cease firing?"

But the second in command plucked him by the sleeve and

"'Fire!' said Speedy."

pointed across the water. Speedy's cannonball had cut the slaver's mainmast clean in two and brought the sails down in a heap upon the deck!

"Holy smoke!" cried the captain. "We've hit him! Look, Bones is flying the signal of surrender!"

Then the captain, who a moment before was all for punishing the man who had fired without orders, wanted to know who it was that aimed that marvelous shot that brought the slaver to a standstill. And the Doctor was going to tell him it was Speedy. But the Skimmer whispered in his ear:

"Don't bother, Doctor. He would never believe you anyway. It was the gun of the man that made the mistake before that we used. Let him take the credit. They'll likely give him a medal, and then he'll feel better."

And now all was excitement aboard the *Violet* as they approached the slave boat lying crippled in the sea. Bones, with his crew of eleven other ruffians, was taken prisoner and put down in the cells of the warship. Then the Doctor, with Zuzana, some sailors, and an officer, went onto the slave ship. Entering the hold, they found the place packed with men with chains on them. And Zuzana immediately recognized her husband and wept all over him with joy.

The men were at once freed from their chains and brought onto the man-o'-war. Then the slave ship was taken in tow by the *Violet*. And that was the end of Mr. Bones's slave trading.

Then there was much rejoicing and hand-shaking and congratulation on board the warship. And a grand dinner was prepared for the rescued men on the main deck. But John Dolittle, Zuzana, and her husband were invited to the officers' mess, where their health was drunk in port wine, and speeches were made by the captain and the Doctor.

The next day, as soon as it was light, the warship went cruising down the coast again, putting the rescued men ashore in their own particular countries.

This took considerable time, and it was after noon before the Doctor, with Zuzana and her husband, were returned to John Dolittle's ship, who still had her lights faithfully burning in the middle of the day.

Then the captain shook hands with the Doctor and thanked him for the great assistance he had given Her Majesty's Navy. And he asked him for his address in England, because he said he was going to tell the government about him, and the queen would most likely want to make him a knight or give him a medal or something. But the Doctor said he would rather have a pound of tea instead. He hadn't tasted tea in several months, and the kind they had in the officers' mess was very good.

So the captain gave him five pounds of the best China tea and thanked him again in the name of the queen and the government.

Then the *Violet* swung her great bow around to the north once more and sailed away for England, while the bluejackets crowded the rail and sent three hearty cheers for the Doctor ringing across the sea.

"The bluejackets crowded to the rail."

And now Jip, Dab-Dab, Gub-Gub, Too-Too, and the rest of them gathered around John Dolittle and wanted to hear all about his adventures. And it was teatime before he had done telling them. So the Doctor asked Zuzana and her husband to take tea with him before they went ashore.

This they were glad to do. And the Doctor made the tea himself and it was very excellent. Over the tea Zuzana and her husband (whose name was Begwe) were conversing about the Fantippo post office.

"Did you send that letter to our cousin?" Begwe asked.

"Yes," said Zuzana. "But I don't think he ever got it. Because no answer came."

The Doctor asked Zuzana how she had sent the letter. And then she explained to him that Bones had offered to let her have Begwe back for a price. And he promised Zuzana that if she got the money in two days' time her husband should be a free man.

So Zuzana had written a letter, begging their cousin to send money to Bones without delay. Then she had taken the letter to the Fantippo post office and sent it off.

But the two days went by and no answer came—and no money. Then poor Begwe had been taken away.

The Royal Mails of Fantippo

NOW, THIS FANTIPPO POST OFFICE OF WHICH Zuzana had spoken to the Doctor was rather peculiar. For one thing, it was, of course, quite unusual to find a post office or regular mails of any kind in an African kingdom in those days. And the way such a thing had come about was this:

A few years before this voyage of the Doctor's there had been a great deal of talk in most parts of the world about mails and how much it should cost for a letter to go from one country to another. And in England a man called Rowland Hill had started what was called "The Penny Postage," and it had been agreed that a penny a letter should be the regular rate charge for mails from one part of the British Isles to another. Of course, for especially heavy letters you had to pay more. Then stamps were made, penny stamps, two-penny stamps, two pence-halfpenny stamps, sixpenny stamps, and shilling stamps. And each was a different color and they were beautifully engraved and most of them had a picture of the queen on them—some with her crown on her head and some without.

And France and the United States and all the other countries started doing the same thing—only their stamps were counted in their own money, of course, and had different kings or queens or presidents on them.

Very well, then. Now, it happened one day that a ship called at the coast of West Africa and delivered a letter for Koko, the king of Fantippo. King Koko had never seen a stamp before and, sending for a merchant who lived in his town, he asked him what queen's face was this on the stamp that the letter bore.

Then the merchant explained to him the whole idea of penny postage and government mails. And he told him that in England all you had to do when you wanted to send a letter to any part of the world was to put a stamp on the envelope with the queen's head on it and place it in a letter box on the street corner, and it would be carried to the place to which you addressed it.

"Aha!" said the king. "I understand. Very good. The High Kingdom of Fantippo shall have a post office of its own. And *my* serene and beautiful face shall be on all the stamps, and *my* letters shall travel faster than any of them."

Then King Koko of Fantippo, being a very vain man, had a fine lot of stamps made with his picture on them, some with his crown on and some without; some smiling, some frowning; some with himself on horseback, some with himself on a bicycle. But the stamp which he was most proud of was the tenpenny stamp that bore a picture of himself playing golf—a game that he had just recently learned from some Scotsmen who were mining for gold in his kingdom.

And he had letter boxes made, just the way the trader had told him they had in England, and he set them up at the corners of the streets and told his people that all they had to do was to put one of his stamps on their letters, poke them into these boxes, and the letters would travel to any corner of the earth they wished.

But presently the people began complaining that they had been robbed. They had paid good money for the stamps, they said, trusting them, and they had put their letters in the boxes at the corners of the streets as they had been told. But one day a cow had rubbed her neck against one of the letter boxes and burst it open, and inside there were all the people's letters, which had not traveled one inch from where they put them!

Then the king was very angry and, calling for the trader, he said:

"You have been fooling My Majesty. These stamps you speak of have no power at all. Explain!"

Then the trader told him that proper post offices had mailmen, or postmen, who collected the letters out of these boxes. And he went on to explain to the king all the other duties of a post office and the things that made letters go.

So then the king, who was a persevering man, said that Fantippo should have its post office anyway. And he sent to England for hundreds of postmen's uniforms and caps. And when these arrived, he dressed a lot of men up in them and set them to work as postmen.

Then when King Koko had his mailmen, the Royal Fantippo Post Office began really working. Letters were collected from the boxes at street corners and sent off when ships called; and incoming mail was delivered at the doors of the houses in Fantippo three times a day. The post office became the busiest place in town.

Some Fantippo dandy even started the idea of using up old stamps off letters by making suits of clothes out of them. They looked very showy and smart, and a suit of this kind made of stamps became a valuable possession among the residents.

About this time, too, one of the things that arose out of all this penny-postage business was the craze or hobby for collecting stamps. In England and America and other countries people began buying stamp albums and pasting stamps in them. A rare stamp became quite valuable.

And it happened that one day two men, whose hobby was collecting stamps, came to Fantippo on a ship. The one stamp they were both most anxious to get for their collections was the "twopenny-halfpenny Fantippo red," a stamp which the king had given up printing—for the reason that the picture of himself on it wasn't handsome enough. And because he had given up printing it, it became very rare.

As soon as these two men stepped ashore at Fantippo a porter came up to them to carry their bags. And right in the middle of the porter's chest the collectors spied the twopenny-halfpenny Fantippo red! Then both of the stamp collectors offered to buy the stamp. And as each was anxious to have it for his collection, before long they were offering high prices for it, bidding against each other.

King Koko got to hear of this and he called up one of these stamp collectors and asked him why men should offer high prices for one old, used stamp. And the man explained to him this new craze for stamp collecting that was sweeping over the world.

So King Koko, although he thought that the rest of the world must be crazy, decided it would be a good idea if *he* sold stamps for collections—a much better business than selling them at his post office for letters. And after that, whenever a ship came into the harbor of Fantippo he sent his postmaster general out to the ship with stamps to sell for collections.

Such a roaring trade was done this way that the king set the stamp-printing presses to work more busily than ever, so that a whole new set of Fantippo stamps should be ready for sale by the time the same ship called again on her way home to England.

But with this new trade in selling stamps for stamp collections, and not for proper mailing purposes, the Fantippo mail service was neglected and became very bad.

Now, Doctor Dolittle, while Zuzana was talking over the tea about her letter which she had sent to her cousin—and to which no answer had ever come—suddenly remembered something. On one of his earlier voyages the passenger ship by which he had been traveling had stopped outside this same harbor of Fantippo, although no passengers had gone ashore. And a postman had come aboard to sell a most elegant lot of new green and violet stamps. The Doctor, being at the time a great stamp collector, had bought three whole sets.

And he realized now, as he listed to Zuzana, what was wrong with the Fantippo post office and why she had never gotten an answer to the letter that would have saved her husband from slavery.

As Zuzana and Begwe rose to go, for it was beginning to get dark, the Doctor noticed a canoe setting out toward his ship from the shore. And in it, when it got near, he saw King Koko himself, coming to the boat with stamps to sell.

So the Doctor got talking to the king, and he told him in plain language that he ought to be ashamed of his post office. Then, giving him a cup of China tea, he explained to him how Zuzana's letter had probably never been delivered to her cousin.

The king listened attentively and understood how his post office had been at fault. And he invited the Doctor to come ashore with Zuzana and Begwe and arrange the post office for him and put it in order so it would work properly.

THE FIFTH CHAPTER

The Voyage Delayed

AFTER SOME PERSUASION THE DOCTOR consented to this proposal, feeling that perhaps he could do some good. Little did he realize what great labors and strange adventures he was taking upon himself as he got into the canoe with the King, Begwe, and Zuzana to be paddled to the town of Fantippo.

This place he found very different from any of the African villages or settlements he had ever visited. It was quite large, almost a city. It was bright and cheerful to look at, and the people, like their king, all seemed very kind and jolly.

The Doctor was introduced to all the chief men of the Fantippo nation and later was taken to see the post office.

This he found in a terrible state. There were letters everywhere—on the floors, in old drawers, stacked on desks, even lying on the pavement outside the post office door. The Doctor explained to the king that this would never do, that in properly run post offices, the letters that had stamps on them were treated with respect and care. It was no wonder, he said, that Zuzana's letter had never been delivered to her cousin if this was the way they took care of the mails.

Then King Koko again begged him to take charge of the post office and try to get it running in proper order. And the Doctor said he would see what he could do. And, going into the post office, he took off his coat and set to work.

But after many hours of terrific labor, trying to get letters sorted and the place in order, John Dolittle saw that such a tremendous job as setting the Fantippo post office to rights would not be a matter of a day or two. It would take weeks, at least. So he told this to the king. Then the Doctor's ship was brought into the harbor and put safely at anchor and the animals were all taken ashore. And a nice, new house on the main street was given over to the Doctor for himself and his pets to live in while the work of straightening out the Fantippo mails was going on.

Well, after ten days, John Dolittle got what is called the *Domestic Mails* in pretty good shape. Domestic mails are those that carry letters from one part of a country to another part of the same country, or from one part of a city to another. The mails that carry letters outside the country to foreign lands are called *Foreign Mails*. To have a regular and good service of foreign mails in the Fantippo post office, the Doctor found a hard problem, because the mail ships which could carry letters abroad did not come very often to this port. Fantippo, although King Koko was most proud of it, was not considered a very important country among nations, and two or three ships a year were all that ever called there.

Now, one day, very early in the morning, when the Doctor was lying in bed, wondering what he could do about the Foreign Mail

Service, Dab-Dab and Jip brought him in his breakfast on a tray and told him there was a swallow outside who wanted to give him a message from Speedy-the-Skimmer. John Dolittle had the swallow brought in and the little bird sat on the foot of his bed while he ate his breakfast.

"Good morning," said the Doctor, cracking open the top of a hard-boiled egg. "What can I do for you?"

"Speedy would like to know," said the swallow, "how long you expect to stay in this country. He doesn't want to complain, you understand—nor do any of us—but this journey of yours is taking longer than we thought it would. You see, there was the delay while we hunted out Bones the slaver, and now it seems likely you will be

"Good morning! What can I do for you?"

busy with this post office for some weeks yet. Ordinarily we would have been in England long before this, getting the nests ready for the new season's families. We cannot put off the nesting season, you know. Of course, you understand we are not complaining, don't you? But this delay is making things rather awkward for us."

"Oh, quite, quite. I understand perfectly," said the Doctor, poking salt into his egg with a bone egg spoon. "I am dreadfully sorry. But why didn't Speedy bring the message himself?"

"I suppose he didn't want to," said the swallow. "Thought you'd be offended, perhaps."

"Oh, not in the least," said the Doctor. "You birds have been most helpful to me. Tell Speedy I'll come to see him as soon as I've got my trousers on and we'll talk it over. Something can be arranged, I have no doubt."

"Very good, Doctor," said the swallow, turning to go. "I'll tell the Skimmer what you said."

"By the way," said John Dolittle, "I've been trying to think where I've seen your face before. Did you ever build your nest in my stable in Puddleby?"

"No," said the bird. "But I am the swallow that brought you the message from the monkeys that time they were sick."

"Oh, to be sure—of course," cried the Doctor. "I knew I had seen you somewhere. I never forget faces. You had a pretty hard time coming to England in the winter, didn't you—snow on the ground and all that sort of thing. Very plucky of you to undertake it."

"Yes, it was a hard trip," said the swallow. "I came near freezing to death more than once. Flying into the teeth of that frosty wind was just awful. But something had to be done. The monkeys would most likely have been wiped right out if we hadn't got you."

"How was it that you were the one chosen to bring the message?" asked the Doctor.

"Well," said the swallow, "Speedy did want to do it himself. He's frightfully brave, you know—and fast as lightning. But the other swallows wouldn't let him. They said he was too valuable as a leader. It was a risky job. And if he had lost his life from the frost we'd never be able to get another leader like him. Because, besides being brave and fast, he's the cleverest leader we ever had. Whenever the swallows are in trouble he always thinks of a way out. He's a born leader. He flies quick and he thinks quick."

"Humph!" murmured the Doctor, as he thoughtfully brushed the toast crumbs off the bedclothes. "But why did they pick you to bring the message?"

"They didn't," said the swallow. "We nearly all of us volunteered for the job, so as not to have Speedy risk his life. But the Skimmer said the only fair way was to draw lots. So we got a number of small leaves and we took the stalks off all of them except one. And we put the leaves in an old coconut shell and shook them up. Then, with our eyes shut, we began picking them out. The swallow who picked the leaf with the stalk on it was to carry the message to England—and I picked the leaf with the stalk on. Before I started off on the trip I kissed my wife good-bye, because I really never expected to get back alive. Still, I'm kind of glad the lot fell to me."

"Why?" asked the Doctor, pushing the breakfast tray off his knees and punching the pillows into shape.

"Well, you see," said the swallow, lifting his right leg and showing a tiny red ribbon made of corn silk tied about his ankle, "I got this for it."

"What's that?" asked the Doctor.

"That's to show I've done something brave—and special," said the swallow modestly.

"Oh, I see," said the Doctor. "Like a medal, eh?"

"Yes. My name is Quip. It used to be just plain Quip. Now I'm called *Quip the Carrier*," said the small bird, proudly gazing down at his little, stubby white leg.

"Splendid, Quip," said the Doctor. "I congratulate you. Now, I must be getting up. I've a frightful lot of work to do. Don't forget to tell Speedy I'll meet him on the ship at ten. Good-bye! Oh, and would you mind asking Dab-Dab, as you go out, to clear away

HUGH LOFTING

"They found the Doctor shaving."

the breakfast things? I'm glad you came. You've given me an idea. Good-bye!"

And when Dab-Dab and Jip came to take away the tray, they found the Doctor shaving. He was peering into a looking glass, holding the end of his nose and muttering to himself:

"*That's* the idea for the Fantippo Foreign Mail Service—I wonder why I never thought of it before. I'll have the fastest overseas mail the world ever saw. Why, of course! That's the idea—*The Swallow Mail!*"

No Man's Land

A S SOON AS HE WAS DRESSED AND SHAVED, the Doctor went down to his ship and met the Skimmer.

"I am terribly sorry, Speedy," said he, "to hear what a lot of trouble I have been giving you birds by my delay here. But I really feel that the business of the post office ought to be attended to, you know. It's in a shocking state—honestly, it is."

"I know," said Speedy. "And if we could, we would have nested right here in this country to oblige you and not bothered about going to England this year. It wouldn't have mattered terribly much to miss one summer in the north. But, you see, we swallows can't nest very well in trees. We like houses and barns and buildings to nest in."

"Couldn't you use the houses of Fantippo?" asked the Doctor.

"Not very well," said Speedy. "They're so small and noisy—with the children playing around them all day. The eggs and young ones wouldn't be safe for a minute. And then they're not built right for us—mostly made of grass, the roofs sloping wrong, the eaves too near the ground, and all that. What we like are solid English buildings, where the people don't shriek and whoop and play drums all day—quiet buildings, like old barns and stables, where, if people come at all, they come in a proper, dignified manner, arriving and leaving at regular hours. We like people, you understand—in their right place. But nesting mother birds must have quiet."

"Humph! I see," said the Doctor. "Of course, myself, I rather enjoy the jolliness of these Fantippos. But I can quite see your point. By the way, how would my old ship do? This ought to be quiet enough for you here. There's nobody living on it now. And look, it has heaps of cracks and holes and corners in it where you could build your nests. What do you think?"

"That would be splendid," said Speedy, "if you think you won't be needing the boat for some weeks. Of course, it would never do if, after we had the nests built and the eggs laid, you were to pull up the anchor and sail away—the young ones would get seasick."

"No, of course not," said the Doctor. "But there will be no fear of my leaving for some time yet. You could have the whole ship to yourselves and nobody will disturb you."

"All right," said Speedy. "Then I'll tell the swallows to get on with the nest building right away. But, of course, we'll go on to England with you when you are ready, to show you the way—and also to teach the young birds how to get there too. You see, each year's new birds make their first trip back from England to Africa with us grown ones. They have to make the first journey under our guidance."

"Very good," said the Doctor. "Then that settles that. Now I must get back to the post office. The ship is yours. But as soon as the nesting is over come and let me know, because I have a very special idea I want to tell you about."

So the Doctor's boat was now turned into a nesting ship for the swallows. Calmly she stood at anchor in the quiet waters of Fantippo harbor, while thousands and thousands of swallows built their nests in her rigging, in her ventilators, in her portholes, and in every crack and corner of her.

No one went near the ship and the swallows had her to themselves. And they agreed afterward that they found her the best place for nesting they had ever used.

HUGH LOFTING

"Thousands of swallows built their nests in her rigging."

In a very short time the ship presented a curious and extraordinary sight, with the mud nests stuck all over her and birds flying in thousands round her masts, coming and going, building homes and feeding young ones.

And the farmers in England that year said the coming winter would be a hard one because the swallows had done their nesting abroad before they arrived and only spent a few weeks of the autumn in the north.

And later, after the nesting was all over, there were more than twice as many birds as there were before, of course. And you simply couldn't get onto the ship for the tons and tons of mud on her.

But the parent birds, as soon as the young ones were able to fly, set their children to work clearing up the mess. And all that mud was taken off and dropped into the harbor, piece by piece. And the Doctor's ship was left in a cleaner state than it had ever been before in its whole life.

Now, it happened one day that the Doctor came to the post office, as usual, at nine o'clock in the morning. (He had to get there at that time, because if he didn't, the postmen didn't start working.) And outside the post office he found Jip, gnawing a bone on the pavement. Something curious about the bone struck the Doctor, who was, of course, being a naturalist, quite a specialist in bones. He asked Jip to let him look at it.

"Why, this is extraordinary!" said the Doctor, examining the bone with great care. "I did not know that this class of animals were still to be found in Africa. Where did you get this bone, Jip?"

"Over in No Man's Land," said Jip. "There are lots of bones there."

"And where might No Man's Land be?" said John Dolittle.

"No Man's Land is that round island just outside the harbor," said Jip. "You know, the one that looks like a plum pudding."

"Oh yes," said the Doctor. "I know the island you mean. It's only a short distance from the mainland. But I hadn't heard that that was the name of it. Humph! If you'll lend me this bone awhile, Jip, I think I'll go to see the king about it."

So, taking the bone, John Dolittle went off to call on King Koko, and Jip asked if he might come along. They found the king sitting at the palace door, sucking a lollipop—for he, like all the Fantippos, was very fond of sweets.

"Good morning, Your Majesty," said the Doctor. "Do you happen to know what kind of animal this bone belongs to?"

The king examined it, then shook his head. He didn't know much about bones.

"Maybe it's a cow's bone," said he.

"Oh, certainly not," said John Dolittle. "No cow ever had a bone like that. That's a jaw—but not a cow's jaw. Listen, Your Majesty, would you mind lending me a canoe and some paddlers? I want to go over to visit No Man's Land."

To the Doctor's astonishment the king choked on his lollipop and nearly fell over his chair backward. Then he ran inside the palace and shut the door.

"How extraordinary!" said John Dolittle, entirely bewildered. "What ails the man?"

"Oh, it's some humbug or other," growled Jip. "Let's go down to the harbor, Doctor, and try to hire a canoe to take us."

So they went down to the water's edge and asked several of the canoesmen to take them over to No Man's Land. But everyone they asked got dreadfully frightened and refused to talk when the Doctor told them where he wanted to go. They wouldn't even let him borrow their canoes to go there by himself.

At last they found one very old boatman who loved chatting so much that, although he got terribly scared when John Dolittle mentioned No Man's Land, he finally told the Doctor the reason for all this extraordinary behavior.

"That island," said he, "we don't even mention its name unless we have to—is the land of evil. It is called"—the old man whispered it so low the Doctor could scarcely hear him—"No Man's Land, because no man lives there. No man ever even goes there."

"But why?" asked the Doctor.

"*Dragons live there!*" said the old boatman, his eyes wide and staring. "Enormous horned dragons that spit fire and eat men. If you value your life, never go near that dreadful island."

"But how do you know all this," asked the Doctor, "if nobody has ever been there to see if it's true or not?"

"A thousand years ago," said the old man, "when King Kakaboochi ruled over this land, he put his mother-in-law upon that island to live, because she talked too much and he couldn't bear her around the palace. It was arranged that food should be taken to her every week. But the first week that the men went there in canoes they could find no trace of her. While they were seeking her about the island, a dragon suddenly roared out from the bushes and attacked them. They only just escaped with their lives and got back to Fantippo and told King Kakaboochi. A famous wizard was consulted, and he said it must have been the king's mother-in-law herself who had been changed into a dragon by some spell. Since then she has had many children and the island is peopled with dragons—whose *food is men*! For whenever a canoe approaches, the dragons come down to the shores, breathing flame and destruction. But for many hundreds of years now no man has set foot upon it. That is why it is called—well, you know."

After he had told this story, the old man turned away and busied himself with his canoe, as though he were afraid that the Doctor might again ask him to paddle him to the island.

"Look here, Jip," said John Dolittle, "you said you got this bone from No Man's Land. Did you see any dragons there?"

"No," said Jip. "I swam out there—just to get cool. It was a hot day yesterday. And then I didn't go far inland on the island. I found many bones on the beach. And as this one smelled good to me, I picked it up and swam back here with it. I was more interested in the bone and the swim than I was in the island, to tell you the truth."

"It's most extraordinary," murmured the Doctor, "this legend about the island. It makes me more anxious than ever to go there. That bone interests me, too, immensely. I've seen only one other like it—and that was in a natural history museum. Do you mind if I keep it, Jip? I'd like to put it in my own museum when I get back to Puddleby."

"Not at all," said Jip. "Look here, Doctor, if we can't raise a canoe, let's you and I swim out to the island. It's not over a mile and a half and we're both good swimmers."

"That's not a bad idea, Jip," said the Doctor. "We'll go down the shore a way till we're opposite the island, then we won't have so far to swim."

So off they went. And when they had come to the best place on the shore, the Doctor took off his clothes and, tying them up in a bundle, he fastened them on his head, with the precious high hat on the top of all. Then he waded into the surf and, with Jip beside him, started swimming for the island.

Now this particular stretch of water they were trying to cross happened to be a bad place for swimming. And after about a quarter of an hour Jip and the Doctor felt themselves being carried out to sea in the grip of a powerful current. They tried their hardest to get to the island. But without any success.

"Let yourself drift, Doctor," panted Jip. "Don't waste your strength fighting the current. Let yourself drift. Even if we're carried past the island out to sea we can land on the mainland farther down the coast, where the current isn't so strong."

But the Doctor didn't answer. And Jip could see from his face that his strength and breath were nearly gone.

Then Jip barked his loudest, hoping that possibly Dab-Dab might hear him on the mainland and fly out and bring help. But of course they were much too far from the town for anyone to hear.

"Turn back, Jip," gasped the Doctor. "Don't bother about me. I'll be all right. Turn back and try and make the shore."

But Jip had no intention of turning back and leaving the Doctor to drown—though he saw no possible chance of rescue.

Presently John Dolittle's mouth filled with water and he began to splutter and gurgle, and Jip was really frightened. But just as the Doctor's eyes were closing and he seemed too weak to swim another stroke, a curious thing happened. Jip felt something come up under the water, right beneath his feet, and lift him and the Doctor slowly out of the sea, like the rising deck of a submarine. Up and up they were lifted, now entirely out of the water. And, gasping and sprawling side by side, they gazed at each other in utter astonishment.

"What is it, Doctor?" said Jip, staring down at the strange

"'Turn back, Jip,' gasped the Doctor."

thing, which had now stopped rising and was carrying them like a ship, right across the strong course of the current, in the direction of the island.

"I haven't the—hah—remotest—hah—idea," panted John Dolittle. "Can it be a whale? No, because the skin isn't a whale's. This is fur," he said, plucking at the stuff he was sitting on.

"Well, it's an animal of some kind, isn't it?" said Jip. "But where's its head?" and he gazed down the long sloping back that stretched in a flat curve in front of them for a good thirty yards.

"Its head is underwater," said the Doctor. "But there's its tail, look, behind us."

And turning around, Jip saw the longest tail that any mortal beast ever had, thrashing the water and driving them toward the island.

"I know!" cried Jip. "It's the dragon! This is King Kakaboochi's mother-in-law we're sitting on!"

"Well anyway, thank goodness she rose in time!" said the Doctor, shaking the water out of his ears. "I was never so near drowning in my life. I suppose I'd better make myself a little more presentable before she gets her head out of water."

And, taking down his clothes off his own head, the Doctor smartened up his high hat and dressed himself, while the strange thing that had saved their lives carried them steadily and firmly toward the mysterious island.

The Animals' Paradise

A T LENGTH THE EXTRAORDINARY CREATURE that had come to their rescue reached the island; and with Jip and the Doctor still clinging to his wide back, he crawled out of the water onto the beach.

And then John Dolittle, seeing its head for the first time, cried out in great excitement:

"Jip, it's a Quiffenodochus, as sure as I'm alive!"

"A Quiffeno-what-us?" asked Jip.

"A Quiffenodochus," said the Doctor, "a prehistoric beast. Naturalists thought they were extinct—that there weren't any more live ones anywhere in the world. This is a great day, Jip. I'm awfully glad I came here."

The tremendous animal, which the Fantippans had called a dragon, had now climbed right up the beach and was standing fully revealed in all his strangeness. At first he looked like some curious mixture between a crocodile and a giraffe. He had short, spreading legs, but enormously long tail and neck. On his head were two stubby little horns.

As soon as the Doctor and Jip had climbed down off his back, he swung his head around on the end of that enormous neck and said to the Doctor:

"Do you feel all right now?"

"Yes, thanks," said John Dolittle.

"I was afraid," said the creature, "that I wouldn't be in time to save your life. It was my brother who first saw you. We thought it was a local and we were getting ready to give him our usual terrifying reception. But while we watched from behind the trees my brother suddenly cried: 'Great heavens! That's Doctor Dolittle—and he's drowning. See, how he waves his arms! He must be saved at any cost. There isn't one man like that born in a thousand years! Let's go after him, quick!" Then word was passed around the island that John Dolittle, the great doctor, was drowning out in the straits. Of course we had all heard of you. And rushing down to a secret cove that we have on the far side of the island, we dashed into the sea and swam out to you underwater. I was the best swimmer and got to you first. I'm awfully glad I was in time. You're sure you feel all right?"

"Oh, quite," said the Doctor, "thank you. But why did you swim underwater?"

"We didn't want the locals to see us," said the strange beast. "They think we are dragons—and we let them go on thinking it. Because then they don't come near the island and we have our country to ourselves."

The creature stretched his long neck still longer and whispered in the Doctor's ear:

"They think we live on men and breathe fire! But all we ever really eat is bananas. And when anyone tries to come here, we go down to a hollow in the middle of the island and suck up the mist, the fog, that always hangs around there. Then we come back to the beach and roar and rampage. And we breathe the fog out through our nostrils and they think it's smoke. That's the way we've kept this island to ourselves for a thousand years. And this is the only part of the world where we are left—where we can live in peace."

"How very interesting!" said the Doctor. "Naturalists have thought your kind of animals are no longer living, you know. You are Quiffenodochi, are you not?"

"All we eat is bananas."

"Oh no," said the beast. "The Quiffenodochus has gone long ago. We are the Piffilosaurus. We have six toes on the back feet, while the Quiffenodochi, our cousins, have only five. They died out about two thousand years ago."

"But where are the rest of your people?" asked the Doctor. "I thought you said that many of you had swum out to rescue us."

"They did," said the Piffilosaurus. "But they kept hidden under the water, lest the people on the shore should see and get to know that the old story about the dragon's mother-in-law wasn't true. While I was bringing you here they were swimming all around you under the water, ready to help if I needed them. They have gone around to the secret cove so they may come ashore unseen. We had better be going on ourselves now. Whatever happens, we mustn't be seen from the shore and have the natives coming here. It would be the end of us if that should ever happen, because, between ourselves, although they think us so terrible, we are really more harmless than sheep."

"Do any other animals live here?" asked the Doctor.

"Oh yes, indeed," said the Piffilosaurus. "This island is entirely peopled by harmless, vegetable-feeding creatures. If we had the others, of course, we wouldn't last long. But come, I will show you around the island. Let us go quietly up that valley there, so we shan't be seen till we reach the cover of the woods."

Then John Dolittle and Jip were taken by the Piffilosaurus all over the island of No Man's Land.

The Doctor said afterward that he had never had a more enjoyable or more instructive day. The shores of the island all around were high and steep, which gave it the appearance Jim had spoken of—like a plum pudding. But in the center, on top, there was a deep and pleasant hollow, invisible from the sea and sheltered from the winds. In this great bowl, a good thirty miles across, the piffilosauruses had lived at peace for a thousand years, eating ripe bananas and frolicking in the sun.

Down by the banks of the streams the Doctor was shown great herds of hippopotami, feeding on the luscious reeds that grew at the water's edge. In the wide fields of high grass there were elephants and rhinoceri browsing. On the slopes where the forests were sparse he spied long-necked giraffes, nibbling from the trees. Monkeys and deer of all kinds were plentiful. And birds swarmed everywhere. In fact, every kind of creature that does not eat meat was there, living peaceably and happily with the others in this land where vegetable food abounded and the disturbing tread of man was never heard.

Standing on the top of the hill with Jip and the piffilosaurus at his side, the Doctor gazed down over the wide bowl full of contented animal life and heaved a sigh.

"This beautiful land could also have been called the 'Animals' Paradise,'" he murmured. "Long may they enjoy it to themselves! May this, indeed, be *No Man's Land* forever!"

"You, Doctor," said the deep voice of the piffilosaurus at his elbow, "are the first human in a thousand years that has set foot here. The last one was King Kakaboochi's mother-in-law."

"By the way, what really became of her?" asked the Doctor. "The natives believe she was turned into a dragon, you know."

"We married her off," said the great creature, nibbling idly at a lily stalk. "We couldn't stand her here, any more than the king could. You never heard anybody talk so much in all your life. Yes, we carried her one dark night by sea far down the coast of Africa and left her at the palace door of a deaf king, who ruled over a small country south of the Congo River. He married her. Of course, being deaf, he didn't mind her everlasting chatter in the least."

And now for several days the Doctor forgot all about his post office work and King Koko and his ship at anchor, and everything else. For he was kept busy from morning to night with all the animals who wanted to consult him about different things.

Many of the giraffes were suffering from sore hooves and he showed them where to find a special root that could be put into a foot bath and would bring immediate relief. The rhinoceroses' horns were growing too long and John Dolittle explained to them how by grinding them against a certain kind of stone and by eating less grass and more berries they could keep the growth down. A special sort of nut tree that the deer were fond of had grown scarce and almost died out from constant nibbling. And the Doctor showed the chief stags how, by taking a few nuts and poking them down into the soft earth with their hooves before the rainy season set in, they could make new trees grow and so increase the supply.

One day when he was pulling out a loose tooth for a baby hippopotamus with his watch chain, Speedy-the-Skimmer turned up, looking rather annoyed.

"Well," said the neat little bird, settling down on the ground at his feet, "I've found you at last, Doctor. I've been hunting all over creation for you."

"Oh hulloa, Speedy," said the Doctor. "Glad to see you. Did you want me for something?"

"Why, of course I did," said Speedy. "We finished the nest-

HUGH LOFTING

"He was pulling out a loose tooth."

ing season two days ago, and you had said you wanted to see
me about some special business as soon as it was over. I went
to your house, but Dab-Dab had no idea where you could be.
Then I hunted all over. At last I heard some gossiping boatmen
down at the harbor say that you came to this island five days
ago and had never returned. All the Fantippans have given you
up for lost. They say you have surely been eaten by the dragons
that live here. I got an awful fright—though, of course, I didn't
quite believe the dragon story. Still, you had been gone so long
I didn't know what to make of it. The post office, as you can
imagine, is in a worse mess than ever."

"Humph!" said the Doctor, who had now taken the loose tooth out and was showing the baby hippo how to rinse his mouth in the river. "I'm sorry. I suppose I should have sent you a message. But I've been so awfully busy. Let's go up under the shade of those palms and sit down. It was about the post office that I wanted to talk to you."

The Swiftest Mail in the World

S
O THE DOCTOR AND JIP AND SPEEDY-THE-Skimmer sat down in the shade of the palm trees and for the first time plans for that great service that was to be known as the Swallow Mail were discussed.

"Now, my idea, Speedy, is this," said the Doctor. "Regular foreign mails are difficult for the Fantippo post office because so few boats ever call there to bring or take the mails. Now, how would it be if you swallows did the letter carrying?"

"Well," said Speedy, "that would be possible. But, of course, we could only do it during certain months of the year when we were in Africa. And then we could only take letters to the mild and warm countries. We should get frozen if we had to carry mail where severe winters were going on."

"Oh, of course," said the Doctor. "I wouldn't expect you to do that. But I had thought we might get the other birds to help— cold-climate birds, hot-climate ones, and temperate. And if some of the trips were too far or disagreeable for one kind of birds to make,

"They sat down in the shade of a palm tree."

we could deliver the mail in relays. For instance, a letter going from here to the North Pole could be carried by the swallows as far as the north end of Africa. From there it would be taken by thrushes up to the top of Scotland. There, seagulls would take it from the thrushes and carry it as far as Greenland. And from there penguins would take it to the North Pole. What do you think?"

"I think it might be all right," said Speedy, "if we can get the other birds to go in with us on the idea."

"Well, you see," said John Dolittle, "I think we might, because we could use the mail service for the birds, and the animals, too, to send their letters by, as well as the Fantippans."

"But, Doctor, birds and animals don't send letters," said Speedy.

"No," said the Doctor. "But there's no reason why they shouldn't begin. Neither did people write nor send letters once upon a time. But as soon as they began, they found it very useful and convenient. So would the birds and animals. We could have the head office here in this beautiful island—in this Animals' Paradise. You see, my idea is, firstly, a post office system for the education and betterment of the animal kingdom, and, secondly, a good foreign mail for the Fantippans. Do you think we could ever find some way by which birds could write letters?"

"Oh yes, I think so," said Speedy. "We swallows, for instance, always leave marks on houses where we have nested, which are messages for those who may come after us. Look"—Speedy scratched some crosses and signs in the sand at the Doctor's feet—"that means *'Don't build your nest in this house. They have a cat here!'* And this"—the Skimmer made four more signs in the sand—"this means *'Good house. Flies plentiful. Folks quiet. Building mud can be found behind the stable.'"*

"Splendid," cried the Doctor. "It's a kind of shorthand. You say a whole sentence in four signs."

"And then," Speedy went on, "nearly all other kinds of birds have a sign language of their own. For example, the kingfishers have a way of marking the trees along the river to show where good fishing is to be found. And thrushes have signs, too; one I've often seen on stones, which means *'Crack your snail shells here.'* That's so the thrushes won't go throwing their snail shells all over the place and scare the live snails into keeping out of sight."

"There you are," said the Doctor. "I always thought you birds had at least the beginnings of a written language—otherwise you couldn't be so clever. Now all we have to do is to build up on these signs a regular and proper system of birdwriting. And I have no doubt whatever that with the animals we can do the same thing. Then we'll get the Swallow Mail going and we'll have animals and birds writing letters to one another all over the world—and to people, too, if they want to."

"I suspect," said Speedy, "that you'll find most of the letters will be written to you, Doctor. I've met birds all over creation who wanted to know what you looked like, what you ate for breakfast, and all sorts of silly things about you."

"Well," said the Doctor. "I won't mind that. But my idea is firstly an educational one. With a good post office system of their own, I feel that the condition of the birds and animals will be greatly bettered. Only today, for example, some deer on this very island asked me what they should do about their nut trees, which were nearly eaten up. I showed them at once how they could plant seeds and grow more trees. Heaven knows how long they had been going on short rations. But if they'd only been able to write to me, I could have told them long ago—by Swallow Mail."

Then the Doctor and Jip went back to Fantippo, carried by the piffilosaurus, who landed them on the shore under cover of night so no one would see them. And in the morning John Dolittle called upon the king again.

"Your Majesty," said the Doctor, "I have now a plan to provide your country with an excellent service of foreign mails if you will agree to what I suggest."

"Good," said the king. "My Majesty is listening. Proceed. Let me offer you a lollipop."

The Doctor took one—a green one—from the box the king held out to him. King Koko was very proud of the quality of his lollipops—made in the Royal Candy Kitchen. He was never without one himself, and always wore it hung around his neck on a ribbon. And when he wasn't sucking it he used to hold it up to his eye and peer through it at his courtiers. He had seen men using quizzing glasses, and he had his lollipops made thin and transparent, so he could use them in this elegant manner. But constant lollipops had ruined his figure and made him dreadfully stout. However, as fatness was considered a sign of greatness in Fantippo, he didn't mind that.

"My plan," said the Doctor, "is this: The domestic mails of Fantippo, after I have instructed the postmen a little more, can be carried by your own people. But the handling of foreign mails as well as the domestic ones is too much for them. And besides, you have so few boats calling at your port. So I propose to build a floating post office for the foreign mails, which shall be anchored close to the island called"—the Doctor only just stopped himself in time from speaking the dreaded name—"er—er—close to the island I spoke of to you the other day."

"I don't like that," said the king, frowning.

"Your Majesty need have no fear," the Doctor put in hurriedly. "It will never be necessary for any of your people to land upon the island. The Foreign Mail post office will be a houseboat, anchored a little way out from the shore. And I will not need any Fantippan postmen to run it at all. On the contrary, I make it a special condition on your part that—er—the island we are speaking of shall continue to be left undisturbed for all time. I am going to run the Foreign Mails office in my own way—with special postmen of my own. When the Fantippans wish to send out

letters to foreign lands, they must come by canoe and bring them
to the houseboat post office. But incoming letters addressed to the
people in Fantippo shall be delivered at the doors of the houses in
the regular way. What do you say to that?"

"I agree," said the king. "But the stamps must all have my
beautiful face upon them, and no other."

"Very good," said the Doctor. "That can be arranged. But it
must be clearly understood that from now on the foreign mails shall
be handled by my own postman—in *my* way. And after I have got
the Domestic post office running properly in Fantippo, you must
see to it that it continues to work in order. If you will do that in a
few weeks' time, I think I can promise that your kingdom shall have
the finest mail service in the world."

Then the Doctor asked Speedy to send off messages through
the birds to every corner of the earth. And to ask all the leaders
of seagulls, tomtits, magpies, thrushes, stormy petrels, finches, penguins, vultures, snow buntings, wild geese, and the rest to come to
No Man's Land, because John Dolittle wanted to speak to them.

And in the meantime he went back and continued the work
of getting the Domestic Mail Service in good running order at the
post office at Fantippo.

So the good Speedy sent off messengers; and all around the
world and back again word was passed from bird to bird that John
Dolittle, the famous animal doctor, wished to see all the leaders of
all kinds of birds, great and small.

And presently in the big hollow in the center of No Man's
Land they began to arrive. After three days Speedy came to the
Doctor and said:

"All right, Doctor, they are ready for you now."

A good strong canoe had by this time been put at the Doctor's service by the king, who was also having the post office houseboat built at the Doctor's orders.

So John Dolittle got into his canoe and came at length to the same hill where he had before gazed out over the pleasant hollow of the Animals' Paradise. And with the Skimmer on his shoulder, he looked down into a great sea of bird faces—leaders all—every kind, from a hummingbird to an albatross. And taking a palm leaf and twisting it into a trumpet so that he could make himself heard, he began his great inauguration speech to the leaders, which was to set working the famous Swallow Mail Service.

HUGH LOFTING

"He began his great inauguration speech."

After the Doctor had finished his speech and told the leaders what it was he meant to do, the birds of the world applauded by whistling and screeching and flapping their wings, so that the noise was terrible. And in the streets of Fantippo people whispered it about that the dragons were fighting one another in No Man's Land.

Then the Doctor passed down among the birds and, taking a notebook, he spoke to each leader in turn, asking him questions about the signs and sign language that his particular kind of bird was in the habit of using. And the Doctor wrote it all down in the notebook and took it home with him and worked over it all night—promising to meet the leaders again the following day.

And on the morrow, crossing once again to the island, he went on with the discussion and planning and arrangement. It was agreed that the Swallow Mail Service should have its head office here in No Man's Land. And that there should be branch offices at Cape Horn, Greenland, in Christmas Island, Tahiti, Kashmir, Tibet, and Puddleby-on-the-Marsh. Most of the mails were arranged so that those birds who migrated or went to other lands in the winter and back again in summer should carry the letters on their regular yearly journeys. And as there are some kinds of birds crossing from one land to another in almost every week of the year, this took care of much of the mails without difficulty.

Then, of course, there were all those birds who don't leave their home lands in winter, but stay in one country all the time. The leaders of these had come under special guidance of other birds to oblige the Doctor by being present at the great meeting. They promised to have their people all the year round take care of letters that were brought to their particular countries to be delivered. So between one thing and another, much of the planning and arrangement of the service was decided in these first two meetings.

Then the Doctor and the leaders agreed upon a regular kind of simple, easy writing for all birds to use, so that the addresses on the envelopes could be understood and read by the post birds. And at last John Dolittle sent them off home again, to instruct their relatives in this new writing and reading and explain to all the birds of all the world how the post office was going to work and how much good he hoped it would do for the education and betterment of the animal kingdom. Then he went home and had a good sleep.

The next morning he found that King Koko had gotten his post office houseboat ready and finished—and very smart it looked. It was paddled out and anchored close to the shore of the island. Then Dab-Dab, Jip, Too-Too, Gub-Gub, the Pushmi-Pullyu, and the white mouse were brought over, and the Doctor gave up his house on the main street of Fantippo and settled down to live at the Foreign Mails post office for the remainder of his stay.

And now John Dolittle and his animals got tremendously busy arranging the post office, its furniture, the stamp drawers, the postcard drawers, the weighing scales, the sorting bags, and all the rest of the paraphernalia. Dab-Dab, of course, was housekeeper, as usual, and she saw to it that the post office was swept properly every morning. Jip was the watchman and had charge of locking up at night and opening in the morning. Too-Too, with his head for mathematics, was given the bookkeeping, and he kept account of how many stamps were sold and how much money was taken in. The Doctor ran the information window and answered the hundred and one questions that people are always asking at post offices. And the good and trusty Speedy was here, there, and everywhere.

"The houseboat post office of No Man's Land"

And this was how the first letter was sent off by the Swallow Mail: King Koko himself came one morning and, putting his large face in at the information window, asked:

"What is the fastest foreign mail delivery ever made by any post office anywhere in the world?"

"The British post office is now boasting," said the Doctor, "that it can get a letter from London to Canada in fourteen days."

"All right," said the king. "Here's a letter to a friend of mine who runs a shoe-shine parlor in Alabama. Let me see how quickly you can get me an answer to it."

Now, the Doctor really had not gotten everything ready yet to work the foreign mails properly and he was about to explain to the king. But Speedy hopped up on the desk and whispered:

"Give me that letter, Doctor. We'll show him."

Then going outside, he called for Quip the Carrier.

"Quip," said Speedy, "take this letter to the Azores as fast as you can. There you'll just catch the white-tailed Carolina warblers about to make their summer crossing to the United States. Give it to them and tell them to get the answer back here as quick as they know how."

In a flash Quip was gone, seaward.

It was four o'clock in the afternoon when the king brought that letter to the Doctor. And when His Majesty woke up in the morning and came down to breakfast, there was the answer to it lying beside his plate!

PART TWO

THE FIRST CHAPTER

A Most Unusual Post Office

NOBODY THOUGHT, NOT EVEN JOHN DOLITTLE himself, when the Swallow Mail was first started, what a tremendous system it would finally grow into and what a lot of happenings and ideas would come about through it.

Of course, such an entirely new thing as this required a great deal of learning and working out before it could be made to run smoothly. Something new, some fresh problem, cropped up every day. But although the Doctor, at all times a busy man, was positively worked to death, he found it all so interesting that he didn't mind. But the motherly Dab-Dab was dreadfully worried about him; for indeed at the beginning he seemed never to sleep at all.

Certainly in the whole history of the world there never was another post office like the Doctor's. For one thing, it was a houseboat post office; for another, tea was served to everybody— the clerks and the customers as well—regularly at four o'clock every afternoon, with cucumber sandwiches on Sundays. Paddling over to the Foreign Mails post office for afternoon tea became quite the fashionable thing to do among the more up-to-date Fantippans. A large awning was put over the back entrance, forming a pleasant sort of veranda with a good view of the ocean and the bay. And if you dropped in for a stamp around four o'clock, as likely as not you would meet the king there, and all the other high notables of Fantippo, sipping tea.

Another thing in which the Doctor's post office was peculiar was its pens. Most post offices, the Doctor had found, always had abominably bad pens that spluttered and scratched and wouldn't write. In fact, very many post offices even nowadays seem to pride themselves on their bad pens. But the Doctor saw to it that *his* pens were of the very best quality. Of course, in those times there were no steel pens. Only quills were used. And John Dolittle got the albatrosses and the seagulls to keep for him their tail feathers, which fell out in the molting season. And of course, with such a lot of quills to choose from, it was easy to have the best pens in the post office.

Still another thing in which the Doctor's post office was different from all others was the gum used on the stamps. The supply of gum that the king had been using for his stamps ran short, and the Doctor had to set about discovering and making a new kind. And after a good deal of experimenting he invented a gum made of licorice, which dried quickly and worked very well. But, as I have said, the Fantippans were very fond of sweetmeats. And soon after the new gum was put into use, the post office was crowded with people buying stamps by the hundred.

At first the Doctor could not understand this sudden new rush of business—which kept Too-Too, the cashier, working overtime every night, adding up the day's takings. The post office safe could hardly hold all the money taken in, and the overflow had to be put in a vase on the kitchen mantelpiece.

But presently the Doctor noticed that after they had licked the gum off the stamps, the customers would bring them back and want to exchange them for money again. Now, it is a rule that all post offices have to exchange their own stamps, when asked, for the price paid for them. So long as they are not torn or marked, it doesn't matter whether the gum has been licked off or not. So the Doctor saw that he would have to change his kind of gum if he wanted to keep stamps that would stick.

And one day the king's brother came to the post office with a terrible cough and asked the Doctor in the same breath (or gasp) to give him five half-penny stamps and a cure for a cough. This gave the Doctor an idea. And the next gum that he invented for his stamps he called *whooping-cough gum*. He made it out of a special kind of sweet, sticky cough mixture. He also invented a *bronchitis gum*, a *mumps gum*, and several others. And whenever there was a catching disease in the town, the Doctor would see that the proper kind of gum to cure it was issued on the stamps. It saved him a lot of trouble, because the people were always bothering him to cure colds and sore throats and things. And he was the first postmaster general to use this way of getting rid of sickness—by serving round pleasant medicine on the backs of stamps. He called it *stamping out* an epidemic.

One evening at six o'clock, Jip shut the doors of the post office as usual and hung up the CLOSED sign as he always did at that hour. The Doctor heard the bolts being shot and he stopped counting postcards and took out his pipe to have a smoke.

The first hard work of getting the post office in full swing was

"Jip hung up the sign."

now over. And that night John Dolittle felt, when he heard the doors being shut, that at last he could afford to keep more regular hours and not be working all the time. And when Jip came inside the registered mail booth he found the Doctor leaning back in a chair with his feet on the desk, gazing around him with great satisfaction.

"Well, Jip," said he with a sigh, "we now have a real working post office."

"Yes," said Jip, putting down his watchman's lantern, "and a mighty good one it is, too. There isn't another like it anywhere."

"You know," said John Dolittle, "although we opened more

than a week ago, I haven't myself written a single letter yet. Fancy living in a post office for a week and never writing a letter! Look at that drawer there. Ordinarily the sight of so many stamps would make me write dozens of letters. All my life I never had a stamp when I really wanted to write a letter. And—funny thing!—now that I'm living and sleeping in a post office, I can't think of a single person to write to."

"It's a shame," said Jip. "And you with such beautiful handwriting, too—as well as a drawerful of stamps! Never mind; think of all the animals that are waiting to hear from you."

"Of course, there's Sarah," the Doctor went on dreamily. "Poor dear Sarah! I wonder whom she married. But there you are, I haven't her address. So I can't write to Sarah. And I don't suppose any of my old patients would want to hear from me."

"I know!" cried Jip. "Write to the Cat's-Meat-Man."

"He can't read," said the Doctor gloomily.

"No, but his wife can," said Jip.

"That's true," murmured the Doctor. "But what shall I write to him about?"

Just at that moment Speedy-the-Skimmer came in and said:

"Doctor, we've got to do something about the city deliveries in Fantippo. My post-birds are not very good at finding the right houses to deliver the letters to. You see we swallows, although we nest in houses, are not regular city birds. We pick out lonely houses as a rule—in the country. City streets are a bit difficult for swallows to find their way round in. Some of the post-birds have brought back the letters they took out this morning to deliver, saying they can't find the houses they are addressed to."

"Humph!" said the Doctor. "That's too bad. Let me think a minute. Oh, I know! I'll send for Cheapside."

"Who is Cheapside?" asked Speedy.

"Cheapside is a London sparrow," said the Doctor, "who visits me every summer in Puddleby. The rest of the year he lives around St. Paul's Cathedral. He builds his nest in St. Edmund's left ear."

"Where?" cried Jip.

"In the left ear of a statue of St. Edmund on the outside of the chancel—the cathedral, you know," the Doctor explained. "Cheapside's the very fellow we want for city deliveries. There's nothing about houses and towns he doesn't know. I'll send for him right away."

"I'm afraid," said Speedy, "that a post-bird—unless he was a city bird himself—would have a hard job finding a sparrow in London. It's an awful big city, isn't it?"

"Yes, that's so," said John Dolittle.

"Listen, Doctor," said Jip. "You were wondering just now what to write the Cat's-Meat-Man about. Let Speedy write the letter to Cheapside in bird scribble and you enclose it in a letter to the Cat's-Meat-Man. Then when the sparrow comes to Puddleby for his summer visit, the Cat's-Meat-Man can give it to him."

"Splendid!" cried the Doctor. And he snatched a piece of paper off the desk and started to write.

"And you might ask him too," put in Dab-Dab who had been listening, "to take a look at the back windows of the house to see that none of them is broken. We don't want the rain coming in on the beds."

"All right," said the Doctor. "I'll mention that."

So the Doctor's letter was written and addressed to *Matthew Mugg, Esquire, Cats' Meat Merchant, Puddleby-on-the-Marsh, Slopshire, England.* And it was sent off by Quip the Carrier.

The Doctor did not expect an answer to it right away because the Cat's-Meat-Man's wife was a very slow reader and a still slower writer. And anyhow, Cheapside could not be expected to visit Puddleby for another week yet. He always stayed in London until after the Easter bank holiday. His wife refused to let him leave for the country till the spring family had been taught by their father how to find the houses where people threw out crumbs; how to pick up oats from under the cab horses' nose bags without being stamped on by the horses' hooves; how to get about in the trafficky streets of London, and a whole lot of other things that young city birds have to know.

In the meantime, while Quip was gone, life went forward busily and happily at the Doctor's post office. The animals—Too-Too, Dab-Dab, Gub-Gub, the Pushmi-Pullyu, the white mouse, and Jip—all agreed that they found living in a houseboat post office great fun. Whenever they got tired of their floating home they would go off for picnic parties to the Island of No Man's Land, which was now more often called by the name John Dolittle had given it, "the Animals' Paradise."

On these trips, too, the Doctor sometimes accompanied them. He was glad to, because it gave him an opportunity to talk with the many different kinds of animals there about the signs they were in the habit of using. And on these signs, which he carefully put down in notebooks, he built up a sort of written language for animals to use—or *animal scribble*, as he called it—the same as he had done with the birds.

Whenever he could spare the time, he held afternoon scribbling classes for the animals in the Great Hollow. And they were very well attended. He found the monkeys, of course, the easiest to teach and, because they were so clever, he made some of them into assistant teachers. But the zebras were quite bright too. The Doctor discovered that these intelligent beasts had ways of marking and twisting the grasses to show where they had smelled lions about—though, happily, they did not have to use this trick in the Animals' Paradise but had brought it with them when they had swum across from the mainland of Africa.

The Doctor's pets found it quite thrilling to go through the mail that arrived each day to see if there were any letters for them. At the beginning of course there wasn't much. But one day Quip had returned from Puddleby with an answer to the Doctor's let-

"He held scribbling classes for the animals."

ter to the Cat's-Meat-Man. Mr. Matthew Mugg had written (through his wife) that he had hung the letter for Cheapside on an apple tree in the garden where the sparrow would surely see it when he arrived. The windows of the house were all right, he wrote; but the back door could do with a coat of paint.

And while Quip had been waiting for this letter to be written, he had filled in the time at Puddleby by gossiping with all the starlings and blackbirds in the Doctor's garden about the wonderful new animals' post office on the island of No Man's Land. And pretty soon every creature in and around Puddleby had heard of it.

After that, of course, letters began to arrive at the houseboat for the Doctor's pets. And one morning, when the mail was sorted, there was a letter for Dab-Dab from her sister; one for the white mouse written by a cousin from the Doctor's bureau drawer; one for Jip from the collie who lived next door in Puddleby; and one for Too-Too, telling him he had a new family of six young ones in the rafters of the stable. But there was nothing for Gub-Gub. The poor pig was nearly in tears at being left out. And when the Doctor went into town that afternoon, Gub-Gub asked could he come along.

The next day the post-birds complained that the mail was an extra heavy one. And when it was sorted, there were ten thick letters for Gub-Gub and none for anybody else. Jip got suspicious about this and looked over Gub-Gub's shoulder while he opened them. In each one there was a banana skin.

"Who sent you those?" asked Jip.

"I sent them to myself," said Gub-Gub, "from Fantippo yesterday. I don't see why you fellows should get all the mail. Nobody writes to me, so I write to myself."

Cheapside

I
T WAS A GREAT DAY AT THE DOCTOR'S POST office when Cheapside, the London sparrow, arrived from Puddleby to look after the city deliveries for Fantippo.

The Doctor was eating his lunch of sandwiches at the information desk when the little bird popped his head through the window and said in his cheeky Cockney voice:

"'Ulloa, Doctor, 'ere we are again! What ho! The old firm! Who would 'ave thought you'd come to this?"

Cheapside was a character. Anyone on seeing him for the first time would probably guess that he spent his life in city streets. His whole expression was different from other birds. In Speedy's eyes, for instance—though nobody would dream of thinking him stupid—there was an almost noble look of country honesty. But in the eyes of Cheapside, the London sparrow, there was a saucy, daredevil expression that seemed to say "Don't you think for one moment that you'll ever get the better of me. I'm a Cockney bird."

"*Cheapside, the London sparrow*"

"Why, Cheapside!" cried John Dolittle. "At last you've come. My, but it's good to see you! Did you have a pleasant journey?"

"Not bad—not 'alf bad," said Cheapside, eyeing some crumbs from the Doctor's lunch, which lay upon the desk. "No storms. Pretty decent travelin'. 'Ot? Well, I should say it *was* 'ot. Quaint place you 'ave 'ere—sort of a barge?"

By this time all the animals had heard Cheapside arriving and they came rushing in to see the traveler and to hear the news of Puddleby and England.

"How is the old horse in the stable?" asked John Dolittle.

"Pretty spry," said Cheapside. "Course 'e ain't as young as

'e used to be. But 'e's lively enough for an old 'un. 'E asked me to bring you a bunch of crimson ramblers—just bloomin' over the stable door, they was. But I says to 'im, I says, 'What d'yer take me for, an omnibus?' Fancy a feller at my time of life carrying a bunch of roses all the way down the Atlantic! Folks would think I was goin' to a weddin' at the South Pole."

"Gracious, Cheapside!" said the Doctor, laughing. "It makes me quite homesick for England to hear your Cockney chirp."

"And me, too," sighed Jip. "Were there many rats in the wood-shed, Cheapside?"

"'Undreds of them," said the sparrow, "as big as rabbits. And so uppish you'd think they owned the place!"

"I'll soon settle *them*, when I get back," said Jip. "I hope we go soon."

"How does the garden look, Cheapside?" asked the Doctor.

"A1," said the sparrow. "Weeds in the paths, o' course. But the iris under the kitchen window looked something lovely, they did."

"Anything new in London?" asked the white mouse, who was also city bred.

"Yes," said Cheapside. "There's always something doing in good old London. They've got a new kind of cab that goes on two wheels instead of four. A man called 'Ansom invented it. Much faster than the old 'ackneys they are. You see 'em everywhere. And there's a new greengrocer's shop near the Royal Exchange."

"I'm going to have a greengrocer's shop of my own when I grow up," murmured Gub-Gub. "In England, and then I'll watch the new vegetables coming into season all the year round."

"He's always talking about that," said Too-Too. "Such an ambition in life to have—to run a greengrocer's shop!"

"Ah, England!" cried Gub-Gub sentimentally. "What is there more beautiful in life than the heart of a young lettuce in the spring?"

"'Ark at 'im," said Cheapside, raising his eyebrows. "Ain't 'e the poetical porker? Why don't you write a bunch of sonnets to the Skunk-Kissed-Cabbages of Louisiana, Mr. Bacon?"

"Well now, look here, Cheapside," said the Doctor. "We want you to get these city deliveries straightened out for us in the town of Fantippo. Our post-birds are having great difficulty finding the right houses to take letters to. You're a city bird, born and bred. Do you think you can help us?"

"I'll see what I can do for you, Doc," said the sparrow, "after I've taken a look around this town of yours. But first I want a bath. I'm all heat up from flying under a broiling sun. Ain't you got no puddles round here for a bird to take a bath in?"

"No, this isn't puddly climate," said the Doctor. "You're not in England, you know. But I'll bring you my shaving mug and you can take a bath in that."

"Mind you wash the soap out first, Doc," chirped the sparrow, "it gets into my eyes."

The next day, after Cheapside had had a good sleep to rest up from his long journey, the Doctor took the London sparrow to show him around the town of Fantippo.

"Well, Doc," said Cheapside after they had seen the sights, "as a town, I don't think much of it—really, I don't. It's big. I'll say that for it. I 'ad no idea they 'ad towns as big as this in Africa. But the streets is so narrow! I can see why they don't 'ave no cabs 'ere—'ardly room for a goat to pass, let alone a four-wheeler. And as for the 'ouses, they seem to be made of the insides of old mattresses.

The first thing we'll 'ave to do is to make old King Coconut tell 'is subjects to put door knockers on their doors. What is 'ome without a door knocker, I'd like to know? Of course, your postmen can't deliver the letters when they've no knockers to knock with."

"I'll attend to that," said the Doctor. "I'll see the king about it this afternoon."

"And then, they've got no letter boxes on the doors," said Cheapside. "There ought to be slots made to poke the letters in. The only place for a postman to put a letter is down the chimney."

"Very well," said the Doctor. "I'll attend to that, too. Shall I have the letter boxes on the middle of the door, or would you like them on one side?"

"Put 'em on each side of the doors—two to every 'ouse," said Cheapside.

"What's that for?" asked the Doctor.

"That's a little idea of my own," said the sparrow. "We'll 'ave one box for the bills and one for sure-enough letters. You see, people are so disappointed when they 'ear the postman's knock and come to the door, expecting to find a nice letter from a friend or news that money's been left them, and all they get is a bill from the tailor. But if we have two boxes on each door, one marked *Bills* and the other *Letters*, the postman can put all the bills in one box and the honest letters in the other. As I said, it's a little idea of my own. We might as well be real up-to-date. What do you think of it?"

"I think it's a splendid notion," said the Doctor. "Then the people need only have one disappointment—when they clear the bill box on the day set for paying their debts."

"That's the idea," said Cheapside. "And tell the post-birds—as soon as we've got the knockers on—to knock once for a bill and twice for a letter, so the folks in the 'ouse will know whether to come and get the mail or not. Oh, I tell you, we'll show people a thing or two before we're finished! We'll 'ave a post office in Fantipsy that really is a post office. And, now, 'ow about the Christmas boxes, Doctor? Postmen always expect a handsome present around Christmastime, you know."

"Well, I'm rather afraid," said the Doctor doubtfully, "that these people don't celebrate Christmas as a holiday."

"*Don't celebrate Christmas!*" cried Cheapside in a shocked voice. "What a disgraceful scandal! Well, look here, Doctor. You just tell the king that if 'e and 'is people don't celebrate the festive season by giving us post-birds Christmas boxes, there ain't going to be no mail delivered in Fantipsy from New Year's to Easter. And you can tell 'im I said so."

"All right," said the Doctor, "I'll attend to that, too."

"Tell 'im," said Cheapside, "we'll expect two lumps of sugar on every doorstep Christmas morning for the post-birds. No sugar, no letters!"

That afternoon the Doctor called upon the king and explained to him the various things that Cheapside wanted. And His Majesty gave in to them, every one. Beautiful brass knockers were screwed on all the doors—light ones, which the birds could easily lift. And very elegant they looked—by far the most up-to-date part of the dwellings. The double boxes were also put up, with one place for bills and one for the letters.

John Dolittle also explained to King Koko that at Christmastime people gave gifts to each other. And among the Fantippo people, the custom of making presents at Christmas became a tradition—not only to postmen, but to friends and relatives, too.

That is why when, several years after the Doctor had left this country, some missionaries visited that part of Africa, they found to their astonishment that Christmas was celebrated there, although the people were not Christians. But they never learned that the custom had been brought about by Cheapside, the cheeky London sparrow.

And very soon Cheapside took entire charge of the city delivery of mails in Fantippo. Of course, as soon as the mail began to get heavy, when the people got into the habit of writing more to their friends and relatives, Cheapside could not deal with all the mail himself. So he sent a message by a swallow to get fifty sparrows from the streets of London (who were, like himself, accustomed to city ways), to help him with the delivery of letters. And around the holiday seasons, the Harvest Moon and the Coming of the Rains, he had to send for fifty more to deal with the extra mail.

And if you happened to pass down the main street of Fantippo at nine in the morning or four in the afternoon, you would hear the *rat-tat-tat* of the post-sparrows, knocking on the doors—*tat-tat*, if it was a real letter, and just *rat!* if it was a bill.

Of course, they could not carry more than one or two letters at a time—being such small birds. But it only took them a moment to fly back to the houseboat for another load, where Too-Too was waiting for them at the "city" window with piles of mail, sorted out into boxes marked CENTRAL, WEST CENTRAL, SOUTHWEST, etc., for the different parts of the town. This was another idea of Cheapside's, to divide up the city into districts, the same as they did in London, so the mail could be delivered quickly without too much hunting for streets.

Cheapside's help was, indeed, most valuable to the Doctor. The king himself said that the mails were wonderfully managed. The letters were brought regularly and were never left at the wrong house.

He had only one fault, had Cheapside. And that was being cheeky. Whenever he got into an argument, his Cockney swearing was just dreadful. And in spite of the Doctor's having issued orders time and time again that he expected his post office clerks and mail birds to be strictly polite to the public, Cheapside was always getting into rows—which he usually started himself.

One day when King Koko's pet white peacock came to the Doctor and complained that the Cockney sparrow had made faces at him over the palace wall, the Doctor became quite angry and read the city manager a long lecture.

Then Cheapside got together a gang of his tough London

"The royal peacock complained that Cheapside had made faces at him."

sparrow friends and one night they flew into the palace garden and mobbed the white peacock and pulled three feathers out of his beautiful tail.

This last piece of rowdyism was too much for John Dolittle, and, calling up Cheapside, he discharged him on the spot—though he was very sorry to do it.

But when the sparrow went, all his London friends went with him, and the post office was left with no city birds to attend to the city deliveries. The swallows and other birds tried their hardest to get letters around to the houses properly. But they couldn't. And before long complaints began to come in from the townspeople.

Then the Doctor was sorry and wished he hadn't discharged Cheapside, who seemed to be the only one who could manage this part of the mails properly.

But one day, to the Doctor's great delight—though he tried hard to look angry—Cheapside strolled into the post office with a straw in the corner of his mouth, looking as though nothing had happened.

John Dolittle had thought that he and his friends had gone home to London. But they hadn't. They knew the Doctor would need them, so they had just hung around outside the town. And then the Doctor, after lecturing Cheapside again about politeness, gave him back his job.

But the next day the rowdy little sparrow threw a bottle of post office ink over the royal white peacock when he came to the houseboat with the king to take tea. Then the Doctor discharged Cheapside again.

In fact, the Doctor used to discharge him for rudeness regularly about once a month. And the city mails always got tied up soon after. But, to the Doctor's great relief, the city manager always came back just when the tie-up was at its worst and put things right again.

Cheapside was a wonderful bird. But it seemed as though he just couldn't go a whole month without being rude to somebody. The Doctor said it was in his nature.

The Birds That Helped Columbus

FTER THE DOCTOR HAD WRITTEN HIS first letter by Swallow Mail to the Cat's-Meat-Man he began to think of all the other people to whom he had neglected to write for years and years. And very soon every spare moment he had was filled in writing to friends and acquaintances everywhere.

And then, of course, there were the letters he sent to and received from birds and animals all over the world. First he wrote to the various bird leaders who were in charge of the branch offices at Cape Horn, Tibet, Tahiti, Kashmir, Christmas Island, Greenland, and Puddleby-on-the-Marsh. To them he gave careful instructions how the branch post offices were to be run—always insisting on strict politeness from the post office clerks; and he answered all the questions that the branch postmasters wrote asking for guidance.

And he sent letters to various fellow naturalists whom he knew in different countries and gave them a whole lot of information about the yearly flights or migration of birds. Because, of course, in the bird-mail business he learned a great deal on that subject, which had never been known to naturalists before.

Outside the post office he had a noticeboard set up on which were posted the outgoing and incoming mails. The notices would read something like this:

NEXT WEDNESDAY, JULY, THE RED-WINGED PLOVERS WILL LEAVE THIS OFFICE FOR DENMARK AND POINTS ON THE SKAGER RACK. POST YOUR MAIL EARLY, PLEASE. ALL LETTERS SHOULD BEAR A FOUR-PENNY STAMP. SMALL PACKAGES WILL ALSO BE CARRIED ON THIS FLIGHT FOR MOROCCO, PORTUGAL, AND THE CHANNEL ISLANDS.

Whenever a new flight of birds were expected at No Man's Land, the Doctor always had a big supply of food of their particular kind readied for their arrival beforehand. At the big meeting with the leaders he had put down in his notebook the dates of all the yearly flights of the different kinds of birds, where they started from and where they went to. And this notebook was kept with great care.

One day Speedy was sitting on top of the weighing scales while the Doctor was sorting a large pile of outgoing letters. Suddenly the Skimmer cried out:

"Great heavens, Doctor, I've gained an ounce! I'll never be able to fly in the races again. Look, it says four and a half ounces!"

"No, Speedy," said the Doctor. "See, you have an ounce weight on the pan as well as yourself. That makes you only three and a half ounces."

"Oh," said the Skimmer, "is that the trouble? I was never good at arithmetic. What a relief! Thank goodness, I haven't gained!"

"Listen, Speedy," said the Doctor, "in this batch of mail we have a lot of letters for Panama. What mails have we got going out tomorrow?"

"Great heavens, Doctor, I've gained an ounce!"

"I'm not sure," said Speedy. "I'll go and look at the notice-board. I think it's the golden jays. . . . Yes," he said, coming back in a moment, "that's right, the golden jays tomorrow, Tuesday, the weather permitting."

"Where are they bound for, Speedy?" asked the Doctor. "My notebook's in the safe."

"From Dahomey to Venezuela," said Speedy, raising his right foot to smother a yawn.

"Good," said John Dolittle. "Then they can take these Panama letters. It won't be much out of their way. What do golden jays eat?"

"They are very fond of acorns," said Speedy.

"All right," said the Doctor. "Please tell Gub-Gub to go across to the island and get the wild boars to gather up a couple of sacks of acorns. I want all the birds who work for us to have a good feed before they leave the main office for their flights."

The next morning when the Doctor woke up, he heard a tremendous chattering all around the post office and he knew that the golden jays had arrived overnight. And after he had dressed and come out onto the veranda, there, sure enough, they were—myriads of very handsome gold-and-black birds, swarming everywhere, gossiping away at a great rate and gobbling up the acorns laid out for them in bushels.

The leader, who already knew the Doctor, of course, came forward to get orders and to see how much mail there was to be carried.

After everything had been arranged and the leader had decided he need not worry about tornadoes or bad weather for the next twenty-four hours, he gave a command. Then all the birds rose in the air to fly away—whistling farewell to Postmaster General Dolittle and the main office.

"Oh, by the way, Doctor," said the leader, turning back a moment, "did you ever hear of a man called Christopher Columbus?"

"Oh, surely," said the Doctor. "He discovered America in 1492."

"Well, I just wanted to tell you," said the jay, "that if it hadn't been for an ancestor of mine, he wouldn't have discovered it in—later perhaps, but not in 1492."

"Oh, indeed!" said John Dolittle. "Tell me more about it." And he pulled a notebook out of his pocket and started to write.

"Well," said the jay, "the story was handed down to me by my mother, who heard it from my grandmother, who got it from my great-grandmother, and so on, way back to an ancestor of ours who lived in America in the fifteenth century. Our kind of birds in those days did not come across to this side of the Atlantic, neither summer nor winter. We used to spend March through September in the Bermudas and the rest of the year in Venezuela. And when we made the autumn journey south, we used to stop at the Bahama Islands to rest on the way.

"The fall of the year 1492 was a stormy season. Gales and squalls were blowing up all the time and we did not get started on our trip until the second week in October. My ancestor had been the leader of the flock for a long time. But he had grown sort of old and feeble, and a younger bird was elected in his place to lead the golden jays to Venezuela that year. The new leader was a conceited youngster, and because he had been chosen he thought he knew everything about navigation and weather and sea crossings.

"Shortly after the birds started they sighted, to their great astonishment, a number of boats sailing on a westward course. This was about halfway between the Bermudas and the Bahamas. The ships were much larger than anything they had ever seen before. All they had been accustomed to up to that time were little canoes.

"The new leader immediately got scared and gave the order for the jays to swing in farther toward the land, so they wouldn't be seen by the men who crowded these large boats. He was a superstitious leader, and anything he didn't understand he kept away from. But my ancestor did not go with the flock, but made straight for the ships.

"He was gone about twenty minutes, and presently he flew after the other birds and said to the new leader: 'Over there in those ships a brave man is in great danger. They come from Europe, seeking land. The sailors, not knowing how near they are to sighting it, have mutinied against their admiral. I am an old bird and I know this brave seafarer. Once when I was making a crossing—the first I ever made—a gale came up and I was separated from my fellows. For three days I had to fly with the battering wind. And finally I was blown eastward near the Old World. Just when I was ready to drop into the sea from exhaustion, I spied a ship. I simply had to rest. I was weather-beaten and starving. So I made for the boat and fell half-dead upon the deck. The sailors were going to put me in a cage. But the captain of the ship—this same navigator whose life is now threatened by his rebellious crew in those ships over there—fed me crumbs and nursed me back to life. Then he let me go free, to fly to Venezuela when the weather was fair. We are land birds. Let us now save this good man's life by going to his ship and showing ourselves to his sailors. They will then know that land is near and be obedient to their captain."

"Yes, yes," said the Doctor. "Go on. I remember Columbus writing of land birds in his diary. Go on."

"So," said the jay, "the whole flock turned and made for Columbus's fleet. They were only just in time. For the sailors were ready to kill their admiral, who, they said, had brought them on a fool's errand to find land where there was none. He must turn back and sail for Spain, they said, or be killed.

"But when the sailors saw a great flock of land birds passing over the ship going southwest instead of west, they took new heart, for they were sure land must lie not far to the southwestward.

"So we led them on to the Bahamas. And on the seventh day, very early in the morning, the crew, with a cry of 'Land! Land!'

"The sailors were ready to kill their admiral."

fell down upon their knees and gave thanks to heaven. Watling's Island, one of the smaller Bahamas, lay ahead of them, smiling in the sea.

"Then the sailors gathered about the admiral, Christopher Columbus, whom a little while before they were going to kill, and cheered and called him the greatest navigator in the world—which, in truth, he was.

"But even Columbus himself never learned to his dying day that it was the weather-beaten bird who had fallen on his friendly deck some years before, who had led him by the shortest route to the land of the New World.

"So you see, Doctor," the jay ended, picking up his letters and getting ready to fly, "if it hadn't been for my ancestor, Christopher Columbus would have had to turn back to please his sailors, or be killed. If it hadn't been for him, America would not have been discovered in 1492—later, perhaps, but not in 1492. Good-bye! I must be going. Thanks for the acorns."

Cape Stephen Light

ON THE COAST OF WEST AFRICA, ABOUT twenty miles to the northward of Fantippo, there was a cape running out into the sea that had a lighthouse on it called the Cape Stephen Light. This light was kept carefully burning by the government that controlled that part of Africa, in order that ships should see it from the sea and know where they were. It was a dangerous part of the coast. There were many rocks and shallows near the end of Cape Stephen. And if the light were ever allowed to go out at night, of course, ships traveling that part of the sea would be in great danger of running into the long cape and wrecking themselves.

Now, one evening not long after the golden jays had gone west, the Doctor was writing letters in the post office by the light of a candle. It was late and all the animals were fast asleep long ago. Presently while he wrote, he heard a sound a long way off, coming through the open window at his elbow. He put down his pen and listened.

It was the sound of a seabird, calling away out at sea. Now,

"There were many rocks and shallows near the end of Cape Stephen."

seabirds don't, as a rule, call very much unless they are in great numbers. This call sounded like a single bird. The Doctor put his head through the window and looked out.

It was a dark night, as black as pitch, and he couldn't see a thing—especially as his eyes were used to the light of the candle. The mysterious call was repeated again and again, like a cry of distress from the sea. The Doctor didn't know quite what to make of it. But soon he thought it seemed to be coming nearer. And, grabbing his hat, he ran out onto the veranda.

"What is it? What's the matter?" he shouted into the darkness over the sea.

He got no answer. But soon, with a rush of wings that nearly blew his candle out, a great seagull swept down onto the houseboat rail beside him.

"Doctor," panted the gull, "the Cape Stephen Light is out. I don't know what's the matter. It has never gone out before. We use it as a landmark, you know, when we are flying after dark. The night's as black as ink. I'm afraid some ship will surely run into the cape. I thought I'd come and tell you."

"Good heavens!" cried the Doctor. "What can have happened? There's a lighthouse keeper living there to attend to it. Was it lighted earlier in the evening?"

"I don't know," said the gull. "I was coming in from catching herring—they're running just now, you know, a little to the north. And, expecting to see the light, I lost my way and flew miles too far south. When I found out my mistake I went back, flying close down by the shore. And I came to Cape Stephen, but it had no light. It was black as anything. And I would have run right into the rocks myself if I hadn't been going carefully."

"How far would it be from here?" asked John Dolittle.

"Well, by land it would be twenty-five miles to where the lighthouse stands," said the gull. "But by water it would be only about twelve, I should say."

"All right," said the Doctor, hurrying into his coat. "Wait just a moment till I wake Dab-Dab."

The Doctor ran into the post office kitchen and woke the poor housekeeper, who was slumbering soundly beside the kitchen stove.

"Listen, Dab-Dab!" said the Doctor, shaking her. "Wake up! The Cape Stephen Light's gone out!"

"Whazhat?" said Dab-Dab, sleepily opening her eyes. "Stove's gone out?"

"No, the lighthouse on Cape Stephen," said the Doctor. "A gull just came and told me. The shipping's in danger. Wrecks, you know, and all that. Wake up and look sensible, for pity's sake!"

At last poor Dab-Dab, fully awakened, understood what was the matter. And in a moment she was up and about.

"I know where it is, Doctor. I'll fly right over there. No, I won't need the gull to guide me. You keep him to show you the way. Follow me immediately in the canoe. If I can find out anything, I'll come back and meet you halfway. If not, I'll wait for you by the lighthouse tower. Thank goodness it's a calm night, anyway—even if it is dark!"

With a flap of her wings, Dab-Dab flew right through the open window and was gone into the night, while the Doctor grabbed his little black medicine bag and, calling to the gull to follow him, ran down to the other end of the houseboat, untied the canoe, and jumped in. Then he pushed off, headed around the island of No Man's Land, and paddled for all he was worth for the seaward end of Cape Stephen.

About halfway to the long neck of land that jutted out into the gloomy ocean the Doctor's canoe was met by Dab-Dab—though how she found it in the darkness, with only the sound of the paddle to guide her, goodness only knows.

"Doctor," said she, "if the lighthouse keeper is in there at all he must be sick, or something. I hammered on the windows, but nobody answered."

"Dear me!" muttered the Doctor, paddling harder than ever. "I wonder what can have happened?"

"And that's not the worst," said Dab-Dab. "On the far side of the cape—you can't see it from here—there's the headlight of a big sailing ship, bearing down southward, making straight for the rocks. They can't see the lighthouse and they don't know what danger they're in."

"Good Lord!" groaned the Doctor, and he nearly broke the paddle as he churned the water astern to make the canoe go faster yet.

"How far off the rocks is the ship now?" asked the gull.

"About a mile, I should say," said Dab-Dab. "But she's a big one—judging by the height of her mast light—and it won't be long before she's aground on the cape."

"Keep right on, Doctor," said the gull. "I'm going off to get some friends of mine."

And the seagull spread his wings and flew away toward the land, calling the same cry as the Doctor had heard through the post office window.

John Dolittle had no idea what he meant to do. Nor was the gull himself sure that he would be in time to succeed with the plan he had in mind. But presently, to his delight, the seabird heard his call being answered from the rocky shores shrouded in darkness. And soon he had hundreds of his brother gulls circling round him in the night.

Then he took them to the great ship, which was sailing calmly onward toward the rocks and destruction. And there, going forward to where the helmsman held the spokes of the wheel and watched the compass swinging before him in the light of a little, dim lamp, the gulls started dashing themselves into the wheelman's face and covering the glass of the compass, so he could not steer the ship.

"The gulls dashed themselves into the wheelman's face."

The helmsman, battling with the birds, sent up a yell for help, saying he couldn't see to steer the boat. Then the officers and sailors rushed up to his assistance and tried to beat the birds off.

In the meantime the Doctor, in his canoe, had reached the end of Cape Stephen and, springing ashore, he scrambled up the rocks to where the great tower of the lighthouse rose skyward over the black, unlighted sea. Feeling and fumbling, he found the door and hammered on it, yelling to be let in. But no one answered him. And Dab-Dab whispered in a hoarse voice that the light of the ship was nearer now—less than half a mile from the rocks.

Then the Doctor drew back for a run and threw his whole

weight against the door. But the hinges and lock had been made to stand the beating of the sea and they budged no more than if he had been a fly.

At last, with a roar of rage, the Doctor picked up a rock from the ground as big as a chair and banged it with all his might against the lock of the lighthouse door. With a crash the door flew open, and the Doctor sprang within.

On the ship the seamen were still fighting with the gulls. The captain, seeing that no helmsman could steer the boat right with thousands of wings fluttering in his eyes, gave the orders to lay the ship to for a little and to get out the hose pipes. And a strong stream of water was turned onto the gulls around the helmsman, so they could no longer get near him. Then the ship got underway again and headed toward the cape once more.

Inside the lighthouse the Doctor found the darkness blacker still. With hands outstretched before him, he hurried forward and the first thing he did was to stumble over a man who was lying on the floor just within the door. Without waiting to see what was the matter with him, the Doctor jumped over his body and began to grope his way up the winding stairs of the tower that led to the big lamp at the top.

Meanwhile Dab-Dab stayed below at the door, looking out over the sea at the mast light of the ship—which, after a short delay, was now coming on again toward the rocks. At any minute she expected the great beam of the lighthouse lamp to flare out over the sea, as soon as the Doctor should get it lit, to warn the sailors of their danger. But instead, she presently heard the Doctor's agonized voice calling from the head of the stairs:

"Dab-Dab! Dab-Dab! I can't light it. *We forgot to bring matches!*"

"Well, what have you *done* with the matches, Doctor?" called Dab-Dab. "They were always in your coat."

"I left them beside my pipe on the information desk," came the Doctor's voice from the top of the dark stairs. "But there must be matches in the lighthouse somewhere. We must find them."

"What chance have we of that?" shouted Dab-Dab. "It's as black as black down here. And the ship is coming nearer every minute."

"Feel in the man's pockets," called John Dolittle. "Hurry!"

In a minute Dab-Dab went through the pockets of the man who lay so still upon the floor.

"He hasn't any matches on him!" she shouted. "Not a single one."

"Confound the luck!" muttered John Dolittle.

And then there was a solemn silence in the lighthouse while the Doctor above and Dab-Dab below thought gloomily of that big ship sailing onward to her wreck because they had no matches.

But suddenly out of the black stillness came a small, sweet voice, singing, somewhere near.

"Dab-Dab!" cried the Doctor in a whisper. "Do you hear that? A canary! There's a canary singing somewhere—probably in a cage in the lighthouse kitchen!"

In a moment he was clattering down the stairs.

"Come on," he cried. "We must find the kitchen. That canary will know where the matches are kept. Find the kitchen!"

Then the two of them went stumbling around in the darkness, feeling the walls, and presently they came upon a low door, opened it, and fell headlong down a short flight of steps that led to the lighthouse kitchen. This was a little underground room, like a cellar, cut out of the rock on which the lighthouse stood. If there was any fire or stove in it, it had long since gone out, for the darkness here was as black as anywhere else. But as soon as the door had opened, the trills of the songbird grew louder.

"Tell me," called John Dolittle, in canary language, "where are the matches? Quick!"

"Oh, at last you've come," said a high, small, polite voice out of the darkness. "Would you mind putting a cover over my cage? There's a draft and I can't sleep. Nobody's been near me since midday. I don't know what can have happened to the keeper. He always covers up my cage at teatime. But tonight I wasn't covered at all, so I went on singing. You'll find my cover up on the—"

"*Matches! Matches!* Where are the matches?" screamed Dab-Dab. "The light's out and there's a ship in danger! Where are the matches kept?"

"On the mantelpiece, next to the pepper box," said the canary. "Come over here to my cage and feel along to your left—high up— and your hand will fall right on them."

The Doctor sprang across the room, upsetting a chair on his way, and felt along the wall. His hand touched the corner of a stone shelf and the next moment Dab-Dab gave a deep sigh of relief, for she heard the cheerful rattle of a box of matches as the Doctor fumbled to strike a light.

"You'll find a candle on the table—there—look—behind you," said the canary, when the match light dimly lit up the kitchen.

With trembling fingers the Doctor lit the candle. Then, shielding the flame with his hand, he bounded out of the room and up the stairs.

"The Doctor lit the candle."

"At last!" he muttered. "Let's hope I'm not too late!"

At the head of the kitchen steps he met the seagull coming into the lighthouse with two companions.

"Doctor," cried the gull, "we held off the ship as long as we could. But the stupid sailors, not knowing we were trying to save them, turned hoses on us and we had to give up. The ship is terribly near now."

Without a word the Doctor sped up the winding steps of the tower. Round and round he went, upward, till he was ready to drop from dizziness.

At length, reaching the great glass lamp chamber at the top, he set down his candle and, striking two matches at once, he held one in each hand and lit the big wick in two places.

By this time Dab-Dab had gone outside again and was watching over the sea for the oncoming ship. And when at last the great light from the big lamp at the top of the tower suddenly flared out over the sea, there was the bow of the vessel, not more than a hundred yards from the rocky shore of the cape!

Then came a cry from the lookout, shouted orders from the captain, much blowing of whistles and ringing of bells. And just in time to save herself from a watery grave, the big ship swung her nose out to sea and sailed safely past upon her way.

THE FIFTH CHAPTER

Gulls and Ships

THE MORNING SUN PEEPING IN AT THE window of the lighthouse found the Doctor still working over the keeper where he lay at the foot of the tower stairs.

"He's coming to," said Dab-Dab. "See, his eyes are beginning to blink."

"Get me some more clean water from the kitchen," said the Doctor, who was bathing a large lump on the side of the man's head.

Presently the keeper opened his eyes wide and stared up into the Doctor's face.

"Who?—What?" he murmured stupidly. "The light! I must attend to the light! I must attend to the light!" and he struggled weakly to get up.

"It's all right," said the Doctor. "The light has been lit. And it's nearly day now. Here, drink this. Then you'll feel better."

And the Doctor held some medicine to the man's lips, which he had taken from the little black bag.

In a short while the man grew strong enough to stand on his feet. Then, with the Doctor's help, he walked as far as the kitchen, where John Dolittle and Dab-Dab made him comfortable in an armchair, lit the stove, and cooked his breakfast for him.

"I'm mighty grateful to you, stranger, whoever you be," said the man. "Usually there's two of us here, me and my partner, Fred. But yesterday morning I let Fred go off with the ketch to get oysters. That's why I'm alone. I was coming down the stairs about noon, from putting new wicks in the lamp, when my foot slipped and I took a tumble to the bottom. My head hit the wall

"The Doctor and Dab-Dab cooked his breakfast for him."

and knocked the senses right out of me. I don't know how long I lay there before you found me."

"Well, all's well that ends well," said the Doctor. "Take this; you must be nearly starved."

And he handed the keeper a large cup of steaming coffee.

About ten o'clock in the morning Fred, the partner, returned in the little sailboat from his oyster-gathering expedition. He was very much worried when he heard of the accident that had happened while he had been off-duty. Fred, like the other keeper, was a Londoner and a seaman. He was a pleasant fellow, and both he and his partner (who was now almost entirely recovered from his injury) were very glad of the Doctor's company to break the tiresome dullness of their lonely life.

They took John Dolittle all over the lighthouse to see the workings of it. And outside they showed him with great pride the tiny garden of tomatoes and nasturtiums that they had planted near the foot of the tower.

They only got a holiday once a year, they told John Dolittle, when a government ship stopped near Cape Stephen and took them back to England for six weeks' vacation, leaving two other men in their place to take care of the light while they were gone.

They asked the Doctor if he could give them any news of their beloved London. But he had to admit that he also had been away from that city for a long time. However, while they were talking Cheapside came into the lighthouse kitchen, looking for the Doctor. The city sparrow was delighted to find that the keepers were also Cockneys. And he gave them, through the Doctor, all the latest gossip of Wapping, Limehouse, the East India Docks, and the wharves and the shipping of London River.

The two keepers thought that the Doctor was surely crazy when he started a conversation of chirps with Cheapside. But from the answers they got to their questions, they could see there was nothing fake about the news of the city that the sparrow gave.

Cheapside said the faces of those two Cockney seamen were the best scenery he had looked on since he had come to Africa. And after that first visit, he was always flying over to the lighthouse in his spare time to see his new friends. Of course, he couldn't talk to them, because neither of them knew sparrow talk—not even Cockney sparrow talk. But Cheapside loved being with them anyway.

"They're such a nice change," he said. "And you should just hear Fred sing 'See That My Grave's Kept Green.'"

The lighthouse keepers were sorry to have the Doctor go, and they wouldn't let him leave till he promised to come and take dinner with them next Sunday.

Then, after they had loaded his canoe with a bushel of rosy tomatoes and a bouquet of nasturtiums, the Doctor, with Dab-Dab and Cheapside, paddled away for Fantippo, while the keepers waved to them from the lighthouse door.

The Doctor had not paddled very far on his return journey to the post office when the seagull who had brought the news of the light overtook him.

"Everything all right now, Doctor?" he asked as he swept in graceful circles around the canoe.

"Yes," said John Dolittle, munching on a tomato. "The man got an awful crack on the head from that fall. But he will be all over it in a little while. If it hadn't been for the canary, though, who told us where the matches were—and for you, too, holding back the sailors—we would never have saved that ship."

The Doctor threw a tomato skin out of the canoe and the gull caught it neatly in the air before it touched the water.

"Well, I'm glad we were in time," said the bird.

"Tell me," asked the Doctor, watching him thoughtfully as he hovered and swung and curved around the tiny boat, "what made you come and bring me the news about the light? Gulls don't, as a rule, bother much about people or what happens to ships, do they?"

"You're mistaken, Doctor," said the gull, catching another skin with deadly accuracy. "Ships and the men in them are very important to us—not so much down here in the south. But up north, why, if it wasn't for the ships in the winter, we gulls would often have a hard time finding enough to eat. You see, after it gets cold, fish and seafood become sort of scarce. Sometimes we make out by going up the rivers to towns and hanging about the artificial lakes in parks where fancy waterfowl are kept. The people come to the parks and throw biscuits in the lakes for the waterfowl. But if we are around, the biscuits get caught before they hit the lake— like that," and the gull snatched a third tomato skin on the wing with a lightning lunge.

"But you were speaking of ships," said the Doctor.

"Yes," the gull went on—rather indistinctly, because his mouth was full of tomato skin, "we find ships much better for winter feeding. You see, it isn't really fair of us to go and bag all the food from the fancy waterfowl in parks. So we never do it unless we have to. Usually in winter we stick to the ships. Why, two years ago a cousin of mine and I lived the whole year round following ships for the food scraps the stewards threw out into the sea. The rougher the weather, the more food we get, because then the passengers don't feel like eating and most of the grub gets thrown out. Yes, my cousin

"The gull caught the tomato skin with a lightning lunge."

and I attached ourselves, as it were, to the *Transatlantic Packet Line*, which runs ships from Glasgow to Philadelphia, and traveled back and forth with them across the ocean dozens of trips. But later on we changed over to the *Binnacle Line*—Tilbury to Boston."

"Why?" asked the Doctor.

"We found they ran a better table for their passengers. With the *Binnacle*, who threw us morning biscuits, afternoon tea and sandwiches last thing at night—as well as three square meals a day—we lived like fighting cocks. It nearly made sailors of us for good. It's a great life—all you do is eat. I should say gulls are interested in men and ships, Doctor—very much so. Why, I wouldn't have an accident happen to a ship for anything—especially a passenger ship."

"Humph! That's very interesting," murmured the Doctor. "And have you seen many accidents—ships in trouble?"

"Oh, heaps of times," said the gull. "Storms, collisions at night, ships going aground in the fog, and the rest. Oh yes, I've seen lots of boats in trouble at sea."

"Ah!" said the Doctor, looking up from his paddling. "See, we are already back at the post office. And there's the Pushmi-Pullyu ringing the lunch bell. We're just in time. I smell liver and bacon— these tomatoes will go with it splendidly. Won't you come in and join us?" he asked the gull. "I would like to hear more about your life with ships. You've given me an idea."

"Thank you," said the gull. "I am feeling kind of peckish myself. You are very kind. This is the first time I've eaten ship's food *inside* a ship."

And when the canoe was tied up, they went into the houseboat and sat down to lunch at the kitchen table.

"Well now," said the Doctor to the gull as soon as they were seated, "you were speaking of fogs. What do you do yourself in that kind of weather—I mean, you can't see any more in the fog than the sailors can, can you?"

"No," said the gull, "we can't *see* any more, it is true. But, my goodness! If we were as helpless in a fog as the sailors are, we'd always be lost. What we do, if we are going anywhere special and we run into a fog, is to fly up above it—way up where the air is clear. Then we can find our way as well as ever."

"I see," said the Doctor. "But the storms, what do you do in them to keep yourselves safe?"

"Well, of course, in storms—bad storms—even seabirds can't always go where they want. We seagulls never try to battle our way against a real gale. The petrels sometimes do, but we don't. It is too tiring, and even when you can come down and rest on the water, swimming every once in a while, it's a dangerous game. We fly with the storm—just let it carry us where it will. Then when the wind dies down, we come back and finish our journey."

"But that takes a long time, doesn't it?" asked the Doctor.

"Oh yes," said the gull, "it wastes a little time. But you know, we very seldom let ourselves get caught by a storm."

"How do you mean?" asked John Dolittle.

"We know, before we reach one, where it is. And we go around it. No experienced seabird ever runs his head into a bad storm."

"But how do you know where the storms are?" asked the Doctor.

"Well," said the gull, "I suppose two great advantages we birds have over the sailors in telling when and where to expect bad weather are our good eyesight and our experience. For one thing, we can always rise high in the air and look over the sea for a distance of fifty or sixty miles. Then if we see gales approaching, we can turn and run for it. And we can put on more speed than the fastest gale that ever blew. And then, another thing, our experience is so much better than sailors'. Sailors, poor duffers, think they know the sea—that they spend their life on it. They don't—believe me, they don't. Half the time they spend in the cabin, part of the time they spend onshore, and a lot of the time they spend sleeping. And even when they are on deck, they're not always looking at the sea. They fiddle around with ropes and paintbrushes and mops and buckets. You very seldom see a sailor *looking* at the sea."

"I suppose they get rather tired of it, poor fellows!" murmured the Doctor.

"Maybe. But after all, if you want to be a good seaman, the sea is the thing that counts, isn't it? That's the thing you've got to look at—to study. Now, we seabirds spend nearly all our lives, night and day, spring, summer, autumn, and winter, *looking at the sea*. And what is the result?" asked the gull, taking a fresh piece of toast from the rack that Dab-Dab handed him. "The result is this: we *know* the sea. Why, Doctor, if you were to shut me up in a little box with no windows in it and take me out into the middle of any ocean you liked and then opened the box and let me look

"*The gull took a fresh piece of toast.*"

at the sea—even if there wasn't a speck of land in sight—I could tell you what ocean it was, and, almost to a mile, what part of it we were in. But, of course, I'd have to know what date it was."

"Marvelous!" cried the Doctor. "How do you do it?"

"From the color of it; from the little particles of things that float in it; from the kind of fishes and sea creatures swimming in it; from the way the little ripples rippled and the big waves waved; from the smell of it; from the taste, the saltiness of it and a couple of hundred other things. But, you know, in most cases—not always, but in most cases—I could tell you where we were with my eyes shut, as soon as I got out of the box, just from the wind blowing on my feathers."

"Great heavens!" the Doctor exclaimed. "You don't say!"

"That's the main trouble with sailors, Doctor. They don't know winds the way they ought. They can tell a northeast wind from a west wind. And a strong one from a weak one. And that's about all. But when you've spent most of your life, the way we have, flying among the winds, using them to climb on, to swoop on and to hover on, you get to know that there's a lot more to a wind besides its direction and its strength. How often it puffs upward or downward, how often it grows weak or grows strong, will tell you, if you know the science of winds, a whole lot."

THE SIXTH CHAPTER

Weather Bureaus

WHEN THE LUNCH WAS OVER THE Doctor took an armchair beside the kitchen stove and lit his pipe. "I am thinking," he said to the gull, "of starting a new department in my post office. Many of the birds who have helped me in this mail business seem to be remarkably good weather prophets. And what you have just told me about your knowledge of the sea and storms has given me the idea of opening a weather bureau."

"What's that?" asked Jip, who was brushing up the table crumbs, to be put out later for the birds on the houseboat deck.

"A weather bureau," said the Doctor, "is a very important thing—especially for shipping and farmers. It is an office for telling you what kind of weather you're going to have."

"How do they do it?" asked Gub-Gub.

"They don't," said the Doctor, "at least they do sometimes. But as often as not they're wrong. They do it with instruments— thermometers, barometers, hygrometers, and wind gauges and

"The Doctor took an armchair beside the kitchen stove."

things. But most weather bureaus so far have been pretty poor. I think I can do much better with my birds. They very seldom go wrong in prophesying the weather."

"Well, for what parts of the world do you want to know the weather, Doctor?" asked the gull. "If it's just for Fantippo or West Africa it will be easy as pie. All you ever get here is tornadoes. The rest of the year is just frying heat. But if you want to prophesy the weather for the Straits of Magellan or Nova Zembla or those countries where they have all sorts of fancy weathers, it will be a different matter. Even prophesying the weather for England would keep you busy. Myself, I never thought that the weather itself knew what it was going to do next in England."

"The English climate's all right," put in Cheapside, his feathers ruffling up for a fight. "Don't you get turning up your long nautical nose at England, my lad. What do you call this 'ere? A climate? Well, I should call it a Turkish bath. In England we like variety in our climate. And we get it."

"I would like," said the Doctor, "to be able to prophesy weather for every part of the world. I really don't see why I shouldn't; this office, together with my branch offices, is in communication with birds going to every corner of the earth. I could improve the farming and the agriculture of the whole human race. But also, and especially, I want to have a bureau for ocean weather, to help the ships."

"Ah," said the gull, "for land weather I wouldn't be much help to you. But when it comes to the oceans, I know a bird who can tell you more about sea weather than any bureau ever knew."

"Oh," said the Doctor, "who is that?"

"We call him One Eye," said the gull. "He's an old, old albatross. Nobody knows how old. He lost an eye fighting with a fish eagle over a flounder. But he's the most marvelous weather prophet that ever lived. All seabirds have the greatest respect for his opinions. He has never been known to make a mistake."

"Indeed?" said the Doctor. "I would like very much to meet him."

"I'll get him for you," said the gull. "His home is not very far from here—out on a rock off the Angola coast. He lives there because the shellfish are so plentiful on the rock and he's too feeble—with his bad sight—to catch the other kinds of livelier fish. It's a sort of dull life for his old age, after all the great traveling he has done. He'll be pleased to know you want his help. I'll go and tell him right away."

"That will be splendid," said the Doctor. "I think your friend should be very helpful to us."

So the gull, after thanking the Doctor and Dab-Dab for a very excellent luncheon, took a couple of postcards that were going to Angola and flew off to get One Eye, the albatross.

Later in the afternoon the gull returned, and with him came the great One Eye, oldest of bird weather prophets.

The Doctor said afterward that he had never seen a bird who reminded him so much of a sailor. He had the rolling, straddling walk of a seafaring man; he smelled strongly of fish; and whenever he spoke of the weather he had an odd trick of squinting up at the sky with his one eye, the way old sailors often do.

He agreed with the Doctor that the idea of a bird weather bureau was quite a possible thing and would lead to much better weather reports than had so far been possible. Then for a whole hour and a half he gave the Doctor a lecture on winds. Every word of this John Dolittle wrote down in a notebook.

Now the wind is the chief thing that changes the weather. And if, for instance, you know that it is raining in the Channel Islands at teatime on a Thursday—and there's a northeast wind blowing— you can be pretty sure that the rain will reach England sometime Thursday night.

The next thing that the Doctor did was to write to all the branch postmasters and have them arrange exactly with the different kinds of birds a time for them to start their yearly migrations—not just the second week in November, or anything like that—but an exact day and hour. Then by knowing how fast each kind of bird flies, he could calculate almost to a minute what time they should arrive at their destination. And if they were late in arriving, then he would know that bad weather had delayed them on the way or that they had put off their starting till storms died down.

The Doctor, the gull, One Eye, Dab-Dab, Cheapside, Speedy-the-Skimmer, and Too-Too the mathematician put their heads together and discussed far into the night, working out a whole lot more arrangements and particulars for running a good weather bureau. And a few weeks later a second brand-new noticeboard appeared on the walls of the Doctor's post office, beside the one for outgoing and incoming mails.

The new noticeboard was marked at the top WEATHER REPORTS, and would read something like this:

THE GREEN HERONS WERE ONE DAY, THREE HOURS, AND NINE MINUTES LATE IN THEIR ARRIVAL AT CAPE HORN FROM THE SANDWICH ISLANDS. WIND COMING SOUTH-SOUTHEAST. BLUSTERY WEATHER CAN BE EXPECTED ALONG THE WEST COAST OF CHILE AND LIGHT GALES IN THE ANTARCTIC SEA.

And then the land birds, particularly those that live on berries, were very helpful to the Doctor in telling him by letter if the winter was going to be a hard one or not in their particular country. And he used to write to farmers all over the world, advising them whether they could expect a sharp frost, a wet spring or a dry summer—which, of course, helped them in their farming tremendously.

And then the Fantippans, who so far had been very timid about going far out to sea on account of storms, now that they had a good weather bureau and knew what weather to expect, began building larger sailboats, instead of their little frail canoes. And they became what is called a mercantile nation, trading up and down the shores of West Africa, and even going as far south as the Cape of Good

Hope and entering the Indian Ocean to traffic in goods with people of foreign lands.

This made the kingdom of Fantippo much richer and more important than it had been before, of course. And a large grant of money was given by the king to the Foreign Mails post office, which was used by the Doctor in making the houseboat better and bigger.

And soon the No Man's Land Weather Bureau began to get known abroad. The farmers in England, who had received such good weather reports by letter from the Doctor, went up to London and told the government that their own reports were no good, that a

"John Dolittle saw him snooping around the post office."

certain John Dolittle, M. D., was writing them much better reports from someplace in Africa.

And the government got quite worked up about it. And they sent the Royal Meteorologist, an old gray-haired weatherman, down to Fantippo to see how the Doctor was doing it.

John Dolittle saw him one day, snooping around the post office, looking at the noticeboards and trying to find out things. But he found out nothing. And when he got back to England he said to the government:

"He hasn't any new instruments at all. The man's a fake. All he has down there is an old barge and a whole lot of messy birds flying around."

Teaching by Mail

T HE EDUCATIONAL SIDE OF THE DOCTOR'S post office was a very important one and it grew all the time. As he had said to the Skimmer at the beginning, as soon as the birds and animals realized the helpfulness of having a post office of their own they used it more and more.

And, of course, as Speedy had foretold, they wrote most of their letters to the Doctor. Soon the poor man was swamped with mail, asking for medical advice. The sleigh dogs wrote all the way from the Arctic Continent to know what they should do about their hair falling out. Hair—which was all the poor creatures had to keep them warm against the Polar winds—was, of course, very important to them. And John Dolittle spent a whole Saturday and Sunday experimenting with hair tonics on Jip to find a way to cure their trouble. Jip was very patient about it, knowing that the Doctor was doing it for the good of his fellow dogs. And he did not grumble—although he did mention to Dab-Dab that he felt like a chemist's shop from all the different hair oils the Doctor had used

HUGH LOFTING

"The Doctor experimented on Jip."

on him. He said they ruined his keen nose entirely for two weeks, so he couldn't smell straight.

And besides the letters asking for medical advice, the Doctor got all sorts of requests from animals all over the world for information about food for their babies, nesting materials, and a thousand other things. In their new thirst for education, the animals asked all manner of questions, some of which neither the Doctor nor anybody else could answer: What were the stars made of? Why did the tide rise and fall—and could it be stopped?

Then, in order to deal with this wide demand for information, which had been brought about by his post office, John Dolittle started, for the first time in history, courses by correspondence for animals.

And he had printed forms made, called "Things a Young Rabbit Should Know," "The Care of Feet in Frosty Weather," etc., etc. These he sent out by mail in thousands.

And then because so many letters were written to him about good manners and proper behavior, he wrote a "Book of Etiquette for Animals." It is still a very famous work, though copies of it are rare now. But when he wrote it, the Doctor printed a first edition of fifty thousand copies and sent them all out by mail in one week. It was at this time, too, that he wrote and circulated another very well-known book of his called "One-Act Plays for Penguins."

But, alas! instead of making the number of letters he had to answer less, the Doctor found that by sending out books of information, he increased a hundredfold the already enormous mail he had to attend to.

This is a letter he received from a pig in Patagonia:

Dear Doctor—I have read your "Book of Etiquette for Animals" and liked it very much. I am shortly to be married. Would it be proper for me to ask the guests to bring turnips to my wedding, instead of flowers?

In introducing one well-bred pig to another should you say "Miss Virginia Ham, *meet* Mr. Frank Footer," or "Get acquainted?"

Yours truly,
BERTHA BACON

P. S. I have always worn my engagement ring in my nose. Is this the right place?

And the Doctor wrote back:

Dear Bertha—In introducing one pig to another I would avoid using the word *meet*. "Get acquainted" is quite all right. Remember that the object of all etiquette and manners should be to make people comfortable—not uncomfortable.

I think turnips at a wedding quite proper. You might ask the guests to leave the tops on. They will then look more like a bouquet.

Sincerely yours,
JOHN DOLITTLE

PART THREE

THE FIRST CHAPTER

The Animals' Magazine

T HE NEXT THING I MUST TELL YOU ABOUT IS the Prize Story Competition: the fame of the Puddleby fireside circle, where the Doctor had amused his pets with so many interesting tales, had become quite a famous institution. Too-Too had gossiped about it; Gub-Gub, Jip, and the white mouse had boasted of it. (You see, they were always proud that they could say they were part of the great man's regular household.) And before long, through this new post office of their own, creatures all over the world were speaking of it and discussing it by letter. Next thing, the Doctor began to receive requests for stories by mail. He had become equally famous as an animal doctor, an animal educator, and an animal author.

From the far north letters came in by the dozen from polar bears and walruses and foxes asking that he send them some light, entertaining reading as well as his medical pamphlets and books of etiquette. The winter nights (weeks and weeks long up there) grew frightfully monotonous, they said, after their own supply of stories had run out—because you couldn't possibly sleep *all* the time, and something had to be done for amusement on the lonely ice floes and in the dens and lairs beneath the blizzard-swept snow. For some time the Doctor was kept so busy with more serious things that he was unable to attend to it. But he kept it in mind until he should be able to think out the best way of dealing with the problem.

Now his pets, after the post office work got sort of settled and regular, often found it somewhat hard to amuse themselves in the evenings. One night they were all sitting around on the veranda of the houseboat wondering what game they could play, when Jip suddenly said:

"I know what we can do—let's get the Doctor to tell us a story."

"Oh, you've heard all my stories," said the Doctor. "Why don't you play Hunt-the-Slipper?"

"The houseboat isn't big enough," said Dab-Dab. "Last time we played it, Gub-Gub got stuck by the Pushmi-Pullyu's horns. You've got plenty of stories. Tell us one, Doctor—just a short one."

"Well, but what shall I tell you a story about?" asked John Dolittle.

"About a turnip field," said Gub-Gub.

"No, that won't do," said Jip. "Doctor, why don't you do what you did sometimes by the fire in Puddleby—turn your pockets out upon the table till you come to something that reminds you of a story—you remember?"

"All right," said the Doctor. "But—"

And then an idea came to him.

"Look here," he said. "You know I've been asked for stories by mail. The creatures around the North Pole wanted some light reading for the long winter nights. I'm going to start an animals' magazine for them. I'm calling it *The Arctic Monthly*. It will be sent by mail and distributed by the Nova Zembla branch office. So far, so good. But the great problem is how to get sufficient stories and pictures and articles and things to fill a monthly magazine—no easy matter. Now listen, if I tell you animals a story tonight, you'll have to do something to help me with my new magazine. Every night when you want to amuse yourselves, we'll take it in turns to tell a story. That will give us seven stories right away. There will be only one story printed each month— the rest of the magazine will be news of the day, a medical advice column, a babies' and mothers' page, and odds and ends. Then we'll have a Prize Story Competition. The readers shall judge which is the best; and when they write to us here and tell us, we'll give the prize to the winner. What do you say?"

"What a splendid idea!" cried Gub-Gub. "I'll tell my story tomorrow night. I know a good one. Now go ahead, Doctor."

Then John Dolittle started turning his trouser pockets out onto the table to try and find something that reminded him of a story. It was certainly a wonderful collection of objects that he brought forth. There were pieces of string and pieces of wire, stub ends of pencils, pocket knives with the blades broken, coat buttons, boot buttons, a magnifying glass, a compass, and a corkscrew.

"There doesn't seem to be anything very hopeful there," said the Doctor.

"Try in your waistcoat pockets," said Too-Too. "They were always the most interesting. You haven't turned them out since you left Puddleby. There must be lots in them."

So the Doctor turned out his waistcoat pockets. These brought forth two watches (one that worked and one that didn't), a measuring

"It was certainly a wonderful collection of objects."

tape, a piece of cobbler's wax, a penny with a hole through it, and a clinical thermometer.

"What's that?" asked Gub-Gub, pointing to the thermometer.

"That's for taking people's temperature with," said the Doctor. "Oh, that reminds me—"

"Of a story?" cried Too-Too.

"I knew it would," said Jip. "A thing like that must have a story to it. What's the name of the story, Doctor?"

"Well," said the Doctor, settling himself back in his chair, "I think I'll call this story 'The Invalids' Strike.'"

"What's a strike?" asked Gub-Gub.

"And what on earth is an invalid?" cried the Pushmi-Pullyu.

"A strike," said the Doctor, "is when people stop doing their own particular work in order to get somebody else to give them what they want. And an invalid—well, an invalid is a person who is always—er, more or less—ill."

"But what kind of work is invalids' work?" asked the white mouse.

"Their work is—er, staying—ill," said the Doctor. "Stop asking questions or I'll never get this story started."

"Wait a minute," said Gub-Gub. "My foot's gone to sleep."

"Oh, bother your feet!" cried Dab-Dab. "Let the Doctor get on with his story."

"Is it a good story?" asked Gub-Gub.

"Well," said the Doctor, "I'll tell it, and then you can decide for yourself. Stop fidgeting, now, and let me begin. It's getting late."

The Doctor's Story

A S SOON AS THE DOCTOR HAD LIT HIS PIPE and got it well going, he began:

"Many years ago, at the time I bought this thermometer, I was a very young doctor, full of hope, just starting out in business. I fancied myself a very good doctor, but I found that the rest of the world did not seem to think so. And for many months after I began I did not get a single patient. I had no one to try my new thermometer on. I tried it on myself quite often. But I was always so frightfully healthy I never had any temperature anyway. I tried to catch a cold. I didn't really want a cold, you understand, but I did want to make sure that my new thermometer worked. But I couldn't even catch a cold. I was very sad—healthy, but sad.

"Well, about this time I met another young doctor who was in the same fix as myself—having no patients. Said he to me: 'I'll tell you what we'll do, let's start a sanitarium.'"

"What's a sanitarium?" asked Gub-Gub.

"A sanitarium," said the Doctor, "is a sort of mixture between a hospital and a hotel—where people stay who are invalids. . . . Well, I agreed to this idea. Then I and my young friend—his name was Phipps, Dr. Cornelius Q. Phipps—took a beautiful place way off in the country, and we furnished it with wheelchairs and hot-water bottles and ear trumpets and the things that invalids like. And very soon patients came to us in hundreds and our sanitarium was quite full and my new thermometer was kept very busy. Of course, we made a lot of money, because all these people paid us well. And Phipps was very happy.

"But I was not so happy. I had noticed a peculiar thing: none of the invalids ever seemed to get well and go away. And finally I spoke of this to Phipps.

"'My dear Dolittle,' he answered, '*go away?*—of course not! We don't want them to go away. We want them to stay here, so they'll keep on paying us.'

"'Phipps,' I said, 'I don't think that's honest. I became a doctor to cure people—not to pamper them.'

"Well, on this point we fell out and quarreled. I got very angry and told him I would not be his partner any longer—that I would pack up and go the following day. As I left his room, still very angry, I passed one of the invalids in his wheelchair. It was Sir Timothy Quisby, our most important and wealthiest patient. He asked me, as I passed, to take his temperature, as he thought he had a new fever. Now, I had never been able to find anything wrong with Sir Timothy and had decided that being an invalid was a sort of hobby with him. So, still very angry, instead of taking his temperature, I said quite rudely: 'Oh, go to the Dickens!'

"Sir Timothy was furious. And, calling for Dr. Phipps, he

"It was Sir Timothy Quisby, our wealthiest patient."

demanded that I apologize. I said I wouldn't. Then Sir Timothy told Phipps that if I didn't, he would start an invalids' strike. Phipps got terribly worried and implored me to apologize to this very special patient. I still refused.

"Then a peculiar thing happened. Sir Timothy, who had always so far seemed too weak to walk, got right out of his wheelchair and, waving his ear trumpet wildly, ran around all over the sanitarium, making speeches to the other invalids, saying how shamefully he had been treated, and calling on them to strike for their rights.

"And they did strike—make no mistake. That night at dinner they refused to take their medicine—either before or after meals.

Dr. Phipps argued with them, prayed them, implored them to behave like proper invalids and carry out their doctors' orders. But they wouldn't listen to him. They ate all the things they had been forbidden to eat, and after dinner those who had been ordered to go for a walk stayed at home, and those who had been ordered to stay quiet went outside and ran up and down the street. They finished the evening by having a pillow fight with their hot-water bottles, when they should have been in bed. The next morning they all packed their own trunks and left. And that was the end of *our* sanitarium.

"But the most peculiar thing of all was this: I found out afterward that every single one of those patients had got well! Getting out of their wheelchairs and going on strike had done them so much good that they stopped being invalids altogether. As a sanitarium doctor, I suppose I was not a success—still, I don't know. Certainly I cured a great many more patients by going *out* of the sanitarium business than Phipps ever did by going into it."

THE THIRD CHAPTER

Gub-Gub's Story

THE NEXT NIGHT, WHEN THEY WERE AGAIN seated around the veranda after supper, the Doctor asked: "Now, who's going to tell us a story tonight? Didn't Gub-Gub say he had one for us?"

"Oh, don't let him tell one, Doctor," said Jip. "It's sure to be stupid."

"He isn't old enough to tell a good story," said Dab-Dab. "He hasn't had any experience."

"His only interest in life is food, anyway," said Too-Too. "Let someone else tell a story."

"No, now wait a minute," cried the Doctor. "Don't all be jumping on him this way. We were all young once. Let him tell his story. He may win the prize. Who knows? Come along, Gub-Gub. Tell us your story. What's the name of it?"

Gub-Gub fidgeted his feet, blushed up to the ears, and finally said:

"This is kind of a crazy story. But it's a good one. It's—er—er—a piggish fairy tale. It's called 'The Magic Cucumber.'"

"Gosh!" growled Jip.

"More food!" murmured Too-Too. "What did I tell you?"

"Tee-hee-hee!" tittered the white mouse.

"Go on, Gub-Gub," said the Doctor. "Don't take any notice of them. I'm listening."

"Once upon a time," Gub-Gub began, "a small pig went out into the forest with his father to dig for truffles. The father pig was a very clever truffle digger, and just by smelling the ground he could tell with great sureness the places where truffles were to be found. Well, this day they came upon a place beneath some big oak trees and they started digging. Presently, after the father pig had dug up an enormous truffle and they were both eating it, they heard, to their great astonishment, the sound of voices coming from the hole out of which they had dug the truffle.

"The father pig hurried away with his child because he did not like magic. But that night the baby pig, when his mother and father were fast asleep, crept out of his sty and went off into the woods. He wanted to find out the mystery of those voices coming from under the ground.

"So, reaching the hole where his father had dug up the truffle, he set to work digging for himself. He had not dug very long when the earth caved right in underneath him and he felt himself falling and falling and falling. At last he came to a stop, upside down in the middle of a dining table. The table was all set for dinner—and he had fallen into the soup. He looked about him and saw, seated around the table, many tiny little men, none of them more than half as big as himself, and all a dark green in color.

"'Where am I?' asked the baby pig.

"'You're in the soup,' said the little men.

"He had fallen into the soup."

"The baby pig was at first terribly frightened. But when he saw how small the men around him were, his fear left him. And before he got out of the soup tureen on the table, he drank up all the soup. He then asked the little men who they might be. And they said:

"'We are *The Cook Goblins*. We live under the ground and we spend half our time inventing new things to eat and the other half in eating them. The noise you heard coming out of the hole was us singing our food hymns. We always sing food hymns whenever we are preparing particularly fine dishes.'

"'Good!' said the pig. 'I've come to the right place. Let us go on with the dinner.'

"But just as they were about to begin on the fish (the soup was already gone, you see), there was a great noise outside the dining hall and in rushed another lot of little men, a bright red in color. These were *The Toadstool Sprites*, ancient enemies of the Cook Goblins. A tremendous fight began, one side using toothpicks for spears and the other using nutcrackers for clubs. The pig took the side of his friends the Cook Goblins, and, being as big as any two of the enemy put together, he soon had the Toadstool Sprites running for their lives.

"When the fight was over and the dining hall cleared, the Cook Goblins were very grateful to the baby pig for his valuable assistance. They called him a conquering hero and, crowning him with a wreath of parsley, they invited him to the seat of honor at the dining table and went on with the meal.

"Never had the baby pig enjoyed a meal so much in all his life as he did that one. He found that the Cook Goblins, as well as inventing new and marvelously tasty dishes, had also thought out a lot of new things in the way of table furnishings. For instance, they served pin cushions with the fish. These were to stick your fishbones in, instead of leaving them to clutter up your plate. Pudding fans were another of their novelties—fans for cooling off your pudding, instead of blowing on it. Then they had cocoa-skin clotheslines—little toy clotheslines to hang the skin off your cocoa on, neatly. (You know what a nasty mess it makes draped over the rim of your cup.) And when the fruit came on, tennis racquets were handed around also. And if anyone at the other end of the table asked you for an apple, instead of going to all the work of handing down a heavy bowl of fruit, you just took an apple and served it at him like a tennis ball, and he would catch it at the other end of the table on the point of a fork.

"These things added a good deal of jolliness to the meal, and some of them were very clever inventions. Why, they even had a speaking tube for things you are not allowed to mention at the table."

"A speaking tube!" the white mouse interrupted. "How was it used? I don't understand."

"Well," said Gub-Gub, "you know how people are always telling you 'You mustn't speak about those things at the table!' Well, the Cook Goblins had a speaking tube in the wall which led, at the other end, to the open air outside. And whenever you wanted to talk about any of the things forbidden at the table, you left the table and went and said it into the speaking tube; then you came back to your seat. It was a very great invention. . . . Well, as I was saying, the baby pig enjoyed himself tremendously. And when the meal was over he said he must be going back because he wanted to get into the sty before his mother and father awoke.

"The Cook Goblins were sorry to see him go. And as a farewell present in return for the help he had given them against their enemies, they gave him the Magic Cucumber. Now, this cucumber, if you cut off even the smallest part of it and planted it, would grow immediately into a whole field of any fruit or vegetable you wished. All you had to do was to say the name of the vegetable you wanted. The baby pig thanked the Cook Goblins, kissed them all good-bye, and went home.

"He found his mother and father still asleep when he got back. So after carefully hiding his Magic Cucumber under the floor of the cow barn, he crept into the sty and went fast asleep.

"Now, it happened that a few days later a neighboring king made war upon the king that owned the country where the pig family lived. Things went very badly for the pigs' king, and, seeing that the enemy were close at hand, he gave orders that all cattle and farm animals and people should be brought inside the castle walls. The pig family was also driven into the castle grounds. But before he left, the baby pig went and bit off a piece of his Magic Cucumber and took it along with him.

"Soon after, the enemy's army closed about the castle and tried to storm it. Then for many weeks they remained there, knowing that sooner or later the king and the people in the castle would run short of food and have to give in.

"Now, it happened that the queen had noticed the baby pig within the castle grounds and, she took a great fancy to him and had a piece of green ribbon tied about his neck and made a regular pet of him, much to the disgust of her husband, the king.

"Well, the fourth week after the enemy came, the food in the castle was all gone and the king gave orders that the pigs must be eaten. The queen raised a great outcry and begged that her pet should be spared. But the king was very firm.

"'My soldiers are starving,' said he. 'Your pet, madam, must be turned into sausages.'

"Then the baby pig saw that the time to use the goblins' magic gift had come. And, rushing out into the castle garden, he dug a hole and planted his piece of cucumber right in the middle of the king's best rose bed.

"'Parsnips!' he grunted, as he filled in the hole. 'May they blossom acres wide!'

"And, sure enough, he had hardly said the words before all over the king's garden parsnips began springing up thick and fast. Even the gravel walks were covered with them.

"Then the king and his army had plenty of food and, growing

"She made a regular pet of him."

strong on the nutritious parsnips, they sallied forth from the castle, smote the enemy, hip and thigh, and put them to flight.

"And the queen was allowed to keep her pet pig, which rejoiced her kind heart greatly. And he became a great hero at the court and was given a sty studded with jewels in the center of the castle garden—on the very spot where he had planted the Magic Cucumber. And they all lived happily ever after. And that is the end of the piggish fairy tale."

THE FOURTH CHAPTER

Dab-Dab's Story

THE ANIMALS NOW BEGAN TO LOOK FORWARD to the evening storytelling—the way people do to regular habits that are pleasant. And for the next night they arranged among themselves beforehand that it should be Dab-Dab's turn to tell a tale.

After they were all seated on the veranda, the housekeeper preened her feathers and in a very dignified voice began:

"On the outskirts of Puddleby-on-the-Marsh there lives a farmer who swears to this day that his cat can understand every word he says. It isn't true, but both the farmer and his wife think it is. And I am now going to tell you how they came to get that idea.

"Once when the Doctor was away in Scotland, looking for fossils, he left me behind to take charge of the house. The old horse in the stable complained to me one night that the rats were eating up all his corn. While I was walking around the stable, trying to think out what I should do about it, I spied an enormous white Persian cat stalking about the premises. Now, I myself have no love for cats.

For one thing, they eat ducklings, and for another, they always seem to me sort of sneaky things. So I ordered this one to get off the Doctor's property. To my surprise, she behaved very politely—said she didn't know she was trespassing and turned to leave. Then I felt sort of guilty, knowing the Doctor liked to be hospitable to every kind of animal, and, after all, the cat wasn't doing any harm there. So I overtook her and told her that if she didn't kill anything on the place she could come and go as she pleased.

"Well, we got chatting, the way people do, and I found out that the cat lived at a farmer's house about a quarter of a mile down the Oxenthorpe Road. Then I walked part of the way home with her, still chatting, and I found that she was a very agreeable individual. I told her about the rats in the stable and the difficulty I had in making them behave, because the Doctor wouldn't allow anyone to kill them. And she said, if I wished, she'd sleep in the stable a few nights and the rats would probably leave as soon as they smelled her around.

"This she did, and the results were excellent. The rats departed and the old horse's corn bin was left undisturbed. Then she disappeared and for several nights I saw nothing of her. So one evening I thought it would be only decent of me to call at her farm down the Oxenthorpe Road, to thank her.

"I went to her farm and found her in the farmyard. I thanked her for what she had done and asked her why she hadn't been around to my place of late.

"'I've just had kittens,' she said. 'Six—and I haven't been able to leave them a moment. They are in the farmer's parlor now. Come in and I'll show them to you.'

"So in we went. And on the parlor floor, in a round basket,

there were six of the prettiest kittens you ever saw. While we were looking at them we heard the farmer and his wife coming downstairs. So, thinking they might not like to have a duck in the parlor (some folks are so snobbish and pernickety you know—not like the Doctor), I hid myself behind a closet door just as the farmer and his wife came into the room.

"They leaned over the basket of kittens, stroked the white cat and started talking. Now, the cat didn't understand what they said, of course. But I, being round the Doctor so much and discussing with him the differences between duck grammar and people's grammar, understood every word they uttered.

"And this is what I heard the farmer say to his wife: 'We'll keep the black-and-white kitten, Liza. I'll drown the other five tomorrow morning. Won't never do to have all them cats running around the place." His grammar was atrocious.

"As soon as they had gone I came out of the closet and I said to the white cat: 'I shall expect you to bring up these kittens to leave ducklings alone. Now listen: Tonight, after the farmer and his wife are in bed, take all your kittens *except the black-and-white one*, and hide them in the attic. The farmer means to drown them and is going to keep only one.'

"The cat did as I bade her. And the next morning, when the farmer came to take the kittens away, he found only the black-and-white one—the one he meant to keep. He could not understand it. Some weeks later, however, when the farmer's wife was spring cleaning, she came upon the others in the attic, where the mother cat had hidden them and nursed them secretly. But they were now grown big enough to escape through the window, and they went off to find new homes for themselves.

HUGH LOFTING

"We'll keep the black-and-white one, Liza."

"And that is why to this day that farmer and his wife swear their cat can understand English, because, they say, she must have heard them when they were talking over the basket. And whenever she's in the room and they are gossiping about the neighbors, they always speak in whispers, lest she overhear. But between you and me, she doesn't really understand a single word they say."

The White Mouse's Story

"**W**HOSE TURN IS IT TO GIVE US A STORY now?**" asked the Doctor, when the supper things were cleared away the following evening.

"I think the white mouse ought to tell us one," said Jip.

"Very well," said the white mouse. "I will tell you one from the days of my youth. The Doctor knows this story, but the rest of you have never heard it."

And smoothing back his white whiskers and curling his pink tail snugly about his small, sleek body, he blinked his eyes twice and began:

"When I was born I was one of seven twins. But all my brothers and sisters were an ordinary mouse color and I alone, out of the whole family, was white. My color worried my mother and father a great deal. They said I was so conspicuous and would certainly, as soon as I left the nest, get caught by the first owl or cat that came along.

"We were city folk, my family were—and proud of it. We lived under the floor of a miller's shop. Across the street from our place was a butcher's shop, and next door to us was a dyer's—where they dyed cloth different colors before it went to the tailor's to be made into suits.

"Now, when we children grew up big enough to go off for ourselves, our parents gave us all sorts of careful instructions about escaping cats and ferrets and weasels and dogs. But over poor me they shook their heads. They really felt that there was not much hope of my leading a peaceful life with white fur that could be seen a mile off.

"Well, they were quite right. My color got me into trouble the first week that I set out to seek my fortune—but not in the way they thought it would. The son of the miller who owned the shop where we lived found me one morning in a bin of oats.

"'Aha!' he cried. 'A white mouse! The very thing I've been wanting!'

"And he caught me in a fishing net and put me in a cage, to keep as a pet.

"I was very sad at first. But after a while I got sort of used to the life. The boy—he was only eight years old—treated me kindly and fed me regularly each day. I grew almost fond of the funny, snub-nosed lad and became so tame that he would let me out of my cage sometimes and I would run up and down his sleeve. But I never got a chance to escape.

"After some months I began to grow weary of the silly life I was leading. And then, too, the wild mice were so mean to me. They used to come around at night and point at me through the wire of my cage, saying:

"'Look at the tame white mouse! Tee-hee-hee! A plaything for children! Good little mousey! Come and have 'ims facey washed!' The stupid little idiots!

"Well, finally I set to work and thought out a clever plan of escape. I gnawed a hole through the wooden floor of my cage and kept it covered with straw, so the boy couldn't see it. And one night when I heard him safely snoring—he always kept my cage at the head of his bed—I slipped out of the hole and got away.

"I had many adventures with cats. It was wintertime and the snow lay thick upon the ground. I started off to explore the world, rejoicing in my liberty. Going around to the back of the house, I passed from the miller's yard into the dyer's yard, next door. In the yard was a dyeing shed, and I noticed two owls sitting on the top of it in the moonlight.

"Entering the shed, I met a rat, very old and very thin. Said he to me:

"'I am the oldest rat in the town and I know a great deal. But tell me, why do you come here into the dyeing shed?'

"'I was looking for food,' I said.

"The old rat laughed a cracked and quavering laugh, with no joy in it at all.

"'There's no food here,' he said, 'only dyes of different colors.' And he pointed to the big dye vats, all in a row, that towered in the half darkness above our heads.

"'Any food there was here I've eaten,' he went on sadly, 'and I dare not go out for more because the owls are waiting on the roof. They'd see my dark body against the snow and I'd stand no chance of escape. I am nearly starved.' And he swayed weakly on his old feet. 'But now that you've come, it's different. Some good fairy

"The old rat laughed a quavering laugh."

must have sent you to me. I've been sitting here for days and nights on end, hoping a white mouse might come along. With your white fur, you understand, the owls can't see you so well against the snow. That's what's called *protective coloration*. I know all about natural history—I'm very old, you see. That is why you managed to get in here without being caught. Go out now, for pity's sake, and bring me the first food of any kind that you can find. The owls by night and the cats by day have kept me shut in here since the snow came without a bite to eat. You are only just in time to save my life.'

"So off I went across the moonlit snow, and the blinking owls on the roof of the dyeing shed never spotted me. Against the whiteness I was nearly invisible. I felt quite proud. At last my white fur was coming in handy.

"I found a garbage can and, picking out some bacon rinds, I carried them back to the starving rat. The old fellow was ever so grateful. He ate and ate—my whiskers, how he ate! Finally he said:

"'Ah! Now I feel better.'

"'You know,' said I, 'I have only just escaped from captivity. I was kept as a pet by a boy. So far, being white has only been a great inconvenience to me. The cats could see me so well that life wasn't worth living.'

"'Well now, I'll tell you what we'll do,' said he, 'you come and live in this dyeing shed with me. It isn't a bad place—quite warm and snug under the floors, and the foundations are simply riddled with holes and corridors and hiding places. And while the snow is here, you can go out and get the food for both of us—because you can't be seen so well against the snow. And when the winter is over and the earth is black again, *I* will do the food hunting outside and *you* can do the staying at home. You see, this is a good place to live in in another way—there is nothing for rats and mice to destroy here, so people don't bother about you. Other places—like houses and food shops and mills—folks are always setting traps and sending ferrets after you. But no one minds rats living in a dyeing shed, see? Foolish young rats and mice go and live where there's lots of food. But not for me! I'm a wise one, I am.'

"Well, we agreed upon this arrangement, and for a whole year I lived at the dyer's with the old wise rat. And we lived high—no mistake! Not a soul ever bothered us. In the winter days I did the foraging, and when summer came my old partner, who knew where to get the choicest foods in town, kept our larder stocked with the daintiest delicacies. Ah, many's the jolly meal I've had under the floor of the dye shed with that old veteran, chuckling in whispers as we heard the dyers overhead mixing the dyes in the great big vats and talking over the news of the town!

"But none of us are ever content for long, you know—foolish creatures that we are. And by the time the second summer was coming, I was longing to be a free mouse, to roam the world and all that sort of thing. And then, too, I wanted to get married. Maybe the spring was getting into my blood. So one night I said to the old rat:

"'Rat,' I said, 'I'm in love. All winter, every night I went out to gather fodder, I've been keeping company with a lady mouse— well-bred she is, with elegant manners. I've a mind to settle down and have a family of my own. Now, here comes the summer again and I've got to stay shut up in this miserable shed on account of my beastly color.'

"The old rat gazed at me thoughtfully a moment and I knew that he was going to say something particularly wise.

"'Young man,' said he at last, 'if you've a mind to go, I reckon I can't stop you—foolish young madcap though I think you. And how I'll ever take care of myself after you've gone, goodness only knows. But, seeing you have been so useful to me this past year and more, I'll help you.'

"So saying, he takes me upstairs to where the dye vats stood. It was twilight and the men were gone. But we could see the dim shapes of the big vats towering above our heads. Then he takes a string that lay upon the floor and, scaling up the middle vat, he lets the string down inside.

"'What's that for?' I asked.

HUGH LOFTING

"Upstairs where the dye vats stood"

"'That's for you to climb out by, after you've taken a bath. For you to go abroad in summer with a coat like yours would mean certain death. So I'm going to dye you black.'

"'Jumping Cheese!' I cried. *'Dye me black!'*

"'Just that,' said he. 'It's quite simple. Scale up that middle vat now—onto the edge—and dive right in. Don't be afraid. There's a string there for you to climb out by.'

"Well, I was always adventurous by nature. And plucking up my courage, I scrambled up the vat, onto the edge of it. It was awful dark and I could just see the dye, glimmering murky and dim, far down inside.

"'Go ahead,' said the old rat. 'Don't be afraid—and be sure you dip your head and all under.'

"Well, it took an awful lot of nerve to take that plunge. And if I hadn't been in love, I don't suppose I'd ever have done it. But I did—I dove right down into the dye.

"I thought I'd never come up again, and even when I did I nearly drowned before I found the string in the dark and scrambled, gasping for breath, out of the vat.

"'Fine!' said the old rat, 'Now run around the shed a few times so you won't take a chill. And then go to bed and cover up. In the morning when it's light, you'll find yourself very different.'

"Well—tears come to my eyes when I think of it—the next day, when I woke up, expecting to find myself a smart, decent black, I found instead that I had dyed myself a bright and gaudy *blue*! That old rat had made a mistake in the vats!"

The white mouse paused a moment in his story, as though overcome with emotion. Presently he went on:

"Never have I been so furious with anyone in my life as I was with that old rat.

"'Look! *Look* what you've done to me now!' I cried. 'It isn't even a navy blue. You've made me just hideous!'

"'I can't understand it,' he murmured. 'The middle vat *used* to be the black one, I know. They must have changed them. The blue one was always the one on the left.'

"'You're an old fool!' I said. And I left the dye shed in great anger and never went back to it again.

"Well, if I had been conspicuous before, now I was a hundred times more so. Against the black earth, or the green grass, or the white snow, or brown floors, my loud, sky-blue coat could be seen as plain as a pikestaff. The minute I got outside the shed, a cat jumped for me. I gave her the slip and got out into the street. There some wretched children spotted me and, calling to their friends that they had seen a blue mouse, they hunted me along the gutter. At the corner of the street two dogs were fighting. They stopped their fight and joined the chase after me. And very soon I had the whole blessed town at my heels. It was awful. I didn't get any peace till after night had fallen, and by that time I was so exhausted with running I was ready to drop.

"About midnight I met the lady mouse with whom I was in love, beneath a lamppost. And would you believe it? She wouldn't speak to me! Cut me dead, she did.

"'It was for your sake I got myself into this beastly mess,' I said, as she stalked by me with her nose in the air. 'You're an ungrateful woman, that's what you are.'

"'Oh, la, la, la!' said she, smirking. 'You wouldn't expect any self respecting person to keep company with a *blue* mouse, would you?'

"Later, when I was trying to find a place to sleep, all the mice I met, wherever there was any light at all, made fun of me and pointed at me and jeered. I was nearly in tears. Then I went down to the river, hoping I might wash the dye off and so get white again. That, at least, would be better than the way I was now. But I washed and I swam and I rinsed, all to no purpose. Water made no impression on me.

"So there I sat, shivering on the riverbank, in the depths of despair. And presently I saw the sky in the east growing pale and I knew that morning was coming. Daylight! That for me meant more hunting and running and jeering, as soon as the sun should show my ridiculous color.

"And then I came to a very sad decision—probably the saddest decision that a free mouse ever made. Rather than be hunted and jeered at anymore, I decided that I would sooner be back in a cage, a pet mouse! Yes, there at least I was well treated and well fed by the snub-nosed miller lad. I would go back and be a captive mouse. Was I not spurned by my lady love and jeered at by my friends? Very well then, I would turn my back upon the world and go into captivity. And then my lady love would be sorry—too late!

"So, picking myself up wearily, I started off for the miller's shop. On the threshold I paused a moment. It was a terrible step I was about to take. I gazed miserably down the street, thinking upon the hardness of life and the sadness of love, and there, coming toward me, with a bandage around his tail, was my own brother!

"As he took a seat beside me on the doorstep I burst into tears and told him all that had happened to me since we left our parents' home.

"'I am terribly sorry for your bad luck,' said he when I had ended. 'But I'm glad I caught you before you went back into captivity. Because I think I can guide you to a way out of your troubles.'

"'What way is there?' I said. 'For me life is over!'

"'Go and see the Doctor,' said my brother.

"'What doctor?' I asked.

"'There *is* only one Doctor,' he answered. 'You don't mean to say you've never *heard* of him!'

"And then he told me all about Doctor Dolittle. This was around the time when the Doctor first began to be famous among the animals. But I, living alone with the old rat at the dyer's shed, had not heard the news.

"'I've just come from the Doctor's office,' said my brother. 'I got my tail caught in a trap and he bandaged it up for me. He's a marvelous man—kind and honest. And he talks animals' language. Go to him and I'm sure he'll know some way to clean blue dye off a mouse. He knows everything.'

"So that is how I first came to John Dolittle's house in Puddleby. The Doctor, when I told my troubles to him, took a very small pair of scissors and cut off all my fur so I was as bald and as pink as a pig. Then he rubbed me with some special hair restorer for mice—a patent invention of his own. And very soon I grew a brand new coat of fur, as white as snow!

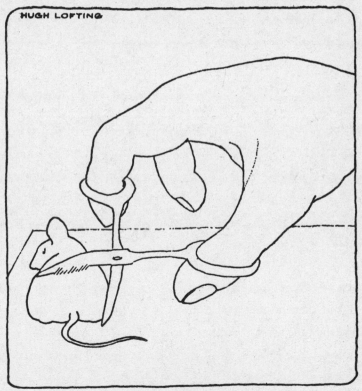

"The Doctor cut off all my fur."

"And then, hearing what difficulty I had had keeping away from cats, the Doctor gave me a home in his own house—in his own piano, in fact. And no mouse could wish for more than that. He even offered to send for the lady I was in love with, who would, no doubt, think differently about me now that I was white again. But I said:

"'No, Doctor. Let her be. I'm through with women for good.'"

THE SIXTH CHAPTER

Jip's Story

THE NEXT NIGHT JIP WAS CALLED UPON FOR A story. And after thinking a moment he said: "All right, I'll tell you the story of 'The Beggar's Dog.'" And the animals all settled down to listen attentively, because Jip had often told them stories before, and they liked his way of telling them.

"Some time ago," Jip began, "I knew a dog who was a beggar's dog. We met by chance one day when a butcher's cart had an accident and got upset. The butcher's boy who was driving the cart was a mean boy whom all the dogs of that town heartily disliked. So when his cart hit a lamppost and overturned, spilling mutton chops and joints all over the street, we dogs were quickly on the scene and ran off with all his meat before he had time to pick himself up out of the gutter.

"It was on this occasion, as I said, that I fell in with the beggar's dog. I found him bolting down the street beside me, with a choice steak flapping merrily around his ears. Myself, I had pinched a string of sausages, and the beastly things kept getting tangled up in my legs, till he came to my rescue and showed me how to coil them up neatly so I could run with them without getting tripped.

"After that the beggar's dog and I became great friends. I found that his master had only one leg and was very, very old.

"'He's most frightfully poor,' said my friend. 'And he's too old to work, you see—even if he had two legs to get around on. And now he has taken to pavement art. You know what that is—you draw pictures on the pavement in colored chalks and you write under them: *"All my own work."* And then you sit by the side of them, with your cap in your hand, waiting for people to give you pennies.'

"'Oh yes,' I said, 'I know. I've seen pavement artists before.'

"'Well,' said my friend, 'my beggar doesn't get any pennies. And I know the reason why: his pictures aren't good enough— not even for pavement art. Myself, I don't pretend to know much about drawing. But his pictures are just awful—*awful*. One kind old lady the other day stopped before our stand—wanting to encourage him, you know—and, pointing to one picture, she said, *"Oh, what a lovely tree!"* The picture was meant to be a lighthouse in the middle of the ocean, with a storm raging around it. That's the kind of an artist my man is. I don't know what to do about him.'

"'Well, look here,' I said, 'I have an idea. Since your man can't work for himself, suppose you and I go into the bone-hiring business.'

"'What on earth is that?' he asked.

"'Well,' I said, 'people hire out bicycles and pianos for rent, don't they? So why can't you and I rent out bones for dogs to chew? They won't be able to pay us in money, of course, so we'll get them to bring us things, instead. Then the beggar can sell the things and get money.'

"'That's a good notion,' said he. 'Let's start tomorrow.'"

"His pictures are just awful."

"So the following day we found an empty lot where people used to dump rubbish, and dug an enormous hole, which was to be our bone shop. Then we went around the back doors of all the richest people's houses early in the morning and picked out the best bones from the garbage cans. We even snatched a few from other dogs who were tied to kennels and couldn't run after us—rather a dirty trick, but we were working in a good cause and were not particular. Then we took all these bones and put them in the hole we had dug. By night we kept them covered up with earth, because we didn't want them stolen—and besides, some dogs prefer their bones buried a few days before they chew them. It gets them seasonedlike.

And then by day we stood over our wares, calling out to all the dogs that passed by:

"'Bones for hire! Beef bones, ham bones, mutton bones! All juicy! Step up, gentlemen, and take your choice! BONES for hire!'

"Well, right from the start we did a roaring trade. All the dogs for miles around heard of us and came to rent bones. And we would charge them according to the length of time they wanted to rent them. For instance, you could rent a good ham bone for one day in exchange for a candlestick or a hairbrush; three days for a violin or an umbrella. And if you wanted your bone for a whole week, you had to bring us a suit of clothes in payment.

"Well, for a while our plan worked splendidly. The beggar sold the things that we got in payment from the dogs, and he had money to live on.

"But we never thought where the dogs might be getting all these things they brought us. The truth is, we didn't bother very much, I'm afraid. Anyway, at the end of our first week of brisk trade we noticed a great many people going through the streets as though they were looking for something. And presently these people, seeing our shop in the empty lot, gathered around us, talking to one another. And while they were talking, a retriever came up to me with a gold watch and chain in his mouth, which he wanted to exchange for a ham bone.

"Well, you should have seen the excitement among the people then! The owner of the watch and chain was there, and he raised a terrible row. And then it came out that these dogs had been taking things from their masters' homes to rent bones with. The people were dreadfully annoyed. They closed up our bone shop and put us

"A retriever came up with a gold watch and chain."

out of business. But they never discovered that the money we had made had gone to the beggar.

"Of course, we hadn't made enough to keep him in comfort for long, and very soon he had to become a pavement artist again and was as badly off as he had ever been—and the pictures he drew were worse, if anything, than before.

"Now it happened one day, when I was wandering around in the country outside the town, that I met a most conceited spaniel. He passed me with his nose turned up in the air in such a cheeky manner that I said to him, I said: 'What makes you so stuck up?'

"'My master has been ordered to paint the portrait of a prince,' he said, putting on no end of elegance.

"'Who is your master?' I said. 'Anybody would think you were going to paint the portrait yourself.'

"'My master is a very famous artist,' said he.

"'What's his name?' I asked.

"'George Morland,' said the spaniel.

"'George Morland!' I cried. 'Is he in these parts now?'

"'Yes,' said the spaniel. 'We are staying at the Royal George. My master is painting some pictures of the country and next week he is going back to London to commence on the portrait of the prince.'

"Now, it happened that I had met this George Morland, who was, and is still, perhaps the most famous painter of farm-life pictures the world has ever known. I am proud to be able to say that I knew him. He was especially good at painting horses in stables, pigs in styes, roosters and dogs hanging around kitchen doors, and things like that.

"So, without letting the spaniel see that I was following him, I went after him, to see where he was going.

"He led me to a lonely old farm out on the hills. And there, concealing myself in some bushes, I watched the great Morland painting one of his famous farm scenes.

"Presently he laid down his paintbrush and muttered to himself: 'I need a dog—by the watering trough there—to fill out the picture. I wonder if I could get that fool spaniel to lie still for five minutes. . . . Here, Spot, Spot! Come here!'

"His spaniel, Spot, came up to him. And George, leaving his painting for a moment, placed the spaniel beside the watering trough and flattened him out and told him to keep still. I could see that George's idea was to have him look as though he were asleep in the sun. George simply loved to paint animals asleep in the sun.

"Well, that blockhead of a spaniel never kept still one minute. First he was snapping at the flies that bit his tail; then he was scratching his ear, then barking at the cat—never still. And, of course, George couldn't paint him at all, and at last he got so angry he threw the paintbrush at him.

"Then an idea came to me—one of the best ideas I ever had. I left the bushes and came trotting up to George, wagging my tail. And how I thrilled with pride as the great Morland recognized me! For, mind you, he had met me only once before—back in the autumn of 1802.

"'Why, it's Jip!' he cried. 'Good dog. Come here. You're the very fellow I want.'"

"Then while he gathered up the things he had thrown at the spaniel, he went on talking to me—the way people do talk to dogs, you know. Of course, he didn't expect me to understand what he said, but I did—every word.

"'I want you to come over here by the trough, Jip,' said he. 'All you've got to do is to keep still. You can go to sleep if you like. But don't move or fidget for ten minutes. Think you can do that?'

"And he led me over to the trough, where I lay down and kept perfectly still while he painted me into the picture. That picture now hangs in the National Gallery. It's called *Evening on the Farm*. Hundreds of people go to see it every year. But none of them know that the smart-looking dog sleeping beneath the watering trough is none other than myself—except the Doctor, whom I took in to see it one day when we were up in London, shopping.

"Come over here by the trough."

"Well now, as I told you, I had an idea in all this. I hoped that if I did something for George Morland, perhaps I could get him to do something for me. But, of course, with him not knowing dog talk, it was a bit difficult to make him understand. However, while he was packing up his painting things I disappeared for a while, just as though I was going away. Then I came rushing back to him in a great state of excitement, barking, trying to show him something was wrong and that I wanted him to follow me.

"'What's the matter, Jip?' said he. 'House on fire or something?'

"Then I barked some more and ran a little way in the direction of the town, looking back at him to show him I wanted him to come with me.

"'What ails the dog?' he murmured to himself. 'Can't be anybody drowning, because there's no river near. . . . Oh, all right, Jip, I'll come. Wait a second till I get these brushes cleaned.'

"Then I led him into the town. On the way there, every once in a while he would say to himself: 'I wonder what can be the matter. Something's wrong, that's for sure, or the dog wouldn't carry on so.'

"I took him down the main street of the town till we came to the place where the beggar had his pictures. And as soon as George saw the pictures, he *knew* what was wrong.

"'Heaven preserve us!' he cried. 'What a dreadful exhibition! No wonder the dog was excited.'

"Well, it happened that as we came up, the one-legged beggar, with his own dog beside him, was at work on a new drawing. He was sitting on the pavement, making a picture on canvas with a piece of chalk of a cat drinking milk. Now, my idea was that the great Morland—who, no matter what people say about him, was always a most kindhearted man—should make some good pictures for the beggar to show, instead of the dreadful messes that he made himself. And my plan worked.

"'Man alive!' said George, pointing to the picture the beggar was doing, 'a cat's spine doesn't curve that way—here, give me the chalk and let me do it.'

"Then, rubbing out the whole picture, George Morland redrew it in his way. And it was so lifelike you could nearly hear the cat lapping up the milk.

"'My! I wish I could draw that way,' said the beggar. 'And so quick and easy you do it—like it was nothing at all.'

"'Well, it comes easy,' said George. 'Maybe there's not so much credit in it for that. But tell me, do you make much money at this game?'

"'Awful little,' said the beggar. 'I've taken only twopence the whole day. I suppose the truth is I don't draw good enough.'

"I watched Morland's face as the beggar said this. And the expression that came into it told me I had not brought the great man here in vain.

"'Look here,' he said to the beggar. 'Would you like me to redraw all your pictures for you? Of course, those done on the pavement you couldn't sell, but we can rub them out. And I've got some spare canvases in my satchel here. Maybe you could sell a few. I can sell pictures in London any day in the week. But I've never been a pavement artist before. It would be rather a lark to see what happens.'

"Then Morland, all busy and excited like a schoolboy, took the beggar's chalk pictures from against the wall and, rubbing them out, did them over the way they should be done. He got so occupied with this that he didn't notice that a whole crowd of people was gathering around, watching. His work was so fine that the people were spellbound with the beauty of the cats and dogs and cows and horses that he drew. And they began asking one another in whispers who the stranger could be who was doing the pavement artist's pictures for him.

"The crowd grew bigger and bigger. And presently someone among the people who had seen Morland's pictures before recognized the work of the great artist. And then whispers went through the crowd—'It's Morland—the great Morland, himself.' And somebody went off and told a picture dealer—that is, a man who buys and sells pictures—who had a shop in the High Street, that George Morland was drawing in the marketplace for a lame beggar.

"And the dealer came down. And the mayor came down—and all the rich folk and poor folk. So, when the whole town was gathered around, the people began offering to buy these pictures, asking the beggar how much he wanted for them. The old duffer was going to sell them at sixpence apiece, but Morland whispered to him:

"'Twenty guineas—don't sell a blessed one under twenty guineas. You'll get it.'

"And sure enough, the dealer and a few of the richer townsfolk bought the whole lot at twenty guineas apiece.

"And when I went home that night I felt I had done a good day's work. For my friend's master, the one-legged beggar, was now rich enough to live in comfort for the rest of his life."

THE SEVENTH CHAPTER

Too-Too's Story

ALL THE ANIMALS HAD NOW TOLD A STORY except Too-Too the owl and the Pushmi-Pullyu. And the following night, a Friday, it was agreed that they should toss a coin (the Doctor's penny that had a hole through it) to see which of these two should tell a tale. If the penny came down heads it was to be the Pushmi-Pullyu, and if it came down tails it was to be Too-Too's turn.

The Doctor spun the penny and it came down tails.

"All right," said Too-Too. "Then that makes it my turn, I suppose. I will tell you a story of the time—the only time in my life—that I was taken for a fairy. Fancy me as a fairy!" chuckled the little round owl. "Well, this is how it happened: One October day, toward evening, I was wandering through the woods. There was a wintry tang in the air and the small, furred animals were busy among the dry, rustly leaves, gathering nuts and seeds for food against the coming of snow. I was out after shrewmice, myself—a delicacy I was extremely fond of at that time—and while they were busy foraging, they made easy hunting.

HUGH LOFTING

"The Doctor spun the penny."

"In my travels through the woods I heard children's voices and the barking of a dog. Usually I would have gone farther into the forest, away from such sounds. But in my young days I was a curious bird, and my curiosity often led me into many adventures. So instead of flying away, I went toward the noises I heard, moving cautiously from tree to tree so that I could see without being seen.

"Presently I came upon a children's picnic—several boys and girls having supper in a grove of oak trees. One boy, much larger than the rest, was teasing a dog. And two other children, a small girl and a small boy, were objecting to his cruelty and begging him to stop. The bully wouldn't stop. And soon the small boy and girl set upon him with their fists and feet and gave him quite a fine drubbing—which greatly surprised him. The dog then ran off home and presently the small boy and girl—I found out afterward they were brother and sister—wandered off from the rest of the picnicking party to look for mushrooms.

"I had admired their spirit greatly in punishing a boy so much bigger than they were. And when they wandered off by themselves, again out of curiosity, I followed them. Well, they traveled quite a distance for such small folk. And presently the sun set and darkness began to creep over the woods.

"Then the children thought to join their friends again and started back. But, being poor woodsmen, they took the wrong direction. It grew darker still, of course, as time went on, and soon the youngsters were tumbling and stumbling over roots they could not see, and getting pretty thoroughly lost and tired.

"All this time I was following them secretly and noiselessly overhead. At last the children sat down and the little girl said:

"'Willie, we're lost! Whatever shall we do? Night is coming on and I'm *so* afraid of the dark.'

"'So am I,' said the boy. 'Ever since Aunt Emily told us that spooky story of the "Bogey in the Cupboard" I've been scared to death of the dark.'

"Well, you could have knocked me down with a feather. Of course, you must realize that was the first time I had ever heard of anyone's being afraid of the dark. It sounds ridiculous enough to all of you, I suppose, but to me, who had always preferred the cool, calm darkness to the glaring, vulgar daylight, it seemed then an almost unbelievable thing that anyone could be afraid merely because the sun had gone to bed.

"Now, some people have an idea that bats and owls can see in the dark because we have some peculiar kind of eyes. It's not so. Peculiar ears we have—but not eyes. We can see in the dark because we practice it. It's all a matter of practice—the same as the piano or anything else. We get up when other people go to bed, and go to bed when other people get up, because we prefer the dark; and you'd be surprised how much nicer it is when you get used to it. Of course, we owls are specially trained by our mothers and fathers to see on very dark nights when we are quite young. So it comes easier to us. But anybody can do it—to a certain extent—if they only practice.

"Well, to return to the children: There they were, all fussed and worried and scared, sitting on the ground, weeping and wondering what they could do. Then, remembering the dog and knowing they were kind to animals, I thought I would try to help them. So I popped across into the tree over their heads and said in the kindliest, gentlest sort of a voice *'Too-wit, Too-hoo!'*— which means in owl language—as you know—'It's a fine night! How are you?'

"Then you should have seen those poor children jump!

"'Ugh!' says the little girl, clutching her brother around the neck. 'What was that, a spook?'

"'I don't know,' says the little boy. 'Gosh, but I'm scared! Isn't the dark awful?'

"Then I made two or three more attempts to comfort them, talking kindly to them in owl language. But they only grew scareder and scareder. First they thought I was a bogey; then an ogre; then a giant of the forest—me, whom they could put in their pockets! Golly, but these human creatures do bring up their children in awful

"What was that?"

ignorance! If there ever was a bogey or a giant or an ogre—in the forest or out of it—I've yet to see one.

"Then I thought maybe if I went off through the woods too-witting and too-hooing all the way, they would follow me and I could then lead them out of the forest and show them the way home. So I tried it. But they didn't follow me, the silly pair—thinking I was a witch or some evil nonsense of that kind. And all I got for my too-witting and too-hooing all over the place was to wake up another owl some distance off, who thought I was calling to him.

"So, since I wasn't doing the children any good, I went off to look up this other owl and see if he had any ideas to suggest. I found him sitting on the stump of a hollow birch, rubbing his eyes, having just got out of bed.

"'Good evening,' says I. 'It's a fine night!'

"'It is,' says he, 'only it's not dark enough. What were you making all that racket over there for just now? Waking a fellow out of his sleep before it's got properly dark!'

"'I'm sorry,' I said, 'but there's a couple of children over in the hollow there who've got lost. The silly little duffers are sitting on the ground, bawling because the daylight's gone and they don't know what to do.'

"'My gracious!' says he. 'What a quaint notion. Why don't you lead them out of the woods? They probably live over in one of those farms near the crossroads.'

"'I've tried,' I said. 'But they're so scared, they won't follow me. They don't like my voice or something. They take me for a wicked ogre, and all that sort of rot.'

"'Well,' says he, 'then you'll have to give an imitation of some other kind of creature—one they're not scared of. Are you any good at imitations? Can you bark like a dog?'

"'No,' I said. 'But I can make a noise like a cat. I learned that from an American catbird that lived in a cage in the stable where I spent last summer.'

"'Fine,' says he. 'Try that and see what happens!'

"So I went back to the children and found them weeping harder than ever. Then, keeping myself well hidden down near the ground among the bushes, I went *'Meow! Me-o-w!'* real catlike.

"'Oh, Willie,' says the little girl to her brother, 'we're saved!' ('Saved,' mark you, when neither of them was in the slightest danger!) 'We're saved!' says she. 'There's Tuffie, our cat, come for us.

She'll show us the way home. Cats can always find their way home, can't they, Willie? Let's follow her!'"

For a moment Too-Too's plump sides shook with silent laughter as he recalled the scene he was describing.

"Then," said he, "I went a little farther off, still taking great care that I shouldn't be seen, and I meowed again.

"'There she is!' said the little girl. 'She's calling to us. Come along, Willie.'"

"Well, in that way, keeping ahead of them and calling like a cat, I finally led the children right out of the woods. They did a good deal of stumbling, and the girl's long hair often got caught in the bushes, but I always waited for them if they were lagging behind. At last, when we gained the open fields, we saw three houses on the skyline, and the middle one was all lit up and people with lanterns were running around it, hunting in all directions.

"When I had brought the children right up to this house, their mother and father made a tremendous fuss, weeping over them, as though they had been saved from some terrible danger. In my opinion grown-up humans are even more stupid than the young ones. You'd think, from the way that mother and father carried on, that those children had been wrecked on a desert island or something, instead of spending a couple of hours in the pleasant woods.

"'However did you find your way, Willie?' asked the mother, wiping away her tears and smiling all over.

"'Tuffie brought us home,' says the little girl. 'She came out after us and led us here by going ahead of us and meowing.'

"'*Tuffie!*' says the mother, puzzled. 'Why, the cat's asleep in the parlor in front of the fire—been there all evening.'

"'Well, it was some cat,' says the boy. 'He must be right around here somewhere, because he led us almost up to the door.'

"Then the father swings his lantern around, looking for a cat; and before I had time to hop away he throws the light full on me, sitting on a sage bush.

"'Why, it's an *owl!*' cries the little girl.

"'*Meow!*' says I—just to show off. '*Too-wit, Too-hoo! Meow! Meow!*' And with a farewell flip of the wing, I disappeared into the night over the barn roof. But as I left, I heard the little girl saying in tremendous excitement:

"'Oh, mother, a fairy! It was a fairy that brought us home. It must have been—disguised as an owl! At last! At last I've seen a fairy!'

"Well, that's the first and last time I ever expect to be taken for a fairy. But I got to know those children quite well. They were a real nice couple of kiddies—even if the little girl did keep on insisting that I was a fairy in disguise. I used to hang around their barn at night, looking for mice and rats. But if those youngsters ever caught sight of me, they'd follow me everywhere. After bringing them safely home that evening, I could have led them across the Sahara Desert and they'd follow—certain in their minds that I was the best of all good fairies and would keep them out of harm. They used to bring me mutton chops and shrimps and all the best tit-bits from their parents' table. And I lived like a fighting cock—got so fat and lazy I couldn't have caught a mouse on crutches.

"They were never afraid of the dark again. Because, you see— as I said to the Doctor one day, when we were talking over the multiplication tables and other philosophy—fear is usually ignorance. Once you know a thing, you're no longer afraid of it. And those youngsters got to know the dark—and then they saw, of course, that it was just as harmless as the day.

"I used to take them out into the woods at night and across the hills, and they got to love it—liked the adventure, you know. And thinking it would be a good thing if some humans, anyway, had sense enough to travel without sunlight, I taught them how to see in the dark. They soon got on to it, when they saw how I always shaded my eyes in the light of a lantern, so as not to get into the habit of seeing in strong light. Well, those young ones became real experts—not so good as an owl or a bat, of course, but quite good at seeing in the dark, for anyone who had not been brought up that way.

"It came in handy for them, too. That part of the country got flooded one springtime in the middle of the night and there wasn't a dry match or a light to be had anywhere. Then those children, who had traveled all over that countryside scores of times in the dark with me, saved a great many lives. They acted as guides, you understand, and took the people to safety, because they knew how to use their eyes, and the others didn't."

Too-Too yawned and blinked up sleepily at the lantern hanging above his head.

"Seeing in the dark," he ended, "is all a matter of practice—same as the piano or anything else."

THE EIGHTH CHAPTER

The Pushmi-Pullyu's Story

ND NOW IT CAME, AT LAST, TO THE PUSHMI-
Pullyu's turn for a story. He was very shy and modest,
and when the animals asked him the following night,
he said in his very well-bred manner:

"I'm terribly sorry to disappoint you, but I'm afraid I don't know
any stories—at least none good enough to entertain you with."

"Oh, come on, Push," said Jip. "Don't be so bashful. We've
all told one. You don't mean to say you've lived all your life in the
African jungle without seeing any adventures? There must be lots
of yarns you could tell us."

"But I've mostly led such a quiet life, you see," said the Pushmi-
Pullyu. "Our people have always kept very much to themselves. We
mind our own business and don't like getting mixed up in scandals
and rows and adventures."

"Oh, but just think a minute," said Dab-Dab. "Something will
come to you. . . . Don't pester him," she whispered to the others.
"Just leave him alone and let him think—he's got two heads to

think with, you know. Something will come to him. But don't get him embarrassed, whatever you do."

For a moment or two the Pushmi-Pullyu pawed the deck of the veranda with his dainty hooves, as if wrapped in deep thought. Then, looking up with one of his heads, he began speaking in a quiet voice, while the other coughed apologetically below the level of the tea table.

"Er—this isn't much of a story—not really. But perhaps it will serve to pass the time. I will tell you about the Badamoshi ostrich hunters. You must know, then, that people have various methods of hunting wild animals. And the way they go about it depends on the kind of animal they mean to hunt. For example, if they want giraffes, they dig deep holes and cover them up with light boughs and grass. Next, they wait until the giraffe comes along and walks over the hole and falls in. Then they run up and catch him. For certain kinds of rather stupid deer they make a little screen of branches and leaves about the size of a man. And the hunter, holding the screen in front of him like a shield, creeps slowly forward until he is close to the deer, and then fires his spear or arrow. Of course, the stupid deer thinks the moving leaves are just trees being swayed by the wind and takes very little notice, if the hunter is careful to approach quietly enough.

"There are various other dodges, more or less underhanded and deceitful, for getting game. But the one invented by the Badamoshi ostrich hunters was perhaps the meanest of them all. Briefly, this was it: Ostriches, you know, usually go about in small herds, like cattle. And they're rather stupid. You've heard the story about their sticking their heads in the sand when a man comes along, thinking that because they can't see the man, the man can't see them. That doesn't speak very well for their intelligence, does it? No. Very well, then. Now, in the Badamoshi country there wasn't much sand for the ostriches to stick their heads in—which in a way was a good thing for them. Because there, when a man came along, they ran away instead—I suppose to look for sand. Anyhow, the running away saved their lives. So the hunters had to think out some trick of coming near enough to the ostriches to get among the herd and kill them. And the way they thought of was quite clever. As a matter of fact, I by chance came upon a group of these hunters in the woods one day, practicing their new trick. They had the skin of an ostrich and were taking it in turns, putting it over their heads and trying to walk and look like a real ostrich, holding up the long neck with a stick. Keeping myself concealed, I watched them and saw at once what their game was. They meant to disguise themselves as ostriches and walk among the herd and kill them with axes that they kept hidden inside the skin.

"Now, the ostriches of those parts were great friends of mine— had been ever since they put the Badamoshis' tennis court out of business. The chief of the tribe some years before, finding a beautiful meadow of elephant grass—which happened to be my favorite grazing ground—had the fine hay all burned off and made the place into a tennis court. He had seen men playing that game and thought he'd like to play it, too. But the ostriches took the tennis balls for apples and ate them—you know, they're dreadfully unparticular about their food. Yes, they used to sneak around in the jungles on the edge of the tennis court, and whenever a ball was knocked out of the court they'd run off with it and swallow it. By eating up all the chief's tennis balls in this way, they put the tennis court out of business, and my beautiful grazing ground soon grew its long grass again and I came back to it. That is how the ostriches happened to be friends of mine.

"So, seeing they were threatened by a secret danger, I went off and told the leader of the herd about it. He was frightfully stupid and I had the hardest work getting it into his head.

"'Now, remember,' I said as I was leaving, 'you can easily tell the hunter when he comes among your herd from the color and shape of his legs.' You see, the skin that the Badamoshis were going to use did not cover the hunters' legs. 'Now,' I said, 'you must tell all your birds when they see an odd-legged ostrich trying to make friends with them, to set on him and give him a good hiding. That will teach the hunters a lesson.'

"Well, you'd think after that, everything should have gone smoothly. But I had not counted on the extraordinary stupidity of ostriches. The leader, going home that night, stepped into some marshy, boggy places and got his long legs covered with mud—caked with it, thick. Then before he went to bed, he gave all the ostriches the careful instructions that I had given to him.

"The next morning he was late in getting up and the herd was out ahead of him, feeding in a pleasant place on the hillside. Then that numbskull of a leader, without bothering to brush the mud off his legs which he had stepped into the night before, comes stalking out into the open space like a king, expecting a grand reception. And he got a grand reception, too—the ignoramus! As soon as the others saw his odd legs, they passed the word around quickly and at a given signal they set on the poor leader and nearly beat the life out of him. The Badamoshis, who had not yet appeared at all, arrived upon the scene at this moment. And the silly ostriches were so busy beating their leader, whom they took for a hunter in disguise, that the men came right up to them and would have caught the whole lot if I hadn't shouted in time to warn them of their danger.

"So, after that, of course, I saw that if I wanted to save my good but foolish friends from destruction, I had better do something on my own account.

"And this was what I thought I'd do: when the Badamoshi hunters were asleep, I would go and take that ostrich skin—the only one they had—away from them, and that would be the end of their grand new hunting trick.

"So in the dead of night I crept out of the jungle and came to the place where the hunters' huts were. I had to come up from the leeward side, because I didn't want to have the dogs get my scent on the wind. I was more afraid of the hunters' dogs, you see, than I was of the hunters themselves. From the men I could escape quite easily, being much swifter than they were; but dogs, with their sense of smell, are much harder to get away from, even when you can reach the cover of the jungle.

"Well then, coming up from the leeward side, I started searching around the huts for the ostrich skin. At first I couldn't find it anywhere. And I began to think they must have hidden it someplace. Now, the Badamoshis, when they go to bed for the night, always leave one of their number outside the huts to watch and keep guard. I could see this night watchman at the end of the row of huts, and of course I was careful not to let him see me. But after spending some time hunting for this ostrich skin, I noticed that the watchman had not moved at all, but stayed in the same place, squatting on a stool. Then I guessed he had probably fallen asleep. So I moved closer and I found, to my horror, that he was wearing the ostrich skin as a blanket—for the night was cool.

"How to get it without waking him was now the problem. On tiptoe—hardly breathing—I went up and began to draw it gently off his shoulders. But the wretched man had tucked part of it under him and I couldn't get it free while he was sitting down.

"Then I was in despair and I almost gave up. But, thinking of the fate that surely awaited my poor friends if I didn't get that skin, I decided on desperate measures. Suddenly and swiftly I jabbed the watchman in a tender spot with one of my horns. With an *'Ouch!'* you could hear a mile off, he sprang in the air. Then, snatching the bird skin from under him, I sped off into the jungle, while the hunters, their wives, the dogs, and the whole village woke up in an uproar and came after me like a pack of wolves.

"Well," the Pushmi-Pullyu sighed as he balanced his graceful body to the slight rolling of the houseboat, "I hope never again to have such a race for my life as I had that night. Cold shivers run down my spine still whenever I think of it—the barking of the dogs and the shouting of the men and the shrieking of the women and the crashing of the underbrush as my pursuers came tearing through the jungle, hot upon my trail.

"It was a river that saved me. The rainy season was on and the streams were in flood. Panting with terror and fatigue, I reached the bank of a swirling torrent. It was fully twenty-five feet wide. The water was simply raging down it. To try and swim it would be madness. Looking backward, I could see and hear my pursuers close upon my heels. Again I had to take desperate measures. Drawing back a little to get space for a run, and still clutching that wretched ostrich skin firmly in my mouth, I rushed at the river at full speed and leapt—as I have never leapt in my life—clear across to the farther bank. As I came down in a heap, I realized I had only just been in time, for my enemies had already come up to the river on the side that I had left. Shaking their fists at me in the moonlight, they were trying to find a way to get across to me. The dogs, eagerest of all, tried, some of them, to swim; but the swift and raging waters swept them down the stream like corks, and the hunters were afraid to follow their example.

"With a thrill of triumph, I dropped the precious ostrich skin before their very eyes into the swirling river, where it quickly disappeared from view. A howl of rage went up from the crowd.

"Then I did something I've been sorry for all my life. You know how my people have always insisted on good manners and politeness.

"I leapt as I have never leapt before."

Well—I blush to recall it—in the excitement of the moment I stuck out both my tongues at the baffled foe across the river. There was no excuse for it—there never is for deliberate rudeness. But it was only moonlight and I trust the Badamoshis didn't see it.

"Well, though I was safe for the present, my troubles were not over by any means. For some time the Badamoshis now left the ostriches alone and turned their whole attention to hunting me. They badgered the life out of me. As soon as I had moved from one part of the country to get away from their pestering, they'd find out where I was and pursue me there. They laid traps for me; they set pitfalls; they sent the dogs after me. And although I managed for a whole year to keep away from them, the constant strain was very wearing.

"Well, after I had been hunted and worried for a long time, I thought I would take a leaf out of the Badamoshis' own book, so to speak, and play something like the same trick on them as they had tried to play on the ostriches. With this idea in mind, I set about finding some means to disguise myself. One day, passing by a tree, I found a skin of a wild ox spread out by some huntsman to dry. This I decided was just the thing I wanted. I pulled it down and, lowering one of my heads, I laid one pair of my horns flat along my back— like this—and drew the cowhide over myself, so that only one of my heads could be seen.

"It changed my appearance completely. Moving through the long grass, I looked like some ordinary kind of deer. So, disguised in this manner, I sauntered out into an open meadow and grazed around till any precious Badamoshis should appear. Which they very shortly did.

"I saw them—though they didn't know it—creeping about

among the trees on the edge of the meadow, trying to get near without scaring me. Now, their method of hunting small deer is this: They get up into a tree and lie along a lower branch, keeping very still. And when the deer passes under the tree they drop down upon his hindquarters and fell him to the ground.

"So presently, picking out the tree where I had seen their leader himself go and hide, I browsed along underneath it, pretending I suspected nothing at all. Then when he dropped on what he thought was my hindquarters, I struck upward with my other horns, hidden under the cowhide, and gave him a jab he will remember the rest of his days.

"With a howl of fright, he called out to his men that he had been stuck by the devil. And they all ran across the country like wildfire and I was never hunted or bothered by them again."

Everybody had now told a tale, and the *Arctic Monthly's Prize Story Competition* was declared closed. The first number of the first animals' magazine ever printed was, shortly after that, issued and circulated by Swallow Mail to the inhabitants of the frozen north. It was a great success. Letters of thanks and votes on the competition began pouring in from seals and sea lions and caribou and all manner of polar creatures. Too-Too, the mathematician, became editor; Dab-Dab ran the Mothers' and Babies' Page, while Gub-Gub wrote the Gardening Notes and the Pure Foods column. And the *Arctic Monthly* continued to bring happiness to homes and dens and icebergs as long as the Doctor's post office existed.

PART FOUR

THE FIRST CHAPTER

Parcel Post

ONE DAY GUB-GUB CAME TO THE DOCTOR and said:

"Doctor, why don't you start a parcel post?"

"Great heavens, Gub-Gub!" the Doctor exclaimed. "Don't you think I'm busy enough already? What do you want a parcel post for?"

"I'll bet it's something to do with food," said Too-Too, who was sitting on the stool next to the Doctor's, adding up figures.

"Well," said Gub-Gub, "I was thinking of sending to England for some fresh vegetables."

"There you are!" said Too-Too. "He has a vegetable mind."

"But parcels would be too heavy for the birds to carry, Gub-Gub," said the Doctor, "except perhaps the small parcels by the bigger birds."

"Yes, I know. I had thought of that," said the pig. "But this month the Brussels sprouts will be coming into season in England. They're my favorite vegetable, you know—after parsnips. And I hear that a special kind of thrushes will be leaving England next week to come to Africa. It wouldn't be too much to ask them to bring a single Brussels sprout apiece, would it? There will be hundreds of birds in the flight, and if they each brought a sprout, we'd have enough to last us for months. I haven't tasted any fresh English vegetables since last autumn, Doctor. And I'm so sick of these yams and okras and other rubbish."

"All right, Gub-Gub," said the Doctor, "I'll see what I can do. We will send a letter to England by the next mail going out and ask the thrushes to bring you your Brussels sprouts."

Well, that was how still another department, the *Parcel Post*, was added to the Foreign Mails office of Fantippo. Gub-Gub's sprouts arrived (tons of them, because this was a very big flight of birds), and after that many kinds of animals came to the Doctor and asked him to send for foreign foods for them when their own ran short. In this way, too, bringing seeds and plants from other lands by birds, the Doctor tried quite a number of experiments in planting, and what is called acclimatizing, fruits and vegetables and even flowers.

And very soon he had an old-fashioned window-box garden on the houseboat post office blooming with geraniums and marigolds and zinnias raised from the seeds and cuttings his birds brought him from England.

A little while after that, by using the larger birds to carry packages, a regular parcel post every two months was put at the service of the Fantippans; and alarm clocks and all sorts of things from England were sent for.

King Koko even sent for a new bicycle. It was brought over in pieces, two storks carrying a wheel each, an eagle the frame, crows the smaller parts, like the pedals, the spanners, and the oilcan.

When they started to put it together again in the post office, a part—one of the nuts—was found to be missing. But that was not the fault of the Parcel Post. It had been left out by the makers, who shipped it from Birmingham. But the Doctor wrote a letter of complaint by the next mail and a new nut was sent right away. Then the king rode triumphantly through the streets of Fantippo on his new bicycle and a public holiday was held in honor of the occasion. And he gave his old bicycle to his brother. And the Parcel Post, which had really been started by Gub-Gub, was declared a great success.

Some weeks later the Doctor received this letter from a farmer in Lincolnshire:

Dear Sir: Thank you for your excellent weather reports. By their help I managed to raise the finest crop of Brussels sprouts this year ever seen in Lincolnshire. But the night before I was going to pick them for market they disappeared from my fields—every blessed one of them. How, I don't know. Maybe you could give me some advice about this.

Your obedient servant,
NICHOLAS SCROGGINS

"Great heavens!" said the Doctor: "I wonder what happened to them."

"Gub-Gub ate them," said Too-Too. "Those are the sprouts, no doubt, that the thrushes brought here."

"Dear me!" said the Doctor. "That's too bad. Well, I dare say, I'll find some way to pay the farmer back."

For a long time Dab-Dab, the motherly housekeeper, had

been trying to get the Doctor to take a holiday from his post office business.

"You know, Doctor," said she, "you're going to get sick—that's what's going to happen to you, as sure as you're alive. No man can work the way you've been doing for the last few months and not pay for it. Now you've got the post office going properly, why don't you hand it over to the king's postmen to run and give yourself a rest? And, anyway, aren't you ever going back to Puddleby?"

"Oh yes," said John Dolittle. "All in good time, Dab-Dab."

"But you *must* take a holiday," the duck insisted. "Get away from the post office for a while. Go up the coast in a canoe for a change of air—if you won't go home."

Well, the Doctor kept saying that he would go. But he never did—until something happened in the natural history line of great enough importance to take him from his post office work. This is how it came about:

One day the Doctor was opening the mail addressed to him, when he came upon a package about the size and shape of a large egg. He undid the outer wrapper, which was made of seaweed. Inside he found a letter and a pair of oyster shells tied together like a box.

Somewhat puzzled, the Doctor first read the letter, while Dab-Dab, who was still badgering him about taking a holiday, looked over his shoulder. The letter said:

Dear Doctor: I am sending you, enclosed, some pretty pebbles which I found the other day while cracking open oysters. I never saw pebbles of this color before, though I live by the seashore and have been opening shellfish

HUGH LOFTING

"Dab-Dab looking over his shoulder"

all my life. My husband says they're oyster's eggs. But I don't believe it. Would you please tell me what they are? And be careful to send them back, because my children use them as playthings and I have promised them they shall have them to keep.

Then the Doctor put down the letter and, taking his pen-knife, he cut the seaweed strings that neatly held the oyster shells together. And when he opened the shells he gave a gasp of aston-ishment.

"Oh, Dab-Dab," he cried, "how beautiful! Look, look!"

"Pearls!" whispered Dab-Dab in an awed voice, gazing down into the Doctor's palm. "Pink pearls!"

"My! Aren't they handsome?" murmured the Doctor. "And did you ever see such large ones? Each one of those pearls, Dab-Dab, is worth a fortune. Who the dickens is this that sent them to me, anyhow?"

And he turned to the letter again.

"It's from a spoonbill," said Dab-Dab. "I know their writing. They are a sort of a cross between a curlew and a snipe. They like messing around lonely seacoast places, hunting for shellfish and sea worms and stuff like that."

"Well, where is it written from?" asked the Doctor. "What do you make that address out to be—at the top of the page there?"

Dab-Dab screwed up her eyes and peered at it closely.

"It looks to me," she said, "like the Harmattan Rocks."

"Where is that?" asked the Doctor.

"I have no idea," said Dab-Dab. "But Speedy will know."

And she went off to fetch the Skimmer.

Speedy said, yes, he knew—the Harmattan Rocks were a group of small islands off the coast of West Africa, about sixty miles farther to the north.

"That's curious," said the Doctor. "I wouldn't have been so surprised if they had come from the South Sea Islands. But it is rather unusual to find pearls of any size or beauty in these waters. Well, these must be sent back to the spoonbill's children—by registered parcel post, of course. Though, to tell you the truth, I hate to part with them—they are so lovely. They can't go before tomorrow, anyway. I wonder where I can keep them in the meantime. One has to be frightfully careful with gems as valuable as these. You had better not tell anyone about them, Dab-Dab—except Jip the watchman and the Pushmi-Pullyu. They must take it in turns to mount guard at the door all night. Men will do all sorts of things for pearls. We'll keep it a secret and send them right back first thing tomorrow morning."

Even while the Doctor was speaking he noticed a shadow fall across the desk at which he was standing. He looked up. And there at the information window was the ugliest man's face he had ever seen, staring in at the beautiful pearls that still lay on the palm of his hand.

The Doctor, annoyed and embarrassed, forgot for the first time in his post office career to be polite.

"What do *you* want?" he asked, thrusting the pearls into his pocket.

"I want a postal order for ten shillings," said the man. "I am going to send some money to my sick wife."

The Doctor made out the postal order and took the money, which the man handed through the window.

"Here you are," he said.

Then the man left the post office and the Doctor watched him go.

"He was an odd-looking customer, wasn't he?" he said to Dab-Dab.

"He was, indeed," said the duck. "I'm not surprised his wife is sick, if she has a husband with a face like that."

"I wonder who he is," said John Dolittle. "I don't much like the looks of him."

The following day the pearls were wrapped up again the way they had arrived, and after a letter had been written by the Doctor explaining to the spoonbill what the "pebbles" really were, they were sent off by registered parcel post to the Harmattan Rocks.

The bird chosen to take the package happened to be one of the thrushes that had brought the Brussels sprouts from England. These birds were still staying in the neighborhood. And though a thrush was a somewhat small bird to carry parcel post, the package was a very little one and the Doctor had nobody else to send. So after explaining to the thrush that registered mail should be guarded very carefully by postmen, the Doctor sent the pearls off.

Then he went to call on the king, as he did every so often. And in the course of conversation, John Dolittle asked His Majesty if he knew who the stranger might be that had called at the houseboat for a postal order.

After he had listened to the description of the man's cross-eyed, ugly face, the king said, yes, he knew him very well. He was a pearl fisherman, who spent most of his time in the Pacific Ocean, where fishing for pearls was more common. But, the king said, he often came hanging around these parts, where he was known to be a great villain who would do anything to get pearls or money. Jack Wilkins was his name.

The Doctor, on hearing this, felt glad that he had already sent the pink pearls safely off to their owner by registered mail. Then he told the king that he hoped shortly to take a holiday because he was overworked and needed a rest. The king asked where he was going, and the Doctor said he thought of taking a week's canoe trip up the coast toward the Harmattan Rocks.

"Well," said His Majesty, "if you are going in that direction, you might call on an old friend of mine, Chief Nyam-Nyam. He owns the country in those parts and the Harmattan Rocks themselves. He and his people are frightfully poor, though. But he is honest—and I think you will like him."

"All right," said the Doctor, "I'll call on him with your compliments."

The next day, leaving Speedy, Cheapside, and Jip in charge of the post office, the Doctor got into his canoe with Dab-Dab and paddled off to take his holiday. On the way out he noticed a schooner, the ship of Jack Wilkins, the pearl fisherman, at anchor near the entrance to Fantippo harbor.

Toward evening the Doctor arrived at a small settlement of straw huts, the village of Chief Nyam-Nyam. Calling on the chief with an introduction from King Koko, the Doctor was well received. He found, however, that the country over which this chief ruled was indeed in a very poor state. For years, powerful neighbors on either side had made war on the old chief and robbed him of his best farming lands, till now his people were crowded onto a narrow strip of rocky shore where very little food could be grown. The Doctor was particularly distressed by the thinness of the few chickens pecking about in the streets. They reminded him of old broken-down cab horses, he said.

While he was talking to the chief (who seemed to be a kindly old man), Speedy swept into the chief's hut in a great state of excitement.

"Doctor," he cried, "the mail has been robbed! The thrush has come back to the post office and says his package was taken from him on the way. *The pearls are gone!*"

The Great Mail Robbery

GREAT HEAVENS!" CRIED THE DOCTOR, SPRING-
ing up. "The pearls gone? And they were registered, too!"

"Yes," said Speedy, "here's the thrush himself. He'll
tell you all about it."

And going to the door, he called in the bird who had carried
the registered package.

"Doctor," said the thrush, who was also very upset and breathless, "it wasn't my fault. I never let those pearls out of my sight. I
flew straight off for the Harmattan Rocks. But part of the trip I
had to go over land, if I took the shortest cut. And on the way I saw
a sister of mine who I hadn't met in a long time, sitting in a tree in
the jungle below me. And I thought it would be no harm if I went
and talked to her a while. So I flew down and she was very glad to
see me. I couldn't talk properly with the string of the package in
my mouth, so I put the parcel down on the bough of the tree behind
me—right near me, you understand—and went on talking to my
sister. And when I turned around to pick it up again, it was gone."

"I put the parcel down."

"Perhaps it slipped off the tree," said the Doctor, "and fell down into the underbrush."

"It couldn't have," said the thrush. "I put it into a little hollow in the bark of the bough. It just couldn't have slipped or rolled. Somebody must have taken it."

"Dear me," said John Dolittle. "Robbing the mails; that's a serious thing. I wonder who could have done it?"

"I'll bet it's Jack Wilkins, the cross-eyed pearl fisherman," whispered Dab-Dab. "A man with a face like that would steal anything. And he was the only one, besides us and Speedy, who knew the pearls were going through the mails. It's Wilkins, sure as you're alive."

"I wonder," said the Doctor. "They do say he is a most unscrupulous customer. Well, there's nothing for it, I suppose, but that I should paddle back to Fantippo right away and try to find him. The post office is responsible for the loss of registered mail, and if Mr. Wilkins took those pearls, I'm going to get them back again. But after this we will make it a post office rule that carriers of registered mail may not talk to their sisters or anyone else while on duty."

And in spite of the lateness of the hour, John Dolittle said a hasty farewell to Chief Nyam-Nyam and started off by moonlight for Fantippo harbor.

In the meantime, Speedy and the thrush flew over the land by the shortcut to the post office.

"What are you going to say to Wilkins, Doctor?" asked Dab-Dab as the canoe glided along over the moonlit sea. "It's a pity you haven't got a pistol or something like that. He looks like a desperate character, and he isn't likely to give up the pearls without a fight."

"I don't know what I'll say to him. I'll see when I get there," said John Dolittle. "But we must be very careful how we approach, so that he doesn't see us coming. If he should pull up his anchor and sail away, we would never be able to overtake him by canoe."

"I tell you what, Doctor," said Dab-Dab, "let me fly ahead and do a little spying on the enemy. Then I'll come back and tell you anything I can find out. Maybe he isn't on his schooner at all at present. And we ought to be hunting him somewhere else."

"All right," said the Doctor. "Do that. It will take me another four hours at least to reach Fantippo at this pace."

So Dab-Dab flew away over the sea, and John Dolittle continued to paddle his canoe bravely forward.

After about an hour had passed, he heard a gentle sort of whispered quacking high overhead and he knew that his faithful housekeeper was returning. Presently, with a swish of feathers, Dab-Dab settled down at his feet. And on her face was an expression that meant great news.

"He's there, Doctor—and he's got the pearls, all right!" said she. "I peeked through the window and I saw him counting them out from one little box into another by the light of a candle."

"The villain!" grunted the Doctor, putting on all the speed he could. "Let's hope he doesn't get away before we reach Fantippo."

Dawn was beginning to show before they came in sight of the ship they sought. This made approaching the schooner without being seen extremely difficult. And the Doctor went all the way around the Island of No Man's Land, so as to come upon the ship from the other side, where he would not have to cross so large an open stretch of sea.

Paddling very, very softly, he managed to get the canoe right under the bow of the ship. Then, tying his own craft so it couldn't float away, he swarmed up the schooner's anchor chain and crept onto the boat on hands and knees.

Full daylight had not yet come, and the light from a lamp could be seen palely shining up the stairs that led to the cabin. The Doctor slid forward like a shadow, tiptoed his way down the stairs, and peered through the partly opened door.

The cross-eyed Wilkins was still seated at the table, as Dab-Dab had described, counting pearls. Two other men were asleep in bunks around the room. The Doctor swung open the door and jumped in. Instantly Wilkins sprang up from the table, snatched a pistol from his belt, and leveled it at the Doctor's head.

"Move an inch and you're a dead man!" he snarled.

The Doctor, taken aback for a moment, gazed at the pistol muzzle, wondering what to do next. Wilkins, without moving his eyes from the Doctor for a second, closed the pearl box with his left hand and put it into his pocket.

While he was doing this, however, Dab-Dab sneaked in under the table, unseen by anyone. And suddenly she bit the pearl fisherman in the leg with her powerful beak.

With a howl Wilkins bent down to knock her off.

"Now's your chance, Doctor!" yelled the duck.

And in the second while the pistol was lowered, the Doctor sprang onto the man's back, gripped him around the neck, and with a crash the two of them went rolling on the floor of the cabin.

Then a tremendous fight began. Over and over and over they rolled around the floor, upsetting things in all directions, Wilkins fighting to get his pistol hand free, the Doctor struggling to keep it bound to his body, Dab-Dab hopping and flying and jumping and flapping to get a bite in on the enemy's nose whenever she saw a chance.

At last John Dolittle, who for his size was a very powerful wrestler, got the pearl fisherman in a grip of iron where he couldn't move at all. But just as the Doctor was forcing the pistol out of his enemy's hand, one of the other men, who had been aroused by the noise of the fight, woke up. And leaning out of his bunk from behind the Doctor's back, he hit him a tremendous blow on the head with a bottle. Stunned and senseless, John Dolittle fell over in a heap and lay still upon the floor.

Then all three men sprang on him with ropes, and in a minute his arms and legs were tied and the fight was over.

When he woke up, the Doctor found himself lying at the bottom of his own canoe, with Dab-Dab tugging at the ropes that bound his wrists, to get him free.

"Where is Wilkins?" he asked in a dazed, sleepy kind of way.

"Gone," said Dab-Dab, "and the pearls with him—the scoundrel! As soon as they had dumped you in the canoe they pulled up the anchor, hoisted sail, and got away. They were in an awful hurry, and kept looking out to sea with telescopes and talking about the revenue cutter. I guess they are wanted by the government for a good many bad deeds. I never saw a tougher-looking crowd of men in all my life. See, I've got the rope around your hands free now; you can do the rest better yourself. Does your head hurt much?"

"It's a bit dizzy still," said the Doctor, working at the rope about his ankles. "But I'll be all right in a little."

Presently, when he had undone the cord that tied his feet, John Dolittle stood up and gazed over the ocean. And there, on the skyline, he could just see the sails of Wilkins' schooner disappearing eastward.

"Villain!" was all he said between his clenched teeth.

Pearls and Brussels Sprouts

ISAPPOINTED AND SAD, DAB-DAB AND THE
Doctor started to paddle their way back.

"I think I'll stop in at the post office before I return
to Chief Nyam-Nyam's country," said the Doctor.
"There's nothing more I can do about the pearls, I suppose. But I'd
like to see if everything else is going all right."

"Wilkins may get caught yet—by the government," said Dab-
Dab. "And if he does, we might get the pearls back after all."

"Not much chance of that, I'm afraid," said John Dolittle.
"He will probably sell them the first chance he gets. That's all
he wants them for—for the money they'll bring in. Whereas the
young spoonbills appreciated their beauty. It's a shame they should
lose them—and when they were in my care, too. Well—it's no use
crying over spilled milk. They're gone. That's all."

As they were approaching the houseboat they noticed a large
number of canoes collected about it. Today was not one of the out-

going or incoming mail days, and the Doctor wondered what the excitement could be.

Fastening up his own canoe, he went into the post office. And inside there was quite a crowd. He made his way through it with Dab-Dab, and in the registered mail booth he found all the animals gathered around a small black squirrel. The little creature's legs were tied with post office red tape and he seemed very frightened and miserable. Speedy and Cheapside were mounting guard over him, one on each side.

"What's all this about?" asked the Doctor.

"We've caught the fellow who stole the pearls, Doctor," said Speedy.

"And we've got the pearls, too," cried Too-Too. "They're in the stamp drawer and Jip is guarding them."

"But I don't understand," said John Dolittle. "I thought Wilkins had made off with them."

"Those must have been some other stolen pearls, Doctor," said Dab-Dab. "Let's take a look at the ones Jip has."

The Doctor went and opened the stamp drawer. And there inside, sure enough, were the three pink beauties he had sent by registered mail.

"How did you find them?" he asked, turning to Speedy.

"Well, after you had set off in the canoe," said the Skimmer, "I and the thrush stopped on our way back here at the tree where he had lost the package. It was too dark then to hunt for it, so we roosted in the tree all night, intending to look in the morning. Just as dawn was breaking we saw this wretched squirrel here flirting about in the branches with an enormous pink pearl in his mouth. I at once pounced on him and held him down, while the thrush took the pearl away from him. Then we made him tell us where he had hidden the other two. And after we had got all three of them, we put the squirrel under arrest and brought him here."

"Dear me!" said the Doctor, looking at the miserable culprit, who was all tied up with red tape. "What made you steal the pearls?"

At first the squirrel seemed almost too frightened to speak. So the Doctor took a pair of scissors and cut the bonds that held him.

"Why did you do it?" he repeated.

"I thought they were Brussels sprouts," said the squirrel timidly. "A few weeks ago when I and my wife were sitting in a tree, we suddenly smelled the smell of Brussels sprouts, awful strong, all about us. I and my wife are very fond of this vegetable and we wondered where the smell was coming from. And then, looking up, we saw thousands of thrushes passing overhead, carrying Brussels sprouts in their mouths. We hoped they would stop so we could get a few. But they didn't. So we agreed that perhaps more would be coming over in a few days. And we arranged to stay around that same tree and wait. And, sure enough, this morning I saw one of these same thrushes alight in the tree, carrying a package. 'Pst!' I whispered to the wife. 'More Brussels sprouts. Let's bag his parcel while he's not looking!' And bag it I did. But when we opened it we found nothing but these wretched gew-gaws. I thought they might be some new kind of rock candy and I was on my way to find a stone to crack them with, when this bird grabbed me by the scruff of the neck and arrested me. I didn't want the beastly pearls."

"Well," said the Doctor, "I'm sorry you've been put to such inconvenience. I'll have Dab-Dab carry you back to your family. But, you know, robbing the registered mail is a serious

"'Pst!' I whispered to the wife."

thing. If you wanted some Brussels sprouts you should have written to me. After all, you can't blame the birds for putting you under arrest."

"Stolen fruit's the sweetest, Doctor," said Cheapside. "If you 'ad given 'im a ton of 'ot-'ouse grapes, 'e wouldn't 'ave enjoyed 'em 'alf as much as something 'e pinched. I'd give 'im a couple of years 'ard labor, if I was you—just to learn 'im to leave the mails alone."

"Well, never mind, we'll forget it," said the Doctor. "It's only a boyish escapade."

"Boyish fiddlesticks!" growled Cheapside. "'E's the father of a large family—and a natural-born pickpocket. All squirrels are like that. Don't I know 'em in the city parks—with their foolish ways that the folks call 'cute'? Cheekiest beggars that ever was—pinch a crumb from under your nose and pop into an 'ole with it before you could get your breath. Boyish hescapade!"

"Come along," said Dab-Dab, picking the wretched culprit up in her big webbed feet. "I'll take you back to the mainland. And you can thank your lucky stars that it's the Doctor who is in charge of this post office. It's to jail you really ought to go."

"Oh, and hurry back, Dab-Dab," the Doctor called after her as she flapped her way through the open window and set off across the sea with her burden. "I'm going to start right away for Chief Nyam-Nyam's country as soon as you are ready."

"I'll take the pearls myself this time," he said to Speedy, "and hand them over to the spoonbill in person. We don't want any more accidents happening to them."

About noon the Doctor started out a second time upon his holiday trip, and as Gub-Gub, Jip, and the white mouse begged to be taken along, the canoe was well loaded.

They reached Nyam-Nyam's village about six o'clock in the evening and the old chief prepared a supper for his guests. There was very little to eat, however. And the Doctor was again reminded of how poor these people were.

While talking with the old chief, the Doctor found out that the worst enemy his country had was the kingdom of Dahomey. This big and powerful neighbor was, it seemed, always making war upon Chief Nyam-Nyam and cutting off parts of his land, making the people poorer still. Now, the soldiers of Dahomey were Amazons—that is, they were women soldiers. They were very big and strong, and there were a terrible lot of them. So whenever they attacked the small country next to them they easily won and took what they wanted.

As it happened, they made an attack that night while the Doctor was staying with the chief. At about ten o'clock everybody was awakened out of his sleep with cries of "War! War! The Amazons are here!"

There was terrible confusion. And until the moon had risen, people were hitting and falling over one another everywhere in the darkness, not knowing friend from enemy.

When it was possible to see, however, the Doctor found that most of Chief Nyam-Nyam's people had fled off into the jungle; and the Amazons, in thousands, were just going through the village, taking anything they fancied. The Doctor tried to argue with them, but they merely laughed at him.

Then the white mouse, who was watching the show from the Doctor's shoulder, whispered in his ear:

"I think I know of a way to deal with them. I'll just go off and collect a few mice in the village and see what we can do."

So the white mouse went off and gathered an army of his own, about two hundred mice, which lived in the grass walls and floors of the huts. And then suddenly they attacked the Amazons and began nipping them in the legs.

With shrieks and howls the soldiers dropped the things they had been stealing and ran helter-skelter for home. And that was one time the famous Amazons of Dahomey *didn't* have it all their own way.

The Doctor told his pet he should be very proud of himself. For he was surely the only mouse in the world that ever won a war.

Pearl Divers

THE NEXT MORNING THE DOCTOR WAS UP early. After a light breakfast (it was impossible to get any other kind in that poverty-stricken country) he asked Nyam-Nyam the way to the Harmattan Rocks and the chief told him they were just beyond sight from here, about an hour and a half's paddle straight out into the ocean.

So the Doctor decided that he had better have a seabird to guide him. And Dab-Dab went and got a curlew who was strolling about on the beach, doing nothing in particular. This bird said he knew the place quite well and would consider it an honor to act as guide to John Dolittle. Then with Jip, Dab-Dab, Gub-Gub, and the white mouse, the Doctor got into his canoe and started off for the Harmattan Rocks.

It was a beautiful morning and they enjoyed the paddle—though Gub-Gub came very near to upsetting the canoe more than once, leaning out to grab for passing seaweed, which he had noticed the curlew eating. Finally, for safety's sake, they made him lie down at the bottom of the canoe, where he couldn't see anything.

About eleven o'clock a group of little rocky islands were sighted, which their guide said were the Harmattan Rocks. At this point in their journey the mainland of Africa was just disappearing from view on the skyline behind them. The rocks they were coming to seemed to be the home of thousands of different kinds of seabirds. As the canoe drew near, gulls, terns, gannets, albatrosses, cormorants, auklets, petrels, wild ducks, even wild geese, came out, full of curiosity to examine the stranger. When they learned from the curlew that this quiet little fat man was none other than the great Doctor Dolittle himself, they passed word back to the rocks; and soon the air about the canoe was simply thick with wings flashing in the sunlight. And the welcome to their home that the seabirds screeched to the Doctor was so hearty and noisy you couldn't hear yourself speak.

It was easy to see why this place had been chosen for a home by the seabirds. The shores all around were guarded by half-sunken rocks, on which the waves roared and broke dangerously. No ship was ever likely to come here to disturb the quiet life of the birds. Indeed, even with a light canoe that could go in shallow water, the Doctor would have had hard work to make a landing. But the welcoming birds guided him very skillfully around to the back of the biggest island, where a bay with deep water formed a pretty sort of toy harbor. The Doctor understood now why these islands had been left in the possession of the poor chief: no neighbors would consider them worth taking. Hard to approach, with very little soil in which crops could be grown, flat and open to all the winds and gales of heaven, barren and lonesome, they tempted none of the chief's enemies. And so for many, many years they remained the property of Nyam-Nyam and his people—though indeed even they hardly ever visited them. But in the end, the Harmattan Rocks proved to be of greater value than all the rest of the lands this tribe had lost.

"Oh, I think this is an awful place," said Gub-Gub as they got out of the canoe. "Nothing but waves and rocks. What have you come here for, Doctor?"

"I hope to do a little pearl fishing," said John Dolittle. "But first I must see the spoonbill and give her this registered package. Dab-Dab, would you please try to find her for me? With so many

"Oh, I think this is an awful place!"

millions of seabirds around, I wouldn't know how to begin to look for her."

"All right," said Dab-Dab. "But it may take me a little time. There are several islands and quite a number of spoonbills. I shall have to make inquiries and find out which one sent you the pearls."

So Dab-Dab went off upon her errand. And in the meantime the Doctor talked and chatted with various seabird leaders who had already made his acquaintance at the Great Conference in the hollow of No Man's Land. These kept coming up to him, anxious to show off before their fellows the fact that they knew the great man personally. And once more the Doctor's notebook was kept busy with new discoveries to be jotted down about the carriage of mail by birds that live upon the sea.

The birds, who at first followed the Doctor in droves around the main island wherever he went, presently returned to their ordinary doings when the newness of his arrival had worn off. And after Dab-Dab had come back from her hunt and told him the spoonbill lived on one of the smaller islands, he got back into his canoe and paddled over to the rock she pointed out.

Here the spoonbill was waiting for him at the water's edge. She apologized for not coming in person to welcome him, but said she was afraid to leave her babies when there were sea eagles around. The little ones were with her, two scrubby, greasy youngsters who could walk but not fly. The Doctor opened the package and gave them back their precious toys; and with squawks of delight they began playing marbles on the flat rocks with the enormous pink pearls.

"What charming children you have," said the Doctor to the

"The young ones were with her."

mother spoonbill, who was watching them proudly. "I'm glad they've got their playthings safely back. I wouldn't have had them lose them for anything."

"Yes, they are devoted to those pebbles," said the spoonbill. "By the way, were you able to tell me what they are? I found them, as I wrote you, inside an oyster."

"They are pearls," said the Doctor, "and worth a tremendous lot. Ladies in cities wear them around their necks."

"Oh, indeed," said the bird. "And why don't the ladies in the country wear them, too?"

"I just don't know," said the Doctor. "I suppose because

they're too costly. With any one of those pearls you could buy a house and garden."

"Well, wouldn't you like to keep them, then?" asked the spoonbill. "I could get the children something else to play with, no doubt."

"Oh no," said the Doctor, "thank you. I have a house and garden."

"Yes, Doctor," Dab-Dab put in, "but you wouldn't be bound to buy a second one with the money you would get for the pearls. It would come in real handy for something else, you know."

"The baby spoonbills want them," said John Dolittle. "Why should I take them away from them?"

"Balls of pink putty would suit them just as well," snorted Dab-Dab.

"Putty is poisonous," said the Doctor. "They appreciate the beauty of the pearls. Let them have them. But," he added to the mother spoonbill, "if you know where any more are to be found, I should be glad to know."

"I don't," said she. "I don't even know how these came to be in the possession of the oyster I ate."

"Pearls always grow in oysters—when they grow at all," said the Doctor. "But they are rare. This is the point that most interests me—the natural history of pearls. They are said to form around a grain of sand that gets into the oyster's shell by accident. I had hoped that if you were in the habit of eating oysters you could give me some information."

"I'm afraid I can't," said the spoonbill. "To tell you the truth, I got those oysters from a pile that some other bird had left on the rock here. He had eaten his fill, I suppose, and gone away. There are a good many left still. Let's go over to the pile and crack a few. Maybe they've all got pearls in them."

So they went across to the other side of the little island and started opening oysters. But not another pearl did they find.

"Where are the oyster beds around here?" asked the Doctor.

"Between this island and the next," said the spoonbill. "I don't fish for them myself because I'm not a deep diver. But I've seen other kinds of seabirds fishing in that place—just about halfway between this island and that little one over there."

"I'll go out with her, Doctor," said Dab-Dab, "and do a little fishing on my own account. I can dive pretty deep, though I'm not a regular diving duck. Maybe I can get some pearls for you."

So Dab-Dab went out with the spoonbill and started pearl fishing.

Then for a good hour and a half the faithful housekeeper fished up oyster after oyster and brought them to the Doctor on the island. He and the animals found opening them quite exciting work, because you never knew what you might discover. But nothing was found in the shells but fat oysters and thin oysters.

"I think I'd like to try a hand at diving myself," said the Doctor, "if the water is not too deep. I used to be quite good at fishing up sixpences from the bottom of the swimming pool when I was a boy."

And he took off his clothes, got into the canoe, and paddled out with the animals till he was over the oyster beds. Then he dove right down into the clear green water, while Jip and Gub-Gub watched him with intense interest.

But when he came up, blowing like a seal, he hadn't even got an oyster. All he had was a mouthful of seaweed.

"Let's see what I can do," said Jip. And out of the canoe jumped another pearl fisherman.

Then Gub-Gub got all worked up, and before anybody could stop him, *he* had taken a plunge. The pig went down so quick and so straight he got his snout stuck in the mud at the bottom, and the Doctor, still out of breath, had to go down after him and get him free. The animals by this time were at such a pitch of excitement that even the white mouse would have jumped in if Gub-Gub's accident hadn't changed his mind.

Jip managed to bring up a few small oysters, but there were no pearls in them.

"Gub-Gub dives for pearls."

"I'm afraid we're pretty poor fishers," said John Dolittle. "Of course, it's possible that there may not be any more pearls there."

"No, I'm not satisfied yet," said Dab-Dab. "I'm pretty sure that there are plenty of pearls there—the beds are enormous. I think I'll go around among the seabirds and try to find out who it was got those oysters our spoonbill found the pearls in. The bird that fished up that pile was an expert oyster diver."

So while the Doctor put his clothes on and Gub-Gub washed the mud out of his ears, Dab-Dab went off on a tour of inquiry around the islands.

After about twenty minutes she brought back a black duck-like bird with a tuft on his head.

"This cormorant, Doctor," said she, "fished up that pile of oysters."

"Ah," said John Dolittle, "perhaps we shall find out something now. Can you tell me," he asked the cormorant, "how to get pearls?"

"Pearls? What do you mean?" said the bird.

Then Dab-Dab went and borrowed the playthings from the spoonbill's children to show him.

"Oh, those things," said the cormorant. "Those come in bad oysters. When I go oyster fishing I never pick up that kind, except once in a while by accident—and then I never bother to open them."

"But how do you tell oysters of that kind from the others?" asked the Doctor.

"By sniffing them," said the cormorant. "The ones that have those things in them don't smell fresh. I'm frightfully particular about my oysters."

"Do you mean to say that, even when you are right down under the water, you could tell an oyster that had pearls in it from one that hadn't—just by sniffing it?"

"Certainly. So could any cormorant."

"There you are, Doctor," said Dab-Dab. "The trick's done. Now you can get all the pearls you want."

"But these oyster beds don't belong to me," said John Dolittle.

"Oh, dear!" sighed the duck. "Did anyone ever see a man who could find so many objections to getting rich? Who do they belong to, then?"

"To Chief Nyam-Nyam and his people, of course. He owns the Harmattan Rocks. Would you mind," the Doctor asked, turning to the cormorant, "getting me a few oysters of this kind to look at?"

"With the greatest of pleasure," said the cormorant.

And he flew out over the oyster beds and shot down into the sea like a stone. In a minute he was back again with three oysters—two in his feet and one in his mouth. The animals gathered around with bated breath while the Doctor opened them. In the first was a small gray pearl; in the second a middle-sized pink pearl, and in the third two enormous black ones.

"Gosh, how lovely!" murmured Gub-Gub.

"Pearls before swine," giggled the white mouse. "Tee, hee!"

"How uneducated you are!" snorted the pig, turning up his snout. "Ladies before gentlemen; *swine* before *pearls*!"

Obombo's Rebellion

L ATE THAT SAME AFTERNOON THE DOCTOR returned to Chief Nyam-Nyam's village. And with him he took the cormorant as well as Dab-Dab and his animals.

As he arrived at the little group of straw houses, he saw that there was some kind of a commotion going on. All the villagers were gathered about the chief's hut; speeches were being made and everyone seemed in a great state of excitement. The old chief himself was standing at the door, and when he saw his friend, the Doctor, approaching on the edge of the crowd, he signaled him to come into the hut. This the Doctor did. And as soon as he was inside, the chief closed the door and began to tell him what the trouble was.

"Great trials have overtaken me in my old age," said he. "For fifty years I have been head of this tribe, respected, honored, and obeyed. Now my young son-in-law, Obombo, clamors to be made chief, and many of the people support him. Bread we have none; food of any kind is scanty. And Obombo tells the tribesmen that the fault is mine—that he, if he is made chief, will bring them luxury and prosperity. It is not that I am unwilling to give up the chieftaincy, but I know this young upstart who would take my place means to lead the people into war. What can he do by going to war? Can he fill the people's stomachs? In wars we have always lost. Alas, alas, that I should ever see this day!"

The old chief sank into his chair as he ended and burst out weeping. The Doctor went up and patted him on the shoulder.

"Chief Nyam-Nyam," said he, "I think I have discovered something today that should make you and your people rich for the remainder of your lives. Go out now and address the tribesmen. Promise them in my name—and remind them that I come recommended by King Koko—promise them from me that if they will abide peacefully under your rule for another week, the country of Chief Nyam-Nyam will be made famous for its riches and prosperity."

Then the old chief opened the door and made a speech to the clamoring crowd outside. And when he had ended Obombo, the son-in-law, got up and began another speech, calling on the people to drive the old man out into the jungle. But before he had gotten halfway through the crowd began to murmur to one another:

"Let us not listen to this forward young man. It would be better to wait and see what comes. Nyam-Nyam has ruled us with kindness for so long. Obombo would but lead us into war, and bring us to greater poverty still."

Soon hisses and groans broke out among the crowd and, picking up pebbles and mud, they began pelting Obombo so he could not go on with his speech. Finally he had to run for the jungle himself to escape the fury of the people.

Then when the excitement had died down and the villagers had gone peacefully to their homes, the Doctor told the old chief of the wealth that lay waiting for him in the oysters of the Harmattan Rocks. And the cormorant agreed to oblige John Dolittle by getting a number of his relatives to do pearl fishing for these people, who were so badly in need of money and food.

And during the next week the Doctor paddled the old chief to the rocks twice a day. A great number of oysters were fished up by the cormorants and the pearls were sorted by the Doctor, put in little boxes, and sent out to be sold. John Dolittle told the old chief to keep the matter a secret and only to entrust the carrying to reliable men.

And soon money began to pour into the country from the pearl fishing business that the Doctor had established, and the people grew prosperous and had all the food they wanted.

By the end of that week the Doctor had, indeed, made good on his promise. The country of Chief Nyam-Nyam became famous all along the coast of West Africa as a wealthy state.

But wherever money is made in large quantities and business is good, strangers will always come, seeking their fortune. And before long the little village that used to be so poor and insignificant was full of traders from the neighboring kingdoms, buying and selling in the crowded, busy markets. And of course, questions were soon asked as to how this country had suddenly got so rich. And, although the chief had carried out the Doctor's orders and had only entrusted the secret of the fisheries to a few picked men, folks began to notice that canoes frequently came and went between the Harmattan Rocks and the village of Chief Nyam-Nyam.

Then spies from those neighboring countries who had always

been robbing and warring upon this land began to sneak around the rocks in canoes. And, of course, very soon the secret was out.

And the emir of Ellebubu, who was one of the big, powerful neighbors, called up his army and sent them off in war canoes to take possession of the Harmattan Rocks. At the same time he made an attack upon the village, drove everybody out, and carrying off the Doctor and the chief, he threw them into prison in his own country. Then at last Nyam-Nyam's people had no land left at all.

And in the jungle, where the frightened villagers had fled to hide, Obombo made whispered speeches to little scattered groups of his father-in-law's people, telling them what fools they had been to trust the crazy doctor, instead of listening to him, who would have led them to greatness.

Now, when the emir of Ellebubu had thrown the Doctor into prison, he had refused to allow Dab-Dab, Jip, or Gub-Gub to go with him. Jip put up a fight and bit the emir in the leg. But all he got for that was to be tied up on a short chain.

The prison into which the Doctor was thrown had no windows. And John Dolittle, although he had been in prisons before, was very unhappy because he was extremely particular about having fresh air. And besides, his hands were firmly tied behind his back with strong rope.

"Dear me," said he while he was sitting miserably on the floor in the darkness, wondering what on earth he was going to do without any of his animals to help him, "what a poor holiday I am spending, to be sure!"

But presently he heard something stirring in his pocket. And to his great delight, the white mouse, who had been sleeping soundly, entirely forgotten by the Doctor, ran out onto his lap.

"Good luck!" cried John Dolittle. "You're the very fellow I want. Would you be so good as to run around behind my back and gnaw this beastly rope? It's hurting my wrists."

"Certainly," said the white mouse, setting to work at once. "Why is it so dark? I haven't slept into the night, have I?"

"No," said the Doctor. "It's only about noon, I should say. But we're locked up. That Emir of Ellebubu made war on Nyam-Nyam and threw me into jail. Bother it, I always seem to be getting into prison! The worst of it was, he wouldn't let Jip or Dab-Dab come with me. I'm particularly annoyed that I haven't got Dab-Dab. I wish I knew some way I could get a message to her."

"Well, just wait until I have your hands free," said the white mouse. "Then I'll see what can be done. There! I've bitten through one strand. Now wiggle your hands a bit and you can undo the whole rope."

The Doctor squirmed his arms and wrists and presently his hands were free.

"Thank goodness I had you in my pocket!" he said. "That was a most uncomfortable position. I wonder what kind of a prison old Nyam-Nyam got. This is the worst one I was ever in."

In the meantime, the emir, celebrating victory in his palace, gave orders that the Harmattan Rocks, which were now to be called the Royal Ellebubu Pearl Fisheries, would henceforth be his exclusive, private property, and no trespassing would be allowed. And he sent out six special men with orders to take over the islands and to bring all the pearls to him.

Now, the cormorants did not know that war had broken out, nor anything about the Doctor's misfortune. And when the emir's men came and took the pearl oysters they had fished up, the birds supposed they were Nyam-Nyam's men and let them have them. However, it happened, luckily, that this first load of oysters had only very small and almost worthless pearls in them.

Jip and Dab-Dab were still plotting to find some way to reach the Doctor. But there seemed to be nothing they could think of.

Inside the prison, the Doctor was swinging his arms to get the stiffness out of them.

"You said something about a message you had for Dab-Dab, I think," peeped the white mouse's voice from the darkness of the corner.

"Yes," said the Doctor, "and a very urgent one. But I don't see how on earth I'm going to get it to her. This place is made of stone and the door's frightfully thick. I noticed it as I came in."

"Don't worry, Doctor, I'll get it to her," said the mouse. "I've just found an old rat hole over here in the corner. I popped down it and it goes under the wall and comes out by the root of the tree on the other side of the road from the prison."

"Oh, how splendid!" cried the Doctor.

"Give me the message," said the white mouse, "and I'll hand it to Dab-Dab before you can say Jack Robinson. She's sitting in the tree, where the hole comes out."

"Tell her," said the Doctor, "to fly over to the Harmattan Rocks right away and give the cormorants strict orders to stop all pearl fishing at once."

"All right," said the mouse. And he slipped down the rat hole.

Dab-Dab, as soon as she got the message, went straight off to the pearl fisheries and gave the Doctor's instructions to the cormorants.

She was only just in time. For the emir's six special men were about to land on the islands to get a second load of pearls. Dab-Dab and the cormorants swiftly threw back into the sea the oysters that had been fished up and when the emir's men arrived, they found nothing.

After hanging around awhile, they paddled back and told the emir that they could find no more pearl oysters on the rocks. He sent them out to look again, but they returned with the same report.

Then the emir was puzzled and angry. If Nyam-Nyam could get pearls on the Harmattan Rocks, why couldn't he? And one of his generals said that probably the Doctor had something to do with it, since it was he who had discovered and started the fisheries.

So the emir ordered his hammock men and had himself carried to the Doctor's prison. The door was unlocked and the emir, going inside, said to the Doctor:

"What monkey business have you done to my pearl fisheries, you villain?"

"They're not your pearl fisheries, you ruffian," said the Doctor. "You stole them from poor old Nyam-Nyam. The pearls were fished for by diving birds. But the birds are honest and will work only for honest people. Why don't you have windows in your prisons? You ought to be ashamed of yourself."

Then the emir flew into a terrible passion.

"How dare you speak to me like that? I am the emir of Ellebubu," he thundered.

"You're an unscrupulous scoundrel," said the Doctor. "I don't want to talk to you."

"If you don't make the birds work for me, I'll give orders that you get no food," said the emir. "You shall be starved to death."

"I have told you," said the Doctor, "that I don't desire any further conversation with you. Not a single pearl shall you ever get from the Harmattan Fisheries."

"And not a bite to eat shall you ever have till I do!" the emir yelled.

Then he turned to the prison guards, gave instructions that the Doctor was not to be fed till further orders, and stalked out. The door slammed shut with a doleful clang and after one decent breath of fresh air, the Doctor was left in the darkness of his stuffy dungeon.

The Doctor's Release

THE EMIR OF ELLEBUBU WENT BACK TO HIS palace feeling perfectly certain that after he had starved John Dolittle for a few days he would be able to make him do anything he wanted. He gave orders that no water should be served to the prisoner either, so as to make doubly sure that he would be reduced to obedience.

But immediately after the emir had left, the white mouse started out through the rat hole in the corner. And all day and all night he kept busy, coming and going, bringing in crumbs of food that he gathered from the houses of the town: bread crumbs, cheese crumbs, yam crumbs, potato crumbs, and crumbs of meat that he pulled off bones. All these he stored carefully in the Doctor's hat in the corner of the prison. And by the end of each day he had collected enough crumbs for one good square meal.

The Doctor said he never had the slightest idea of what he was eating, but as the mealy mixture was highly digestible and nutritious, he did not see why he should mind. To supply his mas-

ter with water the mouse got nuts, and after gnawing a tiny hole
in one end, he would chop the nut inside into pieces and shake
it out through the hole. Then he would fill the empty shell with
water and seal up the hole with gum arable which he got from
trees. The water-filled nuts were a little heavy for him to carry,
so Dab-Dab would bring them from the river as far as the outside end of the rat hole, and the white mouse would roll them
down the hole and into the prison.

By getting his friends, the village mice, to help him in the prepa-
ration of these nuts, he was able to supply them in hundreds. Then
all the Doctor had to do when he wanted a drink was to put one in

"The white mouse would roll them down the hole."

his mouth, crack it with his teeth, and after the cool water had run down his throat, spit the broken shells out.

The white mouse also provided crumbs of soap, so that his master could shave—for the Doctor, even in prison, was always very particular about this part of his appearance.

Well, when four days had passed, the emir of Ellebubu sent a messenger to the prison to inquire if the Doctor was now willing to do as he was told. The guards, after talking to John Dolittle, brought word to the emir that he was as obstinate as ever and had no intention of giving in.

"Very well," said the emir, stamping his foot, "then let him starve. In ten days more, the fool will be dead. Then I will come and laugh over him. So perish all wretches who oppose the wishes of the emir of Ellebubu!"

And in ten days' time he went to the prison, as he had said, to gloat over the terrible fate of the prisoner. Many of his ministers and generals came with him to help him gloat. But when the prison door was opened, instead of seeing the man's body stretched upon the floor, the emir found the Doctor smiling on the threshold, shaved and hearty and all spruced up. The only difference in his appearance was that, with no exercise in prison, he had grown slightly stouter and rounder.

The emir stared at the prisoner openmouthed, speechless with astonishment. Now, the day before this he had heard for the first time the story of the rout of the Amazons. The emir had refused to believe it. But now he began to feel that anything might be true about this man.

"See," one of the ministers whispered in his ear, "he has even shaved his beard without water or soap. Your Majesty, there is surely evil here. Set the man free before harm befalls us. Let us be rid of him."

And the frightened minister moved back among the crowd so the Doctor's evil gaze could not fall upon his face.

Then the emir himself began to get panicky. And he gave orders that the Doctor should be released right away.

"I will not leave here," said John Dolittle, standing squarely in the door, "till you have windows put in this prison. It's a disgrace to lock up anyone in a place without windows."

"Build windows in the prison at once," the emir said to the guards.

"And after that I won't go," said the Doctor, "not till you have set Chief Nyam-Nyam free; not till you have ordered all your people to leave his country and the Harmattan Rocks; not till you have returned to him the farming lands you robbed him of."

"It shall be done," muttered the emir, grinding his teeth. "Only go!"

"I'll go," said the Doctor. "But if you ever molest your neighbors again, I will return. Beware!"

Then he strode through the prison door out into the sunlit street, while the frightened people fell back on either side and covered their faces, whispering:

"Do not let his eye fall on you!"

And in the Doctor's pocket the white mouse had to put his paws over his face to keep from laughing.

And now the Doctor set out with his animals and the old chief to return to Nyam-Nyam's country from the land where he had been imprisoned. On the way they kept meeting with groups of the chief's people who were still hiding in the jungle. These were told the glad tidings of the emir's promise. When they learned that their land was now free and safe again, the people joined the Doctor's party for the return journey. And long before he came in sight of the village, John Dolittle looked like a conquering general coming back at the head of an army, so many had gathered to him on the way.

That night grand celebrations were made in the chief's village, and the Doctor was hailed by the people as the greatest man who had ever visited their land. Two of their worst enemies need now no longer be feared—the emir had been bound over by a promise and Dahomey was not likely to bother them again. The pearl fisheries were restored to their possession. And the country should now proceed prosperously and happily.

The next day the Doctor went out to the Harmattan Rocks to visit the cormorants and to thank them for the help they had given. The old chief came along on this trip, and with him four trustworthy men of his. In order that there should be no mistake in the future, these men were shown to the cormorants and the birds were told to supply them—and no others—with pearl oysters.

While the Doctor and his party were out at the Rocks, an oyster was fished up that contained an enormous and very beautiful pearl—by far the biggest and handsomest yet found. It was perfect in shape, flawless, and a most unusual shade in color. After making a little speech, the chief presented this pearl to the Doctor as a small return for the services he had done him and his people.

"Thank goodness for that!" Dab-Dab whispered to Jip. "Do you realize what that pearl means to us? The Doctor was down to his last shilling—as poor as a church mouse. We would have had to go circus-traveling with the Pushmi-Pullyu again, if it hadn't been

"Do you realize what that pearl means to us?"

for this. I'm so glad. For, for my part, I shall be glad enough to stay at home and settle down a while—once we get there."

"Oh, I don't know," said Gub-Gub. "I love circuses. I wouldn't mind traveling, so long as it's in England—and with a circus."

"Well," said Jip, "whatever happens, it's nice the Doctor's got the pearl. He always seems to be in need of money. And, as you say, Dab-Dab, that should make anybody rich for life."

But while the Doctor was still thanking the chief for the beautiful present, Quip the Carrier flew up with a letter for him.

"It was marked 'Urgent,' in red ink, Doctor," said the swallow, "so Speedy thought he had better send it to you by special delivery."

John Dolittle tore open the envelope.

"Who's it from, Doctor?" asked Dab-Dab.

"Dear me," muttered the Doctor, reading. "It's from that farmer in Lincolnshire whose Brussels sprouts we imported for Gub-Gub. I forgot to answer his letter—you remember, he wrote asking me if I could tell him what the trouble was. And I was so busy it went clean out of my mind. Dear me! I must pay the poor fellow back somehow. I wonder—oh, but there's this. I can send him the pearl. That will pay for his sprouts and something to spare. What a good idea!"

And to Dab-Dab's horror, the Doctor tore a clean piece off the farmer's letter, scribbled a reply, wrapped the pearl up in it, and handed it to the swallow.

"Tell Speedy," said he, "to send that off right away—registered. I am returning to Fantippo tomorrow. Good-bye and thank you for the special delivery."

As Quip the Carrier disappeared into the distance with the Doctor's priceless pearl, Dab-Dab turned to Jip and murmured:

"There goes the Dolittle fortune. My, but it is marvelous how money *doesn't* stick to that man's fingers!"

"Heigh-ho!" sighed Jip. "It's a circus for us, all right."

"Easy come, easy go," murmured Gub-Gub. "Never mind. I don't suppose it's really such fun being rich. Wealthy people have to behave so unnaturally."

A Mysterious Letter

WE ARE NOW COME TO AN UNUSUAL event in the history of the Doctor's post office, to the one which was, perhaps, the greatest of all the curious things that came about through the institution of the Swallow Mail.

On arriving back at the houseboat from his short and very busy holiday, the Doctor was greeted joyfully by the Pushmi-Pullyu, Too-Too, Cheapside, and Speedy the Skimmer. King Koko also came out to greet his friend when he saw the arrival of the Doctor's canoe through a pair of opera glasses (price ten shillings and sixpence) that he had recently gotten from London by parcel post. And the prominent Fantippans, who had missed their afternoon tea and social gossip terribly during the postmaster's absence, got into their canoes and followed the king out to the Foreign Mails office.

So for three hours after his arrival—in fact, until it was dark—the Doctor did not get a chance to do a thing besides shake hands and answer questions about how he had enjoyed his holiday, where he had been, and what he had done. The welcome he received on his return and the sight of the comfortable houseboat with its flowering window boxes, made the Doctor, as he afterward said to Dab-Dab, feel as though he were really coming home.

"Yes," said the housekeeper, "but don't forget that you have another home, a real one, in Puddleby."

"That's true," said the Doctor. "I suppose I must be getting on to England soon. But the Fantippans were honestly pleased to see us, weren't they? And after all, Africa is a nice country, now, isn't it?"

"Yes," said Dab-Dab, "a nice enough country for short holidays—and long drinks."

After supper had been served and eaten and the Doctor had been made to tell the story of the pearl fisheries all over again for the benefit of his own family circle, he at last turned to the enormous pile of letters that were waiting for him. They came, as usual, from all parts of the world, from every conceivable kind of animal and bird. For hours he waded patiently through them, answering them as they came. Speedy acted as his secretary and took down in bird and animal scribble the answers that the Doctor reeled off by the dozen. Often John Dolittle dictated so fast that the poor Skimmer had to get Too-Too (who had a wonderful memory) to come and help listen, so nothing should be missed through not writing it down quick enough.

Toward the end of the pile, the Doctor came across a very peculiar thick envelope, written all over in mud. For a long time none of them could make out a single word of the letter inside, nor even who it was from. The Doctor got all his notebooks out of the safe, compared and peered and pored over the writing for hours. Mud had been used for ink. The signs were made so clumsily they might almost be anything.

But at last, after a tremendous lot of work, copying out afresh, guessing and discussing, the meaning of the extraordinary letter was pieced together, and this is what it said:

Dear Doctor Dolittle: I have heard of your post office and am writing this as best I can—the first letter I ever wrote. I hear you have a weather bureau in connection with your post office, and that a one-eyed albatross is your chief weather prophet. I am writing to tell you that I am the oldest weather prophet in the world. I prophesied the Flood, and it came true to the day and the hour I said it would. I am a very slow walker or I would come and see you and perhaps you could do something for my gout, which in the last few hundred years has bothered me a good deal. But if you will come to see me I will teach you a lot about weather. And I will tell you the story of the Flood, which I saw with my own eyes from the deck of Noah's ark.

Yours very truly,
MUDFACE

P.S. I am a turtle.

At last, on reading the muddy message through, the Doctor's excitement and enthusiasm knew no bounds. He began at once to make arrangements to leave the following day for a visit to the turtle.

But, alas! when he turned again to the letter to see where the turtle lived, he could find nothing to give a clue to his whereabouts! The mysterious writer who had seen the Flood, Noah, and the ark had forgotten to give his address!

"Look here, Speedy," said John Dolittle, "we must try and trace this. Let us leave no stone unturned to find where this valuable document came from. First, we will question everyone in the post office to find out who it was delivered by."

Well, everyone in turn, the Pushmi-Pullyu, Cheapside, Too-Too, Quip the Carrier, all the swallows, any stray birds who were living in the neighborhood, even a pair of rats who had taken up their residence in the houseboat, were cross-examined by the Doctor or Speedy.

But no one had seen the letter arrive; no one could tell what day or hour it had come; no one could guess how it got into the pile of the Doctor's mails; no one knew anything about it. It was one of those little post office mysteries that are always cropping up even in the best-run mail systems.

The Doctor was positively heartbroken. Often in his natural history meditations he had wondered about all sorts of different matters connected with the ark; and he had decided that Noah, after his memorable voyage was over, must have been a great naturalist. Now had come most unexpectedly a chance to hear the great story from an eyewitness—from someone who had actually known and sailed with Noah—and just because of a silly little slip like leaving out an address, the great chance was to be lost!

All attempts to trace the writer having failed, the Doctor, after two days, gave it up and went back to his regular work.

This kept him so busy for the next week that he finally forgot all about the turtle and his mysterious letter.

But one night, when he was working late to catch up with the business that had multiplied during his absence, he heard a gentle tapping on the houseboat window. He left his desk and went and opened it. Instantly, in popped the head of an enormous snake, with a letter in its mouth—a thick, muddy letter.

"Great heavens!" cried the Doctor. "What a start you gave me! Come in, come in, and make yourself at home."

Slowly and smoothly the snake slid in over the windowsill and down onto the floor of the houseboat. Yards and yards

"In popped the head of an enormous snake."

and more yards long he came, coiling himself up neatly at John Dolittle's feet like a mooring rope on a ship's deck.

"Pardon me, but is there much more of you outside still?" asked the Doctor.

"Yes," said the snake, "only half of me is in yet."

"Then I'll open the door," said the Doctor, "so you can coil part of yourself in the passage. This room is a bit small."

When at last the great serpent was all in, his thick coils entirely covered the floor of the Doctor's office and a good part of him overflowed into the passage outside.

"Now," said the Doctor, closing the window, "what can I do for you?"

"I've brought you this letter," said the snake. "It's from the turtle. He is wondering why he got no answer to his first."

"But he gave me no address," said John Dolittle, taking the muddy envelope from the serpent. "I've been trying my hardest ever since to find out where he lived."

"Oh, was that it?" said the snake. "Well, old Mudface isn't much of a letter-writer. I suppose he didn't know he had to give his address."

"I'm awfully glad to hear from him again," said the Doctor. "I had given up all hope of ever seeing him. You can show me how to get to him?"

"Why, certainly," said the big serpent. "I live in the same lake as he does, Lake Junganyika."

"You're a water snake, then, I take it," said the Doctor.

"Yes."

"You look rather worn out from your journey. Is there anything I can get you?"

"I'd like a saucer of milk," said the snake.

"I only have wild goats' milk," said John Dolittle. "But it's quite fresh."

And he went out into the kitchen and woke up the housekeeper.

"What do you know, Dab-Dab," he said, breathless with excitement, "I've got a second letter from the turtle and the messenger is going to take us to see him!"

When Dab-Dab entered the postmaster's office with the milk, she found John Dolittle reading the letter. Looking at the floor, she gave a squawk of disgust.

"It's a good thing for you Sarah isn't here," she cried. "Just look at the state of your office—it's *full of snake!*"

The Land of the Mangrove Swamps

I T WAS A LONG BUT A MOST INTERESTING JOURNEY that the Doctor took from Fantippo to Lake Junganyika. It turned out that the turtle's home lay many miles inland in the heart of one of the wildest, most jungly parts of Africa.

The Doctor decided to leave Gub-Gub home this time and he took with him only Jip, Dab-Dab, Too-Too, and Cheapside—who said he wanted a holiday and that his sparrow friends could now quite well carry on the city deliveries in his absence.

The great water snake began by taking the Doctor's party down the coast south for some forty or fifty miles. There they left the sea, entered the mouth of a river, and started to journey inland. The canoe (with the snake swimming alongside it) was quite the best thing for this kind of travel, so long as the river had water in it. But presently, as they went up it, the stream grew narrower and narrower. Till at last, like many rivers in tropical countries, it was nothing more than the dry bed of a brook, or a chain of small pools with long sand bars between.

Overhead, the thick jungle arched and hung like a tunnel of green. This was a good thing by daytime, as it kept the sun off better than a parasol. And in the dry stretches of riverbed, where the Doctor had to carry or drag the canoe on homemade runners, the work was hard and shade something to be grateful for.

At the end of the first day John Dolittle wanted to leave the canoe in a safe place and finish the trip on foot. But the snake said they would need it farther on, where there was more water and many swamps to cross.

As they went forward, the jungle around them seemed to grow thicker and thicker all the time. But there was always this clear alleyway along the riverbed. And though the stream's course did much winding and twisting, the going was good.

The Doctor saw a great deal of new country, trees he had never met before, brightly colored orchids, butterflies, ferns, birds, and rare monkeys. So his notebook was kept busy all the time with sketching and jotting and adding to his already great knowledge of natural history.

On the third day of travel, this riverbed led them into an entirely new and different kind of country. If you have never been in a mangrove swamp, it is difficult to imagine what it looks like. It was mournful scenery. Flat bog land, full of pools and streamlets, dotted with tufts of grass and weed, tangled with gnarled roots and brambling bushes, spread out for miles and miles in every direction. It reminded the Doctor of some huge shrubbery that had been flooded by heavy rains. No large trees were here, such as they had seen in the jungle lower down. Seven or eight feet above their heads was as high as the mangroves grew, and from their thin boughs long streamers of moss hung like gray, fluttering rags.

The life, too, about them was quite different. The brilliantly colored birds of the true forest did not care for this damp country of half water and half land. Instead, all manner of swamp birds—big-billed and long-necked, for the most part—peered at them from the sprawling saplings. Many kinds of herons, egrets, ibises, grebes, bitterns—even stately anhingas, who can fly beneath the water—were wading in the swamps or nesting on the little tufty islands. In and out of the holes about the gnarled roots strange and wondrous water creatures—things half fish and half lizard— scuttled and quarreled with brightly colored crabs.

For many folks it would have seemed a creepy, nightmare sort of country, this land of the mangrove swamps. But to the Doctor, for whom any kind of animal life was always companionable and good intentioned, it was a most delightful new field of exploration.

They were glad now that the snake had not allowed them to leave the canoe behind. For here, where every step you took you were liable to sink down in the mud up to your waist, Jip and the Doctor would have had hard work to get along at all without it. And, even with it, the going was slow and hard enough. The mangroves spread out long, twisting, crossing arms in every direction to bar your passage—as though they were determined to guard the secrets of this silent, gloomy land where men could not make a home and seldom ever came.

Indeed, if it had not been for the giant water snake, to whom mangrove swamps were the easiest kind of traveling, they would never have been able to make their way forward. But their guide went on ahead of them for hundreds of yards to lead the way through the best openings and to find the passages where the water was deep enough to float a canoe. And although his head was out of sight most of the time in the tangled distance, he kept, in the worst stretches, a firm hold on the canoe by taking a turnabout the bowpost with his tail. And whenever they were stuck in the mud he would contract that long, muscular body of his with a jerk and yank the canoe forward as though it had been no more than a can tied on the end of a string.

Dab-Dab, Too-Too, and Cheapside did not, of course, bother to sit in the canoe. They found flying from tree to tree a much easier way to travel. But in one of these jerky pulls that the snake gave on his living towline, the Doctor and Jip were left sitting in the mud as the canoe was actually yanked from under them. This so much

"The canoe was yanked from under them."

amused the vulgar Cheapside, who was perched in a mangrove tree above their heads, that he suddenly broke the solemn silence of the swamp by bursting into noisy laughter.

"Lor' bless us, Doctor, but you do get yourself into some comical situations! Who would think to see John Dolittle, M. D., heminent physician of Puddleby-on-the-Marsh, bein' pulled through a mud swamp by a couple of 'undred yards of fat worm! You've no idea how funny you look!"

"Oh, close your silly face!" growled Jip, black mud from head to foot, scrambling back into the canoe. "It's easy for you—you can fly through the mess."

"It 'ud make a nice football ground, this," murmured Cheapside. "I didn't know there was this much mud anywhere— outside of 'Amstead 'Eath after a wet bank 'oliday. I wonder when we're going to get there. Seems to me we're comin' to the end of the world—or the middle of it. 'Aven't seen a 'uman face since we left the shore. 'E's an exclusive kind of gent, our Mr. Turtle, ain't 'e? Meself, I wouldn't be surprised if we ran into old Noah, sitting on the wreck of the ark, any minute. . . . 'Elp the Doctor up, Jip. Look, 'e's got his chin caught under a root."

The snake, hearing Cheapside's chatter, thought something must be wrong. He turned his head-end around and came back to see what the matter was. Then a short halt was made in the journey while the Doctor and Jip cleaned themselves up, and the precious notebooks, which had also been jerked out into the mud, were rescued and stowed in a safe place.

"Do no people at all live in these parts?" the Doctor asked the snake.

"None whatsoever," said the guide. "We left the lands where

men dwell behind us long ago. Nobody can live in these bogs but swamp birds, marsh creatures, and water snakes."

"How much farther have we got to go?" asked the Doctor, rinsing the mud off his hat in a pool.

"About one more day's journey," said the snake. "A wide belt of these swamps surrounds the Secret Lake of Junganyika on all sides. The going will become freer as we approach the open water of the lake."

"We are really on the shores of it already, then?"

"Yes," said the serpent. "But, properly speaking, the Secret Lake cannot be said to have shores at all—or, certainly, as you see, no shore where a man can stand."

"Why do you call it the Secret Lake?" asked the Doctor.

"Because it has never been visited by man since the Flood," said the giant reptile. "You will be the first to see it. We who live in it boast that we bathe daily in the original water of the Flood. For before the Forty Days' Rain came, it was not there, they say. But when the Flood passed away, this part of the world never dried up. And so it has remained, guarded by these wide mangrove swamps, ever since."

"What was here before the Flood, then?" asked the Doctor.

"They say rolling, fertile country, waving corn, and sunny hill-tops," the snake replied. "That is what I have heard. I was not there to see. Mudface, the turtle, will tell you all about it."

"How wonderful!" exclaimed the Doctor. "Let us push on. I am most anxious to see him—and the Secret Lake."

THE NINTH CHAPTER

The Secret Lake

D URING THE COURSE OF THE NEXT DAY'S travel the country became, as the snake had foretold, freer and more open. Little by little the islands grew fewer and the mangroves not so tangly. In the dreary views there was less land and more water. The going was much easier now. For miles at a stretch the Doctor could paddle, without the help of his guide, in water that seemed to be quite deep. It was indeed a change to be able to look up and see a clear sky overhead once in a while, instead of that everlasting network of swamp trees. Across the heavens the travelers now occasionally saw flights of wild ducks and geese, winging their way eastward.

"That's a sign we're near open water," said Dab-Dab.

"Yes," the snake agreed. "They're going to Junganyika. It is the feeding ground of great flocks of wild geese."

It was about five o'clock in the evening when they came to the end of the little islands and mudbanks. And as the canoe's nose glided easily forward into entirely open water, they suddenly found themselves looking across a great inland sea.

The Doctor was tremendously impressed by his first sight of the Secret Lake. If the landscape of the swamp country had been mournful, this was even more so. No eye could see across it. The edge of it was like the ocean's—just a line where the heavens and the water meet. Ahead to the east—the darkest part of the evening sky—even this line barely showed, for now the murky waters and the frowning night blurred together in an inky mass. To the right and left the Doctor could see the fringe of the swamp trees running around the lake, disappearing in the distance north and south.

Out in the open, great banks of gray mist rolled and joined and separated as the wailing wind pushed them fretfully hither and thither over the face of the waters.

"My word!" the Doctor murmured in a quiet voice. "Here one could almost believe that the Flood was not over yet!"

"Jolly place, ain't it?" came Cheapside's cheeky voice from the stern of the canoe. "Give me London any day—in the worst fog ever. Look at them mist shadows skatin' round the lake. Might be old Noah and 'is family, playin' 'Ring-a-ring-a-rosy' in their nightshirts, they're that lifelike."

"The mists are always there," said the snake, "always have been. In them the first rainbow shone."

"Well," said the sparrow, "I'd sell the whole place cheap if it was mine—mists and all. 'Ow many 'undred miles of this bonny blue ocean 'ave we got to cross before we reach our Mr. Mudface?"

"Not very many," said the snake. "He lives on the edge of the lake a few miles to the north. Let us hurry and try to reach his home before darkness falls."

Once more, with the guide in front, but this time at a much better pace, the party set off.

As the light grew dimmer the calls of several night birds sounded from the mangroves on the left. Too-Too told the Doctor that many of these were owls, but of kinds that he had never seen or met with before.

"Yes," said the Doctor. "I imagine there are lots of different kinds of birds and beasts in these parts that can be found nowhere else in the world."

At last, while it was still just light enough to see, the snake swung into the left and once more entered the outskirts of the mangrove swamps. Following him with difficulty in the fading light, the Doctor was led into a deep cove. At the end of this the nose of the canoe suddenly bumped into something hard. The Doctor was about to lean out to see what it was when a deep, deep bass voice spoke out of the gloom quite close to him.

"Welcome, John Dolittle. Welcome to Lake Junganyika."

Then looking up, the Doctor saw on a moundlike island the shape of an enormous turtle—fully twelve feet across the shell— standing outlined against the blue-black sky.

The long journey was over at last.

Doctor Dolittle did not at any time believe in traveling with very much baggage. And all that he had brought with him on this journey was a few things rolled up in a blanket—and, of course, the little black medicine bag. Among those things, luckily, however, were a couple of candles. And if it had not been for them, he would have had hard work to land safely from the canoe.

Getting them lighted in the wind that swept across the lake was

"The Doctor saw the shape of an enormous turtle."

no easy matter. But to protect their flame, Too-Too wove a couple of little lanterns out of thin leaves, through which the light shone dimly green but bright enough to see your way by.

To his surprise, the Doctor found that the mound, or island, on which the turtle lived was not made of mud, though muddy footprints could be seen all over it. It was made of stone—of stones cut square with a chisel.

While the Doctor was examining them with great curiosity, the turtle said:

"They are the ruins of a city. I used to be content to live and sleep in the mud. But since my gout has been so bad, I thought I ought to make myself something solid and dry to rest on. Those stones are pieces of a king's house."

"Pieces of a house—of a city!" the Doctor exclaimed, peering into the wet and desolate darkness that surrounded the little island. "But where did they come from?"

"From the bottom of the lake," said the turtle. "Out there," Mudface nodded toward the gloomy, wide-stretching waters, "there stood, thousands of years ago, the beautiful city of Shalba. Don't I know, when for long enough I lived in it? Once it was the greatest and fairest city ever raised by men and King Mashtu of Shalba the proudest monarch in the world. Now I, Mudface the turtle, make a nest in the swamp out of the ruins of his palace. Ha! Ha!"

"You sound bitter," said the Doctor. "Did King Mashtu do you any harm?"

"I should say he did," growled Mudface. "But that belongs to the story of the Flood. You have come far. You must be weary and in need of food."

"Well," said the Doctor, "I am most anxious to hear the story. Does it take long to tell?"

"About three weeks would be my guess," whispered Cheapside. "Turtles do everything slow. Something tells me that story is the longest story in the world, Doctor. Let's get a nap and a bite to eat first. We can hear it just as well tomorrow."

So in spite of John Dolittle's impatience, the story was put off till the following day. For the evening meal, Dab-Dab managed to scout around and gather together quite a nice mess of fresh-water shellfish and Too-Too collected some marsh berries that did very well for dessert.

Then came the problem of how to sleep. This was not so

easy, because, although the foundations of the turtle's mound were of stone, there was hardly a dry spot on the island left where you could lie down. The Doctor tried the canoe. But it was sort of cramped and uncomfortable for sleeping, and now even there, too, the mud had been carried by Dab-Dab's feet and his own. In this country, the great problem was getting away from the mud.

"When Noah's family first came out of the ark," said the turtle, "they slept in little beds that they strung up between the stumps of the drowned trees."

"Ah, hammocks!" cried the Doctor. "Of course—the very thing!"

Then, with Jip's and Dab-Dab's help, he constructed a very comfortable basket-work hammock out of willow wands and fastened it between two larger mangroves. Into this he climbed and drew the blanket over him. Although the trees leaned down toward the water with his weight, they were quite strong and their bendiness acted like good bedsprings.

The moon had now risen and the weird scenery of Junganyika was all green lights and blue shadows. As the Doctor snuffed out his candles and Jip curled himself up at his feet, the turtle suddenly started humming a tune in his deep bass voice, waving his long neck from side to side in the moonlight.

"What is that tune you are humming?" asked the Doctor.

"That's the 'Elephants' March,'" said the turtle. "They always played it at the Royal Circus of Shalba for the elephants' procession."

"Let's 'ope it 'asn't many verses," grumbled Cheapside, sleepily putting his head under his wing.

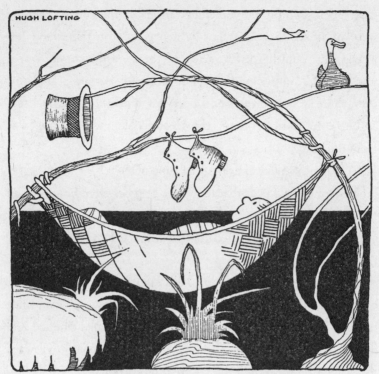

"The trees bent down with his weight."

*   *   *

The sun had not yet risen on the gloomy waters of Lake Junganyika before Jip felt the Doctor stirring in his hammock, preparing to get up.

Presently Dab-Dab could be heard messing about in the mud below, bravely trying to get breakfast ready under difficult conditions.

Next Cheapside, grumbling in a sleepy chirp, brought his head out from under his wing, gave the muddy scenery one look and popped it back again.

But it was of little use to try to get more sleep now. The camp was astir. John Dolittle, bent on the one idea of hearing that story, had already swung himself out of his hammock and was now washing his face noisily in the lake. Cheapside shook his feathers, swore a few words in Cockney, and flew off his tree down to the Doctor's side.

"Look 'ere, Doctor," he whispered, "this ain't an 'olesome place to stay at all. I'm all full of cramp from the damp night air. You'd get webfooted if you loitered in this country long. Listen, you want to be careful about gettin' old Mudface started on his yarn spinning. Tell 'im to make it short and sweet—just to give us the outline of his

HUGH LOFTING

"The Doctor was washing his face in the lake."

troubles, like, see? The sooner we can shake the mud of this place off our feet and make tracks for Fantippo, the better it'll be for all of us."

Well, when breakfast had been disposed of, the Doctor sharpened his pencil, got out a notebook and, telling Too-Too to listen carefully, in case he should miss anything, he asked the turtle to begin the story of the Flood.

Cheapside had been right. Although it did not take a fortnight to tell, it did take a very full day. Slowly and evenly the sun rose out of the east, passed across the heavens, and sank down into the west. And still Mudface went murmuring on, telling of all the wonders he had seen in days long ago, while the Doctor's pencil wiggled untiringly over the pages of his notebook. The only interruptions were when the turtle paused to lean down and moisten his long throat with the muddy water of the lake, or when the Doctor stopped him to ask a question on the natural history of antediluvian times.

Dab-Dab prepared lunch and supper and served them as silently as she could, so as not to interrupt; but for the Doctor they were very scrappy meals. On into the night the story went. And now John Dolittle wrote by candlelight, while all his pets, with the exception of Too-Too, were already nodding or dozing.

At last, about half past ten—to Cheapside's great relief—the turtle pronounced the final words.

"And that, John Dolittle, is the end of the story of the Flood, by one who saw it with his own eyes."

For some time after the turtle finished no one spoke. Even the irreverent Cheapside was silent. Little bits of stars, dimmed by the light of a half-full moon, twinkled like tiny eyes in the dim blue dome that arched across the lake. Away off somewhere among the tangled mangroves an owl hooted from the swamp and Too-Too turned his head quickly to listen. Dab-Dab, the economical housekeeper, seeing the Doctor close his notebook and put away his pencil, blew out the candle.

At last the Doctor spoke:

"Mudface, I don't know when, in all my life I have listened to a story that interested me so much. I—I'm glad I came."

"I too am glad, John Dolittle. You are the only one in the world now who understands the speech of animals. And if you had not come, my story of the Flood could not have been told. I'm getting very old and do not ever move far away from Junganyika."

"Dab-Dab, the economical housekeeper, blew out the candle."

"Would it be too much to ask you," said the Doctor, "to get me some souvenir from the city below the lake?"

"Not at all," said the turtle. "I'll go down and try to get you something right away."

Slowly and smoothly, like some unbelievable monster of former days, the turtle moved his great bulk across his little island and slid himself into the lake without splashing or disturbance of any kind. Only a gentle swirling in the water showed where he had disappeared.

In silence they all waited—the animals now, for the moment, reawakened and full of interest. The Doctor had visions of his enormous friend moving through the slime of centuries at the bottom of the lake, hunting for some souvenir of the great civilization that passed away with the Flood. He hoped that he would bring a book or something with writing on it.

Instead, when at last he reappeared wet and shining in the moonlight, he had a carved stone windowsill on his back, which must have weighed over a ton.

"Lor' bless us!" muttered Cheapside. "What a wonderful piano mover 'e would make, to be sure! Great Carter Patterson! Does 'e think the Doctor's goin' to 'ang that on 'is watch chain?"

"It was the lightest thing I could find," said the turtle, rolling it off his back with a thud that shook the island. "I had hoped I could get a vase or a plate or something you could carry. But all the smaller objects are now covered in fathoms of mud. This I broke off from the second story of the palace—from the queen's bedroom window. I thought perhaps you'd like to see it anyway, even if it was too much for you to carry home. It's beautifully carved. Wait till I wash some of the mud off it."

The candles were lighted again and after the carvings had been cleaned, the Doctor examined them with great care and even made sketches of some of them in his notebook.

By the time the Doctor had finished, all his party, excepting Too-Too, had fallen asleep. It was only when he heard Jip suddenly snore from the hammock that he realized how late it was. As he blew out the candles again he found that it was very dark, for now the moon had set. He climbed into bed and drew the blankets over him.

THE TENTH CHAPTER

The Postmaster General's Last Order

WHEN DAB-DAB ROUSED THE PARTY next morning the sun was shining through the mist upon the lake, doing its best to brighten up the desolate scenery around them.

Poor Mudface awoke with an acute attack of gout. He had not been bothered by this ailment since the Doctor's arrival. But now he could scarcely move at all without great pain. And Dab-Dab brought his breakfast to him where he lay.

John Dolittle was inclined to blame himself for having asked him to go hunting in the lake for souvenirs the night before.

"I'm afraid that was what brought on the attack," said the Doctor, getting out his little black bag from the canoe and mixing some medicines. "But you know you really ought to move out of this damp country to some drier climate. I am aware that turtles can stand an awful lot of wet. But at your age one must be careful, you know."

"There isn't any other place I like as well," said Mudface. "It's so hard to find a country where you're not disturbed these days."

"Here, drink this," the Doctor ordered, handing him a teacup full of some brown mixture. "I think you will find that that will soon relieve the stiffness in your front legs."

The turtle drank it down. And in a minute or two he said he felt much better and could now move his legs freely without pain.

"It's a wonderful medicine, that," said he. "You are surely a great Doctor. Have you got any more of it?"

"I will make up several bottles of the mixture and leave them with you before I go," said John Dolittle. "But you really ought to get on high ground somewhere. This muddy little hummock is no place for you to live. Isn't there a regular island in the lake, where

HUGH LOFTING

"Mixing the turtle's medicine"

you could make your home—if you're determined not to leave the Junganyika country?"

"Not one," said the turtle. "It's all like this, just miles and miles of mud and water. I used to like it—in fact, I do still. I wouldn't wish for anything better if it weren't for this wretched gout of mine."

"Well," said the Doctor, "if you haven't got an island, we must make one for you."

"Make one!" cried the turtle. "How would you go about it?"

"I'll show you very shortly," said John Dolittle. And he called Cheapside to him.

"Will you please fly down to Fantippo," he said to the city manager, "and give this message to Speedy-the-Skimmer. And ask him to send it out to all the postmasters of the branch offices: The Swallow Mail is very shortly to be closed—at all events for a considerable time. I must now be returning to Puddleby and it will be impossible for me to continue the service in its present form after I have left. I wish to convey my thanks to all the birds, postmasters, clerks, and letter carriers who have so generously helped me in this work. The last favor that I am going to ask of them is a large one; and I hope they will give me their united support in it. I want them to build me an island in the middle of Lake Junganyika. It is for Mudface the turtle, the oldest animal living, who in days gone by did a very great deal for man and beast—for the whole world in fact—when the earth was passing through the darkest chapters in all its history. Tell Speedy to send word to all bird leaders throughout the world. Tell him I want as many birds as possible right away, to build a healthy home where this brave turtle may end his long life in peace. It is the last thing I ask of the post office staff, and I hope they will do their best for me."

Cheapside said that the message was so long he was afraid he would never be able to remember it by heart. So John Dolittle told him to take it down in bird scribble and he dictated it to him all over again.

That letter, the last circular order issued by the great postmaster general to the staff of the Swallow Mail, was treasured by Cheapside for many years. He hid it under his untidy nest in St. Edmund's left ear on the south side of the chancel of St. Paul's Cathedral. He always hoped that the pigeons who lived in the front porch of the British Museum would someday get it into the museum for him. But one gusty morning, when men were cleaning the outside of the cathedral, it got blown out of St. Edmund's ear and, before Cheapside could overtake it, it sailed over the housetops into the river and sank.

The sparrow got back to Junganyika late that afternoon. He reported that Speedy had immediately, on receiving the Doctor's message, forwarded it to the postmasters of the branch offices with orders to pass it on to all the bird leaders everywhere. It was expected that the first birds would begin to arrive here early the following morning.

It was Speedy himself who woke the Doctor at dawn the next day. And while breakfast was being eaten, he explained to John Dolittle the arrangements that had been made.

The work, the Skimmer calculated, would take three days. All birds had been ordered to pick up a stone or a pebble or a pinch of sand from the seashore on their way and bring it with them. The larger birds (who would carry stones) were to come first, then the middle-sized birds, and then the little ones with sand.

Soon, when the sky over the lake was beginning to fill up with circling ospreys, herons and albatrosses; Speedy left the Doctor and flew off to join them. There, taking up a position in the sky right over the center of the lake, he hovered motionless, as a marker for the stone-droppers. Then the work began.

All day long a never-ending stream of big birds, a dozen abreast, flew up from the sea and headed across Lake Junganyika. The line was like a solid black ribbon, the birds dense, packed and close, beak to tail. And as each dozen reached the spot where Speedy hovered, twelve stones dropped into the water. The procession was so continuous and unbroken that it looked as though the sky were raining stones. And the constant roar of them splashing into the water out of the heavens could be heard a mile off.

The lake in the center was quite deep. And of course tons and tons of stone would have to be dropped before the new island would begin to show above the water's surface. This gathering of birds was greater even than the one the Doctor had addressed in the hollow of No Man's Land. It was the biggest gathering of birds that had ever been seen. For now not only the leaders came but thousands and millions of every species. John Dolittle got tremendously excited and, jumping into his canoe, he started to paddle out nearer to the work. But Speedy grew impatient that the top of the stone pile was not yet showing above the water, and he gave the order to double up the line—and then double again, as still more birds came to help from different parts of the world. And soon, with a thousand stones falling every fraction of a second, the lake got so rough that the Doctor had to sail back to the turtle's hummock, lest his canoe capsize.

All that day, all that night and half the next day, this continued. At last, about noon on the morrow, the sound of the falling stones

"A never-ending stream of big birds"

began to change. The great mound of seething white water, like a fountain in the middle of the lake, disappeared, and in its place a black spot showed. The noise of splashing changed to the noise of stone rattling on stone. The top of the island had begun to show.

"It's like the mountains peeping out after the Flood," Mudface muttered to the Doctor.

Then Speedy gave the order for the middle-sized birds to join in; and soon the note of the noise changed again—shriller—as tons and tons of pebbles and gravel began to join the downpour.

Another night and another day went by, and at dawn the gallant Skimmer came down to rest his weary wings; for the workers did not need a marker any longer—now that a good-sized island stood out on the bosom of the lake for the birds to drop their burdens on.

Bigger and bigger grew the homemade land, and soon Mudface's new estate was acres wide. Still another order from Speedy; and presently the rattling noise changed to a gentle hiss. The sky now was simply black with birds; the pebble-shower had ceased; it was raining sand. Last of all, the birds brought seeds: grass seeds, the seeds of flowers, acorns, and the kernels of palms. The turtle's new home was to be provided with turf, with wild gardens, with shady avenues to keep off the African sun.

When Speedy came to the hummock and said, "Doctor, it is finished," Mudface gazed thoughtfully out into the lake and murmured:

"Now proud Shalba is buried indeed: she has an island for a tombstone! It's a grand home you have given me, John Dolittle. Alas, poor Shalba! Mashtu the king passes. But Mudface the turtle—lives on!"

THE ELEVENTH CHAPTER

Good-bye to Fantippo

UDFACE'S LANDING ON HIS NEW HOME was quite an occasion. The Doctor paddled out alongside him till they reached the island. Until he set foot on it, John Dolittle himself had not realized what a large piece of ground it was. It was more than a quarter of a mile across. Round in shape, it rose gently from the shores to the flat center, which was a good hundred feet above the level of the lake.

Mudface was tremendously pleased with it; climbing laboriously to the central plateau—from where you could see great distances over the flat country around—he said he was sure his health would quickly improve in this drier air.

Dab-Dab prepared a meal—the best she could in the circumstances—to celebrate what she called the turtle's housewarming. And everyone sat down to it and there was much gaiety, and the Doctor was asked to make a speech in honor of the occasion.

Cheapside was dreadfully afraid that Mudface would get up to make a speech in reply and that it would last into the following day.

"Dab-Dab prepared a meal."

But to the sparrow's relief, the Doctor, immediately after he had finished, set about preparations for his departure.

He made up the six bottles of gout mixture and presented them to Mudface with instructions on how it should be taken. He told him that although he was closing up the post office for regular service, it would always be possible to get word to Puddleby. He would ask several birds of passage to stop here occasionally; and if the gout got any worse, he wanted Mudface to let him know by letter.

The old turtle thanked him over and over again, and the parting was a very affecting one. When at last the good-byes were all said, they got into the canoe and set out on the return journey.

Reaching the mouth of the river at the southern end of the lake, they paused a moment before entering the mangrove swamps and looked back. And there in the distance they could just see the shape of the old turtle standing on his new island, watching them. They waved to him and pushed on.

"He looks just the same as when we saw him the night we arrived," said Dab-Dab. "You remember? Like a statue on a pedestal against the sky."

"Poor old fellow!" murmured the Doctor. "I do hope he will be all right now. . . . What a wonderful life! What a wonderful history!"

"Didn't I tell you, Doctor," said Cheapside, "that it was going to be the longest story in the world? Took a day and half a night to tell."

"Ah, but it's a story that nobody else could tell," said John Dolittle.

"Good thing, too," muttered the sparrow. "It would never do if there was many of 'is kind spread around this busy world. Of course, meself, I don't believe a word of the yarn. I think he made it all up. 'E 'ad nothin' else to do—sittin' there in the mud, century after century, cogitatin.'"

The journey down through the jungle was completed without anything special happening. But when they reached the sea and turned the bow of the canoe westward, they came upon a very remarkable thing. It was an enormous hole in the beach—or rather a place where the beach had been taken away bodily. Speedy told the Doctor that it was here that the birds had picked up the stones and sand on their way to Junganyika. They had literally carried acres of the seashore nearly a thousand miles inland. Of course, in a few months the action of the surf would fill in the hole so that the place looked like the rest of the beach.

But that is why, when many years later some learned geologists visited Lake Junganyika, they said that the seashore gravel on an island there was a clear proof that the sea had once flowed through that neighborhood. Which was true—in the days of the Flood. But the Doctor was the only scientist who knew that Mudface's island, and the stones that made it, had quite a different history.

On his arrival at the post office the Doctor was given his usual warm reception by the king and dignitaries of Fantippo, who paddled out from the town to welcome him back.

Tea was served at once; and His Majesty seemed so delighted at renewing this pleasant custom that John Dolittle was loath to break the news to him that he must shortly resign from the Foreign Mail Service and sail for England. However, while they were chatting on the veranda of the houseboat, a fleet of quite large sailing vessels entered the harbor. These were some of the new merchant craft of Fantippo that plied regularly up and down the coast, trading with other African countries. The Doctor pointed out to the king that mails intended for foreign lands could now be quite easily taken by these boats to the bigger ports on the coast where vessels from Europe called every week.

From that, the Doctor went on to explain to the king, that much as he loved Fantippo and its people, he had many things to attend to in England and must now be thinking of going home. And of course as none of the natives could talk bird language, the Swallow Mail would have to be replaced by the ordinary kind of post office.

The Doctor found that His Majesty was much more distressed

at the prospect of losing his good friend and his afternoon tea on the houseboat than at anything else which the change would bring. But he saw that the Doctor really felt he had to go; and at length, with tears falling into his teacup, he gave permission for the postmaster general of Fantippo to resign.

Great was the rejoicing among the Doctor's pets and the patient swallows when the news got about that John Dolittle was really going home at last. Gub-Gub and Jip could hardly wait while the last duties and ceremonies of closing the houseboat to the public and transferring the Foreign Mails Service to the office in the town were performed. Dab-Dab bustled cheerfully from morning to night, while Cheapside never ceased to chatter of the glories of London, the comforts of a city life, and all the things he was going to do as soon as he got back to his beloved native haunts.

There was no end to the complimentary ceremonies that the good king and his courtiers performed to honor the departing Doctor. For days and days previous to his sailing, canoes came and went between the town and the houseboat, bearing presents to show the good will of the Fantippans. During all this, having to keep smiling the whole time, the Doctor got sadder and sadder at leaving his good friends. And he was heartily glad when the hour came to pull up the anchor and put to sea.

People who have written the history of the kingdom of Fantippo all devote several chapters to a mysterious man who in a very short space of time made enormous improvements in the mail, the communications, the shipping, the commerce, the education, and the general prosperity of the country. Indeed, it was through John Dolittle's quiet influence that King Koko's reign came to be looked upon as the Golden Age in Fantippan history. A wooden statue still stands in the marketplace to his memory.

The excellent postal service continued after he left. The stamps with Koko's face on them were as various and as beautiful as ever. On the occasion of the first annual review of the Fantippo Merchant Fleet a very fine two-shilling stamp was struck in commemoration, showing His Majesty inspecting his new ships through a lollipop quizzing-glass. The king himself became a stamp collector, and his album was as good as a family photo album, containing as it did so many pictures of himself. The only awkward incident that happened in the record of the post

HUGH LOFTING

"A wooden statue still stands to his memory."

office that the Doctor had done so much to improve, was when some ardent stamp collectors, wishing to make the modern stamps rare, plotted to have the king assassinated in order that the current issues should go out of date. But the plot was happily discovered before any harm was done.

Years afterward, the birds visiting Puddleby told the Doctor that the king still had the flowers in the window boxes of his old houseboat carefully tended and watered in his memory. His Majesty, they said, never gave up the fond hope that someday his good friend would come back to Fantippo with his kindly smile, his instructive conversation, and his jolly tea parties on the post office veranda.

The End

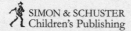 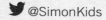